BOOK 2 OF COLONY

SANCTUARY

VERN & SUSAN NORDMAN

BLUE FORGE PRESS

Port Orchard ✪ Washington

Sanctuary (Book 2)
Copyright 2024
By Vern Nordman and Susan Nordman

First Print Edition March 2024
First eBook Edition March 2024

ISBN 979-8-89439-004-8

For information about film, reprint or other subsidiary rights, contact blueforgegroup@gmail.com

Blue Forge Press is the print division of the volunteer-run, federal 501(c)3 nonprofit company, Blue Forge Group, founded in 1989 and dedicated to bringing light to the shadows and voice to the silence. We strive to empower storytellers across all walks of life with our four divisions: Blue Forge Press, Blue Forge Films, Blue Forge Gaming, and Blue Forge Records. Find out more at www.BlueForgeGroup.org

Blue Forge Press
7419 Ebbert Drive Southeast
Port Orchard, Washington 98367
blueforgepress@gmail.com
360-550-2071 ph.txt

ACKNOWLEDGMENTS

Thanks to Neil deGrasse Tyson, Stephen Hawking, Carl Sagan, Albert Einstein, and all scientists dedicated to understanding our world and the space that surrounds it. While we never interviewed you for our Colony series, we did watch a lot of your documentaries.

COLONY

Book 1: Project Voyager
Book 2: Sanctuary

ALSO BY VERN NORDMAN

Uncle Sam, My Sailor, and Me:
Experiences on the Lighter Side of a Long Military Life

ALSO BY SUSAN NORDMAN

Ascension

SANCTUARY

Vern & Susan
NORDMAN

CHAPTER 1

Wakey! Wakey!"

With a groan, John Marshal opened his eyes to see the smiling face of Doctor Nancy Watson. "Oh, good! I'm not dead," he muttered, but due to the brain fog of seven years in cryogenic hibernation, he accidentally said it out loud.

Doc Nancy laughed. This was the third time Marshal had been brought out of cryogenic hibernation during their twenty-year journey through the vastness of space and she thought that he'd probably said the same thing when he had come out of cryogenic sleep both times before.

Not even trying to stifle a massive yawn, Marshal's fuzzy brain had already reasoned that he wasn't dead. If he had been, an angel like Doctor Nancy Watson would have to be dead too and Marshal was pretty sure that whatever hereafter he went after dying, it wasn't likely he would end up in the same place she would.

Marshal gave another huge yawn and then frowned at

the philosophical turn his thoughts had taken. He didn't usually contemplate such things, but then again, cryogenic sleep was weird and had a tendency to scramble one's thinking... or at least that had been Marshal's experience.

The procedure for putting people into cryogenic hibernation was pretty straight forward: Doc Nancy, her husband Doctor John Watson or one of the other medical technicians along with one of the cryogenic specialists had him strip completely naked before laying him down in the seven-foot-long torpedo-shaped cryogenic pod. Once he was settled in the cryo-pod, the curved clear plastic lid that ran the full length of the "bed" was securely fastened down and a wispy yellowish mist was pumped in. Then he went to sleep. After what seemed like just moments, he'd wake up to discover that a year, or two, or several years had passed.

If he woke up. Each time they had put him under, he couldn't shake the feeling that, philosophy aside, he'd experience the afterlife personally.

Of course, everyone *had* woken up, so far anyway. But every time Marshal had been put under, he couldn't get the nagging thought out of his head that maybe this time something would go wrong. This time would be... it.

Thankfully, he remembered that this, his third awakening, would be his last. They were nearly there.

When the Starship Voyager left Earth's orbit on its twenty-year journey to the newly discovered planet their bosses, the Board of Directors of Visions Unlimited, had named Sanctuary, Marshal had been put into cryogenic hibernation along with over six hundred of his fellow travelers. Most of them would remain sleeping all the way to Sanctuary but the big brains who had envisioned Voyager had determined that a watch crew would remain awake during the journey in order to deal with any emergencies the spaceship might encounter. This "watch crew" would rotate in one-year shifts for the duration of the twenty-year journey and would consist of a medical specialist, a cryogenic engineer and a construction robot operator. Yeah, guess who was the construction robot operator? Just about to enter his third and final shift of the watch crew, Marshal still wasn't quite onboard with that decision.

As he came fully awake, Marshal rolled his eyes and wondered for the umpteenth time why in the world VU thought a construction robot operator was needed on the watch team. Sure, having a medical and cryogenic specialist awake during the voyage made sense in case something went wrong with one of the six hundred plus pods that were currently occupied by sleeping colonists... and to bring the watch team out of hibernation for their annual rotation... and to wake up the colonists when they finally reached Sanctuary. But what the heck was he supposed to do if something did go wrong? Get out and push?

It was true that he and Samantha, his own construction robot, and the rest of the construction robots had built Voyager... in space while orbiting the Earth, no less... but they were no longer in a nice, stable orbit around their home planet. Marshal and the rest of the humans fleeing earth were now whizzing through the vast emptiness of space at .98 the speed of light. If by some off chance catastrophe did occur Marshal had no idea what he was supposed to do about it. He really didn't fancy taking Sam outside of Voyager into the vacuum of space to fix whatever had gone wrong. This wasn't like a car chase where he could roll to the curb and hope the worst thing that happened was a serious case of road rash. Voyager was traveling at near-lightspeed. Not only was he not sure if he could repair whatever hypothetical problem had gone wrong, but he absolutely didn't want to find out that if he and Sam went outside, they would remain in close proximity to Voyager. The ship would be long gone before it could even register that he'd been left behind. There were no U-turns at the next gas station to reclaim any stragglers.

It had been different when he was working in orbit around Earth. While Marshal *knew* he, Sam, Voyager and the space station Wisdom were all moving at hundreds of miles per hour around Earth and Earth was moving at thousands of miles per hour around the sun, they were all traveling together at the same speed so he never felt like he was moving at all. Out here in the depths of space nineteen lightyears from home Marshal had no desire to test the theory on whether he and Sam would stay in close proximity to Voyager or if Voyager would just warp away and leave him stranded in the abyss of space.

Marshal gave himself a rueful smile. The Robot Jockeys, or RJs as the construction robot operators had named themselves, were victims of their own success. Having managed to solve every problem thrown at them during the building of Voyager, the big brains at VU probably figured that if there was a problem the RJs would think of something to fix it. But when all was said and done Marshal really didn't want to find out what that something might be.

And it was now his turn to be awake for a year... again. He'd been awake for years three and twelve and, if all was going as planned, this was year twenty, the final year. This was the year that Voyager would arrive at its destination—a planet in another solar system: Sanctuary.

Sanctuary!

Marshal's mind wandered again. Ever since Planet X (Sanctuary's original name) had been discovered by the new Webb space telescope, speculation on what the planet was actually like had consumed most of the human race including a huge multinational cooperation called Visions Unlimited. VU looked at an overcrowded and polluted Earth, looked at Planet X and sensed a potential opportunity. At enormous expense they went forward with plans to actually build an interstellar vehicle that would carry human beings on a forty year round-trip journey of exploration to determine if the planet could be a new home for the human race. Talk about thinking big and long term! Regardless of their altruism of rescuing humanity, Marshal knew that if VU found that Planet X was suitable for human habitation it would be the biggest real estate deal in history.

But that mission of exploration was never to be.

Events on Earth overtook the Voyager Project before the spaceship was completed. As many scientists had been predicting for decades, the climatological tipping point was reached. Earth's planetary life support system collapsed and the rapid disintegration of civilized society quickly followed.

It's ironic, Marshal thought. *We called ourselves Homo Sapiens because it meant 'wise man' in Latin. It described us as the most intelligent species on the planet, yet in the blink of a cosmic eye we turned our Eden into an overcrowded wasteland.*

It wasn't an exaggeration. Through greed, ignorance, arrogance, mis-management and downright stupidity, Earth, the only home that mankind had ever known, was all but uninhabitable for any species, let alone their own. Air, land and sea were irretrievably polluted and it was only a matter of time before everything died. Marshal knew that the Fifth (or was it the sixth) Great Dying had already begun.

With that inevitable disaster looming the Directors of Visions Unlimited sought to save, if not themselves at least some of their descendants and changed Voyager's mission from one of exploration to an attempt at colonization. The result was that over six-hundred men, women and children, a ridiculously small portion of the human race, had cast themselves into the unknown void of space to take their chances on a new world sight unseen.

While Marshal liked to joke that he wasn't the brightest star shining in the cosmos, he was no fool either and was a hell of a lot savvier than many of the other colonists. Having been part of the Voyager Project from the beginning, he knew that Sanctuary was more of a gamble than a sure bet. All anyone really knew about this newly discovered world was that it was probably Earth-like. Key emphasis on "probably."

Sanctuary was the fourth planet from its star which was also remarkably the same age and size as Earth's star Sol, so naturally everyone was unimaginatively calling it Sol II. Marshal didn't really care what they called it as long as it delivered the warmth and energy that all the big brained scientists with all the scholarly letters before and after their names declared it would. But with all their assurances, no matter what they insisted that the math told them, none of them could be sure Sanctuary had everything they needed... and that big gray area left a lot of unanswered questions that worried Marshal even though he and Alex were the first to sign up for this venture.

And these were big, important life-and-death questions.

Did the planet have an oxygen atmosphere that humans could breathe—or did it have any atmosphere at all? Was there liquid water on the planet and if there was would it be suitable for human consumption?

While the scientists insisted it did and it would, there wasn't any guarantee that when they arrived at Sanctuary, they weren't going to land on a barren rock... and that was assuming there was actually something solid to land on. The planet could be all ocean or worse—all lava.

Yeah, that would shorten our trip real fast! Marshal snorted in bitter amusement. If any of those things happened, the colonists would have no choice except to return to Earth. And when they arrived back at Earth forty years would have passed. What would they return to?

Doc Nancy raised her eyebrow at Marshal. In his post-hibernation stupor, he had quite forgotten she was there. Assuring her that he was fine, Marshal swung his legs over the edge of his pod and accepted the tube of fortified fruit juice that Nancy and her husband had concocted to help hydrate the colonists after their long sleep. Marshal snorted again, this time in real amusement at the thought of her husband: Doctor John Watson.

John Watson always made Marshal think of Sherlock Holmes' trusty sidekick. Though he ached to tease him about it, Marshal had refrained as he was sure the guy had heard every crack joke possible since he first enrolled in medical school.

Yeah, the Watsons are great people, Marshal thought to himself as he drank down his juice. The Doctors Watson had had their own medical practice in Sand Flea City long before Project Voyager set up operations in a block of hangars at the big industrial airfield just outside of town. Word of the Watsons spread fast and soon the Voyagers were seeing the Docs for their bumps and bruises, colds and flu. The Voyagers quickly came to love and respect them as much as the local community did. They were the kind of doctors who were never going to retire rich. As compassionate healers of the old school, they determined that everyone was going to be treated regardless of their ability to pay.

After the security situation in Sand Flea City

deteriorated to the point where it was downright dangerous to live anywhere outside of a fortified and guarded complex, Alex made them an offer they couldn't refuse and to everyone's delight they moved into one of Project Voyager's hangers lock, stock and infirmary.

Absolutely one of the best hires Alex ever made.

The thought of Alex immediately removed the remaining fog from Marshal's mind. With a start, he quickly looked over at the next pod where Dr. Alexandria Cummings, possessor of several PhDs, the director, heart and soul and driving force behind Project Voyager and Marshal's ever-loving spouse, still slept in her own cryogenic cocoon.

"She's fine, John." Nancy smiled. "They're all fine. Now, finish your juice and I'll see you up forward after you get dressed."

After thanking her, Marshal looked over again at Alex as his throat tightened with emotion making it difficult to sip his drink. He couldn't really see her through the yellowish mist in her cryogenic pod and he remembered that he hadn't actually seen her since she went into cryogenic hibernation shortly after they left Earth. So, technically, he hadn't *seen* her for nineteen years.

Alex hadn't been woken up once during their journey and still wouldn't be for another six months. Those were her explicit instructions: wake her when they were six months out from Sanctuary. She never said exactly why she wanted to be brought out of cryogenic hibernation at that particular point but there was no doubt that her instructions would be followed.

He took another swig of juice and tried to add the years up. In Earth time, it would have been twenty-two years ago that the huge, multinational conglomerate called Visions Unlimited tapped Alex to be their Project Manager and oversee the building of Voyager. Alex took the job, made sure that her engineer husband was also employed on the project as an operator of one of their experimental space construction robots and in just over three years the brilliant woman had brought the Spaceship Voyager from dream to reality.

Quite a gal, my Alex, Marshal thought with pride.

Loving thoughts of Alex reminded Marshal that he was still sitting on the edge of his cryogenic pod buck naked. Reaching for his flight suit that was stored in the plastic storage locker at the foot of his pod, along with all his other possessions, he managed to hit his head on the metal catwalk that serviced the second tier of cryogenic pods above him. He muttered a small oath and shook his head. *Dumb,* he thought. Every time he woke up, he forgot about the row of pods above him.

Of course, they hadn't always been there. When Voyager had been designed as an exploratory vessel it was constructed on the lines of a wide-bodied 747 passenger plane but without the three-hundred plus passenger seats. In Voyager the section holding cryogenic pods was directly aft of the flight deck right where you would expect to find first-class.

Originally the cryogenic section housed twenty-four pods installed on only one level, twelve on each side of a center aisle. When the exploratory mission morphed into a colonizing mission it was imperative that as many warm bodies as possible be accommodated and a second tier of twenty-two pods, eleven on each side, were added.

Marshal thought he should have remembered that they had been added because he was the one who had added them. Well, he and Sam along with the other RJs and their robots of course. Marshal knew he couldn't have done any of it without his Sam. The construction robots were amazing bits of engineering: spherical balls that were made of some super-secret clear plasti-glass material that the RJ operated from a console inside the sphere. The robots also had four mechanical arms to handle construction material and a beyond state-of-the-art solar power plant that could actually maneuver the robots in the vacuum of space.

John Marshal was rather proud of the fact that he was the original robot operator, the first RJ, the first person in human history to actually operate a construction robot in space.

Though it didn't feel like it, those days were more than two decades and nineteen light years in the past.

Hard to believe.

As he dressed, Marshal looked around and marveled at the changes to Voyager. In the early days when Voyager had been an exploratory vessel, it had been designed to carry twenty-four people the twenty light years through space and once it reached Sanctuary the ship would fly down through the planet's atmosphere and land then the crew would spend a year in exploration and then return to Earth. Because it had to be aerodynamic, it had been built along the lines of a modern, wide-bodied conventional passenger airliner. The only external difference one would have noticed between Voyager and any other large passenger plane was that Voyager had a delta wing configuration.

Of course, inside the ship was another matter. Internally, Voyager was totally unlike any conventional aircraft that was ever built. Instead of the normal first class, business class, cattle car class or whatever sections that standard passenger aircraft had, Voyager was divided into four sections; the command section forward, the cryogenic section where he was standing, a supply section that was accessible from inside the spacecraft and further on an equipment section that was only accessible from the outside.

As Voyager's mission changed from an exploratory vessel carrying twenty-four people into a colony ship carrying over six-hundred humans its design had also evolved... or *mutated* would have been Marshal's opinion.

The current version of Voyager that was sailing through space was almost unrecognizable from its original blueprints. The original wide body passenger aircraft was still there at its core but with a few not inconsiderable additions: attached to the top of the fuselage was the vast tube of a 747-cargo plane that was stuffed full of supplies and equipment and on either side of the fuselage above the wings there were two more large, metal tubes each holding three hundred cryogenic pods to accommodate the six hundred sleeping colonists. To ensure the wellbeing of the sleeping colonists, the cryogenic cylinders were accessible from inside Voyager; however, the supply cylinder was not.

Of course, in order to make Voyager aerodynamic again so it could actually fly in an atmosphere and land on Sanctuary's surface, Marshal and the other RJs would have to remove those three cylinders in space. In order for them to be able to do this R3 had also been brought along on the journey. Robbie's Robot Roost (shortened to R3 and named after Robbie the Robot of TV and movie fame) was the storage and maintenance facility for the construction robots. This cylinder was one-hundred-and-fifty-feet-long, divided into three sections with each section holding four robots. R3 was attached to the underside of Voyager and accessible via a hatch located between the command section and the cryogenic section.

But R3 wasn't alone. Also fastened to the underside of Voyager was Wisdom, a space station that had orbited Earth for years. Convinced that it would be foolish to leave such a valuable resource behind while exploring an unknown world, the RJs had broken down the station into five separate tubes and hitched them to the ever-growing Voyager.

Finally, nestled under Voyager's delta wings were another marvel of Visions Unlimited: four space shuttles that were capable of flying out of a planet's gravity well into space—the Stardusters.

Still shaking his head at how much they had accomplished before leaving Earth, Marshal finished dressing and made his way forward the fifteen or twenty steps up to the command section. As he did, he wondered who the other two members of this year's Day Shift would be.

As Marshal entered the command section, the happy chatter stopped as everyone wished him a cheerful good morning even though the ship's chronometer said it was nearly eleven thirty at night. In space, time was pretty meaningless.

The changeover of watch crews was a happy event that was supposed to take about five seconds with the exchange being little more than...

"Anything happen?"

"Nope."

"Okay, see you in a year or so!"

But it never worked out that way. With the novelty of new faces, the outgoing and incoming crews generally sat around and talked and talked and talked for hours... even days.

With both shifts currently present, six people made the cockpit pretty crowded, but no one minded. Doc Nancy and her husband John were sitting in the pilot's seats deep in conversation. Though Nancy had been the one who woke Marshal up, he wasn't sure which of the two Watsons was just coming out of or going into hibernation, but he was sure that both of them would be awake for a day or two at least. John and Nancy were the only doctors aboard Voyager and, due to the very real possibility that they were going to be the only source of modern medical knowledge available to the colony, they planned to establish a medical school to ensure that their knowledge would be passed on.

Marshal took a seat around the metal card table that had been installed behind the pilot's seats. He still wasn't quite sure who had installed the table, but the list was narrowed down to six possibilities: the people who had been awake in years one and two. When Voyager had left Earth and he'd been placed in hibernation, there had been four first-class type passenger seats behind the pilot's chairs, but when he woke up two years later, someone had taken them out and replaced them with a metal card table and four metal chairs. Marshal had been thrilled. With lots of time on their hands, it was a much more practical arrangement for card games or building puzzles or whatever else they could think of to do while whiling away the next three-hundred and sixty-five days.

Marshal wasn't sure what he'd expected of space travel, but he'd never pictured it as boring.

Live and learn.

With the Docs off in their own little world, Marshal joined cryogenic specialists Dave Allen and Marty Brance and Fred Thompson, the robot jockey he'd be replacing, at the table. He was still getting to know Dave and Marty as they had only joined the Voyager team toward the end of construction when it had finally been time to install the individual pods in the huge cryogenic cylinders, but Fred was an old friend.

Though all of the RJs were pretty tight, Marshal and Thompson, along with Jack (JJ) Jackson and Billy Wright were the originals. The four of them had been the first of Alex's hires and had the dubious distinction of spending a couple of months at a big manufacturing plant just south of Chicago called Ajax Industries assisting, or at least trying to assist, in the development of the space construction robots.

While the concept of the robots was brilliant and way ahead of its time, Marshal and the other RJs thought that the self-absorbed designers at Ajax were morons. The RJs, the men who would actually use the machines in space, couldn't get it through the eggheads' heads that their invention, while brilliant on paper, wasn't exactly practical during operation. It had been a frustrating and futile two months trying to get them to tweak the design in order to make the robots more user friendly, but it was during those fruitless battles that the four of them had become close.

After everyone chatted for a while, Thompson and Marshal went down into R3. Back when they were in orbit around Earth, the robot storage and maintenance facility had been the first thing that the RJs and their robots had actually built-in space and, although Marshal didn't know exactly how he was going to spend the next six months until Alex came out of hibernation, he was pretty certain that most of his time would be spent in R3.

To keep himself busy during the last two times he had been awake, Marshal had rebuilt Sam—twice—and he had already decided that he wasn't going to do that again. But looking around, he sighed when he couldn't see what else he could do. The eleven robots were neatly lined up in their holding/launch racks looking like the metal balls in an old pinball machine.   Due to the mind-numbing boredom of interstellar travel, they had been worked on constantly. They looked like they had just come off the assembly line. Better than brand new, actually.

As did R3. The scattered, jumbled clutter of new, old

and broken spare parts that had originally taken up most of the working spaces were now clean, repaired and organized. Even the tools were neatly racked. Unless he redid stuff that was already done, Marshal couldn't see that there was anything that he could get into to occupy his time.

Thompson laughed as he read Marshal's glum expression. "I know! To kill time this past year, I not only rebuilt my robot, but I cleaned and racked all the spare robot parts."

"You fiend. Thanks a lot," Marshal said. "Now what the heck am I going to do?"

Laughing again, Thompson gave him a thump on the shoulder and said, "Beats me, but at least you only have six months until Alex wakes up. Just think! We're almost there!"

They went back up to the command section and talked with the others for a while, but it was soon evident that the outgoing crew, well Thompson and Brance as the two Doctors would probably just keep talking and comparing notes for at least another couple of days, would just as soon go to sleep realizing that the moment they did so, they'd then open their eyes and their journey would be over. *Lucky them,* Marshal miffed before mentally admonishing himself that he would have done the same if he could have. That meant that Dave Allen would be awake for the next year.

Marshal and Allen sat talking while Doc John and Brance took Fred back into the original cryogenic section just behind the command section. When they returned, Allen went with them to Marty's pod. Brance had been one of the later arrivals to the Voyager Program so his pod was in one of the three-hundred pod cylinders attached to the hull.

Once Thompson and Brance were down and not having anything better to do, Marshall gave his legs a stretch by taking another walk-through Voyager. When they had first begun building Voyager and it had still been an exploratory ship, it would have been a short walk, but with all the additions, you could now walk the length of two three-hundred-foot-long cryogenic cylinders.

He walked. He worried. He wondered.

Even if the Sanctuary was habitable what would it be like? Hot? Cold? Animals? Intelligent life?

No one was sure what would happen to their colony if they encountered an intelligent species on Sanctuary. When the subject was brought up in the bull sessions back on Earth some of the colonists wanted to remain on Sanctuary regardless of the fact that it was already occupied. Voyager certainly carried enough firearms to put up a hell of a fight if anyone objected. Others had insisted that they didn't have the right to do that if the current inhabitants wanted them to leave.

Marshal's opinion was that if the civilization on Sanctuary was anything like the so-called civilizations on Earth, when the UFO called Voyager appeared in Sanctuary's skies the Sanctuarians would probably just shoot first and ask questions later or maybe just let Voyager land and then put the Earthlings in a zoo.

After a very intrusive medical exam, of course.

Another, and potentially even greater problem, were the colonists themselves. When Voyager morphed from an exploratory mission to a colonizing mission the deal Alex struck with Visions Unlimited was that the people who were actually working on the vessel would get an equal opportunity to go to Sanctuary if they so desired. Alex would nominate half the colonists and the Visions Unlimited Board would pick the other half.

Marshal knew most of the colonists that Alex had picked but the large group of colonists that had been nominated by Visions Unlimited were an unknown quantity. They hadn't been involved in the trials and tribulations of actually building Voyager and for the most part they had only arrived at Project Voyager's ground base at Sand Flea Airfield during the final days before Voyager made its wild escape from Earth.

As Marshal walked, he moved quietly through the two cryogenic cylinders. While he knew the inhabitants were all in perfect hibernation, he always got quiet around the pods. It felt as if he was walking through a tomb or a mausoleum and at any moment, he might wake the dead.

He also smiled as he walked. The two cryogenic cylinders should have been identical. They were made to the same specifications. They looked the same from the outside—but inside, like the colonists themselves, they ended up not looking or feeling quite the same.

The first cylinder he walked through the robot jockeys had christened "The Italian Job" because it had been built in a factory just outside of Milan, Italy. The Italian Job had been the first cryo-cylinder to be completed. The Italian Job also had the full complement of three-hundred cryogenic pods, but most importantly, the sleepers in this cylinder were all people from Sand Flea. Friends.

The second cylinder—San Diego Job—had only been delivered to a rocket launch facility for its journey up to Voyagers orbit in the last months before Voyager's departure from Earth. The cylinder itself was fine, but in the chaos of Climate Change and government disintegration, it had been impossible for the factory to build and deliver all three-hundred of the individual cryogenic pods. This cryo cylinder was twenty- seven pods short and of the two-hundred and seventy-three pods that were installed, thirteen were empty.

Marshall didn't know the people who were sleeping

away in hibernation in most of those two hundred and sixty pods, but judging from the stories that he had heard, he didn't think that he was going to like them very much either.

That was probably unfair seeing as he didn't have any personal experience with them but...

Marshal guessed that the people VU picked were probably family members or friends and from what he had heard they were mostly stereotypical rich folk. People of privilege who thought that they were better than everyone else. Even Alex had said that there had been some rather uncomfortable scenes when the rich and obnoxious flew into Sand Flea in their private jets and started complaining about everything and everybody.

The fact that they were going to start a new life on a new world hadn't seemed to have percolated into some of their tiny brains. According to Alex, when some of these would-be colonists arrived at Sand Flea the first conflict was over clothing... or at least, that had been a part of it. The larger issue had been what each individual could take aboard Voyager. Space on a spacecraft is critical so early in the program, Alex had decided that individuals would board Voyager with the clothes on their back and The Project would provide each colonist with a standard storage container that would hold all their personal belongings. And Alex, being Alex, studied the problem and published a list of rugged, utilitarian items that would not only be useful, but essential starting out on a new world: Standard military flight suits, underwear, socks, shoes, coats, hats, etc. Every colonist had their own foot locker with their name stenciled neatly on the side at the foot of their individual cryo-pod.

And with Alex's careful planning, there was even space in the locker left open for any personal items that an individual might want to bring. Not a lot of space but some.

But apparently, some of these fancy ladies weren't having any of that. Some of them had as many as six suitcases and insisted they weren't going to leave anything behind. Not even their evening gowns.

Seriously? Evening gowns? Marshal had no idea where they intended to wear them.

And it hadn't been just the women. A few of the men had some extra baggage as well. Marshal hadn't heard what had been in their suitcases, but he was sure it had been just as dumb.

Naturally, Alex wasn't about to put up with any of that petty nonsense. One storage container per person *only* and if you're smart, you'll step over to our supply section and bring what everyone else is bringing.

Of course, what they could or could not bring onboard Voyager wasn't the only thing that the rich and obnoxious complained about. They didn't like having to eat what everyone else ate in Project Voyager's take-it-or-leave-it cafeteria-style dining. They didn't like the semi-private sleeping arrangements in the hangar dormitories. They didn't like the community bathrooms and they *really* didn't like it when it became painfully obvious to them that no one gave a rat's patootie what they liked or didn't like.

Some didn't like it so much that they actually climbed back onto their fancy executive jets and flew away.

Oh yeah, these people were going to be a joy on Sanctuary.

That morbid thought brought Marshal from the large cryogenic cylinder and into the much smaller cryo section to Alex's pod to reassure himself she was still only asleep. Inside the slick metal tomb, Marshal could just make out her form through the yellow mist.

With a sigh, he told his sleeping wife, "I don't know,

Luv. This shift until you wake up is only half the time of the others, but I think it's going to feel twice as long."

Oblivious to her husband's melancholy, Alex slept on.

CHAPTER 2

Doctor John Watson sat quietly with his earbuds on listening to the London Philharmonic and working a crossword puzzle on his pad but his mind wasn't really on either one. He smiled to himself; what he was really doing was hiding from John Marshal. Today was the day that the clock programmed into the ship's computer said Voyager was six months from its rendezvous with the planet Sanctuary and therefore the day that the duty crew was directed to bring the head of the Voyager Project out of cryogenic hibernation.

And, of course, Dr. Alexandria Cummings was John Marshal's wife.

As the time to bring Alex out of hibernation drew near, Marshal had become as nervous as a long-tailed cat in a room full of rocking chairs. For the last couple of weeks, it seemed that he was constantly asking Watson and Dave Allen if everything was okay with Alex's pod. Were all the readouts, correct? Shouldn't Watson and Allen check this or that?

Should they wake Alex early?

Watson and Dave had just laughed and told him that everything was fine. Both thought Marshal was becoming a bit of a pain in the lower regions, but neither Doc nor Dave could get mad at him. Marshal hadn't seen his wife, except through a yellow mist behind a plexi-glass cover of a cryogenic pod for nineteen and a half years—well, *technically* two and a half years if you just counted the time during the journey that Marshal had been awake, but even that was a long time.

So, today the chance for a little payback presented itself. Of course, the opportunity for practical jokes was rather limited in a spaceship hurtling through space at .98 light speed.

Limited, but not impossible.

Which was why Doc and Dave were hiding in as much as they could on a spaceship. Watson sat quietly working his puzzle in the farthest section of the robot repair and maintenance facility; in fact, the section where he was sitting was currently Marshal's workshop—the place where he had spent all his time over the last six months working on something. He wouldn't say what it was and Watson hadn't pressed him on it. And he was hoping that here tucked away in the farthest corner of R3 was the last place Marshal would think to look.

He was curious about Marshals project and he looked up at Marshal's workbench again and wondered just what the RJ was working on. Oh, not that he wasn't pleased that he was working on *something*. In the early days of their current shift, Doc Watson had become increasingly anxious about Marshal. A year or even six months is a long time and if an individual doesn't have something to occupy their mind during that time their mental and physical health could suffer. Marshal had told him that during his previous two awakenings he had rebuilt his construction robot Sam—twice—but he said that he wasn't going to do that again. For the first couple of weeks that Marshal had been awake, he just kind of wandered the halls from Voyager to the Italian Job, back to Voyager then into the San Diego Job and then back again. Then one evening while Watson was sitting in one of the pilot's chairs working on his school curricula for the Sanctuarian medical school and Marshal and Allen were playing chess, Marshal had what Watson could only describe as a Eureka moment.

The game had been going slowly as Marshal's mind was clearly elsewhere and Allen was becoming increasingly frustrated. Allen said later that he was about to suggest that they call it quits for the night when Marshal sat bolt upright and exclaimed, "Yes! That could work."

Watson looked up and Allen asked, "What could work?"

Marshal looked a little unfocused and said, "What? Oh! Nothing... nothing." Then he mumbled, "Your game Dave," and disappeared down into R3. After that, Watson and Allen had only seen him off and on for the last five and a half months.

Watson laid his electronic puzzle book down and looked around again. So, what was Marshal working on? Whatever it was it was clearly something to do with the construction robots. There was a partially stripped-down robot sitting in the maintenance cradle but Watson was pretty sure that it wasn't Marshal's Sam. No way would Marshal leave a partially disemboweled Sam scattered across R3. No, this one must be one of the general use robots. Watson didn't know squat about the robots, but he sensed that this one was different from the other robots sitting in the launch racks. The doctor looked back and forth between them to see if he could deduce the difference and the only obvious item that he could come up with was that the robot Marshal was working on was only going to have two arms rather than the standard four. But that wasn't really anything unique. During the construction of Voyager when parts were scarce the robots often worked with only two arms. No, it was something else but Watson wasn't familiar enough with the robots to pin it down. He shrugged and went back to his puzzle. John Marshal would reveal his pet project in time.

At about the same moment and practically right over Watson's head in the cryo-section, John Marshal jerked awake from a fitful sleep. He'd been sitting on the edge of his own pod while watching Alex while counting the minutes until it was time for her to wake up. Then he decided to lay down on the comfortable padding just for a moment and two hours had suddenly passed.

Time to get my girl back! Marshal jumped up, hit his head on the overhead walkway... again!... swore... again!... and began looking around for Doc and Dave. Frustrated that there was no sign of them, he bounded into the command section shouting, "Hey guys! Come on! It's time to wake Alex up."

The cockpit was empty and only silence answered his calls.

What the heck? Marshal thought. *Where are those guys?*

Backing out of the cockpit, Marshal entered the Italian Job. Down its cavernous length as far as he could see were nothing but rows of cryogenic pods full of sleeping colonists. The gigantic cylinder was empty.

What the heck? Marshal thought again. He crossed through the command section and looked into the other cryogenic cylinder.

Nothing.

The only other place to look was R3 but he knew they wouldn't be there. They never went down there. Marshal shook his head, climbed down the ladder into section one of the robot storage and maintenance facility and looked down the entire length of R3. Nothing.

Nothing but robots and machinery.

Marshal scratched his head. Where were the guys? Had they been spirited away by the space vampires because they surely hadn't gone out for a walk.

"What the actual heck!" he exclaimed.

Climbing the ladder back into Voyager, Marshal walked the length of the Italian Job looking carefully between each tier of cryogenic pods looking for his crewmates. When he didn't find them, he then did the same in the San Diego cylinder.

Nothing!

Marshal was becoming increasingly concerned and a little paranoid that maybe they really *had* been abducted by space vampires. There were only so many places they could be and he had checked them all.

No, he hadn't!

In a mixture of annoyance and glee, he went back down into R3, only this time instead of just looking down the length of the robot facility, he walked through sections one and two and into his workshop in section three. He was speechless when he saw Watson calmly sitting there tapping his pen in rhythm with the beat in his earbuds while working his crossword without a care in the world.

"Doc!" Marshal cried when he finally found his voice. "Doc! What are you doing here?"

No answer. Watson just sat there quietly working on his crossword. Then Marshal noticed the earbuds and waved a hand in front of Watson's face. Watson looked up, smiled and said, "Hi, John. Good morning."

"Doc, what are you doing down here?"

"Oh, I was just trying to find a quiet place to work on my puzzles. What's a five-letter word for 'caper'?"

Marshal sputtered, "What are you talking about? We're on a spaceship—in space—everyplace is a quiet place." Then he said, "Never mind, come on—it's time. Where's Dave?"

Watson asked innocently, "Time for what? And I have no idea where Dave is. Five letters; starts with 'p'."

Marshal was practically jumping up and down. "Doc, come on! Today we wake Alex up."

"Oh! Is that today?"

"Dooooooc!"

Watson laughed, clapped Marshal on the shoulder and said, "Okay, John. I guess we've pulled your chain enough. Let's go get your good lady. Oh, and the five-letter word for 'caper' I was looking for was 'prank'—as in, practical joke. Har, Har."

Marshal shook his head, laughed and said, "I'm going to get you guys. Just wait. Where's Dave?"

As they climbed the ladder into Voyager, Watson replied, "I honestly don't know, John. We kind of went our separate ways. I'm sure he's not down here. Must be up in one of the cryo-tubes."

Marshal shook his head. "No, I checked them out pretty good. I would have seen him."

"Command!" the two men said together only to be baffled when their missing man still remained missing.

As they stood together in the empty command section trying to solve the new puzzle of where's Dave, Marshal suddenly smacked himself on the forehead. "That sneaky son-of-a- gun! I know exactly where he is." And he headed into the San Diego cylinder and stopped by the pod whose foot locker was neatly labeled "David Allen, Cryogenics."

Marshal looked down at a smiling Dave Allen and said, "You snake. You pulled the plastic cover down."

Allen laughed. "That I did, and you walked right past me—twice! It was all I could do to keep from laughing out loud."

Marshal said, "Well, I already told this other Joker," he jerked his thumb at Watson, "that I'm going to get you guys. Now can we please wake Alex up?"

Laughing back and forth they went to Alex's pod, Doc and Dave did their magic. The mist cleared and Marshal lifted the plastic cover as his wife opened her eyes.

"Hello, Luv," Marshal said, emotion choking his voice.

Alex smiled and then frowned. Her throat dry, she croaked, "What's wrong?"

The three men looked at each other and Watson said, "Rest easy, Alex; nothing's wrong. We are exactly on schedule. I know it seems like you just closed your eyes, but you have been in cryogenic hibernation for nineteen and a half years. According to the ship's computer we're six months from Sanctuary, and we woke you up just as you requested. How do you feel?"

"Groggy. Even though I guess I've been sleeping for a couple of decades, I feel like I've been woken up in the middle of the night."

As veterans of many awakenings, her comment caused Marshal, Doc and Dave to snort in laughter. Marshal said, "Yup, Luv, that's exactly what it feels like." Watson handed her a container of fruit juice, told her to take her time and he and Allen went up into the command section.

Marshal sat down on the edge of the pod and said,

"Take your time, Luv. Here, take a sip of Doc's magic snake oil; it helps."

While they sat holding hands, Marshal filled his wife in on Voyager's journey up to this point. Which didn't take long seeing as nothing untoward had occurred during the last nineteen-and-a-half-years. They chatted for a while about nothing in particular, just glad to be together again until Alex felt sufficiently recovered to get dressed and head up to the command section.

When they joined Watson and Allen, Allen asked, "Alex, why did you want us to bring you out of hibernation now, six months from Sanctuary?"

Alex smiled and answered, "Well, Dave, in the rush to get away from Earth and to keep out of the government's clutches, there was only so much preprograming I could do to get Voyager headed off in the right direction and at the right speed. As it turned out, it's fortunate that I could even accomplish that much considering our rather frantic departure. So, to answer your question, if we continued at this speed in a few days, we would go past Sol II and Sanctuary at .98 light speed and our destination would be just a blur in the rear-view mirror. If we're going to make our rendezvous with the planet, I need to talk to Voyager and start getting us slowed down."

"But I don't have to do it right this minute. I'm hungry."

The guys laughed and Marshal said, "Yup, very common reaction. Grab a chair, Luv. One gourmet, reconstituted, freeze-dried special coming up!"

Alexandria Cummings sat in one of the metal chairs and looked around her command section. She looked at Doc and Dave and, indicating the metal table and chairs that were firmly fastened to the deck asked, "Where did these come from? It seems to me that when I went to sleep there were four first class passenger chairs here."

Watson agreed. "That's the way I remember it too, but when I woke up for my shift in year four, the chairs were gone—they're stored in the front of the San Diego Job by the way—and the metal table and chairs were in their place. I'm still not sure who made the switch. John said that the table was here when he woke up in year three. But it was a good switch. This is a much more practical arrangement, much better for card games or building puzzles or whatever. You'll see! Unless you plan to work on your computer 24/7, a year is a long time. Or in your case six months. That's another reason we are glad you're awake as we're getting tired of playing three handed bridge and whist."

Marshal returned with a steaming plate. "Here you go, Luv: one lousy freeze-dried dinner with some of André's and John Marshal's extra touches."

"It smells wonderful," she said.

The three guys smiled while she ate her first meal in nineteen-and-a-half years. Then she looked up, gave an embarrassed smile and said, "Sorry, but I was so hungry. I must have looked like a starving wolf."

They all laughed and Marshal said, "Not to worry, Luv, we've all been there. Do you want another one?"

Alex laughed. "I feel like I could eat one, but I guess I'd better not. And I guess that I had better get to work. Doc, could I move you out of the pilot's chair and over to the co-pilots? The computers I need are where you're sitting."

Watson looked surprised, looked around and exclaimed, "Really! What computers? I've been sitting in that chair for years. I didn't see any computers."

Alex smiled. "You weren't supposed to see them, Doc, and neither was anyone else. Gustave and I wanted to make sure that if the Vice President's minions got too nosy about how Voyager worked and started poking around in here, all they would see were the ordinary atmospheric flight controls that you would find on any regular passenger plane. Even the on/off switch and the rheostat for his magic engines are just for show. You can play with them all you want because they don't really do anything."

Watson and Allen looked a little blank, but Marshal asked, "Gustave? As in Herr Professor Gustave Gutman? The guy who invented and installed these engines?"

Alex said, "Of course. Now let me think for a moment I'm doing all this from memory."

The three men watched fascinated as Alex started punching seemingly ordinary flight control buttons in a certain pattern and panels slid aside, computer screens appeared and finally a virtual keyboard materialized in front of her.

Marshal sputtered, "Where the heck did all of this come from?"

Alex smiled. "My sweet, this is the Gutman Drive Programming and Control suite and as to where it came from it has been here ever since you installed the engines in Voyager."

Watson and Allen had to laugh because Marshal was sputtering like a mal-functioning bottle rocket.

"But! But!" he sputtered, "I built Voyager. I never installed any of this stuff and the only other people who were in here installing stuff were the engineers from Boeing and the other RJs and I'm pretty damned sure that they didn't either. When did all this happen and who did it?"

Alex smiled again. "Easy, my sweet, you'll blow a gasket. Gustave installed it when you were installing the engines."

"But! But!" Marshal continued sputtering. "I was with

him every minute. On your orders I never let him out of my sight."

"Yes, he said that you were very helpful—you and Sam."

Marshal sat back in his chair. "I don't believe it. That sneaky son of a gun. Right under my nose. While me and Billy and Tony were helping him install the engines he was also installing," and he waved his hand at the computers and screens that had appeared around Alex, "all this. And you...."

"Yes, my sweet."

Marshal shook his finger at his smiling wife and finally said, "Well, I must be a candidate for dummy-of-the-week. I mean, I was right with Gustave all the time and he did all this right under my nose." Marshal shook his head and looked at Dave and Doc. "Don't tell me that you two jokers knew all about this."

Allen said, "Are you kidding? I don't even know what you're talking about. Who's Gustave?"

That brought a laugh from the other three and Alex and Marshal looked at each other. Marshal said "Go ahead, Luv."

Alex steepled her hands under her chin for a moment marshaling her thoughts and began. "Well, Dave, Herr Professor Gustave Gutman is a genius. A man way ahead of his time. He's the one who designed, constructed and installed the engines that are currently driving this ship through space at almost the speed of light."

She paused thoughtfully then gave herself a little shake and went on. "Several years ago, back on Earth, Gustave Gutman just suddenly appeared on the fringes of the scientific community and when he first revealed his 'Gutman Drive', as he called it, everyone wrote him off as a quack. That is everyone except Visions Unlimited. At that time VU was becoming seriously interested in Sanctuary. VU wanted to explore 'Planet X' as it was then called and Gutman's magic engine, if it worked, was the only interstellar drive system in existence, or possibly in existence, that would make a journey of twenty light years possible. So, they took a chance, a very expensive chance! They provided the means, gave Gustave a pile of money—a really big pile of money—and that's how Voyager was born. We, myself and the project support people on the ground at Sand Flea as well as John and the robot jockeys in space, built Voyager to the design specifications that came from VU, but I suspect that they actually came from Gutman. That is, we built everything except the engines. Voyager the ship is pretty straight forward engineering. There are space vessels of one kind or another of fairly similar design running around all over Earth, the Moon and Mars. So, we built Voyager and waited and then one day the engines turned up at one of the rocket launch facilities in Texas and Gutman turned up at Sand Flea. John took the Professor up to Wisdom and Voyager where he directed the installation of the engines."

"And when that was completed," Marshal added, "he just got into one of VUs corporate jets and flew away."

Allen was in awe. "Wow!"

Doc agreed, "Wow indeed. Gutman was only at Sand Flea for a few days before he went up to Voyager, but I did get to talk to him a couple of times. Funny little guy but friendly. He was brilliant, curious about everything. You couldn't help liking him." He turned toward Marshal. "But I guess of all of us you must have known him best, John?"

"Well, maybe." Marshal answered. "I worked with him for over two months, but I don't know if I really knew him. I sure liked him. Smart. Hard worker. I tried my best to get him to go with us to Sanctuary and I think that he was tempted, but he said that he had to go home. That he had obligations."

Allen asked, "Where was home?"

The other three chuckled and Alex replied, "That was a big mystery, Dave. I'm not sure where his home was exactly, but I'm pretty sure that it was somewhere in Central Europe... Germany, Hungary, somewhere around there."

Marshal snorted. "Ha! I know where. He had a castle in Transylvania. A castle with a deep, dark dungeon where he kept aging scientists with long gray beards chained up to their work benches cranking out magical inventions."

Everyone laughed and Alex said, "I wish he was here, maybe he could help me solve another little problem that we are going to have when we land on Sanctuary."

Marshal asked, "What problem's that, Luv?"

"Basically, it's initially getting established," she answered.

Marshal seemed a bit confused. "What's the problem?" he asked.

Alex answered, "As I see it, my sweet, we are going to have a problem getting our supplies and equipment transferred from Voyager to wherever we establish ourselves on the planet."

Marshal scratched his head and said, "I guess I don't see the problem, Luv. We just do it the same way that we loaded Voyager when we were in orbit around Earth only in reverse, instead of loading the shuttles on the ground and unloading in space we load the shuttles here in space and unload them on the ground."

Alex smiled. "Thinking like a spaceman pushing things around in zero gravity. Of course, the unloading of the supply cylinder and the supply and equipment sections in Voyager here in space won't be a problem. Just pull the stuff out, float it over to the nearest Starduster and into the cargo bay. The problem is how do we unload the Stardusters once we're on the ground?"

Marshal still wasn't catching Alex's drift. "Well, we unload them the same way we loaded them back at Sand Flea."

Alex smiled again. "Unload them the same way we loaded them at Sand Flea in Phil Ruston's shuttle maintenance hangar with all kinds of equipment to move stuff around? Back there, we had cranes, moveable stairs and even an overhead gantry to lift some of the very heavy boxes, spare parts and equipment from the ground and into a Stardusters top loading cargo hold. Which I'll remind you is forty feet above the ground. None of which will be available on Sanctuary."

The three men finally nodded in understanding. Without just throwing it over the side they would have to build a whole series of cranes and gantries to get all that stuff out of the cargo bays and down to the ground.

Marshal started to reply, then sat back for a moment, then he jumped up, snapping his fingers and laughing.

Alex gave him a sharp look.

"No! I know! Sorry! Sorry!" Marshal said. "I wasn't laughing at the problem, it's just that I've been working on something. You see... oh hell come on I'll show you." And Marshal disappeared down the ladder into R3.

Alex looked at Watson and Allen. "Do either of you have any idea what my sweet but slightly goofy husband is talking about?"

Allen shook his head and Watson said, "Not a clue, Alex. All I know is that he has been down there in R3 working on something for months."

Alex shook her head. "Well, I guess I had better go see what it, whatever it is, is."

Watson and Allen agreed and followed Alex down the ladder. The three of them walked through the robot maintenance facility into the last section where Marshal was standing next to the half-built construction robot that was sitting in the maintenance cradle.

Not even trying to hide his smug grin, Marshal said, "Welcome Luv, gentlemen. I think I might have a partial answer to Alex's little supply problem." He then turned and gave a flourish wave to the robot. "Alex, Doc, Dave—meet Sam II, or Sam Junior. I think I like 'Junior' best."

Alex gave him an exasperated look and said, "John what are you talking about? This is a construction robot, a *space* construction robot. The supply problem is not at this end but on the ground. How is a robot that can only operate in space going to solve the problem?"

Watson and Allen nodded in agreement and gave Marshal a sympathetic look because his bubble was about to burst.

But Marshal remained all smiles. "Oh, ye of little faith! If Junior here was a space robot, he certainly wouldn't be of any use solving the unloading problem on Sanctuary, but despite outward appearances Junior isn't a space robot... or he won't be when I have him finished. If I've done the math and engineering right, Junior will fly in an atmosphere, in gravity, and on Sanctuary."

"What?" the three people exclaimed at once. When they had calmed down a little Alex gave her husband a squeeze and asked, "John, this is wonderful, but are you sure that will fly on Sanctuary?"

Marshal looked a little embarrassed and said, "Sure? No, Luv, I'm not 100% sure and there is no way to test Junior until we are actually on the planet. But I think Junior will fly, the math checks out, and Gustave thought that it could be done."

Alex asked, "Gustave?"

Marshal answered, "Yeah! One of the many things that he mentioned. It was just a passing remark, you know, one of the many that he made. We were just coming into R3 from a long day of working outside and he looked around at all the robots and said," Marshal paused before continuing with a fair approximation of Gutman's accent, "'Ya know, Yon, mit a little re-engineering of the solar power plant, I think dese robots could operate in a gravity well.'"

Marshal paused as the others stared at him with their mouths slightly open. "It was just a passing thought," he justified to them. "I was tired and I forgot all about it until a few months ago. Well. It turned out that when I started checking the design specifications it was just as Gutman thought, it could be done. I spent weeks on the computers running simulations and all the results said that the robots' solar power plants could be re-engineered to enable them to fly in a gravity well so I went from there. Junior here is the result or will be when I get him put back together again."

Alex wrapped her arms around Marshals neck, gave him a huge kiss and said, "Well, my sweet, you do have your moments, but two questions: If Junior can actually operate on Sanctuary, can he lift heavy loads? And the second question is, what made you think of doing it? I mean re-engineering a robot. I only mentioned the supply problem ten minutes ago."

"As for the first, Luv, will he be able to lift heavy weights?—I don't know—hadn't thought about it. He's certainly no heavy weight himself, but right off the top of my head I think Junior could get all the small stuff from the cargo bay to the ground. Maybe he could even manage a few hundred pounds, but certainly not the big awkward stuff like some of the farm equipment and the pieces for the saw mill.

For that stuff we'll still have to rig a sheerlegs, or something. As for the second question, when I set out to change the robots from space to ground, I wasn't thinking about supplies at all. I was thinking that once we were established on Sanctuary except for performing maintenance on Wisdom the robots and the robot jockeys would be out of business so I set out to give them and us a new life—a new role.

"I was thinking of using them as something like a light scout helicopter. You know, scout for Link and the security team, carry one or two people from place to place, that sort of thing."

Alex smiled, gave him another hug and looked again at what, if it worked, was a true engineering marvel and at her husband again and shook her head. You never knew about big happy-go-lucky John, but when he came through, he came through big time!

"Well," she finally said. "As wonderful as this is, I had better get back to my job and start reprogramming Voyager or we're going to end up somewhere out around Orion."

The guys all laughed as they trooped back up to the command section.

CHAPTER 3

Alexandria Cummings sat in the pilot's seat with her fingers steepled under her chin. To anyone who knew her this was her typical "don't bother me, I'm thinking" position. Actually, at the moment, she was reflecting on space travel. Over the last several days and weeks since she had been brought out of cryogenic hibernation, she had come to realize what a long time a year really was, especially when traveling through the seemingly endless blackness of space with nothing to do unless some disaster struck. No wonder Doc John was worried about the mental health of the watch crews. Alex shook her head in wonder that they hadn't all gone bonkers. But there was never a complaint from any of them. This was the job that she had assigned them and, like the good soldiers they were, they would carry it out.

To make time go by everyone on the watch crews had created a self-assigned project to keep them busy during the long endless hours of boring a hole through space. Doc John was working on the medical school curriculum, her husband, John, was converting a construction robot to planetary operation and Dave Allen had decided that that there probably wasn't a future for cryogenic specialists once the colony was established on Sanctuary so in order to keep himself useful and employed while also making sure the colonists were not going to go down the fossil fuel route, he was reading everything that he could find in the ship's library on renewable energies like water, solar, geothermal and wind.

But an individual could only do so much on their own and Alex marveled at how much they all looked forward to their evenings together even if it was just a reconstituted meal and a card game, or a game of chess, or even building a puzzle.

Live and learn, Alex thought with a self-admonishing sigh. VU had recommended that Voyager have a watch crew and she had gone along with it. She certainly regretted that decision now and vowed that if Voyager ever did make another interstellar flight—like, heaven forbid, a return to Earth—everyone would be in cryogenic hibernation and if they hit a space rock or were boarded by inter-galactic zombies so be it.

But that was for another day. Reaching out, Alex double-checked her computer findings and smiled which didn't go unnoticed by Doc John sitting in the co-pilot's seat. He drew a breath to ask her what was up but didn't get the chance when Marshal came up out of his "hole", what he called the entrance to his robot facility. Sliding around the card table, Marshal wrapped his arms around Alex from the back and kissed her on the cheek.

Alex's smile widened as she reached back and patted him on the arm. "I'm glad you're here, my sweet, I was just about to call you."

"Why?" he asked. "What's up?"

Turning her smile to the three men, Alex announced, "Gentlemen, we are here."

Marshal, Doc John and Dave excitedly looked out the command section windows and then gave each other a glance when all they saw was the seemingly never-ending blackness of space.

"Uh, Luv," Marshal said as the confusion clouded his expression, "just where exactly is here?"

With a patient smile Alex replied, "Here, my sweet, is the outermost reaches of the planetary system of Sol II. If our computer projections are accurate, and I'm just about 100% sure that they are, we are now crossing the orbit of planet number eight, our new star's outermost planet."

They all responded with various forms of "wow" and "gee" then Marshal leaned forward to look out the windows again. Scratching his head he frowned. "Ah, Luv, pardon my asking, but if you and the computers are right, shouldn't there be something kind of big and round out there? Something that looks like, well, you know, like a planet?"

With a chuckle Alex reached back and smacked him lightly on the arm. "There will be, you big oaf. You will definitely see something big and round like a planet out there if you want to wait," she glanced down at a different screen, "ninety-seven years. Planet number eight's orbit currently puts it on the other side of Sol II."

"Okay," Marshal said, "I'll give you that. But if we are in Sol II's planetary system, where's Sol II? I also don't see anything that looks kind of big and bright, you know, like a sun."

"Nor will you for quite some time," Alex replied. "Well, you won't see it 'big and bright' yet, anyway as we are still about four billion miles away from Sol II... 3.8 billion miles to be exact. Look out the lower right-hand edge of Doc's front window," she pointed out so they could better locate the area in the sea of identical stars. "See that little white dot? That's Sol II."

"It's tiny!" Allen seemed disappointed. "It looks like all the other stars. How long until we get there?"

"Still a couple of months; sixty-four days to be exact."

"Why so long?" Marshal asked. "At our speed we should be there in no time."

Alex said, "If we maintained this speed we would be, my sweet, but if we would like to stop for a while at Sanctuary and maybe, you know, go into orbit around the planet, we need to slow down. And don't complain about the rest of the journey taking sixty-four days. If you'll remember it took our namesake Voyager 2—an unmanned probe that the United States launched way back in the 1970s—twelve years to reach our planet number eight and Neptune is a billion miles closer to Sol than this planet eight is to Sol II."

Over the next days and weeks looking out the window at the tiny speck of light became irresistible, but the faint dot that was Sol II never appeared to be getting any closer. It was like watching grass grow or paint dry; they had to wait a long while to discern any real change. However, that didn't stop them from looking. Eventually, the little dot of light did appear bigger and brighter... or at least the Voyagers convinced themselves that it was.

Two weeks after crossing the orbit of planet eight Alex announced that they were passing through the orbital path of planet number seven. Again, there was nothing to see and answering their silent question Alex pointed to the right side of Voyager and said, "About thirty-two years that way. But," she added to dispel their obvious disappointment, "in a few days, I think we might see something of planet six and if these projections are correct, we should pass fairly close to planet five."

While the guys all commented and looked out the windows Alex frowned. "Maybe too close," she muttered. Double checking her computer readouts, Alex sat back and steepled her fingers as she thought and then gave herself a shake as she came to a decision. "Doc, I think I would like you and Dave to bring Al out of hibernation."

At the doctor's shocked expression, she smiled and shrugged her shoulders at his unasked question. "I know, John. There's really no reason to bring him out of hibernation until we reach orbit around Sanctuary and get Wisdom up and running, but he's been a part of Voyager, if only unofficially, since the beginning and he is our senior scientist. You know he would love to be a part of all of this!" Alex waved her hand in the general direction of the blackness outside Voyager's windows. "He has to be a part of this... watching these planets reveal themselves and especially observing Sanctuary as we approach from outer space."

Watson smiled back. "That's a nice thought, Alex. I'm sure he would. Come on, Dave. Let's go get the Professor."

If Doc Watson had any concern about how any of the six-hundred plus individuals on Voyager would react physically to a twenty-year period of cryogenic hibernation his greatest worry was Al Wilson. In addition to being the oldest of the Voyagers at sixty-three, Al had spent most of the last ten years before the departure from Earth in weightless orbit as the senior meteorologist aboard the space station Wisdom.

When he was back on Earth, back in the Project Voyager hangers at Sand Flea, Doc John had spent hours trying to convince Wilson that long periods of weightlessness were not good for bones, muscles and other parts of the human anatomy and that he should spend more time on the ground. But from his perch three hundred miles above him Al had just smiled, said he was fine, that he had a job to do and stayed in orbit aboard Wisdom. Even pressure from Doc Nancy to get the scientist out of orbit for a thorough examination had been futile. Al was always very polite, never outright refusing, but it was clear that if the docs wanted to examine him, they would have to come up to Wisdom. Actually, they had planned to do just that when they were overtaken by the events that led to Voyager's hasty departure from Earth.

By any measure, Professor Al Wilson was planet Earth's weatherman. Broadcasting from the space station Wisdom his forecasts were listened to and trusted all over the world and although Wilson had never been hired by Alex or had actually been a part of Project Voyager, he was certainly a willing co-conspirator helping as much as he could to conceal the fact that a spaceship was being built next to his space station and when he found out that Wisdom was going to make the journey to Sanctuary there was no doubt that Al Wilson was going along.

To maintain the appearance of business-as-usual as Voyager's departure approached, Al had kept up his daily weather forecasts even as Wisdom was being dismantled around him. On the day the spacecraft actually departed for Sanctuary, Al Wilson had broadcast his normal worldwide weather report not from Wisdom but from Voyager's cockpit and then he had gone straight into cryogenic hibernation.

Now Doc John shook his head at the prospect of waking the weatherman up. During Voyager's twenty-year journey through space approaching the speed of light, the spaceship had gravity. That meant Al Wilson had spent ten years in weightlessness orbit followed by twenty years of gravity and the doctor wasn't sure how that was going to work out for Al. At least Al was oblivious as he slept soundly in a nice padded pod. Watson remembered the first time that Marshal had come back to earth after fourteen months in space. His legs were so rubbery that he had to be carried into Alex's office.

On the other hand, he thought, as Alex gradually slowed the ship from .98 light speed to around the twenty-five thousand miles an hour required to obtain orbit around Sanctuary, weightlessness was starting to return so maybe Al would be in his natural environment.

Wilson's pod was in the original cryogenic pod section just behind the command section so they were there in just a few steps and, with Watson and Allen's experience, it only took a few minutes to bring Professor Al Wilson out of cryogenic hibernation.

The mists in the torpedo shaped pod cleared, Watson lifted the plastic lid and Al Wilson blinked his eyes open and with a start, exclaimed, "What's wrong? Didn't we go?"

Allen and Doc John laughed at the common reaction everyone experienced at coming out of hibernation. No matter how long you were in hibernation, days, weeks, months, years it always seemed that when you woke up you had just closed your eyes.

"Relax, Al," Watson reassured him, "everything's okay. I know you feel like you just went to sleep but you have been in hibernation for twenty-years."

Blink. Blink. "Really? We're here?" He tried to struggle up but Watson gently held him down.

"Easy, Al. Take it easy. Your old bod has some adjusting to do."

Wilson sniffed. "My bod's not that old." And they both laughed.

A few minutes later Wilson felt strong enough to sit on the edge of the pod and while he sipped on the magic fruit juice, Doc John gave him a full examination.

Much to Watson's befuddlement Al Wilson was just fine.

"So, we're not there yet?" Al asked as Watson brought him up to date on Voyager's progress.

"No, we're currently passing through planet seven's orbit and we're a few days from six," Doc John told him. "Alex doesn't think that we will see much of planet six but she seems confident that we will get a real close-up view of five. She thought that you would like to be a part of that and our approach to Sanctuary."

Wilson smiled warmly. "Bless her heart. Of course, I would! Ah, Doc, do I go around naked or are there any clothes available?" It was clear that his nudity was the only thing preventing him from dashing into the cockpit to view the new solar system immediately.

Watson laughed. "You old fart. Don't you remember where you put them?" The doctor opened the storage locker at the foot of Wilson's pod and handed Wilson his clothes before warning him, "And be careful as you move around, Al. Voyager is slowing down so we are kind of halfway between gravity and weightlessness. I don't want you to try floating down a hatch and breaking your ankle or neck."

When they walked into the command section Alex bounced out of her chair and fumbled her way around the metal table and chairs in order to give Wilson a big hug. While they chatted and Wilson was brought up to date, Marshal fixed a dinner which Al managed to make disappear in a heartbeat before he and Alex squirmed up into the pilot and co-pilot's seats. The man was in awe and didn't move for more than an hour. Marshal wasn't sure if the professor even blinked.

Alex looked back at Marshal. "My sweet," she said

waving a hand at the table and chairs, "I know that this arrangement has been very useful over the years but I am getting tired of climbing over them. Do you think that you could do something about that?"

Marshal smiled. Of course, he could! And the next morning the metal table and chairs had disappeared and the four first-class passenger seats had been re-installed as Voyager sailed on to intersect the orbit of the sixth planet. It was magnificent! A gas giant with what appeared to be a series of rings much like Saturn, but the Voyagers weren't sure. The planet was just visible and about the size of a basketball just off to their left. Al watched it slowly pass through a pair of binoculars he'd packed in his footlocker. More than once they heard him whisper, "Thank you for waking me!"

But number six was just of passing interest as everyone's attention became focused on the looming presence of planet five—a massive, swirling ball of multi-colored gas that soon filled all the visible space to the front and left of the spacecraft.

Jupiter II, as they were now beginning to call it, was overpowering, breathtaking. A rapidly spinning cloud in various shades of blue and streaked with bands of yellow, brown and gold, the gas giant wasn't anything like Earth's Jupiter. There wasn't the iconic Great Red Spot, but there were dozens of massive storms clearly visible along the boundaries of the colorful bands swirling around the perimeter of the planet.

"What are all those black dots moving across the planet's surface?" Dave asked, squinting as he studied the giant sphere.

"Moons," Alex and Wilson answered almost in unison.

Everyone chuckled and Dave said, "That seems like a

lot of moons. At a quick count I think I can see over twenty."

Al smiled. "I wouldn't be surprised if there weren't more than that. Probably a lot more. Earth's Jupiter has dozens of named moons and four of them are big enough to be called planets. I'm sure that you have heard the names: Io, Ganymede, Calisto and Europa. Heck! Ganymede is bigger than the planet Mercury."

His enthusiasm couldn't be contained. Turning to Alex, Wilson exclaimed, "Just looking at the size of it! I'm sure that the planet serves the same purpose that Jupiter does in Earth's Solar System. It's the gravitational force that balances Sol II and keeps everything from spiraling into it. It's probably also the vacuum cleaner that sucks in a lot of loose debris. The gravitational pull of a planet that size must be enormous."

As if in answer to Wilson's observation a shudder ran through the fabric of Voyager.

The five humans looked at each other as Dave Allen exclaimed, "What the hell was that!"

Before anyone could answer they felt a stronger shudder and then Voyager began to vibrate

"What is it?" Allen asked again, his voice quivering in panic. "What's happening?"

Alex and Wilson looked at each other, looked out at Jupiter II and Alex said, "I was afraid of this. Gravity! Our flight path is too close to the planet. We're getting caught in the planet's gravitational field and like Jupiter II does with everything else in space it's trying to pull us in."

Watson asked, "Can we break free, Alex?"

Alex had all her screens and the virtual keyboard out and her fingers were flying. "I don't know," she said through clenched teeth. "I can't really steer Voyager, you know. The only control I have is through the computers and that's only to aim her at a point in space and to increase or decrease power to the engines. I can try to edge us away from the planet and since we have been slowing down the engines are only at half power so we have plenty in reserve. I'll see if I can break us free."

Marshal, sitting behind her, laid a hand on her shoulder and softly said, "Easy, Luv. Not too fast. Not too much power too quickly."

She looked a question at him. He shrugged. "Two reasons Luv. One if we apply too much power to Gutman's engines and break free too fast it could be like a tug of war when one side lets go, we might go shooting right past Sanctuary. And secondly, and I think more importantly, I'm pretty sure Voyager would hold together in a tug of war with the planet, but I'm not so sure about all our attachments," he added and waved a hand towards the ceiling of the ship "The supply cylinder up top, the two cryo cylinders, R3, Wisdom and especially our Stardusters are just hanging on the outside so to speak. Any sudden stress might break some or all of them loose. And in addition to all our irreplaceable stuff, there's five hundred and fifty-nine people sleeping out there."

Alex nodded and said, "Got it, my sweet, thanks! Nothing sudden or violent. Steady pressure. Right." Then murmured to herself, "if I can!" Again, her fingers flew over the virtual keyboard.

Marshal sat silent. Kind of unfocused as he mentally reviewed the internal and external fabric of Voyager. Suddenly, he got up and, due to Voyager's violent shaking, staggered back to close the hatches leading to the two cryogenic cylinders and R3. When he returned to his seat, he saw the others looking at him and said, "Sorry. I don't mean to seem coldhearted, but if one of those cylinders were to break loose and the hatches were open, it would not only be the end of them," he waved at the cylinders, "but the end of all of us, too."

No one spoke as they sat in silence while Alex continued her solitary struggle with the planetary mass that was Jupiter II. After a few minutes that seemed like an eternity, the vibration in the ship's fabric seemed to diminish slightly. Wilson looked over from the co-pilot's seat and said softly, "Whatever you're doing it's working, Alex. I think we're edging away; keep it up."

More attuned to Voyager than the others, Marshal knew what she was attempting. Through the ship's vibrations he could feel it. With just her keyboard she was jockeying the engines. She would slightly increase power to both engines to keep Voyager from being pulled closer to the planet then she would apply slightly more power to the port engine to edge Voyager a little farther away from Jupiter II. Then both engines. Then slightly more on the port engine. Just a few seconds each time. Small beads of perspiration appeared on her forehead.

Marshal sat behind her trying to lend support without speaking or touching her. Not doing anything that would break her concentration. The minutes seemed like hours but then, suddenly, Voyager seemed to slightly break free of the planet's pull. They could all feel it. The shaking diminished, then after several minutes stopped altogether and Voyager felt like it just kind of staggered forward.

Marshal leaned over the back of Alex's chair, kissed her lightly on the cheek and said, "Well done, Luv."

An exhausted Alexandria Cummings gave him a wan smile.

Then Marshal was out of his chair and back to the hatches. He looked through the hatch window into the Italian Job, mumbled something to himself, and slowly, cautiously opened the hatch, waved to the others to stay put and disappeared inside. It was a full five minutes before he reappeared with a big smile on his face. "Looks good!" he announced, relieved. "No damage that I can detect with a quick look. Let me give the San Diego Job and R3 a quick check and then whenever you're ready, Doc and Dave, we'll give them a thorough going over."

Watson and Allen nodded in agreement. When Marshal returned, the three of them started on the Italian Job and over the course of the next several hours checked the readings on every pod and every seam and joint in the ship's fabric that they could reach.

Their conclusion when they reported back to Alex was that all six hundred and one humans in hibernation were fine and that Voyager hadn't suffered any structural damage from their encounter with the huge planet.

Lucky, Alex thought to herself. *Very lucky. If we had been any closer...!*

CHAPTER 4

It took a full week for Voyager to pass Jupiter II and as the fifth planet faded behind them Marshal asked, "What about the asteroid belt, Luv? Does this star system have an asteroid belt?"

Alex replied, "I don't know, my sweet. That was one of the many questions that the earthbound astrophysicists couldn't answer and I don't know if we'll be able to answer it, either."

Marshal only had to raise an eyebrow at his wife to ask why not.

"Because," Alex answered with a shrug, "it's... well... space. The asteroid belt is always pictured as this great mass of rocky debris moving around the sun, and it is. But space is so vast and the individual hunks of rock floating in it are so small, relatively speaking, and are so far apart that, unless we are extremely unlucky and hit one, we will probably pass through the gap between Jupiter II and Sanctuary without ever seeing anything or answering the question of whether the asteroid belt exists or not."

Marshal looked out into the blackness of space in relieved disappointment. While the adult in him was immensely relieved that the odds were in their favor that the asteroid belt would be another boring non-event, the kid in him had really, *really* wanted to see a bunch of asteroids crashing into each other and had to admit to himself that he was slightly miffed that it wouldn't be as excitingly cool as the movies made it out to be. That being said, Marshal realized he was now more adult than kid when the nagging worry that they'd be unlucky enough to hit a bunch of space rocks dissipated when the asteroid belt was firmly in their rearview mirror... so to speak.

As Voyager sailed on, all attention was directed forward. When Sol II grew from the never changing little white dot into a small glowing ball and finally into a large blazing sun, the focus shifted to the black dot moving across its fiery face that Alex said was the fourth planet. The hunk of space rock that all of their hopes and dreams centered on— Sanctuary.

As Voyager crept up on Sanctuary it didn't seem that anything except their spaceship was actually moving, but they were. Everything was in motion. Sol II, its family of planets— all were racing through space at about a million miles a day and within that movement, Sanctuary was following its own annual 372-day orbital journey around its star.

But as they approached Sanctuary, it was clear that the planet was moving away from them and they had to play catch-up to their new home. The nearer Voyager got to the planet; new discoveries were made every minute. Much to the joy of the watching Voyagers, Sanctuary slowly changed from a black dot against the sun to a blue dot against the void of space.

Blue!

Every human watching from the Voyager cockpit breathed a sigh of relief. Blue was a very good sign as it meant there was probably water.

Then that relief was replaced with consternation as they got closer. Mixed in with the blue was white—a lot of white.

"Ice or clouds, Al?" Allen asked as they all looked to their meteorologist.

Wilson reassured them that it was just clouds, but the others still had their doubts. Even if it wasn't ice, that was still a lot of cloud cover. Three quarters of the planet or more seemed to be covered with swirling white vapors and storms. So, if it was covered in clouds and wasn't covered in ice and snow, what was Sanctuary? A rainy water world? They couldn't land if there wasn't anything to land on.

And they also couldn't seem to get close enough to Sanctuary fast enough to find out. Though they were speeding towards it faster than any person had ever traveled, the planet was still a distant blue-white ball that didn't appear to be getting any bigger. An illusion to be sure, but an annoying one for the impatient Voyagers.

Suddenly Allen pointed off to the right-and side of Sanctuary and exclaimed, "Look, a moon! Sanctuary has a moon!" Then he whispered in awe, "It looks just like our moon."

It did, but the others chuckled anyway and Wilson said, "Dave, this is our moon now."

"Aw, you know what I mean, Al. Quit pickin' on me."

They all laughed again and acknowledged that he was right, it did look like Earth's moon. At nearly the same size, it was a crater covered barren rock that appeared to orbit at about the same distance from Sanctuary as the Moon did from Earth.

Once Voyager was inside the lunar orbit, Sanctuary was plainly visible... or as visible as it could get through the clouds.

Doc John said, "You know, from here Sanctuary looks just like the photographs that the Apollo astronauts took of Earth on their trips to the Moon but with more clouds."

The others agreed and as details of the planet's surface were occasionally observed through the swirling clouds one after the other the five humans voiced their observations.

Marshal was sitting, well standing, floating, behind Alex's chair with his arms wrapped around her and her chair while she monitored Voyager's progress toward orbit. "Look Luv," he said excitedly, "there are patches of green and brown down there."

Before Alex could reply Allen said, "Yeah, just patches."

"Well," Marshal remarked, "At least there is some land. Something we can at least put the shuttles down on and maybe Voyager, too."

Al frowned. "Yes, there appears to be some surface area, but at first glance I think that there is even less land area on Sanctuary than there is on Earth and Earth's land surface area is only about thirty percent of the total."

"Why do you think that?" Alex asked. After a decade of observing Earth from orbit, Alex didn't doubt the weatherman's hypothesis; she just wanted him to explain it.

Wilson shrugged. "Just thinking about weather, Alex. With all that open water to provide the energy the storms generated in that vast ocean could be huge—ferocious! And once a storm did form it could roll all around the planet. It's hard to be certain without any instruments and all that cloud cover, but at first glance it looks like the southern hemisphere is all ocean. I'm trying to compare it to Earth. Imagine what the weather is like in the South Atlantic, the South Pacific or the Great Southern Ocean around Antarctica. Without any land formations to break the storms up—no islands, no tip of South America, no southern tip of Asia and no Australia—that's what the weather could be like here." He chuckled. "The Roaring Forties on steroids."

While Alex and the rest were trying to digest that observation, Dave Allen started jumping up and down in his seat and pointing out the window. "Look! Look!" he exclaimed ecstatically. "A second moon! We have two moons!" It seemed that Dave Allen had a thing for moons.

After giving the second moon its due appreciation, Marshal commented, "Al, is it me or does that second moon look smaller than the first one?"

"Yes," Wilson answered, "it's smaller and I think that it's closer to the planet. Its orbit is a lot faster." Suddenly Al shook his head as if trying to dislodge the thought that had popped in.

"What?" asked Alex.

"Oh, nothing really, Alex. I was just thinking about what I just said about the Roaring Forties. With the gravitational effect of two moons added to the apparent lack of land area on the planet's surface the oceans of Sanctuary could be really, really wild. Just speculating, but any large body of water could be a constantly churning, storm tossed cauldron. Look out your window, Alex, see those large white swirls in the cloud's way off to the south all around the southern hemisphere? Those are storms, big storms! Hurricanes, typhoons, cyclones—whatever you want to call them."

Watson asked, "Al, without landmasses, once they got going what would stop those storms or even slow them down?"

"Nothing!" Wilson answered, "Absolutely nothing. I imagine they would probably just keep going until they ran out of energy. But not all of them will stay in the Southern Ocean, you know. Because of orbital rotation many will swing to the north and hit whatever land they run into. And," he went on. "those bodies of water between what we can see of the land masses are big enough to generate their own storms."

Well, Alex frowned to herself, *if the oceans of Sanctuary are potentially a churning cauldron with the occasional massive storm, so much for settling on the coast and exploiting the Bounty of the Sea.*

Voyager was still too distant from the planet and the cloud cover far too dense to accurately define the shape of the continents, if they were indeed continents and not just scattered large and small islands. It wasn't until they were almost in orbit that they kind of agreed that the visible land areas were connected and not just a separate chain, or chains, of large islands. The more they looked, the more the land areas appeared to be large and small peninsulas running from the northern hemisphere to the Southern Ocean.

Marshal commented that the smaller peninsulas looked like a bunch of Italy's sticking into the Mediterranean Sea and the observation brought a general chuckle and nods of agreement.

Another feature that slowly became visible in and out of the cloud cover was that any land extending far enough south to cross the equator had a wide belt of green. Thick, lush forests ringed the equatorial regions in a broken dotted line. While the storms of the planet were daunting and there wasn't nearly as much land as they would like, Marshal took heart that what was there seemed to be flourishing. Sanctuary was green, blue and white... the three colors humans needed to survive. It seemed to be warm enough for plants to grow and maintain water in liquid, solid and vapor.

Alex had to make a quick decision as to where to put Voyager into orbit and seeing as there appeared to be more land north of the equator than south she slid Voyager into orbit three hundred miles above the center of the northern hemisphere and for the first time in over twenty years Gustave Gutman's wonderful, magic, mysterious engines shut down.

The Earth men and women looked at each other as the reality of their accomplishment sank in. They had traveled across twenty light years of empty space and were now in orbit around Sanctuary. They had done it!

There was a long silence as each of them individually realized that they were really here. That silence was immediately followed by wild excitement. Everyone was out of their seats, hugging each other, laughing, pointing at the planet, chattering and in their weightless environment bouncing off the walls.

The spontaneous joy didn't last very long, however, as the pull of Sanctuary was too strong. Soon each of them was back with their noses pressed against the glass observing the planet.

Watson said, "Those two larger land masses are bigger than I thought."

His comment was followed by general speculation as to whether their initial thoughts had been correct and the bits of land that they could see were all actually connected landmasses. Voyager made two full revolutions around the planet before they were in general agreement that the five peninsula-like continents were indeed connected. Observations through the occasional breaks in the clouds verified that the land masses were two large and three small peninsulas oriented from the north down to the south. Agreeing that there were just five of the peninsula/continents was made more difficult not just due to the density of the clouds but because the two large continents were so large. One appeared to be as wide and as long as Earth's North and South America squashed together without a Caribbean Sea or a Gulf of Mexico.

This continent also had a large body of water in the middle of the northern hemisphere that initially made the continent appear to be divided into two or more separate peninsulas.

Another obvious feature of that large continent was that there was no break in the clouds along what they assumed to be the west coast of the southern hemisphere. A mass of cloud so dense that they couldn't determine for sure where the coast actually was.

They looked toward Al Wilson who shrugged. "I'm not sure. My best guess is that there is a high range of mountains along the coast that's blocking the weather. See the lack of cloud cover to the east and look at the other large land mass, the one that looks to me to be approximately the shape of Africa. Look, along the west coast of both hemispheres the same phenomena, dense black clouds along the coast and almost no cloud cover inland to the east. Something is blocking those clouds and the only thing I can think of is mountains."

Marshal was privately impressed. That must be some mountain range! It was easily twenty thousand miles long and he couldn't even begin to guess how high.

Directing their attention to the far north, the arctic

region was an unbroken expanse of white that covered the entire polar area and extended southward for thousands of miles in a solid, unbroken sheet of ice that covered the northern third of the planet. Creeping from under this snowy polar region were the five peninsulas which extended southward anywhere from a few hundred miles to several thousand. Three of them made it as far south as the equator and had a lush greenbelt, though one only just barely.

Allen was floating in the aisle looking out between Alex and Al when he blurted out, "It's a hand!"

"What?" four voices chorused.

"The planet, the continents; look!" Allen explained. Reaching his left hand in between Al and Alex, he held his hand there with the palm down and his fingers extended. "See? The back of my hand is the polar ice cap and the fingers are the peninsulas."

"He's right!" Al chuckled. "It's a giant hand gripping a ball," which made everyone laugh.

"Good!" Marshal nodded definitively. "That saves us the trouble of thinking up fancy names for them."

"What?" four voices chorused again.

"Sure!" Marshal's smile was half a smirk because he knew he was about to annoy Alex. "Start with the little guy," he explained, pointing to the squat, almost fat peninsula. "We call him Thumb. That will give us Thumb, Index, Middle, Ring and Little."

Everyone laughed while Alex good-naturedly rolled her eyes. "You big oaf. You know if those names stick it'll be just my luck that I'll end up living on Middle Finger."

That brought another laugh while they went back to looking at the wonder that was Sanctuary. It was more than a little crowded as five people jockeyed for a good viewing position out of a cockpit window the size of one on a commercial aircraft, but the fact that they couldn't really see much didn't stop everyone from trying and commenting. One thing they were unanimous on was that Al's first assessment had been correct: the top one third of the planet was one continuous sheet of ice. What they couldn't decide on was if this was normal for Sanctuary or if the planet was experiencing an Ice Age. Al could only shake his head and say that he didn't know.

"I'm an idiot," Marshal suddenly muttered as he slapped himself on the forehead. He'd been standing behind Alex's command chair trying to get a good view of the peninsulas of Middle and Index as they passed below while in the distance at about where Antarctica would be on Earth, all he could see was storm-tossed oceans. It wasn't the kind of view that inspired confidence in the future. It was when he drifted to the other side of the cockpit to try and get a peek around Doc and Dave that he had his sudden inspiration to his own intelligence. Without explaining himself, he reached down and grabbed Alex's hand. "Come on, Luv."

"What?" she squeaked as Marshal pulled her up out of her seat, towed her through Voyager's weightless passageway and down the hatch into R3. "What is it?" she asked again as her husband put her hand on the workbench and told her to wait. Alex's curious frown turned into a massive grin as he floated over to the rack where the construction robots rested and threw some cushions into Sam. Moments later, they went through the outer hatch and popped into space.

"How about this, Luv?" Marshal asked. "For you: the best seat in the house?"

Alex hugged Marshal in delight and then gasped as she looked out of Sam's clear plexi-glass bubble at the unobstructed view of the planet Sanctuary revealing itself before them. They were silent for several minutes taking in the spectacle below them. Then one or the other would comment on some observation. The experience reminded Marshal of the old days back on Earth when they used to fly their own private airplane up and down the East Coast of the United States looking at the aftermath of the latest storm that had blown through.

While Alex was observing Sanctuary, Marshal gently glided Sam all around Voyager looking for possible damage from their twenty-year journey through space, or even worse the possible loss of anything from their encounter with Jupiter II. For several minutes, he drifted under the wings in silence as he checked every fastening on all four Stardusters before he went over all five sections that made up Wisdom, then R3, the cryo cylinders and finally the huge supply cylinder riding on the top of Voyager's fuselage.

Marshal became so engrossed in his task that he jumped when Alex asked, "Well?"

"What?" he stammered and grinned at how startled he was. "Oh no, Luv, nothing. I mean everything's fine." He kind of shook his head in bemusement. "Everything's still attached. As far as I can see we didn't lose anything—not even Brian's junkpile."

They both laughed at that. Brian Anders was a blacksmith who had attached himself to the Voyager Project and was noted for being a man of very few words. That had changed right before they left Earth when he used every last syllable of his daily word allotment in a plea for his junkpile. In fewer words than Marshal thought would have been possible for a man to speak and still get his meaning across, Brian insisted that if he was going to be of any use on Sanctuary, he had to have raw material—scrap iron—to work with. Alex had given in and Marshal and the rest of the RJs had fastened whatever bits and pieces of junk Anders sent up to the underside of Voyager. Turned out there was quite a bit of it.

Alex kissed Marshal on the cheek. "I'm not at all surprised, my sweet, you and the boys built well." Then she asked, "Can I talk to Al?"

"Sure." Marshal flipped a couple of switches and asked, "Al, are you there?"

Marshal and Alex laughed as they listened to the confused bumbling around in Voyager's cockpit and Wilson finally asked, "John, is that you? Where are you?"

"Look up," Marshal said and he and Alex laughed again at the astonished look on the three men's faces as they saw Sam floating out in space.

Alex asked, "Al, do you have any more thoughts on that ice cap? Specifically, is Sanctuary in an ice age?"

"Well, Alex, I'm sure that what we are seeing are glaciers, big glaciers." Wilson answered immediately. "We're over the middle of the northern hemisphere so we're a long way away from the edge of the ice to really see much detail but looking at the way the sun is reflecting off of the ice faces I would guess that they must be at least a mile high. Could Sanctuary be in an ice age?" He asked and then answered himself, "I wonder? And, if Sanctuary is in an ice age is the ice advancing or retreating." Al muttered to himself for a while longer before answering Alex directly that there was no way to tell for sure until they gathered more data. "But one thing for sure I am willing to bet is that the entire arctic is a solid ice cap. It must be thousands of miles across. Uninhabitable. Impassable."

Alex nodded in agreement and thought to herself that a possible ice age was one more thing to consider on where they decided to settle.

Wilson was clearly thinking along the same lines.

"Alex, I've been noticing how the ice extends down each land mass. I think that would make any travel between the peninsulas by land impossible, but I've also been looking at the thousands of miles of churning ocean between the peninsulas. The smallest of those bodies of water is as wide as the Atlantic. Taking the two together—right off the top of my head I would say that these land masses are totally isolated one from the other and have been for a very long time. Thousands of years—maybe longer. Depending on which direction evolution has taken on each peninsula, the flora and fauna on each of those continent-sized peninsulas could be as different from one another as Australia is from Africa."

They were all silent for a few minutes thinking about what Al had said. After a bit Allen said, "No people."

"What do you mean?" Marshal asked.

"There's no people," Allen said again.

"Or at least nothing you would call an advanced civilization," Wilson agreed. "Or I should say that there's nothing that has made a mark on the planet."

Allen nodded. "It's hard to see with all the cloud cover but we have been around the planet twice now. When we were on the night side did you see any lights—any cities? You know what Earth looks like at night—lights blazing everywhere. Great clusters of light where the cities are. The night side of Sanctuary's as dark as the inside of a bowling ball. I've been looking. I don't know how much we could expect to see from up here but even when we're on the day side I didn't see anything that looks, well, man-made to use a term, and there's certainly nothing man-made or advanced civilization made, up here in space with us."

Alex looked at the empty space around them before looking back down at the planet; Allen was right. Not only were there no cities, there didn't seem to be anything that resembled wide-scale agriculture. Even from Earth's past, civilizations like the Egyptians or Rome didn't need electricity to make them great, but they did need to feed their people. The landscape below looked naturally broken between forests and prairies with no indication of farms. There was nothing indicative of any kind of advanced civilization.

Trying to put a more positive spin on their conclusion Doc Watson observed, "Well there could be primitive species present; pre-agricultural, hunter-gathers, something like that."

Wilson said, "That could be true but I think nothing more advanced than that. If there was any higher civilization than hunter-gather we should be able to see signs of it: towns, roads, cleared areas, farming operations, but I don't think that anything earlier than that would be visible."

"What about fires?" Allen asked.

Wilson pointed to the planet below. "Look off to the south, Dave. See those smoke plumes? Those are probably grass or forest fires. Any native fires would be so small that they would be indistinguishable from here."

The five humans were silent for several minutes while each individual processed the fact that potentially they had an entire planet to themselves.

Another consideration in establishing the colony, Alex thought.

Finally, Wilson cleared his throat and said, "Well, to change the subject, look north."

Alex asked, "What specifically, Al? The aurora? Sanctuary has a magnetic field?"

"Most definitely," Wilson answered, "and from what I could see of the northern and southern hemispheres of that big peninsula we just went over Sanctuary also has seasons which indicates an axial tilt."

Alex didn't say anything as she mused how seasonal snows and floods would add even more factors to consider where to establish their colony. Ice ages, axial tilts, stormy oceans... it was daunting.

Voyager with its attendant construction robot continued on around the planet with the five Voyagers, the three men in the command section and Alex and Marshal in Sam, commenting on what they could see or what was most often the case, what they couldn't.

As they had observed before, as far as they could see north and south, the entire west coast of Index was covered by a swirling layer of solid gray-black clouds from a seemingly continuous group of storms blanketing both hemispheres of the continent's western ocean. The thick clouds lit from within by the flashes of innumerable lighting strikes.

Over the interior of the northern half of the continent, the charcoal-like cumulonimbus storm clouds gave way to small, scattered cotton balls before clearing entirely to reveal an unbroken rolling plateau that extended for hundreds maybe thousands of miles before it turned into a range of green mountains and finally disappeared into the ocean to the east.

"I think I see a volcano," Marshal commented.

"Where?" Alex asked.

"Right under us."

"Damn!" Watson grumbled from the cockpit. "I can't see anything straight down."

"I can," said Alex, "and I see what John means, that red glow in the clouds. In fact, looking further south I can see two or three more. Al, I can see the south western coastline a little clearer from here and it does look like a continuous mountain range running all the way from the ice in the north to the tip of the peninsula in the south broken only by the green belt around the equator. That would be what? A continuous mountain range, eighteen to twenty thousand miles long? Is that possible?"

Wilson chuckled. "Who knows what's possible on Sanctuary, Alex. But seriously, it's even possible on Earth, look at the Mid Atlantic Ridge. From where I'm sitting, I can only see the northern hemisphere but now that I am looking, I can see a couple of your volcanos this way, too."

"So, Sanctuary is a tectonically active planet." Alex said.

"It would seem to be," Wilson answered.

Then they went over water again and Alex asked, "My sweet, what were we calling that peninsula that we just went over, the one with the long mountain range?"

"Index."

"Okay! Thanks. I think I'm oriented now. So, the next one should be Thumb."

They didn't wait long for the smallest of the peninsulas to come into view. Thumb was covered with more dark clouds, but they thought they could see that the little, relatively speaking, peninsula was a low rocky land mass that on its southern end disappeared in a jumble of scattered rocks into the ever-churning great Southern Ocean.

And just as quickly the planet turned it was gone. *As they used to say: Nothing to see here,* Marshal thought as Voyager flew on.

They confirmed Wilson's initial impression that each peninsula was separated by at least a couple of thousand miles of ocean and looking to the south the planet was all ocean. Marshal said, "You notice, Luv, there doesn't seem to be any islands. The only dry land is those peninsulas."

"Yes," Alex murmured as she crossed off another idea for where to establish their colony. With those oceans churning away, settling on an island probably wouldn't be a good idea and Alex realized that's probably why there weren't any. In these waters, Islands would be eroded down to rubble in short order.

As Voyager continued its orbit, Little and Ring were almost completely obscured, but what little they could see of Ring, it seemed to be a peninsula of unbroken mountains running north to south and east to west rising straight out of the ocean.

Alex asked, "Al what's wrong with those clouds over Ring? Surely those lighted patches aren't from lighting."

"No." Wilson answered, "And it's more than clouds. It looks to me as if volcanoes are adding their smoke and ash to the cloud cover. But if that's true, that would indicate hundreds of volcanos. The entire peninsula would be volcanic."

The Voyagers were silent. Was that possible? The peninsula was thousands of miles long, maybe a thousand miles wide, reaching, they thought, almost to the equator. They could even make out a hint of green at its southern tip.

Little passed below them with almost no comment to the mountains on both coasts and a solid brown nothingness in the middle. No one said anything, but it was obvious that collectively the group was becoming more and more discouraged as they continued their survey.

As they came up on Middle for another pass Alex sighed and said, "I think that's enough for the first look, my sweet, let's go in."

CHAPTER 5

Later the five of them stood, or more accurately floated, around one of R3s work benches trying to keep their dinners from drifting away while kind of soberly reflecting on all they had observed during their first few orbits around Sanctuary. After listening for a while Alex asked, "Well boys, after comparing all your first impressions what do you think?"

They were all silent for a moment and finally Marshal said, "Well, Luv, personally I guess I don't really know what to think. Sanctuary! Actually, being here—the reality of it. It's so... overwhelming! I know that this is what we planned to do from the beginning—to come to a new planet and establish a colony—but now that we're actually here...."

Allen chimed in, "Yes that's the word—overwhelming." He waved an arm at the bulkhead of R3. "Look at it. Millions of miles of wilderness, vast continents, oceans stretching all around the planet, towering mountains, gigantic, violent storms, volcanos, who knows what kind of wildlife and no sign of any type of civilization. It's hard for me to wrap my mind around the fact that when we go down and land on the planet and establish a colony it will be just us. Whatever problems we may encounter—just us. Not another human being for at least twenty light years in any direction. Its daunting."

Always positive Doc Watson said, "We'll find a way. We'll make it. Right now, we just need to find a place to get started."

Alex smiled. "Doc's right; in fact, you're all right: the planet is big and overwhelming. But Doc is one hundred percent correct in saying that the first item on the agenda is to find a place to establish our colony and to do that we need more information, more data as Sherlock would say. We need better eyes than just us looking out of a cockpit window." With that she turned briskly to Wilson. "Al, does Wisdom have all the bells and whistles that you used to forecast the weather back when you were orbiting around Earth? Things like infra-red and the cloud penetrating weather forecasting instruments that would give us a better look?"

"Sure!" the weatherman answered. Then he hesitated a moment before amending, "Well some. The instruments I have on board won't give us the detail we would have expected when we were in orbit around Earth. Back then Wisdom was tied into dozens of other satellites—now as Dave says it's just us. But, yeah, some"

"That's what I thought. So, I guess the next order of business is to get Wisdom, or at least Al's Meteorological Section of Wisdom operational." She turned toward Marshal, "Well, my sweet, do you think that you could do something about that?"

"Oh, I think that could be arranged, Luv, but it would

go a lot faster if I had some help."

"Well, of course. Will you need all the RJs?"

"Hah! No. That won't be necessary. Just the hard corps: Billy, JJ and Fred. We'll have Wisdom up and running in no time. Well, in a couple of weeks or so, anyway."

Alex smiled at his expected response. Those four—her husband, Jack (JJ) Jackson, Fred Thompson and Billy Wright—were nothing if not reliable. Not only were they the original robot construction operators, they were the engineering brain trust that had come up with the concept of the expanded spaceship that they had used to travel through twenty light years of empty space. There was no question they'd still be limping around Earth without them. "Okay!" Alex smiled again. "Let's go get them."

Marshal kind of hovered around while Doc and Dave brought JJ Jackson out of hibernation and after the usual disorientation and question and answer session, he walked with the large man over to the next cryo pod in the row so he could check on his wife Cathy. Marshal smiled at the thought of the miniature human dynamo. Five feet nothing with high heels on and she couldn't have weighed a hundred pounds if she was carrying an anvil. But as tiny as she was Cathy Jackson was a whirlwind who was constantly in motion radiating energy. She was a Dietician by training but back at Project Voyager's facility at Sand Flea Airfield she had managed the entire food service operation. She made the menus, found and negotiated with suppliers, ordered the food, supervised food storage and preparation, trained the kitchen staff and even managed to keep André, their rotund French chef, pretty much in line.

Compare that with her husband! Not only was JJ Jackson a very good engineer, the man had to have been six foot two or three, two hundred and twenty pounds or so and... quiet! JJ never seemed to say much, but when he did offer an observation or an opinion, whatever he said was worth paying attention to.

Marshal smiled at the couple again. Whoever said that opposites attract surely had those two in mind.

Once assured that his lady was sleeping peacefully JJ was ready to go to work.

Next it was Billy Wright's turn to come out of hibernation and as soon as he was on his feet, he had to stumble over into the San Diego Job to check on the two loves of his life. Erin McPherson and her daughter Judy were Colonel Alexander McPherson's daughter and granddaughter. *The* Colonel McPherson who back on Earth had been Voyager's mole in the White House. For years the colonel had watched Voyager's back, shielding the project from government interference, deflecting inquires, perpetuating the myth that Voyager was just an exploratory mission to Mars and when government flunkies did visit Sand Flea ensuring that they saw nothing while the spacecraft was being constructed three hundred miles over their heads.

Erin McPherson hadn't been a part of the program initially. She was a divorced single mom who only came to Sand Flea to check it out in order to satisfy herself that mom and dad weren't making a terrible mistake racing off to the stars. But when she showed up at Sand Flea and she and Billy laid eyes on each other it was love at first sight.

Her daughter Judy was a tougher nut for Billy to crack. After being the victim of an abusive father, men were definitely not on Judy McPherson's list of preferred individuals. But Billy Wright was no dummy. A trip for Judy up to Voyager in a Starduster shuttle and a ride in Billy's construction robot took care of that. Especially when he presented her with her very own bright blue flight suit with a robot jockey patch that said "Judy." And to put more icing on the cake, he renamed his construction robot after the girl. Marshal wasn't sure what the coupling up norms would be in the colony but one way or another, Judy McPherson had a new daddy.

Once Fred Thompson was on his feet, Marshal fixed his team a meal and while they anchored themselves around one of R3s workbenches he brought them up to date on Voyager's progress so far and what was next on the agenda. Of course, before any work could be started, they had to go up into the Command Section and see Sanctuary despite Marshals pleadings that they would have a much better view from their robots in space.

After the usual bumbling around behind Alex and Al as they tried to peer through the cockpit windows, they finally decided that they really couldn't see anything from inside the spacecraft and they would be better off in the robots.

Marshal rolled his eyes loud enough for each of them to hear his telepathic, "Told you so!"

With a lot of laughing and good-natured joshing they floated back down into R3 and began to ready their robots to go to work: Marshal's *Sam*, JJ's *Cathy* and Billy's *Judy*. If Fred Thompson had ever named his robot no one knew what it was.

While they were prepping their robots, Billy wandered forward into section three which had been John Marshal's work space for the last year. "What the hell is this?" he exclaimed so loudly that the others hurried to find out the cause.

Billy was just staring dumbfounded at the robot in the maintenance rack which caused JJ and Fred's jaws to drop when they saw it. Marshal didn't say a word and just listened to the comments as they explored it like a kitten discovering a ball of string for the first time.

"It's only got two arms."

"The operator's seat is in the middle."

"The solar engine looks different."

"Yeah, and it's in the wrong place too."

"Where's the equipment belt?"

After a few minutes they all turned toward Marshal.

"Is this your work, John?" JJ asked.

Marshal had a huge grin on his face when he replied, "Yup!"

"Well, we can see that you have moved things around but why? How are these modifications going to improve our construction abilities here in space?"

"They won't." Marshal replied. "This construction robot isn't designed to operate in space."

"What?" Three voices said in unison.

With a flourish Marshal said, "Gentlemen, meet Sam II, or Junior... I haven't quite decided. He is the future, I hope, for the robots and us robot jockeys."

Three faces were regarding him like he was two saddlebags short of a full camel load.

"The future?"

"Yup!"

"And it doesn't fly in space?"

"Nope!" Marshal confirmed. "And was never designed to," he reiterated just so they knew he hadn't royally goofed. "Junior here is designed to operate in a gravity well, in the atmosphere, to be precise, on Sanctuary."

The other three stood for a moment in shocked surprise and then they all started talking at once.

"How did you change the solar engine?"

"What made you think of it?"

"What would we use it for on the ground?"

And finally, "John, will it work?"

"Ah! Well," Marshal hesitated, "to take your last question first, will Junior actually work in Sanctuary's gravity? The honest answer is I don't really know. All the computer projections say that it will, but I guess we won't really know until we take it down to the planet and try it. As for your other questions, after I woke up last time and was trying to think of something to do to make my year go by, I got to thinking about what would happen to the robots—and us—after we establish our colony. Once all the supplies and equipment are transferred down and Voyager is taken apart, outside of servicing Wisdom, we're going to be out of business. Our robots will be good for nothing except artifacts in the colony's space museum."

The way the others were nodding, it had crossed more than one of their minds. Marshal continued, "So that's when I remembered a casual remark that Gustave had made about the robots and gravity when we were installing the engines. That got me pursuing the 'what if' idea. Of course, the big question was could the power plant be re-engineered. I spent four weeks doing research before I ever started work. As I said, the computers say that Junior will fly. We will see.

"As to the question of how we would use Junior on Sanctuary? My original thought was using it as a scout helicopter. You know, reconnaissance, ferry individuals from place to place, pick up and deliver small items, that sort of thing. Then Alex mentioned a problem that she was wrestling with which was how to unload the Stardusters once we landed on Sanctuary. I went back to the books, tweaked the engines a little more and although Junior's a bit of a light weight, I think he can manage a few hundred pounds, maybe more, so he should be able to pick most items out of the shuttle's cargo bay. Of course, we'll still have to rig a sheerlegs or some type of crane for the heavier stuff that we can't break down like the farm tractors."

JJ and Billy lit up like sailors on shore leave and were ready to start converting Cathy and Judy on the spot. Marshal laughed. "I know you two Romeos would love to be able to work on the ground close to your honeys, but before you go tearing the robots apart, don't you think that we should wait until we are actually on the ground and see if Junior here really works?"

They all laughed and Fred said, "You're right. Seeing as we haven't even touched down on the planet yet why don't we take care of Al first."

They popped out into space and of course before any work could be done the three newly awakened robot jockeys had to have their look at Sanctuary.

"That's a lot of clouds," JJ commented. "John, is always like that?"

Marshal replied, "I don't know about always, we've only been here a few days, but so far, yes."

"That's a lot of water too," said Billy. "It looks like the entire southern hemisphere is nothing but ocean."

"Yeah! Al thinks so too," Marshal agreed. "That's something he wants to determine. He's guessing 80% or more of the planet's surface is water. Storms and tides around the planet might be really severe. Oh, and added to the climatic uncertainty, look the other way toward space, Sanctuary has two moons."

Billy said, "I only see one."

"Trust me," Marshal replied, "There's two. The little moon must be around on the other side of the planet but it's there and it moves fast, too."

While they pondered that bit of information Fred chimed in, "I sure don't see a lot of land, are those patches of ground I see between the clouds big islands?"

"No. They're all connected forming contiguous land masses but they don't look like any of the continents on Earth. As far as we can tell the land area seems to consist of five large peninsulas that extend south from the white area to the north. Al and Alex are pretty sure that the top third of the planet, anywhere from sixty-five to seventy degrees north latitude on up to the pole, is one giant glacier. In my opinion, Dave came up with the best description of the overall effect, he says that the whole thing looks like a giant hand holding a ball."

They all laughed and Fred said, "Yeah, I can see that. The palm is the glacier and the peninsulas are the fingers."

JJ asked, "John, with all that ice is the planet in some kind of an ice age?"

"Yes, well maybe. Al's pretty sure that the planet has ice ages but he's not sure where Sanctuary is in the cold/hot cycle if you know what I mean. That's the main reason why we, the stalwart robot jocks of the spaceship Voyager, are going to activate Wisdom."

With a smooth efficiency forged over years of working together they proceeded to accomplish just that. The Meteorological Cylinder of Wisdom was detached from the underside of Voyager and maneuvered into a position above the spaceship. With the huge supply cylinder riding on the top of Voyager's hull they couldn't attach Wisdom directly to the spaceship so the flexible plastic personnel tube that had been used to attach Wisdom to Voyager in Earth orbit was utilized again.

When the solar panels were attached a few days later Wisdom began to look like a space station and several days after that as the robot jockeys stood, sat or otherwise anchored themselves around the maintenance bench in R3's first section sharing the evening meal with Alex, Al, Doc and

Dave, Marshal announced "Well Luv, externally Al's Met section is ready to go and once we take care of one small soft internal obstacle Al can go to work.

Alex raised an eyebrow and started to say, "And what would that be?" and she stopped. And then started sniggering as she suddenly remembered. "Oh!"

They all couldn't help laughing as they recalled what had happened twenty years ago when they were in orbit around Earth dismantling and packing Wisdom for the journey to Sanctuary. Originally, they hadn't planned to bring the space station. Never even thought of it. But when Herr Professor Gutman pointed out to them in no uncertain terms what idiots they would be to leave it behind, plans quickly changed and Wisdom was added to the inventory. However, when the supply people saw all that lovely empty space inside each one of Wisdom's five cylinders, they wanted to pack it full of supplies but the scientists weren't having any of it. The scientists saw all those boxes with sharp corners, metal equipment of all shapes and sizes and who knew what else these grubby supply people wanted to bring bouncing around inside the cylinders and banging into their precious, sensitive and irreplaceable scientific instruments and flatly rejected the idea.

While this rather vociferous discussion was going on in space, on the ground Alex was facing a not so minor revolt at Sand Flea. It seemed that several of the ladies who were planning to make the trip to the new colony found out that toilet tissue was not included in the supply inventory and a delegation of rather irate women was sent to confront Alex with this deplorable and highly unacceptable situation. Poor Alex. She, being a lady herself, sympathized with the delegation and tried to explain that TP took up a lot of space and space was limited.

The ladies weren't buying it and much to Alex's chagrin they went away extremely unhappy. That evening when Alex on the ground and Marshal in orbit three hundred miles above her were telling each other their woes of the day, the obvious solution presented itself. As a result, the scientific instruments in the five cylinders of Wisdom were soon well cushioned with thousands of rolls of toilet paper.

That was then.

The problem now was that Wisdom was going to be activated and there wasn't a ground station yet available. So, the question was: where to put several thousand rolls of toilet paper so Al could go to work? They couldn't store it outside of Voyager in space and even if they could, how would they attach thousands of loose rolls of toilet paper so that they didn't just drift away? The more they thought about it, it seemed that that might be the solution—just jettison them into space. Alex was dead set against that for the simple reason that she was the one who would have to face the ladies once they were on Sanctuary.

They thought some more. Suddenly Billy said "What about the San Diego Job?"

Seeing as they had already considered that and rejected it because they would have the same problem of loose rolls of T-P floating around only in another location, they wondered what he meant.

"I mean the front end where we didn't install any cryo pods?"

When the others asked how he expected the rolls to stay put without floating around all over the cylinder Billy reached up and fingered the rolled-up netting that they used to keep their tools and other materials from floating away when they were working on the benches. "What about these? We could stretch these nets across the end of the cylinder where we never installed any cryo pods."

"Brilliant and simple," Marshal smiled.

"The best ideas usually are," Alex added.

As soon as dinner was over, they removed the nets and floated into the San Diego Job. Using whatever anchor points, they could find they created a spider's web of netting across the front end of the huge cylinder.

At least it looked like it would work and it was a plan, so the next morning the eight Voyagers proceeded to transfer several thousand rolls of toilet paper from the Met Section of Wisdom, down the connecting tube into Voyager, through Voyager into the San Diego Job and then into the netted space in the huge cylinder's front end. They planned for the operation to work like a kind of bucket brigade but these weren't buckets and there weren't enough Voyagers to pass anything hand to hand anyway. So, they decided to have weightlessness work for them by stationing themselves at strategic locations and just giving the rolls a little nudge in the right direction.

And it worked—well mostly. Actually, it worked in the finest traditions of Laurel and Hardy, the Three Stooges and the Keystone Cops. The result was the first slapstick comedy show performed either above or on the planet Sanctuary.

The eight Voyagers spread themselves out along the route from Wisdom to the San Diego Job. When everyone was at their stations Marshal swam up the connecting tube to Wisdom. As soon as he opened the hatch rolls of toilet paper started drifting down. Which was kind of the idea but the bucket brigade wasn't quite ready.

The plan was for Marshal to get up into the Met section, float the rolls over to Billy stationed at the entrance to the tube who would then redirect them down the tube.

But before all that could happen Marshal first had to

get into the Met cylinder but he couldn't do that because thousands of rolls of TP were in the way. He tried to push the rolls past and behind him so he could get up into Wisdom but there wasn't enough room for him to do that in the tube and there wasn't enough room for him to squirm out of the tube and into the Met section.

Marshal started digging like a badger going after a ground squirrel pushing rolls behind him and stuffing them down the tube.

This brought a howl from Billy who had followed him up the tube to assume his post at the tube end in the Met section. The tube was soon plugged with Billy Wright and a few hundred rolls of toilet paper. He couldn't go up and the rolls couldn't come down. Billy had to back down into Voyager then they had to get Marshal to stop digging and pushing rolls in from the top. Of course, when Billy dropped back into Voyager a cascade of TP rolls came in after him and proceeded to float around in the Command Section.

That was when the Voyagers discovered that each roll of toilet tissue had its own devious little brain and was determined to float away in any direction except the direction the Voyagers wished it to go.

After several minutes of shouting, laughing and not a little cursing they finally got Marshal to stop sending rolls down the tube and corralled, or thought that they had corralled, all the rolls that had come down into Voyager and sent them through the connecting hatch into the San Diego Job.

After that rather auspicious beginning Marshal established a small pocket in the cylinder and Billy went back up through the tube and took his post at the Met section's hatch. Marshal resumed digging out rolls and sending them in Billy's general direction. Even if Marshal had a better aim and even if the individual rolls didn't want to go their own way Billy would have needed more arms than an octopus to catch them all and send them down the tube.

At the other end of the tube Alex and Al waited to intercept the rolls as they came down the pipe, keep them from drifting forward into the Command Section and re-direct them toward Doc and Dave so they could keep them from going into the cryogenic section and send them through the hatch into San Diego Job where Fred and JJ were waiting to cage them behind the net.

At least the Italian Job and R3 had hatches so they were sealed off.

Several thousand rolls of toilet tissue refused to cooperate. Instead of a nice smooth flow coming down the tube the rolls would bang into each other, slow down or jam up in the tube and Billy would have to float down and knock them loose and get them moving again. This resulted in Alex and Al having to deal with rolls coming in bursts and each roll was determined to go anywhere except toward Doc and Dave. And finally, Fred and JJ would have to intercept each roll as it came into the San Diego Job and send it in a new direction behind the net. Of course, once behind the net the individual rolls didn't want to stay there. Each seemed determined to float out and explore the interior of the cryogenic cylinder, investigate the pods and especially see just how far out of reach they could get. When JJ or Fred tried to push them back in, no easy task given the size of the cylinder, more would come in from Voyager.

It took most of the morning for Marshal to clear the Met section and for he and Billy to push everything ahead of them down into Voyager. When they exited the tube, they found Alex, Al, Doc and Dave frantically trying to capture and direct a cloud of floating rolls into the hatch leading to the San

Diego Job. They joined in the hunt and with six of them working they finally cleared Voyager and pushed everything into the cryo cylinder. Then the six of them joined Fred and JJ in trying to get an even bigger cloud of TP rolls to stay behind the net.

It was well after noon before they declared the job finished and all the rolls safely stored. This proved to be a premature declaration of victory as for days, even weeks afterward, wayward rolls of TP turned up in every unlikely location imaginable. Even when they moved down into R3 for lunch a roll drifted in behind them and as Billy noted they would have to do it four more times as the rest of Wisdom was activated. That brought a groan from everyone and Alex said she refused to think about it—that it was a problem for another day.

"Right now," she said, "Al, Dave and I are going to see what we can learn about Sanctuary. Why don't you RJs see about reassembling the rest of Wisdom without removing the TP."

They all laughed and went to work.

It was only a couple of days later that Alex again called everyone into Wisdom and briefed them on their progress in studying the planetary surface or more accurately their lack of progress.

"The blunt truth," she said, "is that due to our limited coverage with just one space platform coupled with all the clouds and smoke obscuring the planet's surface, we still aren't able to observe large areas. I think the only answer is that we have to get under that cloud layer for a closer look. What I would like to do is mount a couple of the sensors on a Starduster and actually fly down to Sanctuary."

She looked at Marshal, "Can do, my sweet?"

"Can do, Luv, but not without help. I can fly a

Starduster but I need a copilot. Better yet, wake up Ben Riley and I'll be his copilot. He's a hell-of-a-lot better Starduster pilot than I am and I think we'll need a third crew member to operate the sensors."

"Well," Alex answered, "just for the adventure of it, Al and I both thought about accompanying the mission—not that we could really contribute anything except maybe operate the sensors. But we gave that idea up when we discovered that Mr. Allen here, among his other talents, is a bit of a computer nerd and he has already figured out a way to mount the sensors and have repeater screens inside the shuttle. So, he has volunteered and will be available to hopefully deal with any glitches that might arise. And we are going to wake up Dan, Tyler and Ann to help us on the scientific side."

Marshal looked a question at his wife. He knew Tyler West and Dan Macintyre from the months and years spent building Voyager. They were old Wisdom regulars who had spent years doing research when the space station was in orbit around Earth but he had no idea who Ann was.

"Ann Turner," Al answered. "I don't know if you ever met her. She wasn't a regular at Wisdom but she did spend a few months in orbit. A very sharp lady."

Marshal nodded.

Alex smiled and said, "Now let's get Ben and the brain trust up and we'll do some planning."

CHAPTER 6

Ben Riley felt like he was riding a bucking bronco at the county fair as he brought Dusty 1 down through the violent storm. He broke out of the clouds and leveled off at three thousand feet over the turbulent churning ocean and found that flying conditions hadn't improved. Wind driven rain mixed with sleet and snow lashed the shuttle as he flew east between the peninsulas of Little and Thumb. He looked over at John Marshal sitting in the copilot's seat. Marshal just shrugged and nodded and Ben knew John agreed with him—it was like flying inside a washing machine, couldn't see a damn thing except wind driven water—water below and water above. Black ocean below, black clouds above.

"How's it handling?" Marshal asked.

"Not worth a damn," Riley replied.

Marshal nodded in sympatric understanding.

As he approached the west coast of the peninsula that they were calling Thumb, Riley brought Dusty's speed down to five hundred miles an hour. In his opinion, three thousand feet above the ground or water with an air speed of only five hundred miles an hour was too low and too slow to be flying a Starduster space shuttle, but that was the flight profile that Alex, Al, Dave, the brain trust and he and Marshal had finally agreed on for the initial planetary exploration flights that they were calling 'fly—bys'.

Three thousand and five hundred had been a compromise and like most compromises no one was a hundred percent happy with it. Alex and the scientists wanted the flights to be even lower and slower to provide better resolution for their cameras and he and Marshal who had to fly this airborne brick wanted something higher and faster. Ten thousand and one thousand would have been more to their liking.

Riley could understand where Alex and the scientists were coming from. To find a location for the colony or to even find possible areas on the planet's surface that were worthy of investigation the Voyagers required more information than they could obtain from orbit so of course they wanted Dusty to get as close a look at the planet as possible but—Jeez!— there were limits especially in this weather. But any Starduster limits that he and Marshal mentioned fell on deaf ears.

Riley had to agree that Stardusters were marvelous machines way ahead of their time, but they were designed and engineered for a specific purpose: to fly from a planetary surface into orbit and back again and this they did very well. No matter how hard they tried he and Marshal couldn't seem to convince the boffins that a Starduster was not designed and built to be utilized as a conventional reconnaissance airplane.

But Riley also had to agree that if they wanted a closer look at Sanctuary, they had to use the instruments that Al had available in Wisdom because that's all they had. He chuckled to himself when he remembered that when he and Marshal had complained—again—about flying low and slow the six scientists ganged up on them and they had all started talking at once and he and Marshal had been given a crash course in what Voyager could and couldn't see from orbit, what the limitations of the sensors were and why it was essential to get down in the dirt.

Okay! Okay! He got it but that didn't make him feel any better about the mission.

Oh, quit your complaining, Riley, he scolded himself, *you know you can fly this crate like a helicopter if you really want to.*

Yeah, he answered himself, *but not when you can't see crap and the winds blowing fifty miles an hour.*

He chuckled again and Marshal looked over at him. Riley shook his head and said, "Nothing, John. Just thinking about how we got here."

Marshal smiled back. He was pretty sure he knew what was on Ben's mind. Getting the mission organized had been an adventure.

Once the humans had reached their compromise, they decided that one of the space shuttles would be fitted with the cameras and sensors Wisdom had available which turned out to be just two optical cameras, one conventional and one panoramic, and one infra-red sensor. Not much, but it was what they had. As it turned out maybe it was a good thing that that's all they had because even with the robots working outside in space and Ben, Dave and Alex working inside the shuttle mounting the three sensors and the monitoring computers to go with them and get everything working took two full days. Then Riley and Marshal were bombarded with dire warnings from Al Wilson to watch where they were flying and to swear on their grandmothers' graves that they would not damage or lose or otherwise somehow manage to destroy his precious, irreplaceable equipment. Riley and Marshal had laughed and pointed out that if they did happen to encounter something hard—like the ground—and/or some critter big enough and unfriendly enough to damage said equipment, destroying Al's sensors would probably be the least of their worries.

Of course, from the cockpit of the shuttle Riley and Marshal had no idea what the cameras and the infra-red were seeing. What they did know was that they couldn't see a damn thing. Well hardly a damn thing. Even if the weather had been clear and visibility unlimited and they weren't in the middle of this never-ending deluge they couldn't see any more outside of the shuttle than the pilot of a commercial airliner could out of his airborne bus. Their field of vision was mostly high and wide, anything directly below was completely obscured by the Starduster itself. Riley thought to himself, *Not only do the shuttles fly like bricks, they're about as transparent as one as well.*

The only one on board the shuttle who had any real appreciation of what Sanctuary was like was Dave Allen who was sitting in a hastily manufactured jump seat just behind Riley and Marshal and looking at the computer screens monitoring the cameras. And at the speed they were flying, over eight miles a minute, he had only a fleeting glance of Sanctuary's surface. But if there was something of interest, he could recall it.

Even though the flight crew complained that they couldn't see much, Alex, Al and the boffins were happy with the arrangement knowing that once the data was recorded, they could view it all at their leisure back up on Wisdom. At first, they had thought of actually installing the repeaters and monitors in Wisdom but abandoned the idea when they faced the reality that without a supporting web of communication satellites to relay the signal, they would only be able to communicate with the shuttle when Wisdom was in direct line of sight and that was for only about a half hour out of Wisdom's two-hour long journey around Sanctuary. And even if they were in a position to communicate, they couldn't guarantee that Dusty wouldn't be stuck inside a thunderstorm.

Riley and Marshal resigned themselves to only being the chauffeurs whose job was to try to keep the craft straight and level and in the middle of the air.

Alex and the brain trust planned to cover all the peninsulas in turn with three extended fly-bys and the first was a flight over the peninsulas of Thumb and Index. Riley wasn't sure that to get full coverage of all five peninsulas it wouldn't require more flights than just the three. Although Sanctuary didn't have a lot of land mass, relatively speaking, it was still a planet larger than Earth and with an air speed of only five-hundred miles an hour it was going to take over six hours just to fly across the three thousand plus miles of Index. But, of course, Alex and Al were no dummies and they had taken all that into consideration.

Quit wool-gathering and concentrate, Riley admonished himself again. As he approached Thumb from the west Riley tried to distinguish something of the terrain before him. In his humble opinion based on what little he had been able to see from space, Thumb was the runt of all the peninsulas and was nothing more than a miserable, windswept, barren, storm blasted rock surrounded on three sides by a constantly churning stormy ocean. About as attractive as the islands in the north and south polar regions on Earth. Measuring only fifteen hundred miles from where the land appeared out of the glaciers to the north to where it disappeared into the churning waters of the Great Southern Ocean and not more than eight hundred miles at its widest point, it seemed like including Thumb in a fly-by was hardly worth the effort. Definitely not the kind of place to build a vacation home let alone establish a permanent colony.

But Alex was Alex and she would leave no stone, or continent, unturned.

Marshal looked out his side of the cockpit into the murk to the south and said, "It looks like the peninsula just ends in rocks. The cliff just fades away into broken scattered rocks. Rocks sticking out into the ocean as far as I can see being pounded into little rocks by the waves."

Then he pointed forward and said, "Look at that!" and the three men watched in silence as ahead of them, left to the north and right to the south, wave after unending wave smashed into a cliff face that must have been hundreds of feet high. But what was even more astonishing was that in every nook and cranny in that storm-battered cliff face and filling the sky overhead and for miles out to sea there were birds, thousands of birds. In their aerial displays, they seemed to be oblivious to the weather and the pounding waves as they continued wheeling in the air and diving into the churning ocean.

Allen shook his head. "Look at that ocean, and the wind. Those must be some mighty tough birds."

Riley and Marshal chuckled in agreement.

The storm moderated a little as the shuttle crossed the cliff lined coast and visibility improved slightly.

That was the good news.

The bad news was that under scattered patches of windblown snow there wasn't much to see on the peninsula called Thumb. The terrain, what there was of it, consisted of low, rolling, rocky hills covered with some kind of scrub grass broken only by the occasional appearance of a short stubby tree or in protected spots, a small grove of trees. On this rolling rock pile there didn't seem to be any ground elevation higher than a few hundred feet and it was evident that the never-ending west wind blasted every bit of vegetation that dared stick its head up out of the rocky soil. The tufted grass leaned to the east and anything larger than grass that did manage to defy the odds and take root and grow had a sharp, gnarly appearance and a pronounced easterly lean. Ben turned to Marshal and remarked that the angles reminded him of an optical illusion perspective house that played tricks with his senses when he was a kid. He said he kept wanting to tilt his head to one side so the skewed plants and trees looked like they were standing upright.

Marshal chuckled at the image and Allen commented that it looked cold. The others agreed. If cold had a look, Thumb was it. A cold, raw, wet, windy, nasty, miserable cold.

From the crews' point of view, everything they had seen so far confirmed their opinion that Thumb was a complete write off. Marshal added that he couldn't imagine even wanting to try and live in those conditions even though he knew it could be done. Natives of the arctic regions on Earth had lived in a similar environment for millennia.

But want to and had to were different things and Marshal definitely didn't *want* to.

Dusty 1 flew on and in just over an hour completed its transit of the peninsula. The only additional item the crew noted was that the east coast of Thumb appeared to be a mirror image of the west coast—a never-ending avian covered cliff battered by the ocean.

Once they were out over water the storm began breaking up and reforming into a line of squalls that the shuttle flew in and out of. Riley punched Dusty up to Mach 4. At that speed they quickly covered over two thousand miles of open ocean and were coming up on the continent of Index in less than an hour.

Approaching Index from the west, the three Voyagers looked ahead through the rain at the formidable mountainous wall that loomed before them. Marshal commented that they always seemed to be looking through the rain. From orbit, snatching the occasional glimpse through the clouds, Alex and Al had determined that the mountain range that dominated the west coast of Index was possibly as high as thirty thousand feet and maybe as much as twenty thousand miles long but until now, they had no idea that it rose practically straight up out of the turbulent sea.

Marshal mused that the question of what the shoreline was like was answered as there was no shoreline—just the same line of practically unbroken cliffs that had dominated the coasts of Thumb. Only these cliffs were bigger, higher, longer. He wondered if the shorelines of all five of the peninsula-like continents consisted of unbroken cliffs that were constantly being assaulted by the unrelenting ocean.

And, here again, there were birds. Birds in their millions.

As the shuttle got closer to land Riley had to pull back and start to climb. Visibility was lousy through the solid black rain clouds but his instruments were telling him that the mountain range ahead of him was rising almost straight up. Gripping the controls tighter he asked, "Can you see anything, John?"

"Not much. Just rain and rocks." Then a few minutes later Marshal added, "You know, Ben, it can't rain all the time because I can see trees, or what look like trees, down there too. Drippy trees but there's a lot of them."

Riley and Marshal could sense a growing excitement behind them as Allen looked at his monitors. Before today's flight Dave, Alex and Al and the rest of the scientists had been pretty tight-lipped about what they suspected the flora and fauna of Index and the other peninsulas was like but they had caught more than a few snatches of arguments and discussions. They had heard the word dinosaur more than once.

Seriously? They thought there were dinosaurs on Sanctuary?

Right!

Dusty 1 continued up and up the western flank of the great north/south range. Although the clouds remained thick and black above them the rain surprisingly slacked off and then stopped. What passed for a coastal plain proved to be a narrow, practically vertical fringe of foothills that were covered with a dense, dark green forest that continued, unbroken, up the mountain side. The Earthmen tried to relate what they were seeing to what they were familiar with from home. The best they could come up with was what they were looking at was a rainforest. Not a tropical rain forest but a northern rainforest of spruce and fir, hemlock and hickory and higher up were trees that resembled pine.

But they all knew that those labels weren't quite right. The trees kind of looked like the Earth names they had given them but it wasn't right. The three men weren't biologists but they knew enough to know that what they were calling a Douglas Fir wasn't quite a Douglas Fir.

Marshal shrugged. "So what!" he said. "We've got to call this stuff something and unless we want to go and make up new names for everything we see—so no one will know what we're talking about—we might as well give them familiar names even if they are not quite accurate."

The other two nodded in agreement although Marshal knew as soon as he said it that Alex and the boffins would never go for that. New things needed new names and there were enough new things here to keep their grandchildren's grandchildren busy.

Despite the poor visibility it was evident that some of the tall, water drenched trees punching through a thick, low-lying fog were gigantic. Each was maybe a hundred and fifty to two hundred feet high and clung to the sides of the mountain range all the way up to the tree line.

"Well, Dave," Marshal asked, "any dinosaurs?"

Mutter, mutter. "Too much rain and clouds. I can't see anything!" Which caused Riley and Marshal both to laugh.

The Starduster swept up the western face of the range, soon reaching twenty thousand feet above sea level, then twenty-five, and still climbing. The shuttle finally reached the summit and leveled off at the programmed three thousand feet above the ground, thirty-four thousand feet above the churning ocean. *My god*, Marshal thought, *this range of mountains is higher than the Himalayas back on Earth and at least twice as long as the Andes.*

The three men were silent as they looked at the range of mountains that was spreading out to the east as far as they could see. Marshal had figured that once they had cleared the crest there would be a drop off followed by a prairie or lower hills, but to his surprise the massive range continued on and on, mile after mile off into the distance. An immense, snow-covered vista six miles high with hundreds of peaks of bare barren rock and even a volcano or two that stuck up even higher.

They flew on in awestruck silence. After a few hundred miles the clouds disappeared and the air was clear, visibility unlimited. The clouds had finally been sucked dry. Any moisture that managed to make it over the first row of mountains fell as snow on these perpetually frozen peaks, probably staying on the ground forever.

Dusty 1 flew over this mountainous waste land for an hour, over five hundred miles, before the mountains began to diminish in height and fade into equally barren foothills finally giving way to a flat featureless tableland.

Ben followed the mountains down maintaining the proscribed three thousand feet and when he leveled off the shuttle was still seventeen thousand feet above sea level. He looked ahead at a high, dry, unbroken frozen plateau that stretched off into the eastern horizon.

"Kind of like the Tibetan Plateau only flatter," Allen remarked.

The only vegetation was a kind of clumpy, tuft grass and nothing else. No trees. No visible water courses. As far as they could see no water ran east from the mountains and the melt water from the glacier to the north seemed to run east along the foot of the glacier and not south onto this featureless plateau.

But even in this high, dry nothingness there were animals. Small groups of cattle-like creatures were spotted grazing on the sparse vegetation and Dave speculated that they could be like the Yaks on Earth.

The barren vista continued on and on for three hours and over fifteen hundred miles. Trying to compare the land below to something familiar they agreed that it looked like a slightly tilted flat roof. As they progressed further east the ground elevation slowly decreased and as the elevation lowered the terrain gradually changed from barren plateau to high desert. Marshal remarked that it looked like the area around Sand Flea on Earth, not a sand desert but a parched unforgiving land covered with cactus and scrub brush.

Then, finally, some green. Vegetation appeared and became denser as they approached the east coast. The high desert gave way to rolling hills and the multi-hued brown slowly changed to green. There was water; small streams flowing to the west and south. Grass was more abundant and a few trees made their appearance. It wasn't the unbroken forest full of giants that they observed on the west coast but smaller trees of a different nature that resembled maple and alder, dogwood and birch, scattered in small groves along the waterways.

And with the increase in vegetation there were more animals. A lot more animals.

Allen seemed disappointed that they all appeared to be mammals.

With the appearance of vegetation and animals the three men smiled at each other. This was more like it. They could live here.

The trees thickened as the shuttle approached the eastern shoreline and then, abruptly, the hills ended. Ahead was a beach. A gigantic beach. An impossible beach. A beach that ran for thousands of unbroken miles north and south without a bay, harbor or inlet of any kind in sight. But, the most striking feature was the beach itself—a vast expanse of hard sand. Judging by what appeared to be the high tide mark and where the edge of the ocean currently was, the beach had to be at least a hundred miles wide. The crew found it hard to imagine a hundred-mile tide, but that was what it looked like.

As they marveled at that incredible swatch of sand, Dusty 1 continued on out over the ocean. Ben turned to Marshal and said, "Okay, John, your turn."

Marshal took the controls and turned Dusty to the south. Alex had wanted the second leg of the flight over Index to be along the northern edge of the equatorial green belt so Marshal planned to take the shuttle south for over a thousand miles. He was just about to increase speed when Riley pointed out of his side window and exclaimed, "My god! What's that?"

Allen leaned over Riley's left shoulder and Marshal twisted in his seat to try to see what Riley was pointing at. What they saw in the churning ocean was a wall of water. A massive tidal wave moving at incredible speed. Before they could comment the wave crashed onto the impossible beach and swept across the sand stopping at the high tide mark.

They were speechless as the beach went from low tide to high tide in an instant. The water slowly began to recede, but it was clear that it would take hours for the tide to recede fully and return to its previous level. The three of them looked at each other and the unspoken thought was: Was this normal?

Then Allen snapped his fingers. "The little moon!" he exclaimed.

Ben and John looked at him and he hurried on, "The small moon racing around the planet. The gravitational pull of the small moon could be causing that tidal wave."

Well. *Yeah*, Marshal thought. *Could be.* Twice a day? Three times a day?

Riley asked, "If the moon's responsible, why didn't we see it on Thumb?"

Allen answered, "I don't know. Maybe we did and didn't recognize it with the cliffs and the storm. Or maybe we were just in-between tides."

While they continued to speculate on Sanctuary's latest wonder, Marshal flew more than a thousand miles south before that impossible beach gave way to what looked like a kind of mangrove swamp. Thousands of square miles of mangrove that lay under a layer of black clouds that had made it previously unknown to the Earthmen orbiting in Wisdom.

Marshal turned the shuttle west to follow the northern fringe of the green belt and the mangroves quickly turned into a forest. But there was something about the forest that bothered him. It just didn't look right. Although the forest was thick and green the trees didn't quite look like trees. Suddenly, he gasped when he realized what he was looking at. Ferns! Ferns large enough to climb and maybe build a treehouse in. Before he could fully wrap his mind around the protozoic spectacle, Marshal was distracted by another flurry of excitement behind him.

"Look! Look!" Allen shouted pointing out of Riley's window on the port side of the Starduster. "I was right. There are dinosaurs. That's a diplodocus!"

"A what?" Riley asked as both he and Allen crowded against Riley's window.

"What the hell is going on?!" Marshal shouted while trying to fly and simultaneously stand up and look out Ben's window. Fortunately, Ben bailed him out as his amused voice said "Keep flying, John! What we are so excited about is that Dave has found his dinosaurs. He spotted a herd of them. He says they're diplodocus or something close to a diplodocus."

"Wow! Dinosaurs! Really?" Marshal asked excitedly before another thought seeped into his brain. "Wait! How can that be? Didn't we see mammals up north on the first leg?" Then another thought crossed his mind. "Uh, is that a good thing, Ben? We're going to share the planet with dinosaurs? Can we share the planet with dinosaurs?" His confused thoughts rambled on. "Those were mammals that we saw up north, weren't they? We have mammals and dinosaurs both? At the same time?"

"Why the hell ask me?" Riley answered. "I don't know... I never really thought about the possibility. Me just pilot, remember?"

Marshal looked at Dave who just shrugged. "Don't ask me, either. We'll just have to see."

While Marshal would never say it over an open transmission, he thought that that didn't sound very comforting. Before he could come up with an appropriate response there was a solid thump against the side of the shuttle and Ben was shouting, "John! Up! Take it up. Up!"

Marshal didn't waste time asking what the hell was going on, but immediately obeyed by pouring on the speed and pulling the Starduster into a steep climb. Still without knowing what was going on, he leveled the shuttle off at five thousand feet. He still couldn't see what had Ben and Dave so excited.

It wasn't over as Dave frantically began beating on the back of Marshal's chair. "Higher! Higher! Take it up! Up!"

Just as he did so, Marshal felt a second bump against the side of the Starduster. Another bump caused him to really put the pedal to the metal… or rather pull back sharply on the stick. It was, after all, a space shuttle and it could really move when he needed it to. Moments later, they were in a low orbit where nothing except meteors could bash against them.

Apparently, space debris was considered safer than whatever was below. The noise from the cabin settled down enough for Ben and Dave to hear his third yell for them to explain what the hell had just happened.

Ben said, "Sorry, John. Things got a little exciting,"

"We were attacked by Pterodactyls!" Dave's terror over what had just happened was clearly overridden by his excitement over what had caused it. While his eyes were still ringed white with fear, the fool was grinning so wide, Marshal could count every tooth in his head.

"What?" Marshal exclaimed. Actually, he and Ben said

it in unison.

"Pterodactyls! Real Pterodactyls. Or some kind of flying dinosaur."

"I felt something bump against the shuttle," Marshal said. "A dinosaur actually attacked Dusty?"

Ben and Dave both nodded. Ben said, "John, they were big. Probably bigger than anything in Earth's fossil records. I'd say about the size of a light airplane. John, how high were we when they stopped attacking?"

Marshal couldn't help but laugh when he told him that he had no idea. "I never saw them, Ben. Can't see a damn thing in one of these bricks, but we were at three thousand when they first hit us and I was around five thousand when you guys told me to go higher. So, what now?"

Dave asked, "Do you think that it's safe to go back?"

Ben and Marshal looked at him like he was a candidate for village idiot but then Marshal shrugged and said, "Sure, I guess. As long as we stay out of the reach of your flying whatever's."

Ben thought for a moment and finally said, "Okay. Take us back and pick up the route at five thousand feet."

Giving Ben a glance of apprehension, Marshal obeyed and brought Dusty back down into the atmosphere. "Okay! I'm at five thousand."

"Excellent," said Dave. "Take her back out to sea and come in again at this altitude."

Their second approach over the coast was met not only without the aerial bombardment, but with complete indifference as the flying prehistoric animals ignored them. But now that Marshal knew they were there, he kept a sharp eye out in order to see his first living, breathing dinosaur... hopefully before they saw him. Inching forward in his seat so he could get a better view, he saw three of the monsters circling hundreds of feet below.

"I'll be damned," Marshal breathed. They did look exactly like the flying dinosaurs, or at least the critters he remembered from artist renditions. He seemed to remember that scientists now believed many of the ones from Earth had feathers, but these flying beasts were nothing but skin covered wings with wicked looking claws. Marshal chuckled.

"What?" Been asked.

"I was just thinking, my poor little single engine puddle jumper back on Earth wouldn't have lasted thirty seconds against those things."

Now completely ignored by the flying whatever-they-weres, Marshal warned the others to keep a sharp lookout as he gradually brought Dusty 1 back down to three thousand feet and they continued their mission.

From then on, the three Earthmen flew mostly in silence as the wonders of Index revealed themselves. It was just too much. A fern forest of many shades of green stretching off into the distance to their left with thousands of birds milling about overhead. Not dinosaurs this time—just birds like parrots, macaws and a few creatures that they never could have imagined. Off to their right was a rolling savannah well populated with what sure looked like herds of grazing dinosaurs and mammals. Familiar looking animals and some rather bazaar animals. It was hard for the men to wrap their minds around it.

Finally, they approached the great mountain range that dominated the west coast. The forest of giant ferns began to thin out at the base of rolling foothills that gradually rose to a spine of low rounded mountains.

It seemed Index was made up of nothing but mountains, plateaus both dry and wet, and forests. As the shuttle flew on toward the western mountains the clouds thickened and the rain increased in intensity. It was obvious that the mountains on this part of the western coast weren't as high as the ones farther north and the forest below them was different also. It was still densely forested but the trees changed from the giant firs they had seen on their first pass to trees that resembled those found in the northeastern part of North America and western Europe.

Allen said, "I think these mountains are part of that great mass that we crossed up north but the range takes a dip near the equator. There is still a lot of rain, but a lot of water is flowing to the east and not right back into the western ocean. I'd bet that if we went a little further south, we would find the headwaters of a river something like the Amazon." He paused for a moment in thought and continued, "And I wonder what kind of creatures we would find there?"

With that thought in their minds and dusk beginning to encroach on western Index they headed back to Voyager anxious to see the recordings of their flying dinosaur.

CHAPTER 7

Two days later with Ben Riley at the controls, Dusty 1, was three thousand feet above the restless ocean waves of Sanctuary approaching the peninsula/continent of Little Finger. From what they could tell from space the peninsula was about three thousand miles long, north to south, and maybe fifteen hundred miles wide at its widest point. The interior of the peninsula appeared to be nothing but a barren desert bordered on both coasts by thousands of square miles of dense, black clouds as storm after storm assaulted the peninsula. Alex and the boffins suspected that there were mountains hidden under that dense bank of clouds.

They could have made the fly-by the day before but an intense cold front was sweeping across the northern hemisphere pushing some really nasty weather ahead of it so they all agreed (Riley, Marshal and Allen especially) that it would be better to experience the storm with its swirling clouds, rain, sleet, hail, hurricane force winds and who knew what else, from three hundred miles above and inside Wisdom rather than up close and personal inside a Starduster.

Riley reflected that it was nice to have Al Wilson's weather station up and running even if he didn't have all the bells and whistles, but he was still of two minds about today's mission. Not the part about covering the big continent of Middle Finger, that was the whole purpose of the fly-by, but the fact that the peninsulas of Ring and Little had been included.

Originally the boffins planned to do Ring and Little as a separate mission but as more of Sanctuary became visible, relatively speaking, the two peninsulas seemed to have even less potential for a colony than Thumb. For a while they questioned even doing a fly-by over of those two peninsulas at all. But in the end considering the fact that the peninsulas were relatively narrow and considering Alex's determination to not leave a stone, or a peninsula, unturned, the decision was made to do a modified fly-by of Ring and Little before Dusty executed the main mission of gathering data on the peninsula/continent of Middle Finger.

Taking advantage of the Stardusters speed and its ability to fly out of Sanctuary's atmosphere into orbit, the shuttle would make just one pass over Little Finger, execute a high-speed run over the ocean toward Ring before turning south, staying well away from that exploding landmass. Not even John Marshal, as reckless as he sometimes was, was going to fly into a cloud of volcanic ash. Instead of flying directly over Ring, Dusty would fly around the southern edge of the peninsula and push up the west coast all the way to the great northern glacier.

The boffins like that part of the plan. In addition to whatever information they might gain from the flight around

Ring's perimeter this would give them their first real close up look at the great ice field that covered the top of the planet.

After Ring, Dusty would reset the clock with flight into space and a run to the west descending back into Sanctuary's atmosphere in time to greet the sunrise on the west coast of Middle Finger. The remainder of the mission would mirror that of Index—a west to east flight over the middle of the northern hemisphere and a return pass over the northern edge of the equatorial green belt finishing while there was still some daylight on the west coast.

Yeah, Riley thought, *it might work, but it's going to be a long day.*

As they came closer to the outer edge of the black swirling clouds surrounding Little the three men thought they were approaching Index again. The shuttle was still hundreds of miles away from where they thought the coast should begin and they were already flying in dense black swirling clouds with wind and rain beating against the windows. And, at five hundred miles an hour they would be on the coast of the peninsula in no time.

Damn, Riley thought, *I can't see a thing.* He looked over at Marshal who just shrugged.

Suddenly Marshal leaned forward and screamed "Up! Up! Take it up Ben!"

Riley had no idea what Marshal was so agitated about, but he wasn't about to argue. He pulled back on the stick and as he did, he saw the solid wall of rock in front of him. *Damn!* He thought to himself. *I'm at three thousand feet above sea level. The cliff can't be this high!* Riley pulled back as hard as he could to stand Dusty on its tail in order to avoid becoming one with the mass of rock in front of him. The shuttle screamed up the side of a mountain that consisted of a sheer, rain drenched rock wall that rose straight up out of the ocean's battering waves.

When their hearts started beating again, the three men let out a collective sigh of relief. All they could see through the rain was wet bare rock. No trees or vegetation of any kind had grafted itself to the solid rock walls.

They continued to climb. Ten thousand feet, fifteen— and still there was nothing to see except the rain and a bare wall of rock that was being lashed by the wind and rain.

"Geez!" exclaimed Allen. "You'd have to be one of those limpet things to live down there."

That brought a nervous chuckle and a nod of agreement from the other two.

Dusty was at just over twenty thousand feet above sea level when the shuttle broke out of the clouds and cleared the top of that impossible mountain range.

Marshal said, "Look at that, the clouds go right up to the tops of the mountains."

"Yeah," Riley answered, "and look ahead."

Allen and Marshal looked and saw... nothing. The terrain below them dropped away as fast as it had risen. What the boffins had thought might be a range of mountains was just a skinny ridge. A very high skinny ridge. A ridge blasted with a continuous deluge of rain on its ocean side but high enough that not a drop of moisture was making it to the eastern slope. Unlike the vast mountain ranges that they had encountered on Index, this range was barely one mountain wide. Riley flew up one side of the mountain and down the other.

And the terrain went with them, down and down.

"Look at the altimeter!" Marshal exclaimed.

"Damn," Riley answered. "Is that accurate? We're below sea level!"

"It's been accurate so far," Marshal answered as he

watched Riley finally level off at the prescribed three thousand feet above ground. Stunned, he said, "This entire basin is two thousand feet below sea level. Is that possible? Does that explain why it's so dry?"

Ben and Dave both snorted and Riley said as usual, "Me just driver. I haven't got a clue. Let your good lady and the other brains figure that one out."

Dusty 1 flew on for over two hours over something that resembled an artist's concept of the surface of Mars. Unrelieved shades of reddish-brown rocks without a patch of green. Nothing grew here. The entire continent between the mountain ranges appeared to be a vast, barren, dry, desert. Not a sandy desert like the Sahara but a desert of hard baked orange dirt with millions of rocks scattered about, single rocks, clumps of rocks, ridges of rocks. Not mountains, not hills... just rocks.

Why? They wondered. With rain storms battering both coasts, why should the interior of the peninsula appear to be so dry? They weren't sure and were counting on the take from today's mission to answer their many questions. Marshal commented that it was Sanctuary's way. Not counting Ring, (which wasn't even considered for their colony), Little and Thumb were the two other continents that appeared to be the most useless for settlement and were always the ones most cloud free.

As they approached the mountains that lined the eastern edge of the peninsula, Marshal remarked, "Well! That was lovely."

The other two chuckled as Ben brought Dusty up the side of the mountains and into the clouds. What they could see of the west coast was identical to the east: a ridge twenty-thousand-feet high that was barely one mountain wide that dropped straight into the ocean through black, wet storm clouds.

As far as Riley, Marshal, and Allen were concerned, that brief pass confirmed what they already knew: the peninsula/continent of Little Finger was a write-off.

Riley punched the speed up and headed across the restless ocean towards Ring.

The Dusty crew later agreed that their initial impression of Ring was that the entire peninsula was exploding. From space they had determined that the peninsula of Ring Finger was almost five thousand miles long north to south. Just long enough that its southern edge reached the northern edge of the equatorial belt giving the peninsula just a fringe of green at its southern tip. With the constant storms on both coasts, coupled with the solid layer of volcanic ash, width was impossible to determine but the brain trust estimated it to be about eighteen hundred miles.

But the main feature of the peninsula of Ring Finger was the volcanos. Throughout the entire peninsula there were dozens if not hundreds of active volcanoes blowing their tops. Even as low as the Starduster was flying they could see at least a half a dozen volcanoes erupting. Looking at the bright points of light in the dense clouds to the north and south they were sure that there were many more adding to the volcanic smoke and ash that mixed with the thick rain clouds and presented a churning gray black wall before them.

Riley turned the shuttle south paralleling the coast but still staying a couple of hundred miles away before increasing their altitude to twenty thousand feet. There was no need to stay down low, they couldn't stay lower and keep out of the ash cloud, but it didn't really matter because there wasn't going to be anything to see no matter what altitude they flew. The billowing clouds from the erupting volcanoes rose more than thousands of feet above them and extended north and south as far as they could see.

Allen mused, "I wonder just how many volcanoes are cooking on Ring right now. Seems like the whole peninsula is on fire." He scratched his head and chuckled. "I wonder if it's always like this. With all that smoke and cloud, it's no wonder that Al and Alex couldn't see anything from Wisdom."

Marshal laughed. "Hell, we're right here and we can't see anything."

Riley turned west across the narrow belt of green that struggled for a foothold across the southern tip of the peninsula. Then turned the shuttle north to fly up the west coast with the churning ocean to the left and beneath them and an exploding landmass on their right. With nothing to see or record he put the pedal to the metal and an hour later they were passing over the mile-high cliff of ice that marked the southern boundary of the great northern glacier.

The first thing the crew noticed was that the ice sheet that covered the northernmost part of Sanctuary wasn't completely featureless. There were craigs and valleys, peaks of isolated mountains and long ridges and most, but not all, were made of ice. Thousands and thousands of miles of ice that Al had estimated to be at least a mile thick. From Dusty's cockpit, that reading seemed to be a pretty good guess.

Al was also right that nothing could live down there on the ice for there wasn't a bird in the sky.

Riley slowed Dusty down as they passed over the face of the glacier that marked the northern boundary of Ring then did a slow turn to the east so they could look down the length of the peninsula. There was nothing to see except the clouds of volcanic smoke and ash that rose as high as fifty thousand feet and spread east over the ocean between Ring and Little for a thousand miles before it began to lift and break up.

If it were even possible, it seemed that the clouds

were denser and blacker on both coasts where wind and rain fought with volcanic ash for supremacy.

"Well so much for that." Marshal said as he sat back in the co-pilot's chair and started to tick items off on his fingers. "Let's see now. So far, we have flown over four peninsulas or continents, or whatever they are, and one glacier. The glacier is a bumpy ice cube that Frosty the Snowman couldn't live on. On the peninsulas we've seen the Himalaya Mountains and the vast nothingness of Tibet, the bleak frozen lands of Greenland and the North Pole, volcanos (lots and lots of volcanoes), a soggy rainforest, a prehistoric jungle complete with dinosaurs—one of which attacked us, a beach the size of the Sahara and the barren sands of Mars."

"Yup! That pretty much sums it up," Riley laughed while Allen added, "Yeah! What's next?"

Riley took the shuttle up into low orbit and raced off to the west getting ahead of the day line before turning back east and descending to three thousand feet over the ever-churning ocean between the peninsulas of Index and Middle. Perfect timing, he patted himself on the back. The sun, somewhere up there above the clouds, was just coming up.

That was a great thing about the Stardusters—he could race around a planet and have as many sunrises and sunsets as he wanted. But Riley had to admit that he was nervous. Marshal had made a serious point. So far from what they had seen of the planet, they hadn't found what any of them would call a good place to establish the colony. Even before today's fly-by, tensions were high among the Voyagers. No one was openly saying it, but privately many were thinking that if the peninsula/continent of Middle didn't pan out it might mean they would be forced to return to Earth. Riley didn't think that it would come to that mostly because Alex was convinced that Middle Finger, the largest continent at twenty thousand miles north to south and thirty-five hundred miles west to east at its widest point offered the best possibilities for settlement. Riley and the rest had great faith in Alex's leadership and judgment.

From orbit the Voyagers knew, or were pretty sure they knew, that mountain ranges dominated both the east and west coasts running, as far as they could tell, the entire length of the continent north to south. But there were mountains... and then there were mountains! In the northern hemisphere the mountains were low enough on both coasts, topping out at no more than four or five thousand feet they thought, that even after dumping a generous amount of moisture on the coastal slopes the atmosphere had plenty of water left over to push clouds hundreds of miles into the interior creating what seemed to be permanent cloud cover over a lush green landscape on both sides of the continent.

The air was much clearer in the southern hemisphere, that was the good news, but what this enhanced visibility revealed wasn't very encouraging. The west coast range of mountains south of the equator was much higher than the mountains to the north. Allen thought that it was a lot like the Andes Mountains of South America back on Earth. The effect created a narrow coastal rain forest on the west coast and an arid plain that extended from the eastern slopes of the mountains to the cliffs on the eastern ocean.

Kind of like the northern hemisphere of Index but not as severe.

A green jungle rainforest belt surrounded the equator which ran three thousand miles wide north to south and spanned the entire width, east to west, of the continent. But in everyone's opinion the most striking feature of the northern hemisphere of Middle Finger was that a vast prairie, that from space appeared to be teaming with animals, lay between the coastal ranges with an enormous lake or inland sea, the jury was out on what to call it, situated right in the center.

From orbit the scientists still weren't sure how big the lake was and how it drained. The southern end of the lake disappeared from view under a seemingly permanent cloud bank that pushed north from the equator. It was obvious that the lake was fed by thousands of rivers and streams from the mountains to the east and west and from the glaciers to the north and drained to the south but exactly where that tremendous volume of water went was still a mystery.

There were many questions Alex wanted answered: Were the cliffs that fronted the oceans continuous or were there breaks that created bays, inlets, or harbors that would provide protection from the raging seas and still allow the humans access to the ocean's bounty? In addition to where the big lake's water went, she wanted to know if the water was fresh or salt? What was the seasonal nature of the lake? She also wanted to know about the flora and fauna that lived under that perpetual cloud cover. From orbit they could get fleeting glimpses of the animals on the northern plains. Tantalizing glimpses. Mammals all as far as they could tell. But what else was lurking under those clouds? Did Middle have dinosaurs?

So, with the help of her husband, Dave Allen and Ben Riley they had planned today's fly-by to try to answer all the questions. By mutual agreement they decided to make the first pass west to east at thirty degrees north latitude, a little farther south than the first pass over Index. And instead of being right on the northern fringe of the green belt the east-west pass was planned for a few hundred miles north of the green belt and they would stick to their formula of Ben piloting the first run and John the return.

As the shoreline approached Ben, John and Dave

looked ahead into the dark and rainy gloom ahead of them. As far as they could tell, like Index, the west coast of Middle consisted of a wall of cliffs that were being slowly pounded to pebbles by the unrelenting sea. But unlike Index they could see that there were some breaks in the rock wall. Just to their left there was an opening that allowed an inlet that must have been at least a mile wide to flow through the rock wall for ten or twenty of miles before it hooked south to form a huge bay that must have been at least a hundred miles long north to south and fifty miles wide.

Alex will like that, Marshal thought.

Once they crossed the coastline, they flew over a fairly level plain that was densely covered in trees. It was a vast, unbroken carpet of trees most with their branches bare at this time of the year, but with a few evergreens mixed in, that stretched east from the ocean cliffs to the rolling foothills of a range of mountains. It was immediately obvious that this range was much lower than the massive range they had encountered on Index.

"More like the Alleghenies than the Rockies," Allen observed more to himself than to the others.

Dusty 1 flew over hill after tree-covered hill. Hills that gradually rose higher and higher until they topped out in a ridge of mountains that were only about four to five thousand feet above sea level. Marshal remarked that the trees seemed to be like the trees he remembered seeing in the eastern United States.

As the Starduster flew on rising over the coastal range the gray black clouds remained solid overhead and the rain continued. But they noted happily it wasn't the pounding, pouring down rain they had experienced on other peninsulas but just rain.

Gradually the mountains became green rolling hills

again. The dark clouds turned gray then white and the three Earthmen stared in awe as ahead of the shuttle there stretched a prairie covered with scattered patches of snow. The vast grassland was brown this time of year but they could imagine that when spring and summer arrived it would be a waving sea of green broken only by the ribbons of tree bordered streams and rivers that meandered east across the plains toward the big lake.

"North America before the Europeans," Marshal whispered.

"No, John," Riley said. "North America before anyone."

Awed as they were by the pristine scene before them, what really caught their eye was that, even at this time of year spread out as far as they could see over the prairie, there were animals. An unimaginable variety of animals but all mammals as far as they could tell. They seemed to be grazers mostly but occasionally they caught a fleeting glimpse of what could be predators. Wolves, maybe even lions. The Starduster passed by so quickly it was hard to be sure. They passed over a great herd of what at first appeared to be North American Bison but these Bison-like animals were bigger and shaggier than their counterparts on Earth. Another herd they passed were some kind of antlered deer which seemed to resemble a cross between a caribou and a reindeer. There were still others that the crew had no idea what they were. Their best guess was that they were like some of the grazers on the Serengeti of Africa. Wildebeests and gazelles maybe. And this vista went on for over three hours and for sixteen or seventeen hundred miles.

The grassland eventually ended on the shores of the lake they had observed from space. The body of water was a least a thousand miles long from north to south and when they flew over, they estimated it to be at least three hundred miles wide. Where the Mississippi River basin would have been in North America back on Earth, here on Sanctuary there was a gigantic lake. All the rivers from the mountains the Starduster had flown over to the west eventually flowed into this inland sea and unlike the oceans of Sanctuary this huge expanse of water was calm and had lots of heavily forested islands.

From the eastern shore of the lake the grassland continued again with all the waterways now flowing west and emptying into the lake. The prairie on the eastern side of the lake was less than a thousand miles wide, but was just as densely populated with animals as the vast grasslands to the west. After a little more than an hour's flight time the prairie gave way to another line of rolling tree covered hills that continued on gradually rising before they ended in a low coastal range of mountains and an abrupt cliff that marked the eastern coast.

Riley, Marshal and Allen were bubbling with excitement. Here they could live!

Ben took Dusty out over the ocean and turned south. It was no wonder they couldn't see much from space he thought. For the last thousand miles they were never out of the clouds and rain.

Marshal took over the controls and said, "Well, if Alex decides to settle on Middle and the critters aren't poisonous, we sure won't be short of meat."

Allen answered, "Yeah, that's for sure. Did you see those bison-like things? Huge! And there must have been a million of them."

Riley said, "I didn't see any dinos." He sounded disappointed.

"Good" Marshal chuckled. "I never liked dinosaur

steaks anyway."

"You never had a dinosaur steak."

"Beside the point. Besides, they probably taste like chicken."

They all laughed and Marshal asked, "Where do we turn in, Dave?"

Allen looked at his computer screen and said, "Here looks good. If we hold this line we should be pretty much where Alex wants us." Marshal brought Dusty's speed down to five hundred and descended to three thousand feet above the restless ocean. They were still in the rain and under the cloud cover. Visibility wasn't great but at least they could see something. Unlike Index there was no great beach on the east coast of Middle... only the never-ending cliffs with the ocean pounding against them.

Marshal crossed the coast keeping the jungle off to the left with hundreds of varieties of brilliantly colored birds filling the skies above the trees and the green rolling hills to the right as far as the eye could see. Strange planet Marshal thought to himself and then giving himself a shake, he thought, *no, not strange; just different.* To the others he said, "Keep your eyes open for those big flying things."

Riley said, "Well I didn't see any dinos up north so maybe there's none down here."

"There weren't any up north on Index either," Allen added.

Marshal said, "Make me happy. Look anyway."

They all chuckled and Allen said, "I don't see anything and we're five hundred miles north of the green belt so we should be okay. Hell, we don't even know if there even are dinosaurs on this continent. Remember what Al said. That between the oceans and the glaciers these continents are totally isolated and could be as different as Africa is from Australia."

The Starduster flew over the green tree covered rolling hills for a couple hundred miles before the hills gave way to the grasslands. Off to the south a few trees appeared as the flat lands approached the equatorial greenbelt. And, of course, everywhere they looked there were animals, herds of animals, all kinds of animals, millions of animals.

They flew on under the clouds that covered everything. But these clouds were not from the west but were clearly being pushed up from the south. Marshal wondered what was generating all that moisture? There were no great bodies of water bisecting the continent. No Mediterranean Sea, no Caribbean Sea, no Gulf of Mexico. Maybe Al would have an answer.

As Dusty 1 crossed the eastern shore of the big lake under the solid gray overcast, three things caught the crew's attention. The first were the trees that extended hundreds of yards out into the water. Having seen flooded areas like that when he was flying around on Earth, Marshal said that it looked as if the lake level had recently risen and flooded the shore.

The second thing was that the lake itself was covered with even more islands than they had seen up north. Islands large and small and just about every one of them had a fringe of trees standing in the water around them. It made the islands appear to be sinking into the lake or inland sea or whatever it was.

The third and best thing was they could see animals drinking from the lake. Fresh water!

At the southern end of this huge lake there didn't appear to be a river flowing south to drain the vast expanse of water. Instead, the lake gradually gave way to a bayou-like delta marshland that extended south as far as the crew could see.

Suddenly Allen shouted, "Horses! Those were horses!"

"What? Where?" Riley and Marshal said together.

"There, well, back there," Dave answered. "Wait." And he fiddled with the Vid pad. "Here. Look." And he shoved the pad between them.

"Well," Marshal said, "They kind of look like horses."

"Mighty big horses." Riley added.

"Those are horses!" Allen insisted.

Marshal laughed. "Okay, Dave, they're horses."

Allen was almost giddy. "I don't care how big they are. If we can domesticate them, they'll make our lives a whole lot easier!"

Once past the lake the grasslands continued on again, unbroken rolling grass for fifteen hundred miles, three hours flying time, until they came to the foothills of the coastal mountain range. Not a dinosaur in sight.

As the mountains rose the clouds that had never dissipated became darker and soon they were again flying through the seemingly ceaseless rain that seemed to be a permanent fixture of Middle Fingers west coast.

Marshal cleared the coast just as Sol II was sinking below the horizon and set a course to rendezvous with Wisdom.

After a meal and a night's sleep Alex and Al had to laugh at the de-briefing as all Ben, John and Dave could talk about were the animals and west coast rain. Especially Allen's horses.

"Well," Al said, "at least in the middle of Middle it doesn't really rain all the time. In fact, we are very interested in that big bay on the west coast you flew past. We plan to take a closer look at that area. Also, the big lake in the middle of the continent looks like it might have possibilities."

"Al, that big lake," Marshal asked, "is the water rising?"

Al and Alex looked at each other and Alex shrugged. "Yes. We think so and before you ask, my sweet, we have no idea how much more it will rise. That will depend on how much water flows from the mountains and how much more the glaciers will melt and retreat. Without any historical data we can't be sure exactly where Sanctuary is in the glacial cycle but Al seems pretty confident that we are about in the middle, that the glaciers have retreated about as far as they are going to go and we should be moving into several thousand years of fairly stable slightly warming weather until a cooling period starts again."

Marshal scratched his head. "So whatever the climate is now it's probably not going to get any colder for a few thousand years."

Wilson frowned. Weather guessers hated to be pinned down. Finally, he said, "Probably." And everyone chuckled.

CHAPTER 8

The Voyagers had learned all they could from their satellite views of the planet and the fly-bys and now it was time to put boots on the ground.

The "Away Team". That's what the Voyagers ended up calling the team that was going to go down and land on Sanctuary. Alex had originally wanted to call it the Exploration Team because when they shortened to ET, it not only described who they were in relation to Sanctuary but also what they were doing. Then someone (probably Marshal although he'd never admit it) remembered the old Star Trek shows and started calling it the Away Team and the new moniker spread faster than a wildfire through the dry bush. Marshal was certain the name annoyed Alex, but she just rolled her eyes and went with the inevitable.

After much discussion Alex decided that the team would consist of thirteen people; four scientists, four security personnel, their two outdoor survival specialists Grant and

Maryanne Foster, and a medic. Of course, Marshal would have to be included to see if Junior was viable but he could also serve as co-pilot for Riley.

The Fosters were brought out of hibernation and at Doc Watson's suggestion Mike Bennet was revived to fill the medical slot. Alex smiled; Doc was a good man. She knew that he would dearly love to go but he was also an honest man who knew that a young, fit, ex-Navy corpsman was better suited to the task of running around on a virgin planet than a bit-past-middle-age, slightly overweight, general practitioner.

Rather than pick the security personnel herself, Alex had Watson and Allen revive the project's security chief, Bartholomew "Link" Lincoln, and left the selection of the security team up to him. Link selected three of his long-time deputies from Project Voyager back on Earth, Jerry Smith, Kurt Jaeger and Jeff Mason. Alex raised an eyebrow at the selection of Jaeger as he had been shot in the shoulder during Voyagers' wild fight and flight from Earth. Alex remembered watching Audrey McPherson patch him up as he lay on the floor of the Starduster and once the dressings were in place, Jaeger had gone straight into his cryogenic pod when he came up to Voyager. Doc assured her that Kurt would be fine and as Doc predicted he came out of cryogenic hibernation twenty years later looking as if he had never been shot.

Everyone was raring to go but Alex was Alex and before she sent her team to investigate actual sites for the colony, she wanted a test landing. She selected Thumb for obvious reasons: not only was it the smallest of the peninsulas, but as far as they had been able to tell from space and the fly-bys, it was also the one most devoid of life. Well, except the peninsulas of Little and Ring but no one wanted to land and walk around on those wastelands.

For this initial trip, the team packed into Dusty 1 with

Riley at the controls and Marshal in the co-pilot's seat. Junior was tucked away in a cradle that they had built in the shuttle's cargo bay. Maryanne Foster rode in Allen's jump seat just behind them. Back in the passenger section, Link Lincoln, Grant Foster, Mike the medic and the seven scientists and deputies sat in the luxurious seats that space tourists had once paid hundreds of thousands of dollars to ride in. That fact went unnoticed in the giddy expectation that they were about to step onto an alien world.

The expatiation was terrifying, but the terror was downright exciting!

Alex and Al had picked out a landing site on the southwestern edge of the peninsula. With the wind steadily blowing from the west, Ben came in from the east and as best as he could without the benefit of an orbiting web of GPS satellites, set the Starduster down on Alex's coordinates. Not for the first time Ben Riley was grumbling that Stardusters may be marvelous, magical machines for flying in and out of orbit and landing on a nice hard-surface runway, but they really suck when you're trying to land vertically on rough terrain in the face of a steady twenty-five mile an hour wind. But as Marshal noted again, Ben had the touch and set them down with scarcely a bump while Marshal silently admitted to himself that he probably would have jolted everyone into next Tuesday.

Needless to say, even as nasty as the weather was, twenty-five mile an hour wind, squalls of freezing rain and snow with the temperature hovering right around freezing, everyone was anxious to set foot on their new home. Not that they were going to live on Thumb, but the symbolism was there. All they had to do now was decide who was going to take the giant leap for mankind. Seeing as he was kind of the senior Away Team leader, everyone thought that Link should go first, but being the courtly gentleman that he was, Link respectfully demurred and let the ladies, Maryanne Foster and Ann Turner, vie for the honor of becoming the first Earthling to set foot on a planet outside of our Solar System.

Let history record that rock, paper, scissors decreed that Maryanne Foster was the first human to set foot on Sanctuary.

Bundled up in her heavy parka, she couldn't see the ground very well—or at least that was her story later anyway—because as she stepped off the ladder and before she could utter any profound proclamation of discovery, she went up to her knee into a gopher hole—a giant gopher hole. In retrospect, at nearly three feet across, Marshal, coming down the ladder behind her, wondered how even encumbered with all her foul weather gear, how could she have missed seeing it? And as he climbed up the side of the shuttle to the cargo bay, he looked out over the rocks and wind-blown scrub grass and saw that the ground was completely pockmarked with big gopher holes.

"Prairie dogs," one of the scientists nodded knowingly. "Or something like prairie dogs."

Those would have to be some big-ass prairie dogs, Marshal thought as he undid the straps that kept Junior from floating away when they were in space and climbed inside. To himself he added, *well, John, me boy, you're either going to be a genius today or you're never going to be able to live this down.*

He touched the controls and an instant later Junior rose smoothly out of Dusty 1's cargo bay and into the windy, rainy skies of Sanctuary. The rest of the team didn't have to look to see if Marshal's brain child was successful because they were treated to a series of war whoops as the modified construction robot darted to and fro, up and down, overhead.

Everyone laughed and congratulated him as he buzzed

around above.

Link said, "When you're done playing, John, how about doing some real work and scout around for us?"

"Oh yeah! Sorry Chief! Got a little carried away there."

Everyone laughed again. Marshal was just one of those guys that you couldn't help liking and his enthusiasm for everything was contagious.

Hovering about forty or fifty feet above the ground from inside Junior, Marshal had a great view over the landscape and the Away Team. "I can't see anything moving, Link. Outside of Maryanne's prairie dogs it looks like you have the place all to yourself."

"Good. Let's keep it that way."

Then Marshal looked down and saw Maryanne standing by one of the gopher holes gesturing wildly while her husband and Ty West were burrowing away into the ground and he asked, "What the hell are Ty and Grant doing?"

Link replied, "I think they're after one of the critters that live in these holes."

Under Maryanne's coaching, Grant and Ty managed to drag out one of the prairie dogs or whatever they were. The creature was the size of a small dog, many times bigger than a Terran prairie dog. And it was sound asleep. Marshal decided it had to be hibernating for all the care it gave to being dragged from its hole. The excited scientists crowded around chattering and speculating on what it was, what it lived on and what to call the critter when someone wondered what kind of predators might be preying on them.

It was an interesting thought and everyone, Marshal included, started looking around like a herd of deer caught in the headlights. When nothing immediately launched at them from the windblown grass, everyone kind of laughed and the scientists continued measuring and photographing the prairie dog thing and collecting their samples of dirt, rocks and some scrubby little flowers Marshal hadn't even noticed that were trying to grow amongst the grass.

Marshal took Junior up a little higher and moved off toward the northeast as the scientists lost interest in the critter. As they scattered looking for something new to document the security personnel, Link, Jerry, Kurt and Jeff, were trying, mostly unsuccessfully, to keep a loose protective perimeter around them.

One of the first things that Marshal had learned as a scout in the Army was that nothing attracts the eye as much as movement and out on the edge of his vision, something was moving. "Link, I've got movement about a mile to your northeast. I'm going to check it out."

"Okay, John. Keep me posted."

Meanwhile, either due to the handling or the fact that it was no longer happily sleeping in its burrow, the critter that the scientists were calling a prairie dog suddenly came to life.

And it was not a happy critter.

A little prairie dog on Earth might be expected to scurry into the first available hole at the first sign of any sign of danger. Sanctuary, apparently, played by different rules. Once awake and realizing what was going on it flipped out of Grant Foster's hands and when it hit the ground, instead of heading for the nearest hole, it charged. The creature, displaying an impressive set of teeth and claws, fastened itself onto Foster's right boot. Everyone who saw what was happening stood paralyzed by this sudden turn of events—everyone except Jerry Smith. Reacting with the speed of a cobra, Jerry took a half dozen quick steps toward Foster and knocked the creature loose with the butt of his rifle. Before the creature could recover Smith bashed it again and it lay still.

While the Away Team was still trying to catch up on what had just happened another one of the creatures bolted out of the hole, all teeth and claws clearly looking to vent its fury on someone or something. Jerry Smith didn't hesitate. He shot the creature dead.

Oblivious to the excitement, Marshal had taken Junior up a little higher where he could look over the folds of terrain that could easily hide things from ground level. *Yup!* he said to himself, *something is definitely moving around up there.* He flew closer and in a sheltered depression between the rocks he saw what had attracted his attention. *Geeze!* he thought, *Wolves!*

Or at least it looked like a pack of wolves, but then he thought they didn't quite look like wolves. They were about the size of wolves with the same kind of fur but their legs were short with large spade-like feet and they had long thin snouts more like a fox.

Marshal was still puzzling over the wolf-like creatures when he heard the gunshot over the open comm link.

"What the heck was that?" he asked, but before he could get an answer, he saw that the pack of wolf-like animals had also heard the shot and were moving out of the sheltered area and turning toward the sound. Quickly he opened the comm. "Link! Some kind of animals heard that shot and they're looking your way. Looks like a pack of wolves."

"Wolves?" Link asked.

"Well, they kind of look like wolves." Then Marshal paused and said, "Link, they've speeded up. They're coming your way fast."

Heeding the urgency in Marshal's voice, Link yelled for everyone to get back on the shuttle. As they scrambled towards the Starduster, Marshal kept pace with the animals as they raced across the barren wasteland right towards the ship and the exposed Away Team.

As the first of the scientists reached the ladder, Ben went back up to the cockpit and started firing up Dusty. While he didn't know if they were going to take off or not, he was going to be ready just in case. Moments later, Maryanne tumbled into the co-pilot's seat, and Grant slid into the jump seat. "Don't mind us," Grant said, "we're just getting out of the way."

Riley noticed that Foster had a dead Prairie dog in each hand.

Things got all confused after that. Sitting high in the Stardusters cockpit, Riley and the Fosters couldn't see anything up close on the ground. Glancing back into the passenger section, all they could make out was a jumble of bodies as people tumbled over each other as they tried to get up the ladder, clear the entryway and head toward the rear while Jerry Smith, gun ready, stood at the door.

Link was the last one up the ladder but before he could clear the stairs something big and furry landed in the middle of his back knocking him forward onto the shuttle floor and ignoring everything else started ripping at the back of his parka as he lay there.

While Ben and Maryanne couldn't see much, they could hear plenty—mostly humans yelling, animals snarling and then a gunshot.

Riley yelled, "No guns! No guns! Unless you want to stay down here on Sanctuary until they crank up another Starduster, don't go shooting holes in Dusty."

Grant Foster had the best view of what was happening and he came out of his seat with a wicked looking knife that seemed to appear in his hand as if by magic. What he had seen were what looked like two big dogs thrashing with Link as he lay in the passageway. Smith had shot the one that was tearing away at the back of Link's parka and Foster leaned down and slashed at the other one who was trying to fasten onto Link's boot. The critter snarled but let go and dropped away.

"Take off!" Link shouted. "Take off, Ben. Get it up!"

With all the noise and confusion Riley couldn't hear the command. "What?"

Maryanne shouted, "Up! Link says to take it up."

Even though the telltale light said that the door was still open, Riley lifted off anyway. Hell, why worry about the passenger door when the cargo door was still open. As the shuttle wobbled up into the air, he heard more banging and cussing. Then the light went out indicating the hatch had finally been closed but Dusty 1 was still bouncing all over the sky. The cargo door was still open.

John Marshal and Junior were still out there.

Riley looked out and, not seeing the robot, frantically asked, "John, where are you? Are you okay?"

Marshal flew Junior up in front of the shuttle where Riley could see him. "I'm fine," he assured him. "Don't worry about me"

Riley asked, "Where do you want me to land so I can get you back aboard?"

Marshal thought for a minute and said, "Why don't you close up. I'll stay out here."

Riley was quiet for a moment and then shrugged "Okay! If you say so."

"Yeah! Go ahead, Ben. I'm good."

After that, everything was eerily quiet. Riley and the Fosters just looked at each other hoping no one had been left behind in the chaos.

The silence, however, was short lived as everyone in the back started talking at once. Gradually, Riley started to relax when he realized the sounds were ones of excitement and not pain. Giving Maryanne another look, he smiled, relieved that the Away Team seemed to be in one piece if not the worse for wear. Eventually, someone would come forward and fill them in with what they'd missed.

He was right. Link soon leaned in over their shoulders and apologized, "Sorry I took so long."

"What were those things?" Ben asked, swiveling his torso in his seat in order to look at Link. "Geeze, Link! Are you okay?" His parka looked like it had been through a shredder.

Link smiled. "Yeah. Fine. Looks like I lost a parka, but otherwise not a scratch."

Riley said, "Good thing you were wearing that parka. What the hell are those things? They looked kind of like wolves, but not like anything I've ever seen."

"Ann Turner thinks that they are some kind of fox."

Marshal chimed in from Junior, "That's one hell of a big fox."

Link said, "Oh hi, John! Sorry. I guess I kind of forgot about you. You okay?"

"I'm fine," and he said again, "That's one hell of a big fox! And I didn't think that foxes ran in packs."

Grant shrugged. "Earth foxes don't, but on this planet, who knows?"

That made a lot of sense and Marshal had to remind himself that this was a completely new world and he shouldn't compare the biology here or anything else to what they'd left behind on Earth. Already they'd seen pterodactyls the size of airplanes and prairie dogs the size of, well, dogs. He shouldn't expect evolution to work the same way here as it did on Earth so there was no reason to expect that foxes should look or act like Terran foxes.

Grant Foster chimed in, "What scares me though is the

way that they came after us. No hesitation, no milling around. They couldn't have any idea what we were, but it seems that as soon as they were aware of our presence they attacked. And not only attacked us organic types, but they went after the Starduster, too. That's taking aggressiveness or territorialism to the n'th degree."

Riley and Marshal in their separate environments just nodded in agreement. Not being a biologist or a zoologist or any kind of "ist" worth mentioning, Marshal decided that maybe those prairie dog things weren't as easy to catch as they appeared. If food was hard to find for the foxy wolves, anything that looked like it might be edible would be worth going after... even shiny metal Stardusters.

Turning to Link Riley chuckled. "Well, boss, that was exciting. What's next? Now that we know, or kind of know, what to look for, do you want to try to set down somewhere else or call it a day?"

Before Link could answer Marshal exclaimed, "Whoa, Ben! Wait a minute."

"What?"

"It looks like you've got a hitchhiker."

"What?"

"Hang on a minute. It looks like one of those foxy wolf things got himself stuck in one of the landing skids. Hold still a minute."

Junior disappeared below Dusty and a few moments later reappeared with one of the fox wolves clutched in Junior's mechanical claws snapping and snarling at the metal hand that held it. "Got him," Marshal exclaimed. "Do you want him?"

Maryanne laughed. "I don't think so. The scientists already have three carcasses back there. Two prairie dogs and a wolf thing."

Marshal said okay and disappeared again below the shuttle. Maryanne asked, "What did you do, drop him?"

"Nah! I'm not that mean. I set him down as gentle as a baby. He's probably some kind of a god now to the other fox wolf things. So, guys, what's the plan?"

Link scratched his head. "Can we talk to Alex and Al?" he asked.

Riley looked at the board. "Nope. Gone over the horizon. Be another hour or so before they come around again."

Link scratched his head again. "Well, seeing as we're here… I hate to waste the trip…"

The Fosters laughed and Ben smiled. "Right, boss! Where to?"

Sitting in the clear plastic ball that was Junior Marshal also grinned. These were the kind of guys he liked!

"Well, when we first flew in, West had an idea; I'll send him up," Link said. He ducked back into the cabin and soon Tyler West was leaning over their shoulders.

"Hey, Ty!" Riley smiled at the excited grin on Tyler's face. "What's up? Having fun?"

The young man couldn't contain his enthusiasm. "This is amazing! It will take me years to unravel the ecology of this planet, but we can grow stuff—our stuff—here I'm sure of it."

"Well, that's good news," Ben said. "Now all we need to do is find a farm someplace where the ground doesn't attack us."

As they shared a laugh, Maryanne asked, "Link said that you had a place that you wanted to check out?"

"Yeah! As we were flying toward the coast just before we landed, I noticed what looked to be a bird colony up the coast to the north. It's a long way so I couldn't see much but the birds looked normal, or rather they seemed to be more

Earth-sized, so maybe we can get a bird or two."

Ben smiled as Link nodded. "You got it, Ty. Take my place here and when we get close see if you guys can spot us a good landing place."

"Right."

It wasn't hard to decide which way to go; Ben just turned Dusty west and headed for the coast but almost immediately got a wail from Marshal. "Hold up, Ben; we have a small problem."

"What?"

"I can't keep up. It looks like I gave Junior everything except speed. Junior here is a bit of a slow poke. It looks like he can only do seventy, seventy-five miles an hour, tops."

"Ah! Right. What do you want me to do? Do you want me to land and take Junior back on board?"

"Let me think a minute. Ty, how far away is your bird roost?"

West answered, "Not far, maybe a hundred miles up the coast."

Marshal was silent for a moment and then said. "Why don't you go ahead, Ben. I'll follow along. You can always come back and get me if I'm too damn slow."

"Okay! If you say so.'

"Yeah, in fact it will give me a chance to put Junior through his paces."

Riley said, "Right, see you in a few." And he pushed Dusty along to the coast and turned north. In just a few minutes the bird colony was in sight. Several thousand big white birds were wheeling and swooping over the sheer cliffs and out over the churning waves as far as he could see. Not being much of an ornithologist, Riley didn't know if he was remembering his facts correctly, but it occurred to him that as it was winter here in the Sanctuarian Northern Hemisphere, he decided that these birds—hell, maybe all of the millions of birds that they had seen—must be some kind of non-migratory species. He imagined that in the spring breeding season, the cliffs on both coasts from north to south would be swarming with even more birds of all kinds.

Nearing the jagged cliffs, the Voyagers saw that the top of the cliffs looked as if they had been leveled as if a giant had taken a massive scythe and whacked the tops clean off. Short, stubby grass swept across the mesa-like landscape between the rocks giving the crags what appeared to be a military buzz cut. Nudging Ben, West pointed to an area that looked solid enough for the weight of a Starduster. "That looks like a nice big flat rock right on the edge of the colony. See it?"

"Yeah! Got it. Looks good."

Ben brought the Starduster in at about three hundred feet and started to settle—and that's as far as they got before they were suddenly mobbed. A bazillion of the albatross-sized birds suddenly swarmed the shuttle—but they weren't just flying around to warn the intruders off, they were attacking! Hundreds of them were pecking at the windows or beating their wings against the metal hull. Ben just kicked the Starduster out of vertical landing and into drive and headed out to sea at about twice the speed of sound.

Stunned, their mouths open in disbelief, Riley, West and the Fosters just looked at each other in shock. So far, they had met four species on this planet: Pterodactyls, overgrown foxes, these white birds and the giant prairie dogs—and the only ones who hadn't attacked them immediately had been the damned gopher because he'd been asleep! Not a good percentage in Riley's book.

Link was back over his shoulder and everyone in back was yelling and demanding to know what was going on.

Dusty 1 was a couple of hundred miles out to sea before Link got the explanations done and everyone calmed down. Ben throttled back, circled around and headed back toward land, well away from the bird colony while he waited to see what brilliant idea the scientific squints in the back came up with next.

The idea was a beauty presented by no less than Maryanne Foster herself. All bubbly, she turned to Ben and said, "If you come back up the coast and approach low and slow, how close to the bird colony do you think you can get and set down without upsetting them?"

"I have no idea. Why?"

"I think that maybe the birds won't react to someone on foot the same way that they would to something in the air."

Riley said, "You want to go up there on foot?"

"Yes. I'm thinking maybe they won't attack someone on the ground."

"After what just happened that's a pretty big maybe," Riley said in astonishment. "It would be a lot harder for someone on foot to get away from them if they do try to swarm. But as I said, I have no idea how close we can get— this flying brick is not a helicopter. Low and slow is not something that Stardusters do very well and we can't just land anywhere."

Maryanne looked a little chagrined, but the smile and the bubbly enthusiasm was still there. "Sorry, just a thought."

Ben, however, wasn't put off by her suggestion. "Tell you what: If I come up from the south over the cliffs, hopefully we'll be high enough so we don't piss the foxes off, if there are any around, but still low enough that we don't get the birds all excited. I'll get as close as I can, and when it looks like they're starting to stir, I'll set down. Depending on how close that is, you might have a long way to walk. How's that?"

Maryanne and Tyler grinned and pounded him on the back and Maryanne gave him a hug. "You're a sweetheart, thank you."

She squirmed over her husband heading toward the passenger compartment and Ben looked over at Grant. "Don't look at me," Foster countered before Ben could accuse him of being complicit in the plan. "I just go along for the ride."

"Well just for the record I think you're both nuts. And you too, Ty." He shrugged. "What do you want me to do?"

"Watch the birds," Grant grinned. "The minute they flutter, set it down."

Ben brought the Starduster in at two-hundred feet and just barely maintaining air speed, Marshal came up on the comm to ask what was going on. He laughed when Ben told him but he was grateful that he wasn't the one at the controls.

Ben Riley was steady as a rock.

Maryanne came back all bundled up again in her parka and managed to wiggle back into the co-pilot's seat. They all held their breath as Riley inched Dusty toward the bird colony. They were probably inside half a mile when the massive flock started fluttering. "You're over a good spot," Maryanne said enthusiastically as Ben gently set the winged brick down. The moment the Starduster settled on the grassy plateau, she, Grant and Tyler were through the door, down the ladder and off toward the birds giggling like a bunch of school kids on a field trip.

Of course, everyone else wasn't going to just sit in the shuttle while they were gone and in no time, the entire Away Team were scattered all over the rocks collecting their bits of this and that.

Marshal and Junior were still poking their way up the

coast when Voyager and Wisdom came over the horizon. With Ben and all the other would-be explorers out ravaging the countryside no one was monitoring the comm so Marshal tried to explain to his wife just what was going on.

"Hello, Luv," he said brightly, hoping his cheerfulness would throw her off for a few more moments. It didn't work and that was probably the main reason he never gambled. Not only did he not have a poker face, he didn't even have a poker voice and could never bluff Alex.

"John," she immediately demanded, "where are you? Is everything all right?"

"We're fine, Luv," he assured her, but there was no way out of telling her their adventures to date.

"So, they just walked up to the bird colony?" Alex was incredulous. "Are they okay?"

"As far as I know, yes. I haven't heard any screams anyway. Don't worry, Luv, we'll be heading back soon. See you in a couple of hours. By the way, in addition to all the dirt, rocks and other stuff that the boffins collected, they also have three carcasses to keep themselves amused. A couple of big ass prairie dogs and some kind of wolf or fox ... something. Oh, and whatever the Fosters and West pick up."

"Hi, Alex," Riley said.

Alex answered, "John, you didn't tell me that Ben was there."

"Ben is there," Marshal answered, "I'm not there."

"What?"

Riley and Marshal laughed while Marshal explained. And he finished "I'm coming up on Dusty right now and I can see the Fosters and West."

Looking out the Starduster window, Riley noticed with great amusement that Marshal had been right: The Fosters and Ty West weren't leaving the bird colony empty handed. As they struggled to lug their findings back to the shuttle, he also had to hand it to the Fosters; they knew their stuff and Maryanne was right on the money about not being attacked.

Marshal flew up to the Starduster to get a better look at what the Fosters were carrying. So, did everyone else. As the crowd gathered Marshal took Junior up a little just to get out of the way only to get a warning from Ben. "Keep it low, John. Don't excite the birds."

"Yeah! Right!" Marshal answered. "It looks like Grant has a big bird in his arms but what the heck is Maryanne carrying?"

Before Riley could answer Maryanne said, "It's an egg, you big lummox. Don't you recognize an egg?"

"That's a big egg! Must be a pretty big chicken."

"Not a chicken—a sea bird of some kind." She pointed to the carcass in Grant's arms. "Some kind of a Guillemot I think."

While all the scientists chimed in Marshal asked, "Well Luv, did you get all that?"

Alex laughed. "I did, my sweet. What's next?"

"I guess it depends on what you and the team..." and he trailed off.

"What?" asked Alex.

"Hang on Luv, I think we're going to have company. Link, it looks like you've attracted some attention. Look off to the east, about a mile or so. There's a pack of those fox-wolf things headed your way. Better get everyone loaded up."

The Voyagers didn't need any more warning than that and while the team scrambled aboard Dusty, Riley opened the cargo doors and Marshal settled Junior into his cradle. Dusty was already flying up to orbit when the fox-wolves swept over the rocks probably wondering where the whatever it was went.

CHAPTER 9

As soon as Marshal's report on Junior's success reached the robot jockeys in space JJ Jackson and Billy Wright started pestering Alex for permission to convert their construction robots to the ground configuration. Seeing as their lady loves would be living in the colony, Alex had expected that and told them to go ahead then she directed Watson and Allen to bring robot jockeys Tony Simmons and Paul Mahoney out of hibernation.

Alex had always wondered why those two, Tony and Paul, had chosen to leave Earth and come to Sanctuary. They were the youngest of the robot jockey engineers, both single and they loved to party. Time would take care of the first and most likely the second, but the partying? She was sure that there would be plenty of celebrations in their new home, but not the way those boys liked to enjoy life. While the team was building Voyager, Tony and Paul had spent every minute of their ground time up in Las Vegas blowing every dime of the generous pay checks that Visions Unlimited gave them. Alex chuckled to herself; they were going to be mighty disappointed when they found out that there wasn't a Vegas, or even a frontier trading post, on Sanctuary.

Which brought her back to her current challenge. On Earth Alex didn't have to think about dividing construction robots between space operations and ground operations. Now she had to make a couple of decisions. She had eleven robots available but only nine jockeys. She smiled to herself. These were her construction engineers. Her robot jockeys.

Not a problem.

Alex had the six jockeys who were awake meet with her in R3 and she proposed the way forward. Three robots would be converted to ground configuration now, Junior, of course, and Judy and Cathy, two more when the colony was established and the rest as conditions permitted as Voyager was being dismantled. For the immediate future there would be five jockeys working on the ground with five robots, four jockeys and six robots would remain in the space configuration to transfer supplies, service Wisdom and dismantle Voyager. The ground jockeys would be on call to man the spare space robots as needed. Fred Thompson would be in charge of space operations. John Marshal on the ground.

Questions?

No questions.

The jockeys thought that was just fine but Tony and Paul made it clear that they wanted to be the two that finished out the ground contingent. There were no objections and the boys went back to work. Alex smiled to herself. If only everyone was as easy to work with as her robot jockeys.

Once he was back in orbit Marshal kind of split his time between helping Fred and the rest of the RJs assemble the second section of Wisdom and providing help and advice to JJ and Billy while they disassembled and rebuilt their robots.

With three or four RJs working on re-assembling the space station it took less than a week before Fred reported to Alex that section two of Wisdom had been attached and as soon as the "packing material" had been removed it would be ready for the scientists to occupy. Those who had been awake and involved with removing millions of rolls of toilet paper from section one laughed at the bewildered stares and questions that came from those who had still been in hibernation.

Compared to the first TP drill the second one, with a dozen more pairs of hands, went pretty well. At least the bucket brigade part went well. The bad news was that before they were halfway finished, the net cage at the end of the San Diego Job was stuffed to overflowing. As soon as the Voyagers crammed toilet paper rolls in one end, other toilet paper rolls, clearly intent on their own agenda, spilled out around the net at the other end and floated away. For the remainder of their time in orbit, the Voyagers would share space with floating rolls of toilet paper that seemed to turn up in the darndest places.

Even in the sleeping pods.

While it was obvious that the remaining three sections of the space station couldn't be emptied and occupied by the scientists until the TP could go directly into a Starduster and down to Sanctuary Alex directed Fred to go ahead and assemble Wisdom anyway and deal with the TP later.

While those projects were going forward the remainder of the Voyagers huddled around Alex and Al and poured over the computer images of Sanctuary as they tried to identify suitable sites for their colony. The consensus opinion was that their initial assessment was correct, Thumb, Ring and Little weren't worth considering. They agreed that a settlement on Index might be possible but only in the hills along the eastern seaboard or in a narrow band just north of the equatorial green belt. Not a great spot to grow and eventually expand and then there were the dinosaurs to consider.

The Voyagers had high hopes for Middle Finger. By far the largest of the peninsulas, Middle offered not only the greatest variety of topography and climate but also the greatest amount of both biological and ecological diversity. The continent of Middle Finger had everything: prairies, deserts, steppes, forests, lakes, rivers, mountains... and also thousands and thousands of miles of coastline.

But it was so immense it was overwhelming. It was almost impossible to decide where to begin to look.

Alex went back to the basics.

In Earth's history, almost all of the earliest civilizations had settled on or near a water source. Be it rivers, lakes or seas, humans needed water to survive and, in the oceans, or even the lakes and streams, there was a bounty of food. Alex wanted to check these areas first for any viable locations.

Unfortunately, the stormy cloud covered coastlines of Middle Finger were almost impossible to see from orbit and what they could see through the rare breaks in the cloud cover was not encouraging. The fly-by had provided a little more information but not much. The consensus was that the coasts of Middle Finger, both east and west, consisted of continuous cliffs that rose straight out of the ocean. The sheer cliffs were anywhere from one to two-hundred feet high and were being constantly pounded to pebbles by twenty to thirty-foot waves—and that was on a good day. Who knew how high the waves got during the really big storms?

Alexandria Cummings wasn't one to keep playing a losing hand. If Sanctuary wasn't going to provide a coast, what about a sheltered body of water associated with the ocean? She had the scientists turn their attention to finding breaks in the cliff wall that might lead to bays or inland seas and after a search several were discovered in the cliff face on the western coastline.

The one she selected for exploration was the one that Ben, John and Dave had noticed on their fly-by. The break in the coastal cliff was located about halfway between the glacier to the north and the tropical green belt to the south with a gap in the solid wall nearly a mile wide that allowed the churning waters of the Index/Middle Ocean to flow about twenty miles inland before being stopped by solid rock walls to the north and east. But at the eastern end of the inlet a huge bay opened to the south. A sheltered body of water that ran for a hundred miles or so before it seemed to disappear into a marshy kind of bayou.

Alex and the rest were fascinated by this bay but the never-ending cloud cover made it impossible to pin down details. The only things that they all agreed on was that it was a bay, at least a hundred miles long, that it was tidal and seemed to vary from about forty or fifty miles in width. Through the occasional breaks in the usually dense cloud cover they could also see that because it was protected from the ocean by a twenty-mile strip of mountains to the west the water was fairly calm. Compared to the wave tossed oceans that prevailed around the planet the bay was downright peaceful. Other than that, determining specific features of the huge bay were purely guesswork.

Not much to go on.

The idea of another fly-by was rejected and two days after the landing on Thumb the same team that executed the preliminary landing floated into Dusty 1 with Ben Riley at the controls and John Marshal sitting in the co-pilot's seat.

After an uneventful flight through the clouds and a constant downpour, Riley approached the cliff opening at five thousand feet. When Grant Foster leaned forward and asked him why he was so high Ben indignantly replied that he didn't want to disturb any birds that might be nesting in the cliffs.

They all laughed and Marshal said, "Hell, Ben, with this rain I can't even see the cliffs. How could the birds see us?"

They all chuckled again as Riley flew over the gap. Just as they had suspected the opening looked like it had been blasted through the cliff face. A meteor strike maybe—long, long ago. Sheer rock walls lined both sides of the opening and twenty miles ahead the inlet ended in another wall of rock. But before they reached that wall the huge bay opened up to their right.

When Riley turned south over the bay the Starduster was closer to the western shore and Marshal remarked, "Not much more than rocks and trees on this side."

Maryanne laughed. "Don't be so pessimistic, John. There is the odd clearing."

"Yeah!" said Marshal. "But you'd have to be a mountain goat to get there."

Maryanne leaned over Riley's shoulder. "What about the east side?" she he asked, pointing. "That side looked like it had at least some beach. Hang on a minute and let me talk to Ann and Dan."

In a few minutes Ann Turner was leaning over Ben's shoulder. "Yes, that looks a possible site, but, Ben, don't land on the beach. Better go a little way inland until we know more about the beach and especially what's in the water."

Marshal asked, "What's in the water?"

"I have no idea," she answered. "That's why I don't

want to get too close."

Riley and Marshal looked at each other. That was an interesting line of thought.

Riley guided Dusty over the beach and landed the shuttle about a quarter mile away from what looked to be the high tide mark. After their previous experience on Thumb, the entire Away Team held their breath and waited for a few minutes to see if anything was going to attack. When nothing did, they cautiously opened up the hatch and Link and his security team dropped to the ground and took up positions around the shuttle. After a few minutes Link waved Marshal down and told Riley that he could open up the cargo bay.

Marshal scrambled down the ladder and then up Dusty's side. He paused at the top of the cargo hold to look around. As far as he could see the terrain looked just like the approach to any beach he had seen on earth—low rolling sand hills covered with coastal grass.

"See anything, John?" Link asked.

"Nothing. Not even a bird."

Still inside the shuttle the scientists looked at each other. Not even a bird—why?

Marshal slid into Junior and lifted into the air. From a hundred feet or so he made a slow circuit around the area. Nothing except the coastal sea grasses, a few scrubby bushes and sand. It seemed that the Away Team had the area to themselves. Still cautious, Link waved the rest of the team down and soon the scientists began to scatter as they went about investigating the area.

After watching the eggheads blunder around on Thumb, Link realized that perimeter security was impossible so he assigned a deputy to each of the scientists. The scientists might think they were too old for a buddy system but in Link's mind that was the only way to go. The scientists moved around so much and once they fixated on something they were oblivious to everyone and everything—especially to any potential danger,

Keeping their rifles at the ready, the team of Link, Ann Turner and Maryanne Foster followed the team of scientist Dan Macintyre and his security man Jeff Mason as they walked up to the tangled mass of trees, branches and other debris that had piled up at must have been the high tide mark. At Link's question, Macintyre said that he wanted to check out one of the holes in the beach that they had noticed flying in. Maryanne laughed and shook her head as Link waved them on. Those guys were like bird dogs on a scent. Once they got intrigued by something nothing could slow them down.

Link looked at Ann Turner wondering where she wanted to go. With a shrug, she too indicated she was content to burrow around the high tide debris, so Link and Maryanne scrambled to the top of the pile of logs and looked around. As Link had anticipated, the teams had quickly separated. Though Maryanne had joined Lincoln and Turner, the security chief didn't worry about either of the Fosters as he was pretty sure they could take care of themselves. Instead, he turned his attention to the other teams. Macintyre and Mason were walking out onto the beach in front of him and a hundred yards or so to the north Kurt Jaeger had Ty West under his watchful eye. Grant Foster had attached himself to that group. About the same distance to the south Link saw Jerry Smith with the other scientist Glenn Fisher. He turned and looked back at the shuttle which was being guarded by Riley and Mike Bennet.

Not an ideal situation to spread out so much, he thought before admonishing himself to quit worrying. They had to spread out if they were going to accomplish anything.

Maryanne looked down the beach and remarked,

"That's a mighty steep beach. I'd bet that at high tide if you were five or ten feet from here the water would be over your head. Just look at that seaweed!"

"Kelp," Macintyre said over the comm.

Maryanne made a face. Yeah! Whatever. That was one thing about their comms—you could talk to anyone anytime but ears were always listening.

Looking down the rock-strewn beach, Link realized Maryanne was right. The seaweed or kelp that would have floated way above his head in a vast, undulating forest when the tide was in lay like deflated balloons over the rocky shore and emanated a strong scent of salty decay.

Macintyre stood on the beach looking back and up at them and went on. "Look at that high tide mark. When the tide comes in, water is going to fill this entire basin right up to that pile of trees you're standing on. We're okay now, but the moment the tides shift we need to be off this beach. With the dual gravity of two moons, I think that when the tide comes in it's going to come in fast."

A chorus of "Check" and "Right" came over the comm.

Link and Maryanne stood on one of the huge logs that made up most of the debris pile and watched Mason and Macintyre as they neared the hole. Now that they had a better view of the beach Maryanne remarked that while there weren't really all that many of them, the holes were huge. At about eight-feet across, each hole was easily large enough to engulf a human if they accidently slipped on the seaweed and fell in.

They're attention shifted from the beach to the driftwood trees they were standing on. "Look at the size of them!" Maryanne commented while pointing to a particularly large trunk. "The circumference is about the same as some of those holes. Do you think they grew here in this bay and got uprooted by a tsunami?"

"Unlikely," Macintyre said after considering the possibility. "While a tsunami wave could easily destroy a forest, it wouldn't uproot everything. And time and tide would have eventually filled the holes back in."

Maryanne had to agree. "Yeah, now that I think about it, most of the trees are just logs. You're right. These fell somewhere else and the tide pushed them in. They'd be useful, though," she said thoughtfully. "If we settle here, that's a lot of wood just ready for the taking."

As Link and Maryanne discussed ways of using the massive pieces of driftwood, their attention was diverted away from Mason and Macintyre as they approached one of the holes. So, no one was really watching when a massive creature exploded from the opening. The movement caught Link's attention. As he snapped his head back to the beach, he saw what looked like a cross between a crab and a giant tick. The creature had legs like a crab but it was oval in shape rather than flat and as best as he could tell it was about the size of a tank. The creature, whatever it was, was the color of burned charcoal and had two enormous crab-like claws sticking out of its sides. With speed that was shocking for a creature its size, it darted out of the sand, scooped up Jeff and Dan, one in each of its giant claws, and started to drop back into its hole.

It never made it.

To Link's astonishment two great octopus-like tentacles whipped out from the edge of the bay and wrapped themselves around the crab creature. In the blink of an eye, crab, tentacles and the two unfortunate humans disappeared into the water.

It had all happened so fast that Link just caught a blur

of motion. By the time he was fully turned back toward the beach the only thing that remained was the turbulent waves where the tentacles had vanished. Link didn't even have time to bring his rifle up, not that he could have fired with the two men being held in those giant claws.

Belatedly, he yelled for everyone to get away from the holes. As they scrambled up the beach and over the logs everyone was talking at once wanting to know what had happened and as he and Maryanne scrambled down the debris pile, Link tried to explain.

While everyone was making their shocked comments, Marshal flew out over the beach to the edge of the water where the two men had disappeared. "I can't see anything," he said in hushed tones. "They're gone."

Link answered just as subdued, "Yes. Thanks, John. Maybe you should get back here, too. And don't get too close to the water," he added urgently. "Those tentacles must have been two hundred feet long."

"Roger!" Marshal acknowledged as panicked adrenaline rushed through him. "Heading back."

Marshal flew over the debris pile and was about halfway to the shuttle when Jerry Smith yelled, "Look out, John!"

Before Marshal could react, something hit Junior and knocked the robot down and sideways. As he fought for control all he could see were feathers, a beak, big claws and a glaring eye. Then the thing, whatever it was, was gone.

As he got Junior under control, Marshal's head was whipping around all points of the compass and up and down as well. "What the hell was that?" he screamed.

Jerry answered, "It looked like an eagle. A big freaking Eagle! And he's still up there."

"Up where?" Marshal demanded.

"Right above you."

Marshal looked up and finally saw the massive avian. "Geeze, you're right. That's a big damn eagle. What happened?"

"Best as I can tell it tried to grab you—or grab Junior anyway," Smith said.

"Yeah!" Marshal replied. "That must be the sound I heard—sounded like fingernails on a chalkboard. Couldn't get a grip on Junior."

"I guess that explains why we didn't see any birds," Ann quipped as Link shouted, "Heads up John! Here he comes again."

This time Marshal wasn't taken by surprise. *It's funny how the mind works,* he thought later. He suddenly remembered reading somewhere that eagles fought in the air talon to talon. Instinctively, he rolled Junior around until Marshal in the cockpit was on his back looking up. As the huge eagle thing bore down on him, he waved the robot's mechanical arms in the air hoping that he resembled another bird ready to fight.

The bird got fairly close and then swooped away. Marshal crowed, "Ha! You big chicken hawk sissy! Didn't like that did you?"

The team clustered around the shuttle's boarding ladder and even though they were still in shock over the disappearance of Macintyre and Mason they were fascinated by Marshal's battle with the big bird.

Grant said, "Oh! Oh! I think our big chicken hawk has shifted his attention from the robot to us."

That was enough for Jerry Smith. As the bird swooped down toward the humans clustered around the Starduster he brought his rifle up and fired a short burst. Jerry wasn't known to miss and the giant bird staggered in the air and crashed to the ground about twenty yards from the shuttle.

While everyone exhaled and gathered around Big Bird, Marshal lightened the mood by saying, "Good shoot'n', Tex. Put another notch in ole Betsy."

"Yeah!" Jerry chuckled and then shook his head. "Well, kind of hated to do it, but I didn't see where I had much choice."

"Amen to that, Jerry," Grant said then looked up at Marshal hovering in Junior. "John, keep an eye out. This thing might have a mate around somewhere."

"Right! Got it. I don't see anything, but I didn't see it before. Well, fearless leader, what's next?"

Lincoln looked around at the clearly shaken scientific members of the Away Team, pointed to the carcass and shrugged. "Do you want it?"

Ty West kind of gave himself a shake and answered, "Ah yes. If we can."

Link turned to Bennet. "Can you bag it?"

"Too big." Bennet shook his head.

"I can cut it up," Maryanne suggested brightly.

In fact, both Fosters seemed pretty calm about the events of the last few minutes. Link smiled to himself as he realized all those stories about their adventures around the world weren't just stories after all. Riley, Marshal, Bennet and Smith were former military and were no strangers to being out on the sharp end and probably very familiar with things dropping into the pot.

That left the three scientists. Eyes wide and mouths opening and closing from the shock, they reminded Link of a school of carp. "If you want it, say so now and Maryanne will butcher it for you. As to what's next, that's also up to you. Shall we call it a day, pack it in and head back up to Voyager or do you feel up to looking around a little more?"

The scientists looked at each other with mixed emotions. As upset as they were over the deaths of two of the Away Team, they were also not ready to abandon the expedition. But when they hesitated, Marshal made the decision for them. "I think we've got enough information on this side of the bay. Why don't you load up back into Dusty, I'll stay out here, and we'll fly down and check out the southern end of the bay and then the west side?"

That suggestion brought murmured agreement from the team and a silent prayer of thanks from Link. Good man, John Marshal, he thought, cool head, handy to have around.

Then Ann Turner surprised everyone when she asked, "John, can I ride with you?"

"Ah yeah, sure," he said in surprise. "I don't have a passenger seat and I didn't bring any pillows. It might be a bit bumpy."

Everyone chuckled at the prospect of Turner sliding around inside Junior. Ann laughed. "I'll be fine."

Marshal landed and a minute or two later Turner came tumbling down Dusty's ladder with her arms full of equipment, scrambled into Junior and started securing various cameras and recorders to anything that looked like a solid surface. Marshal laughed and said, "Okay, Ben, we're off." And with that he lifted Junior and waited for the shuttle to lift and start south. Ben asked, "What speed, John?"

"Don't worry about us," Marshal replied. "Make whatever speed you're comfortable with. We'll be along. Who knows we might stop and pick some roses?"

Ben chuckled and asked, "Did everyone get that? If you see anything that you want to check out, sing out and we'll send Ann and John in to explore." Then he clicked the mic twice and announced, "Attention Sanctuary Air Traffic Control this is Riley in Dusty 1 with a mixed flight of two proceeding south at a thousand feet along the east shore of a big ass bay that we haven't given a name to yet. Please advise of any conflicting traffic, especially any big ass chicken hawks."

Marshal grinned wickedly to himself. The bay did have a name and he was going to do his darndest to make sure it stuck: Bigass Bay!

Marshal and Turner joined the laughter that came from the shuttle. You had to agree that it was a mixed flight, two totally alien flying machines consisting of a space shuttle and a construction robot flying over the surface of a planet that had never seen a flying machine of any kind. But they didn't remain in company for long as the shuttle rapidly drew away from the robot. Not that Marshal and Turner were trying to keep up. Dusty 1 was almost to the southern end of the huge bay when Marshal and Turner saw a swarm of birds rise up and engulf the shuttle. This was followed immediately by Riley's yell for everybody to hang on and the Starduster disappeared straight up into the cloudy sky.

"You okay?" Marshal asked.

A few moments later Riley answered, "Yeah! Fine! Geeze, those things came after us just like the birds on Thumb."

Ann answered, "Yes, they obviously see the shuttle as a threat."

Ben said, "Yeah! Well! Whatever! John, you be careful down there. You can't get away as fast as Dusty can."

"Gotcha, Papa," Marshal said and he looked over at Ann who nodded and said, "Ben, the birds didn't react to Junior when we were on Thumb and my best guess is that they won't bother us here."

"Are you sure? There were a hell-of-a-lot of birds down there. Big ones too."

"Well, we'll see. I'm pretty sure that if we just cruise up to them nice and easy, they won't even notice us."

Marshal smiled. He couldn't see Ben but he knew he was shaking his head. Riley replied, "And, John, I suppose you're just going to go along with the crazy lady."

"Ugh! Me just driver. Quit worrying; we'll be fine."

As they flew down the beach the landscape turned from rocky beach to marshy bayou and more and more plants started to appear followed by the trees and birds. Ben was right. There were thousand's, tens of thousands of birds, of all sizes and descriptions and, of course, Ann Turner wanted to get up close and personal with each and every one of them.

Marshal was happy to oblige and he quickly got caught up in trying to identify the vast variety of birds that presented themselves. One thing that was immediately obvious was that these were not colorful tropical birds but waterfowl, mostly he decided, ducks and geese, seagulls, stuff like that... and a big awkward bird that looked like a pelican. Of course, none of the birds looked *exactly* like the birds he was used to seeing on Earth. A close resemblance to many of them, not so much in others, but in all cases, they were just... off. The birds he thought he recognized just didn't look right.

He mentioned that to Ann and she chuckled. "Evolution goes in strange directions, John, but in most cases given the same conditions nature's answers to survival should stay pretty close. Survival has to solve certain basic problems for any species to thrive and even though your ducks and geese don't quite look like what you would expect you could still identify them as ducks and geese. The proportions might shift. A little more of this or a little less of that but the building blocks are the same."

Ben came up on the comm. "Hey, where are you guys?"

Marshal answered, "We're in the swamp playing with the birds. Where are you?"

"About five thousand feet over your head. The birds didn't attack you?"

"No. They seem to be ignoring us completely."

"Boy, they sure came after us that's why I'm sitting up here."

"Well, you're a big bad space shuttle and we're just a harmless soap bubble. Have you been up the west side of the bay?"

"Yeah! Not much to see: steep hills, northern rainforest and a few clearings."

"Well why don't you go back up there, find a place to set down and when we're finished here, we'll join you, get Junior aboard and call it a day."

"Will do," Riley answered. "See you in a few."

Marshal looked a question at Ann. She shrugged and said, "Yes, I guess we can call it a day. I have Vids of tons of stuff. Too bad we couldn't collect any samples."

"Yeah! Sorry about that. Junior could collect them but John Marshal the brilliant engineer neglected to provide any external pouches. Of course, you could get out and collect them yourself."

Ann looked down at the black, muddy, waterlogged marsh they were hovering over and laughed. "Not a chance." Then she glanced out toward the bay and shouted, "Up John! Take us up!"

Marshal didn't hesitate and lifted Junior straight up just as a wall of water that was maybe fifty feet high rolled beneath them."

Ben Riley was shouting, "John! Are you two, all right?"

Marshal hesitated a moment and then said, "Yeah, we're okay. What the hell just happened?"

From the back of the shuttle Ty West answered, "I think the tide just came in. I guess you could call it a tidal bore." Then he excitedly said, "Look the waters filled the entire basin. I'll bet that it's right up to that debris pile we were standing on."

Marshal exclaimed, "Well, if Ann hadn't yelled when she did, we would have been part of the debris pile! That wave would have swept us right up to the trees."

Riley added, "Remember, John, just like on the east coast of Index when the tide came in it came all at once."

Marshal said, "Yeah, I remember. I wonder if it's the same all over the planet?"

Half an hour later Junior floated over a large clearing that Riley had parked Dusty 1 right in the middle of. Marshal chuckled; Riley certainly wasn't taking any chances of having something sneak up on him. He set the robot down and as Ann gathered her armful of stuff and started to get into the shuttle, Marshal told her to wait a minute. Before she could ask why Junior was flying up to the top of a huge pine tree. Marshal used one of Junior's mechanical claws to snip off a pine cone.

Ann was delighted! The pine cone was three and a half feet long and a good eighteen inches in circumference. While the Away Team marveled at the cone Marshal took Junior up to the cargo bay.

It was just an automatic reflex that he took a look around their surroundings before he tucked the robot into its cradle. That's when he saw the bear. At least he thought it was a bear.

Link was watching the team load into the Starduster when he heard Marshal's warning shout. He hustled everyone up the ladder while he, Jaeger and Smith took up positions waiting for Marshal to climb down.

It seemed that everything on this planet was huge. The giant bear-thing ignored them for a few moments and then went into the other default setting for Sanctuary animals—attack! The bear-thing started moving towards them.

Damn! Lincoln thought. He didn't want to kill it and yelled to Marshal to hurry up. Maybe they could lift off before the creature got too close. Then much to his surprise Marshal didn't come down the ladder. Instead, Junior was flying straight at the bear thing.

"John, what..."

The animal reared up on its hind legs with its front paws waving in the air. The humans stared in terrified wonder as the massive creature must have been at least fifteen feet tall. Its bellowing roar echoed through the clearing as Junior brushed by its head. The creature seemed confused by Junior as it dropped back onto all four legs. Marshal didn't give it time to react but immediately brought Junior around and flew at the creature again. This strange flying creature was apparently too much for the bear thing. It let out another defiant roar and ambled off into the forest.

Jerry Smith laughed. "John you nut! What the hell are you doing?"

A bit ruefully Marshal replied, "Aw, I just didn't want to see it killed—seen enough of that today."

Lincoln nodded his head. Marshal certainly spoke for all of them when he said that.

CHAPTER 10

Despite bravely carrying on with the mission it was a clearly shaken Away Team that floated into Voyager. The loss of two of their members coupled with the rapid-fire experiences that had beset the team had left them in various stages of shock. While Dave Allen and the RJs fixed a meal, Alex, Doc Watson and Al Wilson spread out and made themselves available to talk or to just listen as the team relived the day's events. Individual emotions and reactions ran the gamut from fear and shock over the deaths, and the manner of their deaths, of Dan Macintyre and Jeff Mason to thrilled excitement over the encounter with the birds and the big bear-thing to laughter over Marshal's encounter with Big Bird as they were now calling it.

After spending a couple of days comparing notes with Al and Doc and going over the reports and Vids of the disastrous landing around what they were now calling Bigass Bay Alex called a meeting of all the revived Voyagers to review previous events and chart a future course.

They crowded into Al's Met section, anchoring themselves as best as they could. Alex looked around at the diverse group of humans around her and said, "Well, ladies and gentlemen, as they say, here we are. We have made two landings on Sanctuary and found ourselves in a life and death struggle with the indigenous wildlife both times, the second encounter ending in the tragic loss of two of our members. So where do we go from here? We have found a planet that I think will support us. A planet that I think will provide for all our needs if we can come to grips with it. Although so far, we haven't encountered any of what we would call intelligent life, the wildlife that we have encountered is, shall we say, formidable. But to be realistic, even though some of the animals that we have encountered are dangerous, so are animals on Earth, we just need to learn the territory. So, unless there are any objections, I suggest that we put our grief for lost members aside and carry on. And by that, I mean that we still have to find a place to live. Al, myself and the rest of the team have identified two more possible sites for our colony and I think we should go ahead and explore them."

There were some worried sighs but in the end nods all around.

"But first I think we need to bring the Away Team back up to strength. Link, have you thought about a replacement for Jeff?"

Lincoln kind of smiled. "I have, Alex. As a matter of fact, I would like to bring two out of hibernation: Linda and although it might sound strange, I think I would like to wake McPherson."

"The Colonel?" blurted Marshal.

"No, John, his son. The big guy we picked up the night we left Earth. I know we don't know a lot about him but he was an active-duty soldier I think on the promotion list for Major." He paused and Alex and John both nodded. "And he certainly handled himself well when you pulled us out of that fire fight."

Marshal said, "Yeah, that's true." He laughed. "He's sure big enough." He turned toward Jackson. "Bigger than you JJ."

Questioning glances went around. They all knew Linda Murphy—Murph. She was one of Link's long-time deputies back at Sand Flea but only about half of those present had been awake during their wild escape from Earth so McPherson was an unknown quantity.

Marshal went on. "Six-seven, maybe six-eight, two seventy-five at least with a hand like ten-pound ham. I was flying so I didn't really get a good look when he came up into the cockpit and thanked me for picking him and his family up."

Link chuckled. "That description's pretty close."

Kurt spoke up. "His wife is okay, too. She's the one who patched me up that night."

Alex said, "Well it's up to you, Chief."

Link nodded. Murph and Captain Andy McPherson would join his team.

Alex then turned to the scientists. "Any thoughts on who you would like to replace Dan on the Away Team?"

The scientists looked at each other and finally Ann said, "Well, not really. I mean we haven't talked about it but I think Jules would be a good choice."

"Really?" Wilson asked, "Professor Rosen? You've got to be kidding."

Ann looked a little miffed but smiled and said, "Oh I know he can be a little absent minded..."

"Absent minded!" Al said, "Look, I know Professor Rosen is brilliant, but... but...." When he trailed off Alex raised an eyebrow for him to continue. Heaving an exasperated sigh Al explained. "We had him up on Wisdom once about two years before Voyager got started and after only two days, we had to arrange to have him sent back down. I swear he'd forget where he was. He kept trying to push buttons, open doors—he even tried to go for a walk! No spacesuit, no gravity and he wanted to open the hatch and take a stroll around the corner. And these were the days before the Stardusters. Cost Visions Unlimited a bundle to send up a rocket with a capsule to take him home."

Turner blushed at the general laughter and started to say something when Ty West said, "He was a professor at Southern California when I was a student there but he didn't teach for long. It was so easy for us to get him off the subject that he never covered the course material and at the end of the semester he gave everyone an A.

Everybody laughed and Fisher said, "I heard that he once got lost in his own lab."

Everyone looked at Ann but she stuck to her guns, "As I said," she said rather stiffly, "I know he can be the stereotypical absent-minded professor but no one knows more about plants and animals than Julius Rosen."

Wilson and the scientists looked at each other. Well, when you put it that way Ann was right and it was decided that Professor Julius Rosen would join the Away Team.

Of course, when Linda Murphy and the two men were brought out of hibernation, they were a bit disoriented but that didn't stop Andy McPherson from checking on the wellbeing of the entire McPherson clan. His pod was surrounded by the pods holding his wife Audrey who was the nurse that had patched up Kurt, his two children Peter and Sally, and his father, Colonel Alexander McPherson—the man who had done so much back on Earth to shield the Voyager project from government scrutiny, or even government notice.

That was the easy part. That group of McPhersons were all together with the other late arrivals in the San Diego Job. To find his mother, sister and niece they had to go to two other capsules. Link escorted him into the cryogenic section of Voyager and past all the floating rolls of toilet paper. As they floated through the ship, Link explained that McPherson's sister, Erin, was part of the Command Team and one of the joint managers of the colony's food system. As soon as they found a suitable spot on the planet to settle, she would be one of the first to be brought out of hibernation.

Having assured himself that his sister and niece were fine the two men floated into the Italian Job to find his mother, Joan. McPherson said, "Thanks, Chief. I appreciate you taking me around and for thinking that I'll be an asset to your security team."

"Don't thank me yet," he laughed. "Wait till you see what we're up against."

They floated down into R3 where Marshal and Billy Wright had already prepared meals for the three new arrivals. McPherson was introduced to Linda Murphy and the rest of the security team, the RJs and Professor Rosen who, McPherson noticed, was trying mightily and unsuccessfully to keep himself and his meal from floating away. When the introductions were made McPherson looked hard at Billy Wright and said, "So, you're Billy Wright. Well Mr. Wright, Erin did mention you a few times in her Vid screens."

With his mouth full of food, Billy could only open his eyes wide as he wondered if Andy's scowl meant he was about to get pounded.

Then McPherson grinned as he stuck out his hand. "Since you've already passed Mom and Dad's inspection, all I can say is welcome to the family."

Billy swallowed and smiled as he shook McPherson's giant hand. "Thanks, Captain. That means a lot."

Alex drifted down into R3 and said, "Welcome to Sanctuary Orbit, lady and gentlemen. I hope that you are being well cared for." There were murmurs in response and Rosen said, "Ah, yes of course, Alexandria Cummings, this is your project. You were going into outer space or something." That brought a big laugh and Alex said, "Yes, or something." When the chuckle died down, she went on. "When you've finished your dinner, Julius, I'll show you what we have in store for you." Then she turned to McPherson. "Well, Captain, after our rather wild first meeting which must seem like just yesterday to you but was actually twenty years ago, welcome again and thank you again for helping to pull Link and the boys out of a pretty tight spot."

Big Andy McPherson actually blushed. "Ah, Director Cummings."

"Alex please."

"Ah yes! Thank you, and please, it's just Andy. And I should be the one thanking you for saving my entire family."

Linda Murphy looked at Link and said in mock anger, "Looks like I missed all the fun... again."

Alex laughed again. "That was a wild night Linda and Andy, don't be too hasty with your gratitude. You haven't seen what we have in store for you yet." McPherson grinned and Murph made a face as Alex continued. "I'll just leave you two with the Chief and I'm sure all will be revealed." Then she turned to Rosen. "Come on, Julius. I'll show you your new domain."

They drifted up into the Command Section and the professor stared in awe at Sanctuary for a very long time. While he did try to push a few buttons, he thankfully didn't try to open any doors.

Over the next two days, Alex picked everyone's brains before the third landing expedition got under way. After weighing all the options, she settled on still using just one Starduster with Riley at the controls, her husband John in the co-pilot's seat with Junior tucked away in the cargo bay. Maryanne occupied the jump seat just behind them as the eleven other Voyagers squeezed into the ten very comfortable chairs in the passenger section.

Marshal looked back past Maryanne at the four scientists (Julius Rosen was so excited he was bubbling over like a teapot), expedition chief Lincoln and his four security personnel (with newcomers Murph and Andy containing their giddiness only slightly better than the professor), the former Navy corpsman Mike Bennet while the last seat was occupied by Maryanne's husband Grant Foster.

"Not too shabby a crew," Marshal said as they disengaged from Wisdom and started their descent to Sanctuary. Ben and Maryanne nodded in agreement.

It was going to be a busy day. If time permitted the Away Team was going to investigate two sites. The first location that Alex, Al, the scientists and the security team had picked was right in the middle of the peninsula/continent of Middle Finger. The site was on the western bank of the big lake that dominated the center of the continent about a thousand miles north of the tropical green belt. After a bumpy ride through the ever-present clouds, Riley spiraled Dusty 1 down toward the spot that Alex had designated.

As they cruised slowly around the location Ben, Marshal and Maryanne had to agree that the place had possibilities. A large river flowing from the west had cut a high bank, maybe fifty to seventy-five feet high, on its south side where it emptied into the big lake creating a bluff that was practically treeless. The prairie grass was just starting to grow now in the early spring and there were scattered copses of trees stretching away over the rolling plains to the west. The banks of the river were heavily forested as was the bank of the lake starting about a mile south from the river junction. About twenty miles upriver to the west a smaller stream had separated from the main river to flow southeast entering the big lake about ten miles to the south creating a kind of triangle shaped island twenty miles long by ten miles wide with rivers on the two long sides and the big lake forming the base.

"Not bad," Maryanne said. "I can see where Alex and the rest are coming from. If we can secure the area between the rivers and keep all those grazing critters off, it would make good farmland. Of course, securing it will depend on how much of a water barrier those rivers really are."

Ben had Dusty in a slow circuit around the island. "Maryanne?" he asked. "This is early spring, right?"

"That's what Al said," she answered.

"So," Riley went on, "will those two rivers get much higher? Because looking at all the animals down there right now the rivers don't seem to be much of a deterrent to grazing in our triangle."

"Yeah!" chimed in Marshal. "I saw at least two big groups of those big bison in the triangle and look at that herd of wildebeest or whatever they are, right in front of us."

Maryanne frowned. "Good point." She paused in thought then answered, "I think Alex and the rest have the right idea but if the herds can move freely across the rivers, establishing a colony here is probably not going to work."

Just then Link leaned into the cockpit and said, "I think we've seen everything useful on the aerial tour, Ben. Did you see a good place to set down?"

Riley answered, "Yeah, we saw a place back on the bluff." He looked at Marshal who nodded. "But I don't want to get too close to the trees if that's all right with you."

"Sounds good," Link said and went back to the passenger section.

Riley approached the bluff from the south flying as low and slow as he dared over the great belt of trees that bordered the lake. Outside of the cloud of birds that rose up in righteous indignation to challenge the Starduster's intrusion into their domain, the humans had the place to themselves.

"Okay!" Ben said over the comm. "Keep your eyes peeled." And he set Dusty down about equidistant from the trees, the lake and the river. As soon as the shuttle touched down the birds seemed to lose interest and flew away.

After the surprises that they had had in the past, Link and the others weren't taking any chances. Everyone seemed to hold their breath as they looked out of their individual windows for a good five minutes.

Link finally asked, "Anyone see anything?"

"Hell," Marshal answered looking out of the cockpit windows, "with the way that this prairie rolls I can't even see that bunch of big bison that are just west of us."

Everyone murmured that that was true. A flat prairie wasn't really flat.

Well, Lincoln thought, they weren't going to colonize the planet waiting on the shuttle for something to come. With his eyes scanning for anything moving that might be larger than a real Earth-sized gopher, he opened the passenger door and lowered the steps and he, Jerry, Kurt, Murph and Andy dropped to the ground and took up positions around the Starduster. After a few minutes he said, "Okay, Ben, open the cargo bay. John, you ready?"

Marshal scrambled down the ladder, took a quick look

around then climbed up Dusty's side to the cargo bay. He paused at the top of the ladder forty feet above the ground for another 360-degree scan. "Link, there's a small herd of big bison, maybe twenty-five or thirty strong. They're tucked into the back side of a hill due west of us. I can give you a better description when I get Junior up."

"Good, John. Anything else?"

"That big herd of wildebeest or whatever they are that we flew over are out past the bison and there's another small group of something way off the south. Outside of that it looks clear." Marshal looked again at the rain squalls that were scudding along from the west underneath the slate gray overcast sky and added. "Oh, by the way, you are all going to get wet in a few minutes."

Link chuckled. "Thanks, John. Okay, folks, except for the rain shower it looks clear."

As the scientists came down the steps, Link assigned one of his security team to each one. He nodded to Kurt and pointed to Professor Rosen. "And don't let him wander too far off."

Kurt smiled and asked his charge, "Well, professor, what would you like to see?"

"Oh my, oh my!" came the bewildered response. "There's so much to see! Is this Kansas?"

To his credit, Kurt didn't laugh and just gave the absent-minded man a patient smile. "No, professor, we're not in Kansas anymore."

However, everyone within hearing distance began to snort their amusement.

Junior rose smoothly out of his cradle and Marshal made a slow circle around the shuttle. "Clear as far as I can see, Chief."

With the Away Team starting to spread out away from

the shuttle, Marshal gradually widened his circle. As always, the sheer size of everything on Sanctuary amazed him. The mountains, the prairie, the animals... everything. He shook his head as he observed the thousands of miles of prairie that stretched out to the north, west and south as far as he could see. The grass was just starting to grow after the winter frost but in his mind's eye he could see that in just a few weeks these vast plains would be covered in a chest high green blanket that would ripple like the ocean in a summer breeze. His thoughts were interrupted when Ann asked, "John, can you do something for me?"

"Ah sure," he answered looking around. "Uh, where are you?"

"On the edge of the bluff by the river."

Marshal finally spotted her. She, Maryanne and Linda—the girls were teaming up—seemed to be peering over the edge of the bluff. "Okay, gotcha. I'm way over on the other side of Dusty. Be there in a minute."

And in a minute Junior was hovering over the trio and he asked, "What's up? Drop something?"

They all chuckled and Ann said, "John, this bank doesn't seem very stable to me. Could you take Junior down toward the river and get me some soil samples?"

"Sure, give me a shovel and a bucket."

Ann stuck her nose into the air, sniffed and said, "We, sir, are scientists. We do not deal in shovels and buckets."

Everyone laughed and Marshal said, "Well, as you might have noticed Junior has rather large hands. I don't think he would do too well with one of your test tubes."

Ann smiled. "I have a small container and a scraper; will that be all right? Do you need to land to pick them up?"

"Nah! Just hold them up."

She did and Marshal hovered Junior over her and

those large mechanical hands gently plucked the container and scraper from her fingers. Shaking her head in amazement she exclaimed, "Those robots truly are amazing machines!"

"Okay, madam we-don't-deal-in-buckets scientist. Where would you like me to take the sample?"

"Down by the river if you can."

"No problem. How much?"

"Not much. About half of that container will be fine."

"Right." Marshal dropped Junior over the edge of the bank, hovered a few feet above the riverbank and began scraping. "Seems like pretty soft sand," he said looking up at the bluff above him. "I wouldn't stand too close to the edge if I were you. The river is really undercutting that bank. I wouldn't be surprised to see the whole thing come down."

Just as Ann started to reply the entire outer edge of the bluff collapsed. Marshal described it later as watching a glacier collapse. And while he was trying to move Junior away from the falling dirt and rocks the three women were frantically scrambling away from a cliff edge that kept crumbling underneath them.

Bedlam reigned. The ladies were shouting to each other as Murph and Maryanne pulled Ann away from the edge. Marshal was yelling at Junior as he struggled to keep the robot away from the falling debris. To add to the noise and confusion everyone on the comm, including Link, wanted to know what was happening.

Before Marshal and the ladies could reassure the chief and each other that everyone was okay they were interrupted by a shout, a string of some very colorful language and the sound of an automatic rifle blast."

"What the hell was that?" asked Marshal as he pulled Junior away from the bank, shedding dirt and small rocks, and swept up over the top of the bluff. He was relieved when he saw the three women getting to their feet ten yards from the collapsing sand bluff.

"Keep going!" He shouted and was relieved that they heard him ever the overlapping comm demands of: 'What was the shooting?' 'What was that noise over by the river?' 'Did the bluff just collapse?' 'Is everyone alright?'

Link was on the comm. "Everyone! Quiet please. John, what happened?'

Marshal answered, "The bluff collapsed. Everybody's okay."

"Good." Then he asked, "Who fired?"

"Me, Chief. Jerry," came the answer

"You, okay?"

"Yep, fine; but some big chicken isn't."

"What? Where are you?" Link asked. "And who's with you?"

"I'm with Ty West. We're south of Dusty toward the woods by the lake."

"On my way," Link said. "What happened?"

Jerry was quiet for a minute obviously getting his thoughts together. "Well, Chief, Ty and I had stopped to check out what looked like one of those big gopher holes like the ones we saw on Thumb. I heard something and when I looked up here was this big bird-like thing running at us and coming fast. Mean looking thing—huge! Must have been fifteen or twenty feet tall with a wicked looking beak. So, I shot it. Went down easy, too. I hit it with a burst in the chest or what looked like the chest and it went down like a puppet with its strings cut."

As Smith was giving his account of the incident the rest of the Away Team were converging on the scene. Marshal hovered overhead with Junior's mechanical hands still full with a container of dirt and the scraper. Link asked, "See anything, John?"

Marshal slowly turned Junior in a full circle. "No, nothing," he answered.

Just then the rain squall hit them and visibility was reduced to practically zero. While the Away Team crouched in a rain-soaked circle with guns pointing in all directions Link asked if anyone else had seen what happened. As it turned out no one had. Marshal looked down and asked, "What the hell is that thing? Looks like an Ostrich on steroids."

West answered, "Well back on Earth archeologists called them 'Terror Birds'."

"We had these things on Earth?" Marshal asked.

"Yes," Ann answered, "until quite recently in geologic time. They went extinct just a couple of thousand years ago. Last reported in South America if I remember right. But not this large. Never this large."

Lincoln looked down at the bird-like thing with its massive head, powerful legs and curved serrated beak. "Carnivorous?"

West answered, "Oh yes! Carnivores and scavengers. Top of the food chain. They would take on any large herbivore. Look at those legs! The ones on Earth could run forty to fifty miles an hour and I would guess that this one would be even faster. They would run next to their prey and slash at its neck until they hit an artery and then just let it run until it bled out."

"Nasty," someone said.

While they were talking and looking at the big ostrich-like bird the rain squall passed. Marshal said, "Here, Ann, let me give you your bucket back and I'll have a look around."

Turner sniffed and elevated her nose again. "Container. We scientists do not deal in buckets."

That broke the tension and everyone chuckled.

Marshal did a slow three-sixty as Junior rose in the air. "Ah crap!" he exclaimed. "Chief, that bunch of bison that was just to the west of us is starting to drift your way. Maybe you had better get everyone back on board Dusty."

"You heard the man," Lincoln said. "Let's go." And everyone started moving toward the shuttle. Everyone that is except professor Rosen who seemed particularly engrossed with a small flowering bush. "Come on, professor," Kurt said pleasantly but firmly so there would be no room for debate. "When the Chief says go, we go." He took Rosen's arm and started to usher him toward the Starduster.

"But the bush. My flower," Rosen protested as Jaeger hurried him along.

After his initial warning Marshal had flown west closer to the big bison. "Damn!" he exclaimed. "Link, get aboard and get out of there. There's a pack of wolves after the bison and they're starting to run. Running right at you."

Half of the Away Team was already on board and the rest didn't need Link's urging to pick up the pace. "Come on, Professor!" Kurt exclaimed, "We've got to go!" He jogged along with Rosen puffing mightily beside him when suddenly to Kurt's surprise the Professor wasn't there anymore. Jaeger turned to see Rosen calmly walking back the way that they had come.

"Professor!" Kurt yelled.

"My flower," Rosen muttered. "I forgot my flower."

"Professor!" Jaeger shouted again as he sprinted back, caught Rosen, spun him around and started half carrying the sputtering professor back toward the shuttle. *He wasn't going to make it,* he thought. He was going to get ground to mush under the hooves of those two-ton monsters. Then suddenly there was big Andy McPherson on the other side of the professor and between the two of them they lifted Rosen up by his armpits and carried him to the ladder. With a shove, they propelled him up into the waiting arms of Link who tumbled backwards into the Starduster with Rosen on top of him followed immediately by Jaeger. McPherson was clinging to the ladder and everyone was yelling at Riley to get the shuttle off the ground.

"What about, John?" Riley yelled.

"I'm in Junior!" Marshal replied. "Don't worry about me. Get the hell out of there."

Dusty 1 lifted, though just barely. With the cargo bay and the passenger doors opened and the ladder still extended with two-hundred and seventy-five pounds of Andy McPherson hanging on the end of it, the Starduster wobbled and finally staggered into the air. McPherson swore later that he felt the hump of the lead bison brush the sole of his boot as the herd went thundering by underneath.

McPherson was finally able to scramble inside, get the ladder up and the door closed while Riley closed the cargo door and tried to stabilize the shuttle and get his heart rate back to normal.

"Ben, where are you going?" Marshal asked. "You're heading out over the lake."

"What? I don't know. Anywhere away from there."

Lincoln asked, "John, what do you see?"

"Everything's quieting down, Chief. It looks like the wolves cut out a young bison. They're about a mile off to the southwest having lunch. The rest of the bison are about a mile off to the south and slowing down."

West asked, "John, is there anything left of the Terror Bird?"

"The Terror Bird!" Marshal exclaimed. He started to say how the hell do I know but thought better of it and said, "Umm, give me a minute... Yeah, there it is. The herd went right over it. From what I can see it looks pretty ground up, Ty, but the head looks like it's still intact."

West said, "If you don't mind, Chief, I'd like to go back and collect that head and anything else that might be salvageable."

Link smiled at the relentless focus of the scientists. "Sure, we have to go back and pick up John anyway."

Ben Riley landed the shuttle in practically the same spot that it had occupied before, the security team deployed and West and Turner went out and collected what was left of the Terror Bird. Marshal settled Junior into his cradle in the cargo bay, took his seat next to Riley and Dusty 1 with the Away Team safely on board flew off to the west toward the second landing site on the agenda. Back in the passenger section the Away Team looked at each other with nervous smiles.

Just another day at the office.

CHAPTER 11

Ben Riley turned Dusty 1 away from their near disastrous landing by the big lake and, just because he could, he kicked the shuttle up to Mach 2 treating the millions of animals that covered the vast plains of northern Middle Finger to their first sonic boom.

The grazing herds didn't seem to notice. If anything, they probably wondered why thunder came out of a fairly clear sky.

After that initial burst Riley kept the speed down so the team could marvel at the seemingly endless herds of animals that covered the grasslands visible on both sides of the shuttle. The rolling prairie soon gave way to the foothills that stretched mile after tree covered mile up toward the vast mountain range that dominated the west coast of Middle Finger. Looking forward all Riley, Marshal and Maryanne could see was an unbroken carpet of many shades of green. Not the solid green that they could imagine seeing later in the spring and summer when all the trees were covered in leaves but still, it was a lot of green. Passing below them as far as the eye could see were thousands of square miles of lush forest hosting a wide variety of firs and other evergreens mixed in with the leafy deciduous kind. The carpet of trees was occasionally broken by strips of blue and white from the many rivers and streams that flowed through the forest toward the east.

Riley maintained speed and brought Dusty down to five hundred feet over the river. No one spoke awestruck by the sheer power and beauty that surrounded them. Intellectually they knew that the western third of the continent was covered in forest but that knowledge didn't translate to the reality of coming face to face with this magnificent spectacle.

"Back on Old Earth," Maryanne said. "This would be called an old growth or cathedral forest."

Whatever you called it, Marshal thought, it was awe inspiring. Nature the way nature was supposed to be. As far as they could see, north, south and west, a solid canopy of trees that kind of resembled cedar and spruce, oak and ash but each tree was bigger—much bigger. Trees that looked like oak and spruce had grown to over a hundred and fifty feet high and must have been ten to fifteen feet in diameter. And the trees became even larger as the shuttle flew further west up the hillsides.

"Wow!" Marshal murmured looking out the window. "Magnificent. North America before Columbus."

Maryanne quietly answered, "No, John. North America before anybody."

Marshal nodded his head. "Yeah!"

Someone back in the passenger exclaimed, "Look at the river!"

Everyone looked. The river had changed.

When they reached the foothills the brown slow moving meandering river that they had followed across the plains had been transformed into a swift moving mountain stream and it was swarming bank to bank with fish. Thousands of fish; millions of fish.

Riley said, "I thought fish went upstream in the fall."

Maryanne chuckled. "It looks like the fish on Sanctuary didn't get that memo because there are sure a lot of them going somewhere."

Marshal smiled to himself and thought maybe that bounty of fish would make Alex feel better about not being able to settle by the ocean. He looked at Riley and asked, "How are we going to find the spot that Alex picked in this sea of trees?"

Ben answered, "I don't know without a GPS system to guide us but the rough coordinates that Al gave us should get us in the ballpark anyway."

"Actually," Maryanne said, "Alex described the location pretty well. She said that our destination should appear as a brown slash in the trees right next to a fairly good sized river. She said that what we were looking for was a cliff—a sheer cliff in the forest more than a mile long." She shook her head. "A mile long cliff! Can you imagine?"

"Well," said Marshal. "We've already seen a lot of crazy stuff on this planet so, yes, I can imagine it." He turned back to Riley. "Ben we've been following this river all the way from the big lake. Are you sure this is the right river?"

Riley looked down at the instrument panel and said, "I think so. At least that's where Al's program is taking us."

They kept following the river higher and higher as it cut a blue and white path through the endless carpet of green forested hills. Marshal's fear that they might not be able to find Alex's spot proved to be unfounded because suddenly, right in front of them standing out stark and clear was Alex's cliff.

The scientists and security people crowded the Stardusters windows when Riley turned the shuttle south and slowly flew parallel to the cliff. It was just as Alex had described: a sheer cliff at least a hundred-and fifty-feet high right in the middle of the forest. What had caused this particular geological formation Marshal couldn't begin to guess and as luck would have it of the four scientists onboard there was not one geologist to explain it to him.

It was as if a giant knife had sliced through a portion of the tree covered hills and then scraped the debris away to the east like you would cut and spread butter on a slice of bread, leaving the cliff with a clear space in front of it.

Smooth, flat rock stretched out from the cliff face for a hundred yards or more before it turned into a vast bushy meadow that was almost bare of trees. Marshal estimated the meadow to be twenty miles long west to east and a mile wide.

At the northern end of the cliff the river had cut a rocky gorge nearly thirty yards wide. The Away Team smiled. If the colony was going to be established here the river would be a plus not just for food and fresh water, but the fast-moving stream made it a potential power source.

But the river was soon forgotten as the team marveled at the cliff itself. The cliff face was honeycombed with cave openings—even great caverns. Dozens of them. Some at ground level but many more scattered across the face of the cliff. Maryanne laughed and when Ben and John looked a question at her she said, "I wonder if we will settle here? When I left Earth, I didn't really expect to become a cave girl."

Marshal laughed along with Ben but on the other

hand, he reasoned, considering what had jumped out of the hole on the beach, fox-wolves, tentacles, charging two-ton buffalo, the big bird that had come after Junior and the Terror Bird, having a nice solid cave for shelter actually sounded pretty attractive.

He tried to remember what he knew about caves. It wasn't much. There were stalagmites and stalactites and, thanks to his father, he never had a problem remembering which was which.

"Johnny, my boy," Marshal remembered his dad answering his four-year-old self, "stalactites stick tight to the ceiling and stalagmites might one day grow to reach the ceiling."

Yup! No problem.

The only other thing Marshal really knew about caves was that they were usually damp but that cavern temperatures were easier to regulate. Caves generally stayed cool in the summer and warm in the winter... a boon his caveman ancestors had clearly taken advantage of.

Link stuck his head into the cockpit. "Is this the place?" he asked.

"According to the coordinates Alex gave us this is the place," Ben said and he started to set the shuttle down onto the wide fat stone shelf in front of the cliff face.

"Wait!" Maryanne cautioned. "We don't know what kind of critters might be calling those caves home. I wouldn't land too close."

"Ah! Right." Riley said and lifted Dusty into the sky again. "John, did you see a good landing spot away from the cliff?"

"Sorry, Ben, I wasn't really looking. Make a swing out to the east."

Riley continued on for a minute or two then turned

the shuttle east. Where the rock shelf ended and the grassy, bush covered meadow stretched away, Riley turned north. There was a tangle of small bushes at the edge of the rock shelf and Marshal said, "Looks like you could put it down anywhere past those bushes, Ben."

"Is this far enough away?" Link asked, trusting Maryanne's judgment.

"I think so, Chief. At least it's far enough away that we can see anything coming at us."

Riley set the shuttle down and the Away Team, remembering all their past landing experiences, sat there looking out of their windows waiting for something to happen. When nothing big, mean, and ugly challenged their right to be there they opened up and went through the landing routine. But no one was comfortable until Marshal and Junior had made a full circuit of the immediate area including a fly-by along the cliff face.

After the tragedy on the beach, and the excitement of terror birds and stampeding big bison no one was inclined to wander off on their own, so the teams stood in a tight group by the shuttle for several minutes before they kind of heaved a collective sigh and separated to make their cautious way toward the cliffs.

Kurt took Professor Rosen, or to be more accurate, the professor took Kurt north toward the river. Link gave Grant a nod and he joined them. In their brief acquaintance in space Jerry and Andy seem to hit it off pretty well so they teamed up and had Ty and Glenn under their wing as they drifted off to the south. That left Link, Murph and Ann in the center.

"Lincoln and the ladies." Marshal said.

Link joined in the general chuckle but then looked around and asked "Where's Maryanne?" just as the intrepid adventurer came out of the Starduster carrying the biggest rifle Lincoln had ever seen.

The security chief dropped his jaw and just stared. At first, he thought she was carrying a double-barreled shotgun but those weren't shotgun shells that Maryanne had tucked in the loops of the bandoleer she had slung over her shoulder, they were bullets. Big bullets. Each one was a good six inches long and an inch and a half in diameter.

"What the hell is that thing?" Link blustered. "A cannon?"

Maryanne smiled. "This is my elephant gun. After this morning's excitement I thought that I would trot out 'Ole' Betsy' here."

"You didn't really name it 'Betsy,' did you?"

"Of course! I think it's a law. Elephant guns are always called Betsy in the movies."

Marshal chimed in from overhead knowing that Maryanne was a committed conservationist jokingly asked, "Did you ever shoot an elephant with it?"

Before she could answer her husband said, "You better believe it, John. We were in Kenya leading a camera safari when we got word that big bull elephant had gone rouge. Tore up a couple of villages and killed three people. The local game rangers asked us if we would help in the search. We were just setting up camp when we got word that the rogue had been spotted in a village just a couple of miles away. We jumped into the cars and were lucky to arrive before he faded away into the bush. Maryanne dropped him with one shot." Grant paused in his story. "But you're right, John. My lady would never go hunting for sport. Hell, she'd probably shoot the hunters."

Maryanne blushed as everyone chuckled and said "Well, I didn't like shooting the rogue either, but sadly it had to be done."

Link looked impressed and pointing to her 'hand cannon' as he called it, said "That thing must have a kick like a Georgia mule."

Maryanne smiled and replied, "It does take some getting used to and my hubby made sure my vest has extra padding in the shoulders."

While they were talking the other teams had fanned out. With a little sigh Link said, "Well, ladies, we're not going to see what's in those caves standing here."

The women gave him a smile and the four started moving across the flat rock toward the cliff with Maryanne, Murph and Link in front and Turner walking slightly behind. They had only gone a few steps when Maryanne held up her hand and hissed, "Wait. Everyone be quiet. Listen."

At first, they didn't know what Maryanne had heard but gradually they thought they could hear a kind of a cross between a whuff and a grunt.

"I can hear it," Link whispered, "but I can't pinpoint where it's coming from. Can you see anything, John?"

Before Marshal could answer Maryanne pointed. "John, look there—that large cave to the right of the big cavern. Can you see anything moving in there?"

Marshal took Junior about halfway between Link's group and the cliff. "Um... I think so." Then *something* moved again within the gaping cavern mouth. "You're right, Maryanne. There is something inside that cave."

Then the *something* suddenly came into view, scaring the hell out of everyone on the Away Team including Marshal riding high in Junior. Initially he thought it was another bear-like creature like the one they had seen at Bigass Bay. The thick fur and foot-long claws resembled a grizzly, but where this creature differed was that it was at least a thousand pounds heavier and four times the size of any grizzly that he had ever heard of. And the head was all wrong. It had an elongated and very un-bear like snout with a jaw more like a crocodile's and full of nasty looking teeth. The hind legs were bigger than the front and the front paws seemed to curve inward as it raked the bare rock with its huge claws.

Everyone froze as the massive creature slowly emerged from the cave entrance. It stood upright in the opening and began sniffing and whuffing while swinging its massive head from side to side.

Fortunately, the rest of the team took their cues from Maryanne Foster who stood her ground while calmly studying the beast. Quietly she spoke into the comm. "Everyone be quiet and keep still. The wind is blowing directly from us to it, whatever it is, so it must smell us and it's trying to figure out the new smell. If it's working its way through its fight or flight options you know how that's going to turn out."

That statement brought a nervous titter over the comm.

Quietly Maryanne went on. "The way the animal is acting I don't think it sees very well. It doesn't seem to have caught sight of us yet."

The whiffing and grunting continued while it shook its enormous head from side to side. Suddenly, or finally, the huge creature became aware of the intruders into its territory. Raising its mass up onto its haunches it looked straight at the humans and, true to the initial reaction of every other creature that they had encountered on Sanctuary, its default setting was attack. The creature let out a roar, dropped back down onto all four legs and charged straight at Link and his ladies.

Without even flinching, Lincoln raised his rifle and fired a full magazine into the rampaging beast. Linda Murphy was blazing away also and though both were certain their rounds were hitting the giant animal; the creature gave no sign that it even noticed the projectiles hitting its thick hide.

Remembering the encounter with the big bear Marshal recklessly dove Junior right at the creature but either the creature didn't see him or it just ignored him and kept bellowing its challenge while charging toward Link, Maryanne, Turner and Murph.

The giant bear-thing was about twenty-five yards away from the group of humans when Link was almost deafened by a loud boom beside his left ear. He looked over and saw Maryanne looking down the sights of her elephant gun.

Her first shot staggered the bear thing but the bullet only seemed to stun it and really piss it off. Enraged, it shifted its focus from the group in general to Maryanne in particular. As it charged straight for her, her hand-held cannon boomed again and this time the great beast folded up like an accordion. Its front legs collapsed as it fell forward. Landing on its chest and chin, the thing skidded forward and finally stopped with that mouth full of teeth only about three inches from Maryanne's right boot. With one last grunting effort to reach her, the creature hissed out the last of the air in its lungs and didn't move again.

Stunned, the four humans just stood there staring at the massive creature. Marshal didn't know about the rest of them, but even from his secure perch fifty feet up in the air he was shaking like a palm tree in a Florida Hurricane.

"What the hell is that thing?" he demanded.

Before he could get an answer, Jerry Smith who had never stopped watching the cave said, "Chief, I think you should get away from that carcass. There's something else moving in the cave."

No one had to be told twice. Guns at the ready, the entire Away Team inched backwards to where the rock shelf ended and the terrain took a slight dip. From behind a fringe of thick bushes they spread out and watched the entrance like a bunch of bystanders unable to turn away from watching a train wreck as another of the creatures came out of the cave. While this one wasn't as big as the first one, it was still plenty big.

The bear thing stood up in the entrance of the cave and went through the same sniff-whuff-grunt sequence that the first one had while swinging its head from side to side. It took a few minutes for the creature to notice the motionless form of the first bear thing. When it did become aware of it, the beast began to move toward the carcass. It didn't charge but moved slowly, hesitantly, stopping every few steps to sniff and look around until it reached the carcass. After sniffing the carcass and prodding it with a huge fore paw, the beast looked around and fixed its eyes on the bushes that shielded the humans. Based on what Maryanne had said earlier the humans didn't think the animal could see them but that didn't stop sweat from forming and knees from shaking. Then to the petrified onlookers' astonishment, the bear thing abruptly turned and shuffled its way back towards the cave. It didn't go in, but gave a new series of whuffs and grunts and two very much smaller versions loped into the open. The three creatures then ambled off to the north along the cliff face and when they reached the river they turned to the west, climbed the broken rocks lining the river to the top of the cliff and disappeared into the forest above.

The Away Team let out its collective breath.

"Well," Marshal said, "Papa bear, mama bear and two little baby bears and Maryanne just knocked off Big Daddy."

Most of the team hadn't realized they'd been just

standing motionless until Grant said, "Well let's get a look at this critter," and started walking towards it.

"What the hell is it?" Marshal asked from his perch above them.

West answered, "The closest thing I can think of is a cave bear or a sloth but the proportions and the head are all wrong."

Marshal exclaimed, "What? That thing is no sloth."

Ann Turner laughed. "John, I'm sure you are thinking of the small slow moving arboreal animals back on Earth that everyone always made fun of."

Tyler laughed. "No! No! John. Not those. I was referring to Ground Sloths. They were part of the megafauna that went extinct on Earth at the end of the last ice age. They were very large, but our fossil records don't have anything nearly as big as this thing and ours were herbivores. With that mouthful of teeth this critter is no herbivore!"

Tyler's knowledge of the ancient sloths got everyone speculating about how these creatures differed from Earth animals as they poked the giant carcass. Maryanne suddenly brought everyone up short when she announced that she wanted the head. Her declaration brought out laughter which died quicker than the bear thing when she suddenly whipped out a vibro-knife and started sawing away.

Link gaped at the vibrating laser knife. "That's a vibro-knife! Those things are illegal in all fifty states."

Grant laughed. "Yup! Just like mine." And he produced one exactly like Maryanne's. Link probably had been too busy fighting for his life to notice at the time, but it was the same knife Foster had used to cut the fox/wolf off of Link's boot back on Thumb.

"Actually," Foster said, "they were presented to us by the Maharaja of Bruni..."

"Raipur," Maryanne corrected.

"Yeah, that's right; Raipur," Grant nodded. "When we captured a couple of tigers that had been snacking on his villagers. Handy things."

No one said a word, not even Lincoln. The vibro-knife seemed to work like a Star Wars lightsaber and Maryanne had the head off in no time flat.

Link wondered not only what she was going to do with the head, but how she intended to get it back up to Voyager. The only option was in the Stardusters cabin which made him groan at the thought. Riley wasn't going to like that. The fox/wolf, the gophers and Big Bird were bad enough. The bear thing wasn't exactly daisy-fresh now and the decapitated head would probably stink up the machine for a week.

At least Maryanne's laser knife mostly cauterized her morbid prize as she cut and there was little blood for them to deal with. She smiled sweetly at Bennet and asked, "Mike, could you bag this for me, please?"

Mike did so using one of the body bags he had brought along and he thought, *Maryanne Foster is something else.*

"Are we leaving?" someone asked, but Link wasn't sure who it was.

"Hell, no!" Grant Foster shot back with a grin. "We came here to check out the caves, so let's get checking." Then he laughed at the general hesitation. "Don't worry, it's safe," he said as he nodded toward the carcass. "A predator that size would have killed or driven off any competition. Am I right, Maryanne?"

"Absolutely!" Maryanne said with complete confidence. "And depending on how long the family was established here there might not be any other animals of any size for quite a distance." She paused and then chuckled at the thought that everyone was thinking. "But on this planet, who knows?"

Grant and Maryanne started walking toward the caves while the rest followed with obedient trepidation. With rifles and elephant gun at the ready, the Fosters tossed stones inside what had been the bear thing's cave. When nothing big and nasty or even little and nasty charged out of the opening and the only sounds were the diminishing echoes of rocks ricocheting down the passage, everyone heaved a relieved sigh that the Fosters had probably been right in their assessment that the caves were now uninhabited.

Their attention then shifted to the enormous cavern that was located right next to the bear's cave. A great gouge in the cliff that looked to be easily a couple of hundred feet wide and maybe twenty-five or thirty feet high.

The humans spread out as they moved into the cavern marveling at its size and the smoothness of the cavern's floor and sides. After just a few minutes of exploration the Away Team was convinced that the caves were perfect for human habitation. Of course, Alex, Al and the rest would make the final judgment but the more the Away Team looked the more enthusiastic they became. The caves would not only give them protection from any would-be predator, but from the elements as well and as a bonus they were close enough to the river that obtaining fresh water wouldn't be a burden. The big cavern alone was probably large enough to shelter the entire colony and now that the caves had also been relieved of their previous tenants, the team thought the site seemed ideal.

While the Fosters went to explore the bear's den, Link and the rest stood in the entrance of the huge cavern.

"Damn," Murph said looking around. "This cavern is as

big as one of the hangars back at Sand Flea."

Testing the size Marshal flew in with Junior. "Bigger, wider, but not as high."

McPherson asked, "Why is the rock floor so smooth? This doesn't seem like any other cave I've ever been in. The caves that I'm familiar with are all jumbled with rocks and the roof and walls are uneven. This cavern's smooth, open, and then there's that smooth shelf of rock outside."

Ann answered, "I'm not sure. I'm no geologist but it could be that it was hollowed out by lava although I didn't notice any volcanoes around here or it could have been smoothed by water over many thousands of years. The water's long since gone now, though."

"There's water back here," announced Jerry who had wandered toward the back of the vast opening. When the others joined him, he pointed to a fair-sized waterfall that tumbled down the rocks and disappeared somewhere underground.

"How about that?" Jaeger muttered. "Our own water supply."

"Yes... potentially," West cautioned. "Let me get some samples for testing."

The team wandered in and out of the various caves and caverns for another hour becoming more and more enthusiastic about the possibilities of the site until Wisdom came into communications range. Alex caught their enthusiasm and said that she looked forward to hearing their observations and seeing the images.

The Fosters were as enthusiastic about the prospect of using the caves as the rest but while the team had been exploring, they had been standing in front of the large cavern watching the carcass of Big Daddy. Large birds that resembled vultures were already circling overhead. Grant said, "Alex, I don't mean to be a wet blanket and dampen enthusiasm but if you are serious about occupying these caves, we have an immediate problem. We are probably going to have to fight for them."

Before Alex could answer the rest of the Away Team was talking all at once and the rest of their rebuttal to Foster was that it wasn't true. They had already fought and won. Big Daddy was dead and his family was gone.

Of course, Alex had no idea who Big Daddy was and that story had to be told. When Alex felt that she was up to speed she asked, "Grant, it would seem that the battle is over and you control the caves. Who or what are you going to fight?"

Maryanne touched her husband's arm and said, "We don't know, Alex, but Grant and I are pretty sure that Big Daddy's not done with us yet."

"What do you mean?" Alex asked puzzled. "I'm afraid I still don't understand."

Marshal broke in, "What they're saying, Luv, is that right in front of these caves there's a ton of fresh meat sitting out in the open just waiting for the scavengers."

"And not just scavengers." Maryanne said. "By sundown every meat-eating creature with a nose will converge on this spot." And waving back toward the caves she continued, "There's not just a fresh supply of food here, but a very enticing home ready for the taking."

"So, what are you suggesting?" Alex asked.

The Fosters whispered together for a moment and Maryanne said, "I know that you haven't had time to make a decision, but if we want to occupy these caves Grant and I think that there are two things we need to do: First, we have to get rid of Big Daddy and fast. And secondly, we don't think that we should come back up to Voyager. These caves are empty now but if we leave for even one night who knows what might move in."

Alex was silent for a few minutes and she asked, "Link?"

Link Lincoln kind of gave a half chuckle. "Well, Alex, we haven't really had time to talk about it but as usual Grant and Maryanne make a lot of sense." He paused for a moment and went on. "At first glance this cave complex does appear to be an ideal site for the colony and having said that I'd say that it's worth hanging on to, at least until you get a look at it."

Alex could see the rest of the teams' nods on her vid and she heard their murmurs of agreement. "Good enough for me," she said. "We'll be down with reinforcements as soon as we can."

The ex-military members of the team, Link and the Fosters all spoke at once.

"What?" Alex asked.

Link pointed at Marshal to be spokesman. "What we're saying, Luv, is we know you want to get help down to us as quickly as possible but we don't think that it's a good idea for you to try to join us at night. Wait till it's daylight here. We'll be okay tonight."

Alex was silent for a moment before she gave a reluctant, "You take care of yourselves. I'll be there first thing in the morning."

Link knew who to listen to when it came to survival and turned to the Fosters. "Okay. What do we do?"

Maryanne pointed and said, "Big Daddy. Before we do anything else, we have to get rid of Big Daddy."

"Done!" Link stated then looked out at the carcass. "And just how the hell do we do that?"

Grant looked at Marshal and asked, "Can Junior move

that carcass?"

Marshal snorted. "Not a chance. That critter must weigh a ton at least. Junior can handle maybe three hundred pounds tops."

Maryanne said, "That's what we thought. Grant and I can take care of cutting him up but we will need Junior's help to dispose of the pieces." She paused, smiled a little smile, and looked at Andy McPherson. "And I think we could use the captain's help too."

Marshal grunted in agreement but McPherson was clearly puzzled as he gave a jerky nod. Maryanne laughed, slipped her arm through his and started walking toward the carcass. Maryanne Foster was not a small woman but she didn't come up to McPherson's shoulder.

With another laugh at Andy's expression, Maryanne said, "Grant and I will do the cutting but with your permission we would like you to do the heavy lifting."

McPherson was still puzzled but he just smiled and let Maryanne Foster lead him toward Big Daddy.

Grant looked at the rest of the Away Team and said, "The second thing we need to do is keep the critters out of the caves and I can't think of any better way to do that than fire. We'll need as many fires as we can build in front of the caves and for that we are going to need lots of firewood." He pointed off toward the forest bordering the river and continued. "Between now and sundown drag as much wood as you can up here."

The Away Team headed toward the forest and Grant walked up to McPherson and his wife and said, "It's going to be messy."

Maryanne didn't say a word, she just started taking her clothes off. A startled Andy McPherson looked at Grant and saw that he was doing the same. Maryanne laughed. "You heard my hubby, captain. If you want to keep your clothes clean, you'd better strip down."

They started to work and McPherson quickly realized why the Fosters wanted him. At the moment Big Daddy was just a two-thousand-pound mound of flesh that had to be transformed into something that Marshal and Junior could handle. One of the Fosters would tell McPherson where to lift and the big man would heave and the vibro-knives would go to work. As a chunk of carcass was worked free Marshal would reach in with Juniors mechanical claws and lift it away.

"Where would you like me to dump it?" Marshal asked.

Foster thought for a minute and said, "Anywhere on the other side of the river. Downstream, as far as you can get."

"Right," Marshal said and flew off on the first of the innumerable trips that it took to dispose of Big Daddy.

Dusk was settling when the Fosters decided that they had accomplished all they could. Big Daddy wasn't completely gone. The rock shelf was covered with guts and gore but a good rain would take care of that. The Fosters and McPherson were also covered in a fair amount of blood, guts and gore. The vibrio knives might mitigate the bleeding but they certainly didn't eliminate it. As they walked off toward the river Marshal and Junior followed along and while the humans tried to clean themselves, Marshal daintily washed Juniors mechanical claws in the stream and having had his laugh went off to help the rest of the Away Team drag logs up to the caves.

They walked back to the caves and Maryanne pointed up. The buzzards or whatever they were that had been circling around all day were coming down to try to snatch a bite before darkness set in. "The birds will go away at night," she said, "but who knows what else is going to show up."

Under Link's direction fires were built in front of as many caves as they felt they could handle and the Away Team settled in for a long uncomfortable night.

CHAPTER 12

Alex Cummings sat on the very edge of the Starduster's hastily installed jump seat behind Stan Robertson and Barry Johnson looking out at the vast unfamiliar—yet familiar—landscape of Sanctuary. When dawn had finally arrived on the planet and her Away Team was still intact the urgency of getting down to the ground had subsided and Alex decided that she was going to enjoy the ride—which she mostly did. This was the first time that she had actually seen Sanctuary up close and personal and not even the cool and collected always calm and in charge director of Project Voyager was immune to the excitement of stepping onto a new planet for the first time.

But her mind wasn't entirely at rest, either. It still seemed strange to not have Ben Riley and her husband in the pilot and co-pilot's seats—not that she had ever actually flown with them, but they had been the flight crew of all the fly-bys and the first landings on Sanctuary. However, after landing at the cliff yesterday and exploring the caves, the entire Away Team, shuttle pilots included, had been adamant that they were staying on the ground to protect the caves until she and the rest of the so-called brain trust came down to physically check the place over. That, of course, required new pilots so she had Doc John and Dave Allen revive Stan and Barry. She also had the rest of the scientists and a half dozen of Link's security personnel brought out of hibernation. And after thinking it through even more, this morning Alex had also brought Bjorn Sorenson who had become the kind of unofficial leader of the farmers out of hibernation. Doc John insisted that they also wake up his wife Doc Nancy to which Alex had wholeheartedly agreed.

It had been a busy twelve hours in orbit once she had made up her mind to support Cliffside as the location of the colony. A second Starduster was detached from under Voyager's delta wing, made serviceable and positioned next to Voyager. The RJs operating in space opened up Voyager's equipment compartment and loaded the shuttle's cargo bay with all that it could carry to support their initial foothold on the planet.

So, Dusty 2 was now descending through Sanctuary's atmosphere crammed full of supplies and people. In addition to herself and the two pilots, Dusty 2 carried the three remaining scientists. Alex sighed. The scientific community was never heavily represented on Voyager and with the death of Dan Macintyre there were now only seven. Technically, she thought, Voyager had eight, but Al Wilson wasn't about to leave Wisdom. Alex imagined that when the time came, they'd have to send a Starduster up to retrieve his bones. Her other four scientists were already on the ground. Alex was pleased that the entire scientific community would be represented in the evaluation of the site. Also on board were

Docs John and Nancy Watson as neither one was willing to stay behind and Link's security people—everyone of which was excitedly chattering as they pointed out the windows at the amazing vistas of their new home.

At the thought of Dusty 2, Alex snorted and quickly pretended she was stifling a sneeze when Doc Nancy looked at her questioningly. She didn't want to let her amusement show at how the Voyager's lacked imagination when it came to naming things. As far back as recorded history went explorers on Earth were putting their marks on the world naming things after themselves, their families or their kings and queens but so far here on Sanctuary the colonists were just calling things what they were. If it looks like a duck, it's a duck. Their Starduster shuttles were Dusty 1 and 2, so when the others were activated, they'd probably be 3 and 4. The new sun in the new planetary system was Sol II, though that one wasn't actually the Voyagers doing. Their new star had been called Sol II long before Voyager had left Earth. The moon was always going to be called the Moon, but now that there were two of them, they were Big Moon and Little Moon. Bigass Bay and the continents... she didn't even want to go there.

Now there was Cliffside. At least from the Away Team's description and the Vids that they had sent up to Wisdom, the name was accurate if only slightly more original. And from what Alex had already seen, she could appreciate their enthusiasm for the site. Cliffside did seem to be an ideal location for Earth's first colony on Sanctuary. Down the road the location probably wouldn't do for a city or even a town but for an initial foothold on the planet the location had much to recommend it.

Smiling again at the prospect, Alex reminded herself that she'd better not get too carried away. She did have an image to maintain, after all, she was the cool, calm, focused project director.

"Stan," Alex said, leaning forward, "before we land, I'd like to take a look over the local countryside. Let's continue on up the river past the cliffs then turn to the south for a way and then to the east."

"You got it, boss," Stan answered and turned Dusty 2 west.

They quickly left the endless grasslands and flew up into the foothills. Stan had followed the wide meandering river over the plains, a river which now changed into a rushing turbulent mountain stream as it cut its blue and white path down the rocks and through the solid green of a virgin forest.

No, Alex thought, *that's not quite right, the forest is all green but the forest to the north of the river is denser with bigger trees and has a solid canopy. The forest to the south of the river is sparser. The trees are smaller with more open areas and meadows.*

She wondered, and not for the last time, what event or combination of events could have caused that.

When they reached the cliffs, the river was still thirty yards wide and moving even faster as it cascaded through the crevasse that it had carved in the rocks. Wilson had said that it was early spring here in the northern hemisphere, so maybe that volume of water was just spring runoff, but Alex didn't think so and her smile widened. With that kind of power available, she could envision water powered mills and even a hydroelectric power plant. Better and better.

Following Alex's request, the Starduster continued on up the river past Cliffside which didn't go unnoticed by her husband "Uh, did you miss us, Luv?"

"No, just doing a little sightseeing."

"Just going to keep the peons waiting," Marshal

admonished, but his wife caught his amusement over the comm.

"Now, now, my sweet. I would never do *that*," Alex answered, matching his mocking tone. "Be there in a few."

Marshal chuckled again. He knew that, as focused as his wife was, once she got on the ground and went to work, she might never have another chance to just go sightseeing.

Alex hoped that the Away Team wouldn't take it the wrong way. She was sorry to keep everyone waiting but she just couldn't help herself. Viewing this pristine planet from above was intoxicating.

Stan turned the shuttle south and flew along the top of the cliff face so Alex could look down at the almost perfectly flat apron of rock. She noticed that above the cliff the forest didn't grow right to the edge. It was very strange.

The shuttle continued south toward the large river that they had observed from space that lay a couple of hundred miles away. When they reached it they turned and followed it east, Barry couldn't help exclaim, "Now, that's a river!"

Indeed! Big River, as they ended up calling it, flowed out of the western coastal range. At this point the slow-moving river was at least a mile wide and already turning a muddy brown. Two hundred miles to the north Little River that flowed past Cliffside was a swiftly moving mountain stream. Alex shook her head again, curiouser and curiouser, she smiled to herself.

From what she had seen from space as Big River flowed east it got wider—much wider. In another three hundred miles the river turned to the southeast, flowed into a tropical jungle that was covered by perpetual clouds and was lost from view from above.

Probably reading Alex's mind Robertson continued

flying the Starduster down the river and another phenomenon of Sanctuary revealed itself—the river was another dividing line. As Little River divided the temperate forest into separate environments, Big River separated the temperate forest to the north from a semi-tropical rainforest to the south.

"Well," Alex smiled. "another mystery for Al to solve. But I guess I had better quit sightseeing before our friends on the ground have any more kittens."

That brought a general chuckle as Robertson swung Dusty 2 to the northwest and in just a few minutes they were settling into place on the rock apron beside Dusty 1.

After three months of weightlessness, Alex was a little wobbly as she came down Dusty 2's personnel ladder. When she finally got her feet on the ground, she leaned against her husband, looked around, looked up at the almost cloudless sky and took a deep breath of the first clear, fresh, non-polluted air that she had breathed in over thirty years. Well over fifty years if you counted the twenty years that she had been in hibernation.

Chief Lincoln quickly gathered his deputies and the security team spread out around her. Although it had been a full day since their landing and the encounter with Big Daddy, they weren't taking any chances that some other Nasty Critter hadn't moved into one of the caves when they weren't looking.

Alex smiled at the team's obvious concern for her safety. She thought about telling them that they were being over solicitous but she knew that it wouldn't have done any good.

"Where's the big bear?" she asked, looking around.

Her husband laughed. "In about two dozen pieces scattered about ten miles east on the other side of the river.

Grant and Maryanne said that a carcass that size would attract every scavenger within twenty miles and he was way too big for Junior to move in one piece so the Fosters and Andy," he nodded toward McPherson, "cut it into more manageable hunks and me and Junior spent most of yesterday afternoon distributing the remains."

Alex shook her head and asked, "Did Maryanne really shoot that thing?"

"You better believe it. Come here and take a look." Marshal walked over to the side of the cavern and unzipped a body bag. "Maryanne said that she wanted the head. Geeze, Luv, that bear thing was huge!"

Alex looked at the massive head and gave a little shudder. If they were going to share the planet with creatures like this, what did the future hold?

She quickly shook off that thought and started looking around again while weighing the possibilities for a settlement. She was the boss and would make the final decision as to whether this site would be the location of the Earth colony but she was an experienced administrator who knew how to work with a staff. Her decision would depend on the opinions of the Docs, the scientists, the security people, the Fosters and especially the farmers whose opinion of the suitability of the land that stretched out to the east for raising crops was critical. Leaning on John's arm she walked back over to the shuttle to have a word with Bjorn before he went off to check the land to the east of the rock shelf.

Bjorn Sorenson was Ole Sorenson's eldest son and Ole had been the unofficial leader of the little farming community of Junction back on Earth. From Alex and Ole's first accidental meeting in a supermarket back in Sand Flea City, Ole Sorenson and the farmers at Junction had supplied Alex and Project Voyager with their fresh vegetables. But when it came time for Voyager to actually leave Earth for Sanctuary, the farmer and his wife Helga had declared that they were too old to go gallivanting off to the stars, but Bjorn, two of his brothers and all their families had enthusiastically signed up. Also, joining the Voyager crew was Bjorn's younger sister Olga who was the very official leader of the drone patrol and the Geek Squad.

"Ready, Bjorn?" Alex asked.

Bjorn was enthusiastic. "Ja, Miz Cummings. I give it a good look but it looks like a fine country." He nodded toward Little River flowing out to the east. "Plenty of water."

"Good! Take your time and if you want anyone else out of hibernation just say so. I'll send Andy and Jerry with you. And," she wagged a finger under his nose, "you listen to Andy. There are some very large and unfriendly critters around here."

Bjorn, who was no shrimp himself, looked at big Andy McPherson and laughed. "Ja! You bet I listen."

They all laughed and as Bjorn and his security team moved off the rock shelf and into the brush Alex turned to John. "Okay, my sweet, let's see this cave of yours."

But after only a few minutes of walking Alex's legs were getting wobbly so Marshal said, "Here, Luv, just sit on this rock. I'll get Junior." And in just a few minutes Alex, well-cushioned with a couple of Dusty 1's pillows, was looking at the cavern from the inside of a construction robot. *Oh yes,* Alex thought, *this is better. Much better.*

Sitting inside of the robot with her husband actually flying her around inside this enormous cave made her really appreciate the possibilities. Marshal drifted to the back of the cave where the small waterfall tumbled down and disappeared underground. "Where does that come out?" she asked.

"No idea," Marshal answered. "I took a quick run off to the east but I couldn't see any sign of a river. Maybe it goes deep and hits an aquifer somewhere."

Looking at the waterfall, Alex couldn't believe their luck. Our own private water supply! She spotted Ty West. "Have you tested the water, Ty?"

"Yup, 100% pure H2O."

Alex shook her head again. Amazing!

Marshal coasted along the south side of the cavern and said that he saw no reason why food service, storage and preparation couldn't be recreated along this wall just like it was in Hangar 1 at Sand Flea. Alex readily agreed. If anything, her food service specialists, Cathy Jackson and Erin McPherson, would have more room than they had back on Earth.

Marshal flew across the vast expanse of the cavern opening and said, "It will be a job closing this off to make the cavern weather proof but it can be done." He waved out to the east. "Plenty of trees. Did Al say anything about the weather in these parts?"

"No. Not that I remember."

"Well, it's nice now and if you put your office where you had it back at Sand Flea you can look out over the countryside."

Alex thought that would be fine and there was plenty of room on that side of the cavern for billeting also. Better and better.

"John, my sweet, I think I could walk a little. I'd like to take a look at some of the other caves."

"No problem, Luv, and you won't have to walk; the caves are huge." With that, Marshal flew Junior out of the great cavern and into the large cave to the north. As the robot drifted through the large open area, he explained that this was the cave that had been used by the giant sloths and she was lucky that she couldn't smell it.

Alex laughed but her mind wasn't on smelly sloth-bears. *Supply; this cave would be ideal for supply.*

Marshal said, "Oh by the way, Luv, down at the other end of the caves there's another cavern like the one we were just in. Not as big but I figure that it would be big enough for the shuttles and the robots. Come on, I'll show you."

As Junior drifted across the face of the cliffs Alex stopped trying to count the numerous large and small openings the place contained. She noticed that the height of the cliff diminished as the robot progressed southward. By the time they reached the cavern her husband had indicated the cliff was only about fifty feet high and as she looked off to the south it got lower and lower and eventually just faded away into the forest. They flew on into Marshal's cavern. She smiled and gave her husband a hug. The cavern was just as large as he had said, easily large enough to house all four Stardusters, the shuttle maintenance facility, and the robots.

"Enough, my sweet," Alex said happily. "If Bjorn puts his chop on it, this is the place. How about taking me back to the shuttles?" Then she spoke into the comm. "Bjorn where are you?"

The *Pop, Pop* sound of a rifle came back from the vid and Sorenson said, "Can't talk, Alex."

"What…?"

Andy McPherson said, "We've got a bit of a situation here."

Marshal looked up the toward the shuttles and saw that Dusty 1 was lifting off and moving east across the open area. Marshal didn't wait to find out what was happening as Junior was already moving across the open area toward where he thought the action was. Sitting on her pillows, Alex held on as best she could.

Alex asked, "Chief! What's going on?"

"Andy and the boys ran into a pack of wolves." Link answered.

Alex and Marshal looked at each other and Marshal murmured, "Wolves!"

Alex didn't say a word as her husband sent Junior hurtling out over the meadow toward where he thought the scouting party might be. "Do you see anything, Luv?" he asked.

"No." A pause. "Yes! Over there—to the right."

Marshal swung Junior around. "See them Luv?" he asked.

She hesitated a moment and exclaimed, "Yes! In that big thicket."

Marshal said, "Yeah! Got 'em. Good eyes, Luv."

McPherson, Smith and Sorenson were in the middle of the thicket hunkered down in a small hollow surrounded by high brush. Their positioning was terrible as they probably couldn't see more than a few yards in any direction. Marshal could see indistinct but large shapes moving through the dense brush all around them, but there was no way he could maneuver Junior in to help. "Damn it, Andy, I can't get at them. The brush is too thick."

Link said, "Clear off, John. We're coming in right behind you."

Immediately, Marshal pulled Junior up and hovered at a hundred feet which gave him and Alex a ringside seat of the action. From above they could see one wolf carcass draped half in and half out of the hollow where the men sheltered. Marshal pointed and whispered to Alex, "It's a standoff position. If the wolves try to get into the little hollow the guys will pick them off but as long as the wolves stay in the bush surrounding the hollow, they can't get a clear shot and they can't get out."

Alex nodded she understood the situation but remained quiet as she watched the scene play out. The shuttle landed about thirty yards from the thicket. The gamble worked. True to the nature of every other species that the Voyagers had encountered on Sanctuary, the default response when encountering anything new or strange was to attack it. As soon as the Starduster touched ground the wolves poured out of the thick tangle of bushes and attacked it. Even inside Junior, Marshal could hear their rumbling snarls of defiance as they charged straight for the shuttle and threw themselves against Dusty 1's metal skin.

McPherson, Sorenson and Smith crawled out of their hollow and quickly moved to the edge of the thicket but they couldn't fire because the wolves were between them and the shuttle. With Lincoln and the rest still buttoned up inside and Ben Riley screaming at everyone to not shoot holes in his Starduster the situation was a standoff again.

Alex was wide eyed. This was so far outside her normal experience that she could only watch fascinated but Marshal laughed and whooped. "Hang on, Luv. Airpower to the rescue." Then to Alex's shocked squeak of surprise Marshal swooped Junior down and grabbed a wolf. But he didn't fly away with it; instead, he dragged the massive canine over the ground as it kicked and growled while trying to bite the mechanical claws that held it.

Marshal dragged the wolf thirty yards away from the shuttle and about the same distance from the thicket. It had the desired effect. Sensing the new threat, the rest of the wolves rushed to the defense of their struggling comrade. When the pack was well clear of the shuttle Marshal let go of the wolf and zoomed upward. Now that the way was clear

Andy, Jerry, and Bjorn opened up while Lincoln, his deputies, and Grant and Maryanne Foster tumbled out of Dusty to add their fire power. In less than a minute all the wolves were down.

Marshal grounded the robot. Seeing the look on his wife's face, he tried to relax her by saying brightly, "Well, that was exciting!"

"Not over yet," Maryanne said as she reloaded.

"What do you mean?" Link asked as he surveyed the pile of dead wolves. The only things he saw moving were humans.

"Maryanne's right," Grant answered. "There's probably a den back in that thicket."

Jerry smith said, "I don't recommend walking through that thicket looking for a wolf den, that might have more wolves."

"Nor do I," Grant agreed. "Maryanne, swap places with Alex and take a little ride with John."

Alex didn't ask any questions and immediately climbed out of Junior to let Maryanne in.   Maryanne directed Marshal to hover a few feet above the bushes.

"What are we looking for?" Marshal asked.

"A den," the woman responded. "A hole in the ground, maybe in the side of a hill… there!"

Marshal followed her pointing finger to a clear space in the middle of the thicket. There was indeed a Sanctuary-size wolf hole dug into the side of a small rise. He started to set Junior down but Maryanne stopped him and had him take a slow circuit around the immediate area. They didn't see anything that looked like a wolf so they flew back to the den site and this time Maryanne had him land. Cautiously, she exited Junior and poked around the den area for several minutes even crawling into the den a little way. She was frowning when she climbed back into the robot and didn't say a word until they were back at the shuttle.

After speaking earnestly with her husband for a few minutes, Grant nodded and turned to the group. "As far as Maryanne can tell, there's good news and bad news. The good news is that there are no wolves in the immediate area. The bad news is that we didn't get all of them. Two adults, maybe more, escaped off to the south with at least four cubs."

Alex asked, "Is that bad?"

Grant shrugged and answered, "Well it could be. The wolves might remember the site and come back and then again, they might not. To be sure I recommend we destroy the den. Does anyone have a stick of dynamite in their pocket?"

That brought a general chuckle and Sorenson said, "Don't worry, Grant. We get fields cleared and planted, you'll never know that bushes or wolves were here."

Alex grinned at Bjorn's approval of the land for his farm. Taking charge again, she said, "Well, that was certainly exciting! Now that we're sure that everyone is still all in one piece, Ben, would you take us back to the cliff?" And over the comm she ordered everyone to meet at the shuttles after they landed.

As the Voyagers gathered around her at Cliffside she said, "Good work all of you. Despite our recent excitement I can't imagine that you could have found a more perfect location for our initial colony." She paused and spoke into her Vid. "Al, are you there?"

From three-hundred miles overhead Al Wilson said, "Yup! Good for another twenty minutes."

"Right!" and she turned to everyone. "According to Al it is now spring in this part of our new world. We have many things to do and if we want to get some crops into the ground this year there is not a lot of time to accomplish them. In two weeks, I want the colony up and running. One week to get food and shelter established; one week to have everyone down here on Sanctuary."

Before the Voyagers could process that she went on. "Cathy and Erin will take the south side of this cavern for food service. We'll use Hangar 1 as a model with billeting on the far side and supply in Big Daddy's cave."

Without breaking her stride, Alex turned to the two doctors. "I think the large cave on the other side of the cavern would do for your infirmary but I'll leave that decision up to you.

"Grant and Maryanne, I don't have the billeting people out of hibernation so until they arrive, I'd appreciate it if you would handle seeing that everyone has a place to sleep. Oh, and until Hank gets down here, please take care of storing the supplies also. Chief, please make any security arrangements that you feel are necessary and Bjorn I want to see seeds in the ground."

"All of you feel free to bring anyone you need out of hibernation. But remember we have to feed them and find them a place to sleep. No need to ask me if you can bring someone out of hibernation, just comm Wisdom."

Everyone nodded as they heard their name and their orders.

"Fred," Alex said, "are you there?"

Fred Thompson up in Wisdom replied, "Yes, boss."

"I want the last two Stardusters activated; check with Ben Riley for crews and after you empty out the supply and equipment sections of Voyager start sending everything that we have in the supply cylinder down. Don't worry about priorities, just take it as it comes and make sure that each shuttle has a full load."

This was Alexandria Cummings in her element.

"JJ, Billy. How are your robots coming?"

"Done," they answered in unison.

"Good. Get down here."

"Ah, Alex," Wright asked. "Do you want us to modify any more shuttles with cradles for the robots?"

That was a serious question. The cradles took up space that could be used for supplies. She looked over at her husband. Marshal shook his head. "No Billy, don't do that. Dusty 1 will be up; use it. Oh, tell Tony and Paul that as soon as Voyager is empty, they can start converting their robots."

Alex smiled when all the RJs grunted in agreement.

"Dave, are you there?"

"Yes, Ms. Cummings."

"You're in charge of bringing everyone we need out of hibernation. The Docs will tell you who to wake up to help you. For starters I want Hank Ferguson and anyone that he wants."

Alex looked around at a slightly stunned crowd. "Okay, that should get us started. Any questions? Good," she said to the numerous negative responses. "If you need me, I'll be in my office." And she pointed to the northeast corner of the cavern. Turned and walked away.

Marshal had to stifle a laugh at the half-stunned expressions on the group of Voyagers. He was used to Alex Cummings when she swung into action, they weren't. They all looked at him and he said, "I think she meant now." It was as if a dam burst and a dozen Voyagers scattered to their assigned chores.

The next two weeks seemed to go by in a chaotic flash. On the ground at Cliffside everyday was like Christmas with the Stardusters as Santa Claus. A shuttle would land, an expectant crowd would gather around, its clamshell doors would open and the colonists would be surprised at the contents. If it was food or kitchen supplies a line of human ants would form leading to the food service area while the robots ferried boxes overhead. The next shuttle might have sleeping bags, and the ant line would shift to the other side of the Great Cavern as they were starting to call it.

But not even having the right twenty-first century tool at hand didn't slow the colonists down. Using whatever they had on hand, the colony quickly began to take shape and by the second day, food service was providing three meals a day. Nothing fancy, mostly Army rations augmented with a couple of the antelope type creatures that had gotten too curious about what the humans were doing, but edible and more than welcome after hours of hard work. Everyone had a sleeping bag and a designated place in the great Cavern to stretch out in.

The small herds of grazing animals were more of a nuisance than a danger. The first day, for apparently no reason at all, a group of the big bison charged across the stone shelf in front of the caves scattering people and supplies but after that the animals ignored them and just got in the way. They would probably figure out pretty soon that it wasn't healthy to be around humans as more and more of them went into the pot.

Link and his deputies kept watch and at night had three large fires going across the opening of the Great Cavern. The local wildlife might not be familiar with people and guns but they understood fire.

CHAPTER 13

Nine-year-old Peter McPherson was living the dream. Well he was almost nine. If this was March like Mom said, he wouldn't be nine for a couple of weeks in April, but nine sounded so much better than eight. You were just a little kid at eight but at nine you were getting somewhere. Yesterday when he told Mom that he was almost nine she laughed and told him that they had been traveling in space for twenty years so maybe he was really twenty-eight soon to be twenty-nine. He told Mom that couldn't be right. He looked down at his arms and legs. They looked the same. No! If he was twenty-eight, he would be an old man and he didn't look or feel like an old man. But Mom never lied to him or tried to fool him. Dad might try to joke sometimes, but not Mom.

Well, whatever his age, the last few weeks of his young life had been fantastic. So many exciting things had happened that it was hard to keep them straight or even remember them. He tried to sort out the last three weeks, or twenty years and three weeks if Mom wasn't kidding him, in his mind.

He, Mom and Dad and his little sister Sally had been living at the big Army post in Georgia. Dad was a captain in the Army and on the general's staff and Mom said that he was on the promotion list for major which was a big deal. Mom was a nurse and worked at a big hospital in town. It seemed to Peter that they had been living there for a long time. A couple of years, he thought, which was almost all his life. He kind of remembered living at another Army base but he was just a little kid then. Army kids moved around a lot and sometimes the places got mixed up in your mind. But this base was cool. He had two real good friends who lived on the same street, Harv and Eddie, and the three of them did everything together: went to school, rode their bikes, played ball and sometimes even got into trouble.

Every day after school they would all go to Mrs. Henry's house to do their homework and play video games until their parents got home then after supper, if it wasn't stormy and raining which it seemed to do a lot, they would be outside playing until the streetlights came on.

It was great fun, but over the last few months Peter noticed that things had started to change. Parents might not want to tell kids that things aren't going right or that something was wrong, but kids always know. One thing Peter was sure of was that it wasn't something wrong between Mom and Dad. No, it was something else. Something outside the house. Mom and Dad would be talking and then they would suddenly stop when he or his little sister Sally came into the room. It wasn't Christmas or one of their birthdays, so they weren't talking about presents and it wasn't the happy or excited mood they got when keeping secrets. They were worried about something. They watched the news a lot which was normal, but if Peter came around, they would change channels. That was not normal.

Then one evening Dad told him to pack his camping bag and keep it ready. Peter thought that that was great. He loved camping. Loved being outside in the woods.

He packed his bag but Dad never said when they were going camping.

And kids were disappearing. It seemed that every day when he went to school there were fewer and fewer kids. And a lot of the houses on his street were empty too. On an Army base people moved a lot, but they usually said goodbye. No one did.

And then one day Eddie didn't show up to walk to school with him and Harv. When they checked on his house there was no answer when they rang the bell. They looked through the windows and all the furniture was still there but no one answered the door.

A couple of days later he had just got to Mrs. Henry's house after school when Dad came to take him home. That was really strange because Dad never got home before five and sometimes not until after six. Dad talked to Mrs. Henry and they hugged. Then she cried a little bit and hugged Peter. And then he and Dad left.

Peter wondered what that was all about, but when they got home there was another surprise because Mom was there—and she never got home until six or seven. Mom had the camp coolers out and she was making sandwiches. They were going camping after all, but it somehow scared Peter. It was all wrong. Mrs. Henry didn't hug him goodbye when they went camping, Mom and Dad didn't leave work early for it and they never, never left in the evening. They left in the morning so there was still time to set up camp and have some fun before toasting marshmallows over the fire.

Dad told Peter to come and help and they started putting all their camping gear into the car. Dad even stuck in two gasoline jerry cans that he had in the garage. Dad told him to get his and Sally's camp bags then they all piled into the car and drove off post. Peter was sure that Mom was crying a little as they drove out through the gate.

No one had told Peter anything but he knew—just knew—that they wouldn't be coming back. That he would never see Harv and Eddie again.

They hadn't gone far. Peter remembered that it was getting dark when he saw a bunch of lights and cars up ahead. There were pick-up trucks parked so they were blocking the road and guys with guns standing around them. Dad told everyone to sit tight and he got out and walked up to the roadblock guys. Mom didn't say anything but she opened the glove compartment and took out Dad's pistol. Mom didn't like guns. She said that she had patched up too many people with holes in them. But she did know how to use them. Even Peter had been out to the rifle range, twice, and Dad had let him shoot a little twenty-two rifle. That had been cool, but serious. Dad made sure that everyone knew how to use guns—and respect them.

Mom sat there with the pistol in her lap and never took her eyes off Dad. A few minutes later Dad shook hands with some of the men, came back to the car and they wove their way through the trucks. Dad said that the roadblock guys told him that with all the gangs running around it wasn't safe to drive at night and there was a motel up ahead that was still open. So, they stayed at the motel and had the sandwiches that Mom had made for dinner. The next morning, they had breakfast in a real restaurant and Peter had a stack of pancakes. That was unusual. Mom wasn't big on pancakes or cereal with sugar or a lot of things that she said weren't healthy. Peter certainly wasn't going to argue with Mom but the pancakes sure were good and he ate the whole stack.

They had to try three gas stations before they found one that was open and had gas to sell. Dad complained about the price for twenty miles.

Peter thought he remembered that they went through one more road block before they got on the Interstate. It was weird. Even on the Interstate they couldn't go very fast. Every few miles or so there were cars and trucks parked right in the middle of the road and lots more by the side of the road, some of them with people around them. Dad drove by most of them but when he saw two older ladies holding up a sign that said 'gas' Dad stopped and emptied a jerry can into their tank. Mom smiled and said he was an old softy.

Peter wondered where it was that they were going camping. Usually, it was just a couple hours' drive until they were up in the mountains. He remembered sleeping off and on and when he was awake, he played little kids computer games with Sally. Mom smiled and Dad said that he was a good trooper. Peter remembered that it was getting dark when they came to a big city. Birmingham Dad said. There weren't any roadblocks but there were cars all over both sides of the road and some cars were just parked on the highway. Some were wrecks and it didn't look like anyone was clearing them up. Peter asked what was going on and Mom sighed and said that she was afraid that that's the way things were these days.

They found a motel that was open but the lady wouldn't take Dad's credit card so he had to pay cash and then he had to sleep in the car because there were so many people prowling around the parking lot. The next day Mom drove and Dad slept in the passenger seat. Peter remembered going through Memphis. He knew it was Memphis because of the big sign and he remembered it because he could see smoke from a couple of really big fires right in town and because they crossed the Mississippi River. Peter asked Mom if they were now in the west. Mom laughed and said that maybe they weren't quite in the wild west yet but they were now on Interstate Forty and the west was where we were going.

Peter remembered thinking that that was cool, he'd never been to the west before. He kept looking for buffalo and cowboys, but he never saw them.

The next three, or maybe it was four, days became a jumble in his mind. They drove during the day and tried to find a motel at night. They went through Oklahoma but he didn't see any cowboys there, either. One night they slept in the car in a picnic area by the side of the road. Dad said he liked the spot because there was a grove of trees between the picnic area and the road and you couldn't see the car from the road. Peter also remembered that it was getting harder and harder to find gas. If they found an open gas station Dad would stop and fill up even if the tank was only half empty... and then he would complain about the price of gas for the next twenty miles.

Mom took Sally up front with her and let Sally sit in her lap. That was really unusual. Mom was always on about seat belts.

They drove all the way to California and one evening just as it was starting to get dark Dad pointed ahead to a bunch of bright lights sitting right out in the middle of the desert.

"Well, there it is, Sand Flea City!"

Peter laughed at the name as he looked ahead and saw the lights and asked if that's where they were going.

Mom said yes and as they got closer Peter could see that most of the lights and especially the brightest lights, weren't coming from the town but from someplace just outside of town.

Dad pulled over and took out his phone. After he talked for a minute or so Peter jerked up. Grandpa! Dad was talking to Grandpa. Peter liked Grandpa; he was cool. They had gone up to Grandma and Grandpas house in Virginia last Christmas. That was great! Grandpa was a colonel in the Space Force and he worked in the Pentagon. One day Grandpa had taken the whole family into the Pentagon and they met Grandpa's boss—a real four-star general named Hunter. He seemed happy to meet Dad. While the grownups talked Peter had looked at all the airplane models that were lying around. Grandpa said that between him and the general they had flown just about all of them. Then the general took the whole family to lunch in what was called the general's dining room. After lunch Grandpa had taken them into Washington past all the monuments and right into the White House where the President lived. Grandpa said that he worked there too. Then they went out to a big Air Force base and they saw the big fancy airplanes that the president flew around in. Yeah! That was great.

They waited in the car for a little while and then Dad looked over at Mom and whispered, "He's here."

Mom looked surprised and said, "Really?"

Cool, Grandpa was here. Peter could only hear Dad on the phone and Dad asked if they should come to the air base. Peter guessed that's where all the lights were. "No!" His dad said and then he listened for a bit. "Yes, we just passed it." He turned to Mom and told her that he thought Grandpa was talking to somebody else.

Then Dad said, "What? Okay, if you say so. Bye."

Mom looked at Dad and he said, "Dad said that we shouldn't go anywhere near the airfield. He said that there were hundreds of people milling around outside the gates and it was getting ugly."

Mom asked what we were supposed to do and Dad kind of sighed and said, "He wants us to take that road that we just passed, the one that went off to the north. Drive fifteen miles or so, find a clear space with no trees, and wait, and he'll come for us."

Mom asked, "What do you think we should do?"

Dad kind of gave a half smile and said, "I guess we'll do what Dad said. I sure don't know what else to do."

Dad turned the car around and they found the road. It was just a two-lane road that went off into the pitch blackness. Now Peter was really worried and he told Dad so. Peter had seen many times on the Vid that this was the kind of dark lonely road that the space aliens kidnapped people on. The flying saucers came down, grabbed them and they were never seen again. Mom and Dad tried not to laugh and Dad said that he thought that they were pretty safe from alien abduction.

"But Dad…." Grown-ups! What do they know?

After fifteen minutes or so Dad stopped right in the middle of the road and turned on the spotlight. After he looked at both sides of the road, he told Mom that he didn't see any trees and he turned the car off and they just sat there in the middle of the dark lonely road. Peter was really worried now. Talk about being alien bait!

They'd been sitting in the middle of the road in the dark for about an hour when Dad's phone rang. Dad listened for a minute and said, "Right, Okay." He hung up and started the car and not only turned on the headlights but the spotlight too.

Peter remembered thinking that the aliens would spot them for sure and sure enough, not a minute later he saw lights in the sky up ahead. Holding his breath Peter watched what he was sure was a flying saucer come closer and closer until it hovered over the road and finally landed in the road right in front of them. For a minute nothing happened then he could see a figure moving around but when the figure stepped into the headlights to Peter's shocked surprise it was Grandpa.

Grandpa was an alien! No, that couldn't be right. Grandpa was cool.

Mom and Dad got out and hugged Grandpa. Then they all walked back to the car and Grandpa said, "Well, Peter, are you ready to take a ride in a spaceship?"

Ha! He knew it.

Dad got their packs and as they got closer to the flying saucer Peter could see that it wasn't a flying saucer at all it looked more like an airplane. A funny looking airplane, though. It was fat and had delta wings. Peter felt braver when Mom didn't hesitate but climbed right up the little ladder. There was a smiling lady up there. She seemed nice and she welcomed them all aboard. Dad went forward to talk to the pilot. That was all the people who were on board: just Grandpa, the smiling lady and the pilot. Peter was all confused. This wasn't like the stories that he had read or seen on the Vid about spaceships at all. He was more confused when the smiling lady took them into the passenger section. It had regular cushy seats like on the front posh section of an airplane. There were only ten seats and they were more like big comfortable reclining chairs than airplane seats. The nice lady took them to the back and told them to take a seat. Mom and Sally took one but Peter grabbed one on the other side where he could look out the window.

While they were doing that the pilot called to Dad and Grandpa and they went up front and talked for a minute then Dad and Grandpa went back outside. For a moment Peter couldn't see them because the wing was in the way, then he could see them walking toward the car. Peter thought that maybe they were going to get the rest of the camping gear. But after a few minutes he saw them walking back toward the shuttle, the nice lady had called it, and they weren't carrying anything. Peter jumped and let out a squawk when *whoosh* the car burst into flames.

He blurted, "Mom! Dad and Grandpa just burned up our car."

Mom just sighed. "I liked that car."

Dad and Grandpa came back on board and closed the door and the airplane (shuttle, Peter corrected himself) just went straight up in the air into the dark. Peter stared out the window at the blackness. By now he was beyond being amazed at anything. Dad and Grandpa and the nice lady came back and she told them to make themselves comfortable that they had one more pick-up to make and then they would be on their way to Voyager.

Like everything else that had happened Peter had no idea what "Voyager" was, but it sounded cool. They flew through the blackness for about an hour and the nice lady— Peter later found out that her name was Ms. Cummings and she was the boss of everything—came back and talked to Mom. Peter caught that one of the people that they were going to pick up had been hurt and could Mom take care of him. Mom put Sally in the seat with him and went with the nice lady up toward the cockpit. When she came back, she had a big metal box with a red cross on it.

Peter looked ahead and saw lots and lots of bright lights. Ms. Cummings called to Dad and Grandpa and opened a panel in the wall. Peter's eyes went wide—in the panel there were guns! Real rifles like the kind the Army used and Dad and Grandpa each took one.

The shuttle flew slowly toward the lights then turned away, went back out into the darkness, turned again and approached the lights from another direction. Peter looked down and could see that they were over a big open area and they landed right in the middle of it. Dad opened the door and he and Grandpa disappeared. Peter pressed his face against the window and tried to look forward. He couldn't see much but with the door open he could hear Pop, Pop, Pop. He knew that sound: guns. It sounded just like when he was on the rifle range.

Peter saw three people running toward the shuttle. When they came up the ladder, he could see that it was two guys supporting the guy that was hurt. Mom got up and told them to lay the hurt guy down and she went to work. His name was Kurt and he had been shot, right through the shoulder. While Mom was bandaging Kurt two more soldiers came onboard, or at least Peter thought they were soldiers because they all wore the same kind of uniform. The same one-piece suit that Ms. Cummings wore.

Soon the cabin was full of soldiers and guns. Dad and Grandpa came back on board and the shuttle lifted off and headed back out into the darkness. The soldiers started to relax, do high fives, and one by one they all came back to thank Mom for taking care of Kurt and thank Ms. Cummings, though they called her Alex, for coming to get them.

Dad came back to see that they were all okay. By this time Peter was beyond amazed. He started to ask Dad the first of a million questions when he started to float out of his seat.

"Daaad! What's happening?" Peter was terrified, but it

was also so awesome he didn't care. He was flying!

All the soldiers were laughing and Dad told him that they were flying out of the Earth's atmosphere and what he was experiencing was weightlessness. Once he got over his shock Peter thought that weightlessness was great. Dad let him go and he floated up to the ceiling and when he pushed himself off one of the soldiers gave him a little shove and he drifted toward the front. Before he could drift into the cockpit, another soldier caught his ankle, turned him around, and he drifted the other way. Everyone was floating and Sally was also enjoying it as she giggled and "Wanted to play Supergirl some more."

The grown-ups let him float around for a while then Dad pulled him down and said that they were arriving at Voyager. Peter looked out the window and saw a great shadow against the blackness of space.

The Mother Ship. They really were aliens! But as he got closer, he could see that it didn't look like a flying saucer either. It kind of looked like a big 747 airplane, but with big, funny-looking tubes stuck all over it.

Everything happened so fast after that that he never had a clear memory of what actually did happen. The soldiers all got up and floated out of the shuttle, then Ms. Cummings and Grandpa. Peter didn't know where they went. Then another lady floated in. She said she was a doctor and took a look at the wounded guy, told Mom that she had done a great job and that she would be a great addition to the team. Then they just floated him out. That just left Peter and Mom and Dad and Sally.

Someone else stuck their head in. "Captain McPherson?"

Dad nodded.

"Would you all come with me, please."

Peter remembered that they floated out into some kind of machine shop then up into what looked to be the back end of a small passenger section that was full of people all laughing and talking. Then they went into another section, a huge tube that had long torpedo-like things on both sides. The lady who said she was a doctor said he would go to sleep in the tube and when he woke up, they would at Sanctuary. Peter didn't know what that was but Mom and Dad said it was okay. But before he could get into the tube, he had to take all his clothes off. That was kind of embarrassing with all those people around but he had done it.

He was never sure if he had gone to sleep or not. It seemed that he just closed his eyes and then opened them. Mom and Dad were still there but the other people were different. He got dressed and they floated through a tube into a lab of some kind. He didn't remember that when he first got there before he went to sleep and there were rolls of toilet paper floating around all over the place. That was weird. They went back into the shuttle and there were two other families with kids and then they flew down through the clouds and Peter could see the ground. A huge flat field with millions of animals then a forest.

They had landed in front of a great cliff and he was now living in a cave with Mom and Dad, Sally, Grandpa and even Grandma was there, too. One of the biggest surprises was when they went to eat in the big dining hall that was on the other side of the great cave there was Aunt Erin and cousin Judy.

Everything happened so fast. He was taken into a cave where they gave him clothes, the one piece overall that everyone was wearing, shoes, coat, everything. Then he was shown where the school was, right in the back of the big cave where they slept. They told him that he was now a member of the Bug Brigade. He had no idea what that was but it turned out to be cool.

That had been three days ago. Today before breakfast and before he had to go to school, he had something to do. The teachers had told him that they were not on Earth anymore but on a different planet. Peter wasn't sure that he believed that but he was sure that he knew how to find out. His teacher Ms. Henderson, she was nice, and the other teacher Mrs. Porter, she was the boss and really mean—told the class that this planet had two moons. So, before there were any grownups to stop him, he was going to look outside and check to see if they were really two moons and he was on a different planet.

Mom and Dad and the other grownups had been on and on about how this was a dangerous planet with lots of wild animals and you couldn't wander around outside. There were even three big bonfires set every night across the front of the big cave with guards to make sure no wild animals got in and no one went outside. Well, he wasn't going to go far—just pop out to take a quick look at the moon or moons.

He was in luck. The fire over on this side of the cave wasn't as big as the other two in fact it had burned down so low that the side of the cave was in deep shadow.

Peter slipped along the wall then stopped close to the entrance. He couldn't see the guard. There were guards at the other two fires but not here. Great! He looked out into the darkness. It was really black. He couldn't see anything. He took a deep breath and ran out several steps and crashed into something big and hairy and smelly. He didn't mean too but he let out a squawk as he bounced back and sat down hard.

He must have squawked louder than he thought because lots of grownups were running towards him. Some snatched up torches and he could see what it was that he had bumped into. A big deer like thing from the wild west that he had seen pictures of and there were a lot of them. Oh boy! Peter thought he was in big trouble now. But once someone had jerked him back inside the cave and the grownups were busy waving torches at the deer and driving them away from the cave and they were all yelling at each other too.

"Where was the guard?"

"Why was the fire allowed to go out?"

"Why were we here in this wilderness?"

"Why do I have to pull guard duty?"

As the crowd grew and the shouting got louder and as Ms. Cummings tried to bring order out of the confusion young Peter McPherson quietly faded into the back of the crowd.

It was only later that he remembered that he had forgotten to see if there were two moons.

CHAPTER 14

Alex stood in front of her "desk," such as it was. A desk stuck in the northeast corner of the Great Cavern created from two large plastic containers that had once held freeze-dried veggies and looked out at the over five hundred and fifty earthmen and women who milled around the Great Cavern. The group was so large, the overflow spilled out onto the rock shelf that fronted it. The only Voyagers missing were the children who were in the makeshift school house at the back of the cavern under the firm control of their teachers Evie Porter and Mary Henderson. Also absent were the few scientists and robot jockeys who were still working up in orbit.

It would have been nice if everyone had a chair but chairs were one of the many things that would have to wait.

The morning's event with the young boy, Peter McPherson (*my goodness,* she thought, *another McPherson! How many of them are there?*) had roiled the colony and made a general meeting imperative so Alex had asked everyone to gather in the Great Cavern right after lunch. Everyone was present and most of them were just plain confused. Many of them had only been out of hibernation a few weeks to a few days while others had only been awake and shuttled down to the planet just yesterday. It was natural for the colonists to be apprehensive and even a little frightened. Alex had her advance team, the Voyagers who had been awake to participate in the initial survey of Sanctuary, who had done the fly-bys and made the first landings, circulating among them trying to keep everyone calm and answer their millions of questions, but it was time for her to address everyone directly.

Which proved to be another challenge. Alex wasn't a small woman, but she wasn't all that tall, either, and the fact that Chief Lincoln and his deputies insisted on providing a protective shield around her to keep her from being jostled or even trampled by the throng of edgy colonists didn't help. Even when she was standing in front of her make-shift desk, Alex couldn't see over the people in front of her and she doubted that anyone could see her. Several times she tried to address the crowd to no avail.

"It's no good, Ms. Cummings!" Andy McPherson shouted into her ear. "No one will hear you from there or even know that you are speaking. Here, you need to get on the packing crates or even better up on this rock."

She started to say that she wasn't going to climb up on packing crates or on a rock but instead she let out a shocked squeak when McPherson effortlessly lifted her and set her on the chunk of rock that projected from the side of the cave.

She shook her finger at the grinning McPherson before regaining her composure. She smiled when she realized that putting her up here on the rock had worked and that the colonists could at least see her and she was even more pleased when the crowd began to quiet. With all eyes now on her, Alex saw the confused apprehension clearly and drew in a breath and said, "Ladies and gent..." she began and then stopped in shock. The acoustics from this particular spot were amazing. The word 'ladies' reverberated around the Great Cavern like a bell in an echo chamber. If she didn't have everyone's attention before, she definitely had it now.

Alex started again a little more relaxed now knowing that everyone could not only see her but could hear her as well. "Good afternoon, ladies and gentlemen and welcome to Sanctuary!"

Some cheers rang throughout the cavern, but it was a mixed reaction.

Everyone, even those who had just come out of hibernation, knew the bottom line: Not only was there no higher civilization on Sanctuary, but as far as they could determine there was no civilization at all and the only life that they had encountered were vicious wild animals the size of tanks. The exciting adventure of getting here was wearing off with the cold hard realization that the humans from Earth were alone on a primitive planet twenty light-years from home. Many were anxious; more than a few were frightened. Most were eager to get on with settling down and establishing their new life, but others were so scared that they wanted to chuck it all in right now and return to Earth.

"I know that most of you are anxious and confused," Alex continued, "and who could blame you? What your internal clock is telling you is that yesterday you were standing on Earth and today you're standing in a cave on a strange planet. You want to know where you are, what's going on and what the future holds." She paused to let the ripple of ascents fade away. Not only was her rocky perch an excellent place for the people to hear her, but she could hear them as well. "So, to ensure that we all start from a common understanding of the facts, I have prepared a little presentation that I hope will answer many of your questions and give you a complete and factual picture of where we are and what we are up against."

Before she could continue, she was interrupted by a harsh voice saying, "Whatever dog and pony show you might have cooked up to cover this disaster is just a phony distraction. What we should be doing is organizing our immediate return to Earth."

That statement caused a stir to ripple through the colonists with some nods of agreement and more than a few "shut ups" and "don't interrupt" mixed in.

However, Alexandria Cummings had directed far too many meetings to be phased by this. Calmly looking out over the crowd, she spotted the speaker. "And you are, sir?"

"Lasseter. Ryan Lasseter."

Alex remembered him; Lasseter had arrived right before they had left Earth and had been one of the loudest voices complaining about everything and everyone at Sand Flea.

"Mr. Lassiter, if I understand you correctly, you're saying that we should immediately return to Earth."

"That's right!" the man stated with a definitive nod to those closest to him. A few nodded back and Lassiter smirked, taking it that they were in agreement with him.

"Might I ask why you feel that way?"

"Look around," Lasseter said. "We left Earth on a promise of a better life, a modern civilized life and you expect us to be primitive cavemen on a primitive planet with no future except minimum survival."

That misinformed statement brought a growl from a

few hundred voices. Voyager had left Earth to escape from a polluted, overcrowded and dying planet. The men and women who had labored on and above Earth for over three years to put Voyager together knew that and said so. And what made him think they'd have modernization on a planet that humans had only just stepped foot on?

Alex just smiled. "Mr. Lasseter, it would appear that you are not very well informed on Sanctuary, Voyager or the entire Voyager Project. Might I ask why you volunteered to join this colony?"

Lasseter glared back at her. "My reasons are my own."

"Very well," Alex said shrewdly before she turned her attention to the colonists. "Ladies and gentlemen, I am sure that Mr. Lasseter's feelings are shared by many of you and with this presentation I hope I can clear up any misunderstandings of where we are, what our assets are and what the future holds."

That statement brought a wave of agreement and a small grumble of protest.

"Please don't misunderstand me. I'm not saying that we won't return to Earth. Maybe at the end of what Mr. Lasseter calls my 'dog and pony show' you will still want to return but let's make that decision an informed decision." She glanced back at Lasseter and thought *Damn! That jackass probably did me a favor.* "Please bear with me now and I'll bring you up to date on our current situation then you can decide for yourselves the way forward."

A wave of mumbled agreement filled the cavern. With their attention fully on her, Alex opened her Vid and as if on signal five hundred and fifty people did the same.

For dramatic effect she looked up and asked, "Professor Wilson, are you there?"

A very familiar baritone filled the Great Cavern and the space outside as over five hundred Vid communicators displayed the distinguished silver haired image of Professor Al Wilson. "Good afternoon to one and all down there on Sanctuary from your orbiting meteorological space station three hundred miles above you."

Almost involuntarily over five hundred pairs of eyes looked up to the rocky cavern ceiling and then back to their Vids.

Al went on. "I can see that you are having a pleasant spring afternoon at Cliffside there on the continent of Middle Finger. And don't blame me for the name," Al laughed at the shocked chuckle from the colonists. "Blame the jokers on the exploration team, but let me show you why our new continents got their names."

Images of Sanctuary from space filled their Vid screens as Al explained the shape of each of the giant peninsulas and why they were called Index, Middle, Thumb, Little and Ring and went on to further refine the Voyagers current location on the south eastern slope of the great mountain range that covered the western edge of the continent of Middle Finger.

"As I was saying, yes, it is spring where you are, about the end of March I would say if measured by an Earth calendar. But you are on a new and different planet. You don't have to call it March. You can call it anything you like. I might suggest calling it New Year's Day, day one of year one."

Al paused to let the people study the images before continuing. "Like Earth, Sanctuary has an axial tilt so there at Cliffside you will experience all four seasons and as you will have already noticed spring is cloudy and wet—expect fall to be the same. Summer will be warm, mid to upper seventies on average, with occasional rain and the winters mild, in the mid-forties and rain. For a comparison to Earth the climate at

Cliffside will be pretty much like the Pacific Northwest of North America with occasional snow, but overall, not bad.

"Unfortunately, without a supporting network of satellites, I don't have all the bells and whistles for weather forecasting that I had in orbit around Earth but I should be able to provide you with a pretty good daily and five-day forecast."

The more the familiar voice of Al Wilson went on the more visibly relaxed the colonists seemed to become. Al then went on to give the size and shape of the planet, the two moons and other information that would be of interest.

The fact that the orbital year was three hundred and seventy-two days didn't seem to trigger a reaction until Al suggested that they could have twelve thirty-one-day months. The revelation of a twenty-six-hour day had everyone looking at their Vids wondering how that was going to work.

Al then said, "Well my half hour is about up. Without a network of satellites, we can only communicate when Wisdom is in line of sight with Cliffside. So, as they used to say back in the twentieth century, 'I'll catch you on the flip side.' I'll see you when I come around again. Al Wilson signing off for now."

The Voyagers applauded and Alex smiled to herself. That was well done. Al Wilson's familiar face and voice had gone a long way toward calming everybody down.

Next up was her husband, another individual that everyone except the late arrivals from VU knew. Marshal being Marshal threw himself into it and had the audience alternately gasping and laughing as the Vids flashed by one after the other. The fly-bys, dinosaurs on Index, the raging oceans, vast mountains and baren plateaus. The great herds of animals located less than a thousand miles to the east. The volcanoes of Ring and the desolation of Little. After the crowds had absorbed the fly-by images, Marshal went on to describe the landings—the close calls on the peninsula of Thumb and by the big lake fifteen hundred miles to the east. He didn't skip the horror by the bay a thousand miles to the west where they lost Macintyre and Mason or the Terror Birds and big bison; Marshal told it all. He spoke for over an hour and the colonists were hanging on every word.

Then to everyone's surprise he pointed to Maryanne Foster and called her up onto the rock with him. Probably anticipating what was to come she clearly didn't want to go but with five hundred pairs of eyes on her what could she do. She stood blushing to the roots of her hair while Marshal told the story of how the previous occupants of the caves were evicted. When he finished—to thunderous applause—he nodded to big Andy McPherson who jumped up on the rock and held up the skull of the great bear thing that Maryanne had killed.

Shock and awe don't begin to describe the reaction.

Alex had planned to have one of the Watsons review the medical aspects facing the colony but after her husband's presentation and a hastily whispered conversation with Doc Nancy, who was in total agreement, they quickly scrubbed that part of the presentation.

Instead, she started to lay out her plan for the colony but was again interrupted by Lasseter who didn't want to hear anything about the colony but only wanted to discuss an immediate return to Earth. And from those gathering around him, there were a few who supported the idea.

Alex said, "I understand your feelings but to me it would seem a shame to have come all this way without even giving Sanctuary a chance." Even in the echo chamber she had to raise her voice over Team Lasseter's shouts. "Having said that... having said that, let me be clear that that is just my feeling. It is up to you as a group to decide whether we stay or go. However, I do want to set the record straight: It has been said that we are cast adrift on a primitive planet without resources and we will be a primitive society. That is not entirely true. We do have resources. We have all the accumulated knowledge of thousands of years of human development in our computers and stuffed away in Voyager there's quite a bit of twenty-first century machinery. We have, among other things, a dozen solar powered generators plus one of Gutman's. We have modern computer-controlled manufacturing equipment. Not as much as we would like perhaps but some. We have two three-dimensional printers and can create items that we need as we come to them. And yes, there are no super markets here. If we want to eat, we will have to be farmers so we have two of what they call the Little Giant farm tractors with all the attachments and a saw mill. We also have a complete industrial size kitchen and for shelter we have the caves. Even if the planet supplied us with nothing, we have enough food to feed the colony for a couple of years. But the planet does provide. You can see that right in our own neighborhood we have steaks on the hoof pushing through the cavern entrance."

That got a laugh and Alex went on. "Locally we have already identified varieties of blackberries, blueberries, huckleberries, apples, pears, plums, walnuts, hazelnuts and onions and, like everything else on Sanctuary, they're all big. Walnuts the size of your fist."

Lasseter interrupted. "So if we stay, we revert to a pre-industrial society of hunters and gathers."

"For now," Alex smiled. If Lasseter expected her to bristle at that he was disappointed. "Let's say it's a mix of pre-industrial and late twenty-first century technology. As I said we have some modern implements and manufacturing equipment. We also have spare parts for our machinery—as many as we could cram into Voyager. And as I said, we have the 3D copiers. It is true that we are years away from being able to manufacture anything that any of us would call modern. We don't have the machines or the machines to make the machines to do that and probably won't have for a while, but we are far from a primitive society. Bottom line, the colony can live on its own resources for a couple of years but it is still unclear if we can live on Sanctuary permanently and we won't know unless we try. And one last item for your consideration when you are deciding if you want to return to Earth—remember the Earth we left and why we left."

That statement brought a reflective silence. Most of the colonists did remember, and a few of Lasseter's new supporters nodded as they remembered that their home planet was dying. But Lasseter would not be deterred and kept pushing for an immediate return to Earth.

Go or stay? It seemed that all five-hundred people were talking at once.

Alex held up her hands for silence. "Let me suggest this: I propose that we give the planet a chance. One year to see if we can not only exist on Sanctuary but if we could really thrive and grow as a civilization. During that year I will leave Voyager in space, intact, and capable of taking as many as wish to go on their twenty-year journey back to Earth."

Most thought that was fair, though Lasseter of course wanted to return immediately.

Alex paused to let this conversation ripple through for a moment. "But as you take the next year to decide," letting them subtly know that the trial year was non-negotiable, she said, "here is also another thing to consider: As we stand here no older than we were when we left our home world, twenty years have passed on Earth—and if we return it'll be another twenty. If we left today, everyone we ever knew would be forty years older by the time we got back."

The crowd was silent as they thought of the implications. A few started crying as they obviously *hadn't* considered that fact. Marshal had trouble mustering any sympathy for them, after all, what did they expect, everything to stay the same?

Alex went on. "Let me clarify one point: I said that I would leave Voyager intact and that's true—except for the large supply cylinder which we will salvage for the material once it's emptied. So, there it is. As best and as honestly as I could present it, you know our situation so the decision is up to you. It's a hard decision, I know, but now that you have all the facts," and she looked directly at Lasseter, "the straight facts, I think you should take a little while to think about it and to talk it over. We'll meet here tomorrow at the same time right after lunch and decide: Do we give Sanctuary a year and then decide whether to stay or go or take the shuttles back up to orbit, board Voyager and return to the Earth we left? The choice is yours."

Before Alex could get off the rock a hundred discussions and probably as many arguments broke out and they continued all that afternoon and well into the evening. Some of the people sat up all night around the large fires in front of the Great Cavern and the several smaller ones that had been built inside to discuss the pros and cons of staying or going.

When Alex climbed back onto the rock the next day it seemed clear that just about everyone had made up their minds. It was also clear that they were far from unanimous.

Without any preamble Alex said, "Well, ladies and gentlemen, you've had a day to think about it and reach your own decision. The choice is do we give Sanctuary a year or do we board Voyager and return to Earth." Without waiting for the arguments of persuasion to begin again, Alex simply pointed to Lasseter and said, "Would everyone who wants to return to Earth step over here with Mr. Lasseter and those who are willing to give the planet a year step over by the food service line."

There was a shuffling of people but not too much. Lasseter had about a hundred people standing around him and the rest were over by the service line.

Slightly depressed that so many had joined Lasseter, Alex was inwardly pleased that so many had decided to stay. Alex started to say that the results were clear when Lasseter shouted over her.

"What does this prove? You people are being given a false choice. This whole thing has been rigged!"

There were shouts of protest at his words as people declared they had a choice and voted the way they saw fit.

"Sheep!" Lasseter snarled and jumped onto the rock and pointed to Alex. "What authority does she have? Ms. Cummings was hired by Visions Unlimited as project director to build the spaceship. Nothing else. She has no authority here on Sanctuary!"

That brought a knee-jerk and mostly angry response from everyone who knew Alex and had worked with her over the past few years. The two sides began to push towards each other in protest but before anyone could act Alex stepped forward and her voice boomed out through the Great Cavern.

"Mr. Lasseter is absolutely correct."

A shocked silence filled the cavern as Alex went on. "The terms of my contract; in fact, all of your contracts were to build Voyager. We did that and having fulfilled such terms; we are now unemployed. At least we're not getting paid." which brought a chuckle from the assembled Voyagers. "Mr.

Lasseter is quite correct when he says that I have no leadership position here on Sanctuary. This is a new planet and whatever form of government the colony has, will have, or indeed if you want any government at all, is up to you."

The cavern filled with a stunned silence.

"Then what do you suggest?" someone asked. Marshal thought it might have been Lasseter, but he wasn't sure. No one was moving and the only person they were looking at was Alex.

And she merely shrugged. "I would suggest that due to the uncertainties of the immediate future, you continue with the director/staff arrangement that we had back at Sand Flea. Having said that, I hereby resign as Project Director."

The stunned silence was replaced as total bedlam broke out in the great cavern. As Alex jumped down from the rock, Lasseter wasted no time in shouting that he should be appointed director while several hundred voices protested Alex's resignation.

In the chaos, Alex went into a huddle with the Colonel and Andy McPherson, Marshal and Chief Lincoln. After a few whispers, the men nodded and separated. Marshal went into the crowd gathering the veteran Voyagers as he went. He spoke briefly with them and they too spread out through the rest of the colonists. Link was quietly gathering his deputies and forming a cordon around the speaker's rock.

Lasseter had never shut up. He was still extolling the colonists with his wonderfulness while denigrating anyone who might challenge his right to lead the colony. At a nod from Alex the two McPhersons climbed up on the rock. Big Andy just walked to the front and crowded Lasseter to the side much to the delight of most of his unwilling listeners.

When Lasseter had no choice but to step to the back end of the rock, the Colonel stepped forward. "Fellow

Voyagers, I think that Mr. Lasseter is getting a little ahead of himself. I think that before we decide on a director we have to decide if the director/staff arrangement is what we want to run the colony."

That's when Marshal's cadre of old hands spread out through the cavern started shouting 'Yes! The director/staff arrangement. It's worked for us before."

If there were any protests to that, no one heard them.

McPherson acknowledged, "Alright. I propose that we continue the existing arrangement of a director supported by a staff. Are we in agreement?"

There was a wave, led by Marshals cadre of yeses.

"Are there any objections?"

Lasseter's people, probably figuring that their man would be nominated, were silent.

"No objections!" the Colonel went on. "Good. Then the next order of business is to select the director. I gather from his last tirade that Mr. Ryan Lasseter has put his name forward." He looked at Lasseter who was still trying to keep a foothold on the rock as Andy McPherson crowded him.

"Yes," Lasseter said, "and I move that the nominations be closed."

"Object!" Marshal shouted from the floor. "I nominate Alexandria Cummings and not just because she is my wife." That brought a chuckle from most of the colonists. Of course, many of the late arrivals probably didn't know that they were married. "Her leadership has brought us this far."

A wave of cheers echoed through the Great Cavern as the motion was seconded.

"Very well," said McPherson. "We have two nominations for the directorship of the colony: Mr. Ryan Lasseter and Ms. Alexandria Cummings. Are there any other nominations?"

The colonel looked out over the crowd and waited.

"No?" He asked and waited some more. No one was going to be able to say later that he rushed the process. "Is there any discussion? Does anyone wish to speak in favor or in opposition to any of the candidates?" And he pointed a finger at Marshal. "Not you, John."

That got a laugh and the Colonel went on. "Then let's decide. Would everyone in favor of Mr. Ryan Lasseter join him here by the rock and, Alex, would you please step over to the serving line and everyone in favor of Ms. Cummings join her there."

A very unhappy Ryan Lasseter watched as Alex made her way across the cavern, smiling, greeting people and gathering the crowd with her as she went. By the time she reached the serving line almost five hundred people were on her side of the cavern.

Before Colonel McPherson could announce the winner, Lasseter was already loudly complaining that the election was illegal, that it was rigged, that there should be a revote in a few days and so on. It seemed that outside of his few followers no one was paying any attention to him.

Alex made her way back across the cavern through a happy crowd. A huge cheer rose as she stepped back onto the rock. "Thank you," she said. "I hope that you're all just as happy after I've worked you half to death."

A laugh rolled around the Great Cavern.

She went on. "As all of you who worked on the Voyager Project know I did not—I could not—manage Project Voyager on my own. I had a lot of help. My staff consisted primarily of the heads of the various functional departments, food service, supply and so forth. So, while we are all here, I would like to appoint a staff to assist me on Sanctuary. As I call your names would you please step forward so everyone will know who you are. The staff will represent the major functions that will keep our colony running. First Security: Chief Lincoln."

The mention of the popular Chief's name brought a roar of approval from the colonists as Link moved in front of the rock.

Alex went on. "Food Service: Cathy Jackson."

Cathy went to stand beside Lincoln amidst another roar of approval.

"Get up here Cathy so people can see you." And a blushing Cathy Jackson joined Alex on the rock. "I would like to have a representative from the farming community on the staff," Alex continued looking at the knot of farmers standing just outside the cavern opening. "I'll leave it up to you to appoint your representative."

A voice that Alex thought might have been Lars Nielsen answered, "No need to wait, Ms. Cummings. Bjorn will speak for us." And Bjorn Sorensen walked over to stand beside Link.

Alex looked down at the Watsons and raised an eyebrow.

"Depends," Doc John said, "but one of us will try to attend. If we can't, we'll send Audrey." *Another McPherson!* Alex thought as she remembered the nurse.

Out loud she replied, "That's fine, John. For now, why don't both of you come forward." Then she looked out over the crowd and said, "For those who don't know them, Doctors John and Nancy Watson. The clinic will be one cave to the south. In charge of supply will be Hank Ferguson and, Al, are you there?" she asked, looking at her Vid.

"Yup! Just passing overhead."

"Al, I would like someone from the scientific community to be on the staff."

"Thought you might. We already talked about it and we selected Ann Turner. Ah—Ann doesn't know that yet so if you see a rather confused lady out there that's probably her."

Everyone who had been monitoring the conversation on their Vid laughed as a slightly flustered Ann Turner made her way to the staff group.

Next Alex pointed at the shuttle pilots, RJs and mechanics standing as a group on the fringe of the crowd. "I'll probably regret it but I need someone on the staff to represent you lot also." She almost laughed out loud as the group went into a huddle around Marshal and she saw him shaking his head vigorously no. Her husband hated meetings but she knew that if the shuttle group wanted him to represent them, he would give in. Sure enough a couple of minutes later Marshal was walking toward the staff group.

Alex then turned to Whitley Latham, an old-time lumberman from Oregon who was already setting up a water powered sawmill on the banks of Little River to speak for the lumber industries and Colonel McPherson for the artisans. That group would consist of machinists, woodcarvers, potters, wavers and blacksmiths.

While Latham and McPherson joined the group Alex went on. "I don't want the staff to get too big but I would like to appoint what I guess would be members at large. Individuals who don't represent a particular discipline or trade but whose advice I feel would be valuable. I'm sure that all of you are familiar with these two from their many adventures back on planet Earth. Grant and Maryanne Foster would you serve on the staff?"

The Fosters looked at each other in surprise and Grant answered, "Of course, if you think we can be useful. We'd be glad to do it."

"Good," Alex smiled. "Now for my last at-large

appointment I would like Mr. Ryan Lasseter to sit on the staff." At that announcement a wave of shocked surprise swept through the cavern. Even Lasseter was speechless. Alex went on. "Good. Very good. The first staff meeting will be tomorrow morning in my," and she nodded toward the packing crates, "office." As the colonists started to disperse, she said, "Remember we're all in this together. I expect everyone to find a job. If you have trouble deciding on where your interests lie," she waved to the staff, "these are the people to talk to."

As she jumped down from the rock, she saw a middle-aged couple who seemed a bit befuddled. Alex didn't remember ever meeting them. She thought that they were probably VU nominees who showed up at Sand Flea just before they departed Earth. "Hello," she said extending her hand. "Alex Cummings. I don't believe we've met."

The man who was of medium height, trim, very well groomed even after twenty years in cryogenic hibernation, replied, "Jordan Roberts, Ms. Cummings. My wife Roberta."

"Pleased to meet you and welcome to Sanctuary. If you will pardon me for saying so, you seem a bit confused."

The man answered, "Ah, yes ma'am…"

"Alex, please."

"Uh, Alex. Uh, thank you. We understand what you said about everyone working for the colony but we are already employed."

A more than slightly confused Alex Cummings asked, "Employed? What do you do?"

"I am a valet."

Alex blustered, "A valet, here on Sanctuary. Mr. Roberts, I can't imagine that anyone would require a valet here on Sanctuary. Who do you work for?"

Roberts answered, "Actually Ms. Cum—Alex, I work

for Mr. Lasseter."

Alex gave herself a shake. Lasseter. Of course, now it began to make sense. That jackass didn't just want to bring his tuxedos and his wife's evening gowns to Sanctuary he brought his valet as well. Trying hard to keep from laughing she said, "Well, Jordan, look around. As you can see just about everyone is wearing the same kind of one-piece jumpsuit that you and I have on. I don't think Mr. Lasseter will require the services of a valet here."

"But, Ms. Cummings," Jordan protested. "Mr. Lasseter paid for our relocation here. We have a contract with him."

"If Lasseter said he paid anything for passage on Voyager he lied. Voyagers were nominated and any contract you might have had with him is just like my contract with Visions Unlimited, ended. Money is worthless here and we don't think that we are going to have indentured servants. He has no money to pay you nor you to pay him back. I would say that your employment has ended and you're free to pursue any trade you desire."

Before her husband could protest further, Roberta Roberts, who had remained silent through the conversation, grinned and said, "Actually, Ms. Cummings, Jordan is quite an accomplished tailor."

That was some of the best news they could give her. "Excellent!" she said. "These flight suits are not going to last forever and we are going to need a clothing industry down the road." She looked around and spotted the Colonel just leaving the cavern. "Jordan, you see that gentleman there? The one that I said was going to speak for the artisans. That's Colonel McPherson. The lady walking with him is his wife, Joan; she's a weaver as well as a potter. I suggest that you go and talk to her."

Then Alex turned toward Roberta Roberts and asked, "Were you employed by the Lasseter's also?"

"Yes, I'm their—was their—cook." Roberta seemed all too happy for the past tense verbiage.

"Excellent again," beamed Alex. She took Roberta's arm and pointed her across the crowded cavern toward the food service area. "Do you see that tiny woman talking and waving her arms like a windmill?"

"Yes."

"That's Cathy Jackson. When you tell her you're a cook, you'll be busier than you could ever imagine for the rest of your life."

The Roberts looked at each other and then back at the people Alex had indicated. Without saying a word, they both gave a little smile. It was the kind shared between long established couples that registered an entire conversation in mere moments. Giving each other's hand a quick squeeze, they thanked Alex and went their separate ways to find their new bosses.

Smiling to herself on a job well done, Alex went about her own business wishing everything else would go off as smoothly.

Of course, when Lasseter found out that his domestic help had resigned, he was furious.

CHAPTER 15

Alex Cummings and John Marshal stood leaning against the side of Alex's brand-new desk looking out of the Great Cavern's opening at a beautiful day in May—or, month 2 as they called it here on Sanctuary. As Al had predicted it didn't rain all the time at Cliffside but like the rest of the planet the skies were almost always cloudy. But not this morning. This morning the sun was rising bright and clear over the great forest to the east of the farms. Two months, Alex thought, they had only been here on Sanctuary for two months and in that two-month period so much had happened to help the colony dig their roots into the planet.

With very little direction from her and the staff the colonists from Earth were making Sanctuary their home. Almost everyone had found a job. Stock brokers and clerks were becoming farmers, lumberjacks, weavers, even security officers. Some were still stubbornly refusing to adapt, insisting that they should return to Earth but their ranks were becoming fewer by the day.

The farms and the Great Berm, as they called it, that was eventually going to completely surround the farm, made of fallen trees and brush to protect the crops from the wandering herds, were visible even from here.

Almost every cave or cavern of any size was now occupied. Brian Anders had established his blacksmith shop in the cave nearest the swiftly moving waters of Little River. The next three caves housed the artisans as they called themselves, the woodworkers, weavers, potters, and machinists. Then came Hank Ferguson's supply storage area in the big cave that had formerly housed Big Daddy and his family.

On the other side of the Great Cavern the Docs had established their medical clinic and beyond them Evie Porter kept insisting that the walled off area at the back of the Great Cavern was unsuitable and wanted a cave for a real school. Even Alex had her eye on a cave that she could use for a conference room so the staff wouldn't have to stand around her desk for a meeting.

Along the river Whit Latham had his saw mill up and running. At the moment he was using a solar generator for power but he promised her that he would convert to water power as soon as the carpenters finished building his under-shot water wheel. She had told him that he could keep the generator but he was adamant that he was going to use Sanctuary power. And that went for the kiln he was constructing to dry the wood. No one else seemed to mind that the products coming out of the mill weren't completely dry but Whit felt bad that everything that they were currently building, walls, tables, benches, etc., was being built with green, uncured wood. Alex hadn't even tried to convince him that that wasn't quite true and that it was okay. She had just sighed and got out of the way.

Most of the wood that was being used were just logs anyway. Logs that were slowly building individual houses and walling in the entrances to the caves so heating and air conditioning could be installed.

But not in all the caves.

Brian the Blacksmith was leaving his open. Warm enough as it is, he said. Plus, he informed her, he was opening up two new forges. Alex had just shaken her head and smiled. That was the first she had heard of that advancement. Brian hadn't asked for permission—not that he needed to—hadn't asked for any help or additional resources, just went ahead and did it.

The Starduster cavern on the far southern end of the cliffs was also going to be left open. The Starduster shuttles had to be moved in and out and without a sliding hangar door walling up the entrance wouldn't have been practical.

On the other hand, the artisans, the weavers, the woodworkers, the machinists, wanted a climate-controlled work environment so those three caves would be closed in and heating and air conditioning installed.

Hank Ferguson was going half way for his supply cave. Just narrowing the entrance but leaving plenty of room to move supplies in and out.

Alex sighed again as she thought about walling in the Great Cavern. It had to be done of course. The Great Cavern was where the colony lived, where they ate and slept. They deserved to live in as comfortable an environment as possible. But she sighed again, not only would walling in the cavern be a monumental task but when it was completed, she would have lost the view from her desk and she loved to be able to look up from her work and look out over the great meadow toward the farm and the forest far to the east. Olga and the

Geek Squad had assured her that they could install a vid looking out to the east that would give her the same view right on her desktop. Alex sighed again, she knew that, but somehow it just wouldn't be the same.

As these thoughts flowed through her mind Alex was torn between enjoying the gorgeous sunrise and running her hands over the beautiful swirling pattern of the desk's grain. Alex smiled to herself as she admired the craftsmanship. Colonel McPherson and his cabinet makers had recreated out of wood her desk back at Sand Flea complete with retracting computer shelves. At the moment the desk was a flat surface but at the trip of a mechanical lever her computer screens would rise as if by magic. The computers, Vids and comms were the only electronic items. The desk itself was entirely handmade from wood and so beautifully polished. Every time she thought about it, she choked up. The entire colony had been in on its construction and installation and they had made it just for her.

John Marshal smiled. Everyone in the colony had been a participant in the great conspiracy, and it had worked. The desk had come as a complete surprise to Alex.

Yesterday Alex had planned to visit the farm and the farmers had gone all out to show off their progress and successes. They also made sure that she spent the whole day down at the farm while the colonel and his gang installed the desk.

So, Alex had spent yesterday at the farm looking at the buildings that were under construction, not just farm buildings either—a few cabins were also going up because many of the farm families planned to move out of the Great Cavern.

Alex took that as an encouraging sign that the colonists were beginning to think of themselves as

Sanctuarians and not just temporary visitors from Earth.

The farmers took great delight in showing off the rows and rows of greenhouses, well they weren't really greenhouses but long curved Quonset-like structures covered with whatever material the farmers could find. These rough structures would be replaced, they said, with metal tubing and cloth covers when Alex started taking Voyager's supply cylinder apart.

Alex smiled and said that it was all wonderful but inwardly she gave a small grimace, a lot of people had their eye on salvaging the supply cylinder. She hoped that there would be enough bits and pieces of the supply cylinder to go around.

Bjorn and his farmers were most enthusiastic about the various crops that they had under cultivation and their methods of cultivation.

"Ja Miz Cummings," Bjorn said, "it will be all natural here on Sanctuary. No pesticides. No chemical fertilizers. Permaculture they called it back on Earth. We will work with nature." Then he laughed. "Of course, first we have to figure out what nature is here. But you will see, Miz Cummings. Tomatoes the size of coconuts." He laughed again. "Don't you worry. Even with just our experimental crops here we'll produce enough vegetables to feed the colony for the winter."

Alex smiled. Said that that was wonderful and quietly hoped that it was true.

Then they had lunch and Alex was surprised again. They didn't go up to Cliffside, to the Great Cavern to the cafeteria. The farmers had built their own kitchen and dining hall. Sorenson laughed again. "A 'cook house' they called it back in the pioneer days, Good for meetings and movies and dances too."

That brought laughter and shouts of agreement from the farmers around him.

"Ja." Bjorn went on. "We draw some supplies from Miz Jackson and some we gather for ourselves. Miz Jackson even sent us a cook. Good cook."

Alex wondered who the good cook was when a smiling Roberta Roberts walked out of the kitchen wiping her hands on her apron. "Ms. Cummings," she said. "It's good to see you. I hope you enjoyed your meal."

A slightly flustered Alexandria Cummings said, "Yes. It was wonderful." Then she went on. "Ah, Roberta. When did all this happen?"

An obviously happy Roberta Roberts said, "Just the other day. Isn't it wonderful? Mr. Sorenson talked to Ms. Jackson and she asked me if I wanted the job. Just like running a big house, only much more fun and these young people are such good eaters!"

That brought a roar of laughter and a round of applause from all the farmers who had been listening.

Someone said, "She's a great cook Alex, we think we'll keep her."

That brought another roar of approval and Alex said, "Well of course. I wouldn't want a munity on my hands."

As the laughing crowd stacked their trays and started out the door Alex thought, this is wonderful, management 101. Find good people. Point them in the direction you want to go and get the hell out of the way. Then she gave a small grimace. But it would be kind of nice to know what's going on.

"Well Roberta, what does Jordan think about all this?"

"Oh, he thinks it's wonderful. In fact, he's going to move his shop down here and when we can we'll build a cabin."

Alex frowned. "Won't that be inconvenient for him? I

mean all the textiles and the looms are up in the caves."

Yes," she answered, "but he says that for the near future he's going to be working on establishing a tannery so he can make heavy gloves for the farmers and lumbermen. Most of the people working cutting down trees and working on the farm are all city people and some of their hands are getting terribly blistered. So, Jordan's going to make them gloves."

Don't try to get out in front Alex, she told herself, *just try to keep up.*

She asked, "What's he going to use for material?"

Roberta answered, "Leather."

"Leather? Does Jordan know how to tan leather?"

"No. Not yet. But Maryanne and Grant and a young fella named Bob Sullivan do, and they're going to teach him and a few others, too."

Alex decided that she was going to have a word with her staff. She wouldn't have disapproved of any of these marvelous endeavors indeed she would have eagerly embraced them but she would like to know what was going on.

She walked outside to find Bjorn Sorenson. "And what," she asked, " O Wizard of the East, are you going to dazzle me next?"

Sorenson was obviously enjoying himself. He had been told to keep Alex busy as long as possible but he was proud of his farmers achievements and overjoyed that Alex was finding them impressive.

"Animals," he said. "We are attempting to domesticate animals." He paused and smiled. "Well, so far, one animal." He went on to admit that the farmers had only captured one species that they hoped to domesticate and was a kind of a pig.

Alex was dubious about that and said so. Lincoln and his security team had described in great detail the encounter they'd had with a five-hundred-pound boar with tusks ten inches long. How could they hope to domesticate something like that?

No! No! Bjorn had insisted. Not a boar. They had captured a sow with a litter. They would raise the young ones and over time, many generations probably, Alex would have bacon for breakfast.

Alex had smiled and congratulated them, thinking that it was an encouraging sign that they were thinking in the long term and also for thinking that she would still be around to enjoy bacon after many generations.

It was late in the afternoon when she took her leave of the farm and the farmers after thanking them profusely for their hospitality and their accomplishments. Her head was spinning as she walked up the road that paralleled the river leading up to Cliffside (the river road the colonists had naturally named it) thinking of all she had learned that day. Well, she said to herself you told them to just get on with it and boy did they ever. She laughed and thought, I wonder what's going on in all the other sections of the colony?

As she walked up toward the Great Cavern, she saw that it was full of what could only be described as chattering happy people. He saw her husband sitting with the McPherson clan and they were all looking at her. Then she realized that everyone was looking at her. *What's going on?* she wondered. *Is my jumpsuit unzipped?*

She came closer and something, she never could explain what it was later, made her look over to the corner of the Great Cavern that she called her office, and there it was. An absolutely magnificent desk, that she later found out was walnut, was sitting where her packing crates had been. And not just the desk. Behind the desk was an executive chair with two matching chairs in front.

Alex was so surprised she stopped dead in her tracks and her mouth fell open.

That must have been the desired response because the entire cafeteria erupted into cheers and laughter. Alexandria Cummings, the boss, the leader of the colony, holder of many PhDs, an accomplished speaker and lecturer was speechless.

The Voyagers went wild.

Later Alex learned that the desk had been built and installed by Colonel McPherson and the wood carvers including, surprisingly, Ryan Lasseter. *A strange man*, Alex thought and not for the first time. Once he was convinced that the colony really would throw him out if he didn't contribute, he turned up at the Cabinet Cave as the wood workers were calling their work space, and announced that he was a cabinet maker and according to the Colonel a damn good one too. Seems that woodworking was his hobby back on Earth and according to the Colonel once he was involved in a wood working project he was as pleasant a co-worker as one could ask for. Very strange. Alex still didn't like or trust him so, while the Colonel and Lasseter were Alex and Ryan, with her it was Ms. Cummings and Mr. Lasseter.

Yes, she thought, yesterday had been quite a day.

Just as she and her husband were about to go their separate ways for the day's activities, Marshal looked up and exclaimed, "What the hell is that?"

Alex answered, "What the hell is what?"

Marshal pointed toward what they were now calling the river road, the cleared tract between the woods that bordered Little River and what would soon be fields of crops, and said, "What's that coming up the road?"

Alex looked again. At first, she just saw a group of men and women walking up the tract. She looked again—there was something odd there. It still took a couple of minutes to realize what her husband meant. It looked like the colonists walking up the road were carrying a log. A big log. No, she thought, they couldn't possibly be carrying it. That thing must weigh tons. But she couldn't deny what her eyes were seeing. There were two files of people walking and laughing and between them was a log.

Marshal exclaimed, "It's floating!"

Before Alex realized she was moving she was halfway across the stone shelf heading toward the group on the road with Marshal right beside her. The smiling laughing group of colonists saw them coming and stopped as Alex and John skidded to a halt in front of them. A completely flabbergasted Alex Cummings just stared at the dozen or so humans and the forty-foot log that seemed to float unsupported in their midst.

Before she could voice her astonishment Fred Thompson said, "Pretty neat uh boss?"

"Fred," she exclaimed, "what are you doing down here? I thought you were working on unloading the supply cylinder."

Fred replied, "Oh yeah, I am. Don't worry boss, that's all going along fine. But I had to come down to see if my brainchild here really worked." And he pointed to what looked like a small motor that was clamped to the underside of the log.

Marshal asked, "Anti-grav?"

"Yup! Got the idea from you. Same principle as Junior."

Marshal protested, "But Fred, the weight. Junior's a light weight. It could never lift something like this." And he waved to the log.

Thompson laughed. "True but you made Junior capable of doing other things like fly, hover, in addition to lifting things—all DAGM here has to do is push against gravity."

"DAGM?" Marshal asked.

"Dumb Anti-Gravity Machine." Everyone laughed and Marshal said, "It looks like you have two of your whatever's..."

"DAGMs," Fred said.

"DAGMs," Marshal repeated, "on here."

Thompson went on. "Yeah. We quickly found out that if you tried to use just one DAGM on something like this log it would slew around all over the place so we put one on each end and that seems to have worked out pretty well but as you can see, we still have to guide it or it would float off to who knows where. It's like one of those big balloons in the Macy's parade."

Marshal asked, "How many did you make?"

"Four. I cannibalized the two red-lined robot motors we had in R3 and used just about everything in the spare parts pile. So, I don't know if we can make any more."

Alex said, "Fred, this is wonderful." She paused, pointed to the log, and asked, "Are you taking it to the sawmill?"

"Yup."

Marshal asked, "Does Whit know you're coming?"

"Not a clue. Want to come along and watch?"

Alex and Marshal joined the group and Whitley Latham's reaction at the sight of the floating log made the trip well worthwhile.

Fred Thompson joined Alex and John on their walk back to the Great Cavern and the shuttle unloading area happy in the knowledge that his brain child worked but Alex knew he was anxious to get back to work in space. Not just to do his job but to get away from the colonists at Cliffside who were always asking where this item or that item was. Alex had decided long ago that it wasn't worthwhile to try to go digging around in the supply cylinder for specific items but to just take things as they came.

That made sense from an operational point of view but that didn't make the lumberjacks any happier sharing just one solar powered chain saw when they knew that there were two more in the supply cylinder. Alex snorted, Fred could get away into space but she had to stay here and answer the same questions. In fact, she reflected, the allocation of resources had become the biggest part of her job. She was the project director or maybe the mayor would be more accurate, but she didn't have to direct anyone. She didn't, in fact couldn't, begin to tell Bjorn Sorenson how to farm. Bjorn and the farmers knew that the colony had to grow its own crops to survive and they got on with it.

No, it was her job to preside over the staff meetings and to try to balance the competing requirements from dedicated people who were trying to do their best.

Her job was to set the priorities. What project was more important or given that they were all important which task had the more immediate impact on the colony. Of course, each member of the staff wanted to fight for their people so everyone insisted that their particular project should receive first consideration.

But they weren't fooling anyone. The job, whatever it was, was going to be accomplished. What they were really squabbling over was who got to use the modern equipment that was slowly coming down to Sanctuary from Voyager that would make the task easier.

The discussions were always serious but they were

always good natured too

When Alex decided that the chainsaw for the next five days of wood cutting would go to the craftsmen so they could build up a stockpile of lumber that would enable them get on with building the kitchen, the cafeteria, the infirmary and a dozen other projects, the farmers who wanted to use the chainsaw to create a berm of fallen trees around their fields to keep the big grazers out said fine we'll do it with hand axes. When they found out that there were no hand axes, they went to Brian Anders the blacksmith and so the man who back on Earth had earned tens of thousands of dollars creating high end medieval armor for wealthy roll players was turning out long handled axes.

Alex smiled to herself again. You couldn't go wrong with people with that kind of attitude.

CHAPTER 16

Alex was enjoying lingering over her last cup of coffee with her husband and friends before they broke up to pursue the day's activities. After almost three months living on Sanctuary, the colony was slowly abandoning the twenty-first century disciplines of office routine and settling into the mindset of an agrarian type society—up at dawn and work until dusk. With over four hundred people doing the exact same thing, the cafeteria of the Great Cavern was buzzing like a hive of bees before setting out on their daily chores. She picked up her coffee and she and Marshal headed to the cave mouth when they were startled by a shout from up on the cliffside.

"Mr. Lincoln! Mr. Lincoln!"

Link Lincoln and the small group of people that he was with all looked up at the shout to the observation platform that the colonists had carved out of the rocks high above the Great Cavern. The observation platform was really just a large ledge that had been improved and was there for two reasons: to post a lookout that could warn everyone if groups of large grazers had broken through the barriers that were being constructed around Cliffside and the farms away to the east. The second (and never officially mentioned) reason was to give the older teenagers a job. The platform was reached by a well-woven rope ladder that the teens had made themselves under the direction of Joan McPherson and Evie Porter. It was manned during daylight hours by older members of the Bug Brigade and they took the duty very seriously indeed.

"What is it, Jimmy?" Link called back.

"Mr. Lincoln, there are people out there in the field." And he pointed off to the south. Link and everyone else looked to the south but the field in question was screened by the Great Berm, the barrier of trees and other vegetation, and a belt of forest that began a couple hundred yards from where the rock shelf that fronted the cliffs ended.

Link looked at the people around him with an inquiring glance. For a moment no one said anything then Bjorn Sorenson kind of coughed and said, "Ah, yes, Chief. I guess I forgot to mention that."

"Mention what?"

"Stephen and Gregory were going down there this morning to see if that meadow would be suitable for planting something this winter or maybe next year."

Yes, Link thought sourly, and you conveniently forgot to tell me because you knew that I would insist that they had some of my security people along. He sighed to himself, it had been almost three months since they had settled here in the caves and cleaned out the last of the predators in the immediate area and with nothing but the big grazers to contend with it was becoming increasingly difficult to get people to take security seriously.

But he decided to not say anything, instead he shouted back up to Jimmy, "It's okay Jimmy! Just a couple of farmers checking out the meadow."

"No! No! Mr. Lincoln. There are a lot of people in the field. Funny looking people."

Bartholomew "Link" Lincoln might be a middle-aged former cop who was getting a little thick around the middle and would never see fifty again, but there was nothing wrong with his agility or reaction time as he swarmed up the rope ladder like a Barbary ape. Taking the binoculars from Jimmy he looked to the south and just as quickly climbed back down while Jimmy Paterson began whaling away on the alarm bell that Brian the Blacksmith had knocked together. Resembling an oversized cow bell, it was big and clunky and anything but musical but it sure made one hell of a racket.

Theoretically, every one of the colonists knew what to do when the bell sounded, get their weapons and stand by. Of course, and also theoretically, everyone was supposed to have their weapons close at hand wherever they were working. Those augmented to the security force were to report to Link or one of his two deputies, Andy McPherson or Jerry Smith, the kids were to stay in the classroom while everyone else went into the caves or to the cook house down at the farm, whichever was closer.

That's the way it was supposed to work and they had run drills to make sure the entire colony knew what to do. But this was the first time the alarm bell had ever sounded for real. The regulars on Link's security force were rapidly congregating, but he figured only about half of the augmentees were assembling and only about half of them had their weapons. Even worse, instead of taking shelter in the caverns most of the colonists were milling around on the stone apron in front of the cave. Link had also noticed as he looked through the binoculars that several of the farmers were making their way up the river road towards Cliffside and only half of them were armed. He was going to hold one hell of a meeting later, but right now he had to get the colony under control.

"All security personnel who have their weapons with me—everyone else, please, back into the caves." He looked at Sorenson. "Bjorn, can you turn your people around?"

He pulled out his com. "I don't think so. But I'll try."

Link looked back up to the ledge. "What do you see, Jimmy?"

"I think that the funny-looking people are coming toward us, Mr. Lincoln. They were just standing around in the field but when they heard the bell, they started looking our way."

"Okay, Jimmy. Thanks. Remember what I told you—stay down and stay quiet."

"Yes, sir."

Link and his deputies moved south toward the brush pile barrier where he surveyed the area again. Pointing to a bunch of security people he said quietly, "Andy, take that group about fifty yards down the barrier and spread them out."

McPherson nodded. "Right, Chief."

"Jerry, about twenty yards down. The rest of you right here. Spread out."

While Link had been taking charge of the situation and deploying his men Alex stood quietly by. Now she asked, "Link, what did you see?"

"What? Oh, Alex sorry. Didn't mean to cut you out of the picture."

Alex smiled. "Don't you worry about that. In an emergency you're in charge. Now what did you see?"

Lincoln scratched his head. "Ah well, as to that—I'm not sure. There are some creatures down there in the field. Ten of them. Never seen anything like them. They kind of look humanoid. I mean they are standing upright and have a head, a body, two arms and two legs. But they sure don't look human. Very tall and skinny. Proportions are all wrong. Arms and legs very long and head and body too small. They seemed to be naked—well it looks like they are not wearing any clothes except for a vest like thing... and they had spears."

Alex frowned but before she could say anything Sorenson asked, "Stephen and Gregory?"

"Sorry, Bjorn. I didn't see them. The grass is already about knee high down there so if they were down. . ." He trailed off, then asked, "Ah, Alex, what do you want to do now?"

Alex shrugged. "We'll try diplomacy first. If they're coming our way, I guess we'll just have to wait and see if we can talk to them."

Several voices rose in protest and Marshal quietly said, "Luv, I'm not sure that talking or reasoning with the... whatever they are... is possible. Remember the normal response of creatures on this planet and it looks like they may have already killed two of us."

Alex sighed and said, "I know, I know. But I think that we should try. I mean, if they have vests and spears, they should have some kind of society. Some kind of intelligence, cooperation." Alex stopped as everyone stared at her. "I mean, we should try. If we're going to share this planet we should try."

Marshal recognized the stubborn tone in her voice and didn't say anything but Link motioned to Kurt Jaeger and he moved to stand close to her.

Jimmy called, "Mr. Lincoln, they've gone into

the trees."

At least two dozen sets of binoculars were now trained on the edge of the woods a couple of hundred yards away when the creatures emerged. Lincoln's brief description had been pretty accurate. Tall and skinny, they looked like the stick men that kids draw. The creatures stopped at the edge of the woods and Link turned his head to see what they were looking at. He didn't think that they could see his men and women hidden down in the brush and trees that formed the barrier but when he looked behind him there were still twenty or thirty people milling around in front of the Great Cavern.

"Damn!" he spat and turned to Marshal. "John, do you think you could shoo those people inside?"

"I'll try Chief," and he jogged toward the milling Voyagers.

Then without saying anything Alex stepped up on the barrier and, holding her empty hands out wide, shouted, "Hello! Friends, we are friends!"

The response was immediate as one of the creatures whipped his arm back and then forward launching his spear straight at Alex. Jaeger lunged forward and swept her feet out from under her. They both fell heavily into the brush just as a spear whispered through the space that she had occupied a second before. Marshal let out a yell and jumped as the spear skidded along the rocks next to him and the people that he was going to talk to disappeared into the Great Cavern like a puff of smoke.

In that same instant there was a gunshot. The creature that had thrown the spear collapsed with a hole in its chest. Jerry Smith lowered his rifle.

So much for negotiations, Link thought bitterly and then pointed to the spear as he cut Alex off before she could speak. "Before you say anything you'll regret later, just remember if Kurt hadn't moved fast enough that thing would be sticking out of you. I know where you're coming from Alex. I'm a cop; serve and protect. My first inclination was to talk, too, but we can't always do that."

Alex just stared at him for a moment, her expression unreadable. "Can I say something now?"

Link nodded.

"Good. What I was going to say was thank you. And especially to you, Kurt. It was a really dumb move."

Link snorted in agreement, but he understood where she was coming from. "You're a passionate woman who hates conflict and I agree. The first possibly intelligent species we meet and we're already at war."

"I know," Alex said sadly. "It's not our fault. Not your fault. They struck first and we were defending ourselves, but still…" She trailed off and sighed. "Can I get up now?"

"Sorry, boss," Jaeger said as he and Link reached down to help her up. "I hope I didn't hurt you."

"I'll live and it hurts a lot less than that spear would have. What's happening?"

Ty West answered her. "There are still nine of those things out there and each one has a spear. They're still confused. They heard a noise, maybe they thought it was thunder, and one of them dropped, probably dead. They're probably still trying to process that."

"I think they've processed," Smith said. "They're looking our way again. What the hell? I hit that critter square in the chest and it's getting up!"

The colonists stared at the seemingly impossible scene. To those with binoculars the hole in the creature's chest was clearly visible but with just a little assist from its comrades it was standing up and moving. The humans heard some kind of clicking and whistling sounds coming from them.

The one Jerry had shot reached for another spear, but before the creature could throw it, Jerry Smith fired again, this time hitting the creature in the head.

The creature went down again but this time it stayed down.

The other creatures were jumping around, alternately trying to raise the one that was down and making threatening gestures toward the humans. Their indecision didn't last long, however and they resumed their advance towards the humans.

"Damn!" said Link. "I hate to just shoot them." He thought for a minute and said, "Andy, Jerry, have your people hold their fire. My section, when I give the command fire one round—one round only—over their heads. Let's see if we can get them to stop and think about this."

Alex quietly said, "Thank you, Link," but Link thought that she hadn't realized that she said it out loud.

The creatures were still a hundred yards away and walking slowly toward them. Looking through his binoculars Jerry Smith said, "Wedges, Wedgies."

"What?" Someone asked.

"Their heads and bodies look like two inverted triangles, wedges, stacked on top of each other with stick arms and legs sticking out."

That brought a general chuckle but the name Wedgies stuck.

The Wedgies kept on walking.

"Damn!" Link said again. "Okay. My section, one round—fire!"

A long rolling *bammmm* echoed along the cliff face.

The Wedgies stopped. But instead of staying stopped the noise seemed to have the opposite effect. The natives clearly heard the noise and looked around at each other.

Realizing that none of them had mysteriously died, maybe they figured that they had conquered the noise. Giving a high-pitched clicking whistle shout, they launched their spears. Fortunately, everyone was burrowed into the barrier or safely inside the caves and the spears passed harmlessly overhead to clatter onto the rocks.

Then the Wedgies started running toward the colonists.

"Damn!" Link said for the third time.

Alex softly said, "Do what you have to do, Chief."

Lincoln shut his eyes before giving the order he dreaded. "Okay, people; pick a target."

But before he could give the order to fire a War Whoop split the air as a construction robot flew out of the maintenance cave, over the humans crouched behind the barrier and right at the natives. Alex looked up. What the... she thought then laughed as she realized that it was John, her wacky, goofy husband, in Junior.

That did it. The Wedgies could process strange creatures that they had never seen before, mysterious noises that came out of nowhere, even one of their members suddenly dropping dead with its head blown apart apparently from nothing, but strange creatures flying through the air in a bubble was one magical event too many. To the cheers of the humans the Wedgies turned as one and fled back toward the trees.

Link called, "What do you see, Jimmy?"

"Nothing yet, Mr. Lincoln. Wait! They're just coming out of the trees." He whooped, "Mr. Marshal and a couple of drones are right behind them! They're crossing the field. They're gone sir, into the trees."

"Good job, Jimmy. Now just keep an eye on the edge of the meadow."

"Yes sir."

"John," Link said into his comm, "can you see anything?"

Marshal answered, "Nah! Trees are too thick. They hit the trees and disappeared."

"Can we help, Mr. Marshal?" A new voice crackled over the comm.

"What? Is that you Olga?"

"Yes, sir. With three drones. We followed you across the field. What would you like us to do?"

"Excellent!" Marshal looked to his right and left and saw three drones spread out around him. "Umm, let me think. What have you got?"

"Visual and infra-red."

"Okay! Good. When they went into the trees, they were heading kind of southwest," and he pointed with one of Junior's arms, "that way. Why don't you spread out and see if you can see anything moving or see if you can pick up anything on the IR? But don't go too far and if you do see them don't get too close, one of those spears could knock down one of your drones in a heartbeat."

"Yes, sir. Got it." Olga said as the three drones fanned out over the dense woods.

Alex had remained quiet during the exchange; now she asked, "John, can you see our two farmers?"

Marshal turned Junior and flew slowly over the field. It only took a minute to spot the two bodies. "Ah, yes, Luv. They're both down. Not moving. I'll land and check."

"You be careful!" Alex said at the same time Lincoln chimed in, "Those creatures might still be around, John. Maybe you had better wait until we get down there."

"Where are you?"

Alex answered, "We're just walking up on the

downed creature."

"Okay, I'll wait."

As Alex, Link, the two docs and the rest of the security team got closer and could see the creature clearly the humans realized that they were looking at something completely unknown. The plants and animals that they had encountered so far on Sanctuary might be slightly different than similar species on Earth but they were similar. This creature was totally alien. As they had observed through the binoculars it was exceedingly tall, Alex estimated it at least seven and a half feet, maybe eight, and very thin. The long, skinny arms and legs did remind her of the stick drawings that children made, just thin appendages stuck on at the shoulders and hips. As Jerry Smith had observed the head and body were like two inverted triangles, or wedges, stuck one on top of the other. The top of the head, what was left of it, was flat and covered not with hair or fur but with what looked like a kind of mossy substance that also grew down the sides of the face. The two forward facing eyes were barely horizontal slits and the nose did not protrude but consisted of two vertical gashes in the face, almost like a 'V'. If the creature had ears, they were not visible.

But the most bizarre feature of the creature's face was the lipless mouth that was full of what looked to be very human-like teeth.

Except for the vest-like garment that the Wedgie was wearing the creature was completely naked and most obviously male. The muscles of the long thin arms and legs were like ropes or vines and the four fingered hands (three fingers and a thumb) were long and thin like the twigs at the end of a tree branch. The legs were very long in proportion to the body, probably accounting for two thirds of the Wedgies total height. And as if all of that wasn't weird enough the most striking features were the creature's skin and blood. Alex shook her head. What covered the creature's body probably acted like skin but it looked and felt (when she steeled herself to touch it) more like a parchment or like the bark of a birch tree and the substance that oozed out the wounds where Jerry's bullets had penetrated was not red but a yellowish color. Well, Alex corrected herself, the substance oozed out the chest wound but the top of the triangular head was completely shattered.

Link looked at the two doctors and asked, "What do you think?"

Doc John snorted and Nancy replied, "Are you serious? John and I don't know any more about this critter than you do." Doc John looked at Alex and said, "Well, boss, we'll take it back to the dispensary and see what we can find out."

Alex patted him on the arm and smiled at Nancy. "I know you will." She paused. "And would you please look after our two farmers too?"

Nancy grimaced. "Sorry, Alex. Should have thought of that." She turned. "Mike, would you see to recovering them please?"

"Sure, doc." Mike Bennet waved to the half dozen students of the medical college that had trailed wide eyed behind. "Let's go."

West spoke up. "Ah doc, Alex, before you take whatever it is away, I'd like to have the vest and the other stuff to take up to Wisdom. See what we can determine from the garment, the weapons and whatever it has in its pockets."

Alex said, "Of course, Ty. I should have thought of that myself."

Marshal's voice came over the com. "Link, Alex, where are you? I could use some help down here."

Link answered, "What's up?"

"What's up is that I landed when I saw people coming through the trees and now, I have a dozen very pissed off farmers down here who seem determined to take off into the woods after the whatever-they-weres."

"No, John, don't let them do that." Lincoln said.

"I agree but I don't know how much longer they will listen to me."

Alex said, "We're coming, my sweet, hang on."

While they were talking Link had motioned to his deputies and a half dozen of them led by McPherson and Smith had already disappeared into the woods. Alex and Link followed at a trot and by the time they broke into the field and spotted the grounded robot the situation was pretty much under control. The farmers weren't happy but they all respected and trusted Alex especially when she explained that once they had a chance to examine the—she gave a fleeting smile—the Wedgie, a fully equipped expedition would be mounted.

While Alex got everyone moving back toward the caves, Link, Marshal and the deputies hung back. Andy McPherson said, "Chief, why don't Jerry and I go take a look? At least we can make sure that they, whatever they are, are still running and not regrouping to come back at us. John and Olga can give us some top cover."

Link nodded and while McPherson and Smith disappeared into the trees and the various robots spread out over the forest, he informed Alex what steps he had taken.

Alex walked up to the crowd of nervous, anxious colonists that was milling around in front of the Great Cavern and as soon as they became aware of her presence a hush fell over them. Alex smiled to herself, *they trust me to know what's going on and what's best for the colony and I don't know any more than they do. Well as my sweety always says never let on. Bold front and all that.*

She found a crate of freeze dry that was waiting to be moved into storage, climbed up on it and looked out at a couple hundred anxious faces.

"Before rumors get out of hand let me reassure you that the creatures, whatever they are, have gone. Yes, we were attacked, unprovoked and without warning, and two of our number were killed and while we attempted to make peaceful contact with them, they attacked again and in self-defense we were forced to kill one of them. At the moment we have no idea exactly what these creatures are. While they appear humanoid, they are definitely not human. They seem to have some level of group organization and intelligence but until we learn more, I can't tell you much more than that."

She went on. "After the confrontation the creatures disappeared back into the trees. Chief Lincoln has a scout force pursuing them through the forest south of here at this moment. Our medical team is examining the body of the creature we killed and Dr. West has taken the physical artifacts up to Wisdom to see what can be learned from them.

"Hopefully by tomorrow we'll know more so I would like Chief Lincoln, the Doctors Watson and the scientists up in Wisdom to be ready to give a report to the staff at say 1000 tomorrow morning. Thank you and please try to be patient."

Alex jumped down from the box and the crowd slowly started to disperse into smaller groups. The anxiety was high as they hung together for mutual reassurance and support.

CHAPTER 17

Alex looked around the Conference Cave that she had selected to be the staff meeting room. She looked down the long table that the cabinet makers had knocked together (much to their embarrassment and with promises that a real conference table would be forthcoming) at the anxious faces of her staff. She glanced up at the Vid screen that showed the same faces. The same picture that several hundred very nervous colonists were watching on the two big screens in the Great Cavern and on the single screen down in the farm's cook house. The benches along both sides of the council cave behind the staff members were full and several dozen colonists were clustered around the cave entrance.

She doubted that anyone had gotten much sleep last night with the startling revelation that not only were they not alone on Sanctuary, but that the natives were definitely unfriendly. *Well, better get on with it,* she thought but before she could speak Ryan Lasseter made his usual demand that in light of these new developments the colony should be abandoned and the Earthlings should return to Earth.

However, this time his demand didn't engender the scorn that it usually provoked. The Wedgies had changed the dynamic. There was a pause before several staff members started to answer but Alex wasn't about to let the meeting be deflected from its original purpose. Before anyone could speak, she rapped smartly on the table.

"Please, ladies and gentlemen," she said. "Before we go off on many tangents let's listen to the reports from the security, scientific and medical communities so we all at least have a common understanding of what facts we have and we can determine the way forward based on knowledge and not rumor and speculation."

She looked at Olga Sorenson who was sitting on the bench behind Chief Lincoln. "Olga, is Wisdom in communications range?"

"Not for a few minutes, Ma'am," Olga answered.

"Alright." Alex turned to the doctors. "Medical?"

Doc Nancy walked over to the Vid screen and replaced the staff's faces with the body of the dead Wedgie. Using a laser pointer and being aware that practically the entire colony had watched all or at least part of the examination of the Wedgie on the Vid she quickly reviewed the creature's anatomy and general features. Then she gave a half smile and shook her head and said, "From a medical point of view John and I are fishing in unknown waters here. Up to now the animals that we have encountered here on Sanctuary have had at least some semblance to Earth animals but this creature is completely out of our experience."

She paused and gave her head a little shake as if she was reluctant to go on. She looked at Alex and continued. "The creature seems to combine the features of a mammal like ourselves with the characteristics of a... well, a tree."

That revelation brought a gasp from the watching colonists.

Nancy went on. "I know that's hard to digest but as you can see the creature is humanoid, two arms, two legs, head, etc. It has a digestive system and judging by its teeth and the contents of its stomach, like us, it's an omnivore but from there..." she trailed off before continuing.

"When we examined the creature's head, we found that the 'Wedgie' has two forward looking eyes located pretty much where our eyes are but we can't determine how keen its vision is or exactly what portion of the light spectrum it perceives. As many of you have noticed and more than a few have commented on," she used her laser pointer and that brought a laugh, "the creature is male. John and I can only surmise that they reproduce the same way all mammals do."

Her comments brought a chuckle from the listeners and Nancy smiled with them. "I mentioned those things first because they are more or less the mammalian features that we, humans and Wedgies, have in common. From here on we are in alien territory."

That half pun brought a small laugh.

"If it has ears, we haven't found them but judging from its reaction to the warning bell it must be able to hear. We have no idea what the V shaped slit in the middle of the face, where our nose would be, is for. What we are sure of is that it's not for breathing—the creature has no lungs. It seems to have some kind of circulatory system but it has no heart we're not sure how the blood, or more accurately that sap-like substance, is moved about the body. The absence of most internal organs probably accounts for the fact that Jerry's first shot had so little effect. We can only guess that it would be like shooting a tree. The Wedgie has no bones but the rope-like muscles that wind throughout its body are incredibly dense and tough, and the outer covering where our skin would be seems to be more like the bark of a birch tree."

Nancy turned toward Alex. "I'm sorry, Alex, I'm sure you have a million questions but it will probably be years before we have any answers."

Alex thanked her and said, "A tree-like mammal that can communicate. At least I think it can communicate. We did hear them making some kind of odd click, it sounded like they were whistling noises at each other."

She gave her head a shake. "Al, are you there?"

Instead of Al Wilson, from three-hundred miles overhead Ty West answered, "Yes, we're here."

Alex asked, "did you hear Nancy's presentation?"

"Yes. Most of it anyway."

"So, what can you tell us about our Wedgies?"

West pointed to the artifacts that were anchored to a work bench. "Well, our best guess is that the Wedgies would fall into what we would call late Stone Age back on Earth. The vest that the creature was wearing is made from a partially tanned animal hide—probably some kind of deer—cut with a sharpened stone, or flint, and sewn together with animal sinew. The vest has a pouch pocket that contains flints that as far as we can tell are both for tools and for fire starting. There were also two bone needles, a couple of spare flint points for their short spears and some strips of singed meat, a kind of crude jerky. The short spears, javelins I guess we could call them, are made from straight shafts of some kind of incredibly hard wood that we are not familiar with. The wooden tips of the javelins are grooved to hold the flint points and the points are tied on with animal sinew. The carrying case for the javelins, the quiver, is put together the same way as the vest with a strap added so it could be carried over the shoulder."

West walked to the end of the bench and picked up what looked to be just a stick and went on. "But probably the most interesting item is this," and he held up the stick. A shaft of wood the watchers could now see had a long groove cut into it and a strip of material attached to one end. "This is a throwing stick. Its purpose is to increase the distance and velocity of the spear. The way it works is that you fit the javelin into the groove here and throwing with an overhand motion you could probably launch one of these javelins over two hundred yards with accuracy."

Alex and Lincoln grimaced as they remembered the javelin just missing Alex.

"So," West went on, "the Wedgies seem to have fire but no metal. They have progressed to the making of vests and quivers to carry their tools but apparently not clothing. Maybe trees don't require clothing. They have spears and the throwing stick but they are probably not to the bow and arrow stage. As far as social organization goes, and we're just guessing here, if these Wedgies we encountered were all young males they probably belong to a clan or a tribe rather than just a family. Again, that's just a guess."

Lincoln asked, "From what you said, Ty, would we expect to find a village somewhere?"

West hesitated. "Well if we were talking about Earth, I would say yes but we've flown all over the area around Cliffside, all over Sanctuary for that matter, and we've never seen a sign of a village or any habitation. Not even a fire at night."

Alex frowned. That was certainly true. She thanked West and the rest of the scientists and turned back to the conference table.

"Chief Lincoln?" she asked.

Link turned toward the people sitting behind him and

said, "If you don't mind, Alex, I'll let Andy speak on the security aspect."

"Of course. Captain?"

Andy McPherson stepped up to the Vid screen and the scene changed to handheld Vid shots of a forest and overhead views of a forest canopy. "Ms. Cummings, ladies and gentlemen, as soon as Jerry and I arrived at the scene of the Wedgie attack and we determined that the area was secure from immediate threat we entered the forest to see if we could track the Wedgies. John Marshal and the Geek Squad provided top cover. I'm sorry to report that we had no success in tracking the Wedgies on the ground or from the air."

That pronouncement caused a stir around the conference table and Colonel McPherson asked, "Nothing?"

"Nothing, Dad. John had marked the spot where the Wedgies entered the forest and the direction they were headed. We followed that general direction for more than an hour and we saw no sign of them, not even a broken leaf." He nodded toward Marshal. "John?"

Marshal said, "I followed Andy and Jerry from above the trees, the tree cover was too dense for Junior or even the drones to get below the canopy. Like Andy said, we went on for about an hour and finally gave it up. The Wedgies could have been miles ahead of us or gone off in any direction."

"Or just stopped." Smith added, "Hell! Looking at the body the Docs have if they just stopped and stood still Andy and I could have walked right past them."

That caused another stir around the table.

Invisible Wedgies.

"Not invisible," Andy told them. "Just incredibly in tune with their environment. But we don't believe that that's what happened—that they stopped. We're confident that the Wedgies kept on going, wherever they went."

While everyone was trying to digest that piece of information Marshal said, "There's one more thing. Olga?"

A very nervous Olga Sorenson stood up and said, "Ms. Cummings, they didn't register on infra-red,"

"Are you sure?" Alex asked.

"Pretty sure, Ma'am." Olga answered. "Two of the drones were fitted with infra-red and we were right behind the Wedgies when they were running across the field toward the forest but the only heat signatures we recorded were the two bodies lying in the grass."

Before poor Olga could be bombarded with questions John Watson chimed in. "I'm not surprised. I don't think that they would register on infra-red any more than a tree would."

Doc's last pronouncement seemed to break the dam and everyone was talking at once with a dozen or more ideas on the way forward. Everything from Lasseter's let's pack up and leave to arm everyone and go wipe them out.

The "let's leave now" people pretty much quieted down when Marshal asked if twenty-first century Earthmen were going to let themselves be kicked off the planet by a couple of spear-chucking Neanderthals. The other extreme of "let's go wipe them out" ran out of things to say when Jerry Smith said that he thought it was a great idea but shouldn't they know where they were going first if they wanted to find the Wedgies and wipe them out.

The same arguments were rolling around the crowd outside the council cave and in the other gathering places. Alex let it go on for over an hour before she called the staff to order. That call rippled out through the Great Cavern, the cook house and the watchers outside the Council Cavern. That was the kind of respect that Alexandria Cummings commanded. As one the colonists quieted and turned their attention toward Alex.

For most of the time that the debate, if one could call a shouting match a debate, had been going on Alex had been silent just sitting listening with her fingers steepled under her chin. When things had more or less quieted down, she said. "Correct me if I'm wrong but if I have heard you all correctly the consensus seems to be that we are certainly not going to abandon Sanctuary but we do need to take steps to protect ourselves."

That brought nods from those seated around the table and a murmur of agreement from those gathered outside the cave and she assumed from those gathered in the Great Cavern and the cook house as well. Then she smiled and said, "Okay, Chief, I'm sure that since yesterday you and your merry men," she gestured toward McPherson and Smith and toward Kurt Jaeger and Linda Murphy who were all clustered behind Lincoln, "and woman," she added with a smile, "have spent the last twenty-four hours giving this some serious thought."

Link smiled and said, "We have, Alex." He said it with a straight face too Marshal thought. Just as if he and Link and Alex and a half dozen other security people hadn't been up half the night deciding on a way forward.

Link went on. "Since yesterday and now knowing what to look for, we have run two full sweeps around Cliffside and the farm and I am confident that there are no Wedgies in our area. "

That brought a nervous murmur from the colonists.

Lincoln went on. "From a security standpoint the best advice I can give everyone is to carry on doing what we have been doing—but," he paused looking sternly around, "carry on taking security more seriously. Every adult was issued a weapon when you landed on Sanctuary. I urge you again to become familiar with your weapon and keep it close at hand. We have a gun shop set up down in the shuttle cavern so anyone who has any questions on the care and maintenance of your weapon come on down and see us."

That's all Lincoln said on that subject but there were a lot of shamefaced people both inside and outside the cave who had poo pooed the Chief's calls to always carry their weapons and be constantly aware of their surroundings.

Link looked at Alex and continued. "I would also like to recommend that we make some changes in our security force."

Marshal had a hard time keeping a straight face himself when Alex innocently asked what he had in mind.

"First, I think that we should expand our security force. At the present time I have two dozen deputies. I would like permission to recruit ten or twelve more. The reason I would like more deputies is that in light of yesterday's events I would like to double our routine patrols and push them out further from the colony and I recommend that we maintain a permanent watch on the top of the cliff above the caves. Finally, I plan to create a sub group within the security force— call them 'the scouts'."

Right on cue Colonel McPherson asked, "What would the role of the scouts be?"

"Long range patrol, Colonel. To go out beyond the forty, fifty miles that we normally cover and see what's out there. Also, to respond to emergencies like the one we are currently facing."

Alex looked around the table at her staff who seemed to be pretty much in agreement and said, "First of all, Chief, I think that how you organize the security forces is your preview. I don't think that you need permission from this council to establish your scouts." She looked around the table again and asked, "Does anyone have any objections to expanding the security force?"

No one did and Whit Latham chuckled and said, "Hell Alex, I don't remember that we ever set a number on the number of deputies in the first place."

That brought a general chuckle and Alex asked, "So, Chief, who are our scouts?"

Link pointed his thumb over his shoulder. "Andy and Jerry. I know they are my two senior deputies but I have two solid replacements in Kurt and Murph and yes there are other possible candidates for the scouts but at the moment they have other important jobs. Your sweetie for one." And he paused as everyone looked at a suddenly very embarrassed John Marshal.

"For those who didn't know," Link continued, "John was a Ranger in the Army—a scout and a sniper who has already been on more than one mission for Voyager."

"He's pretty good, too," Jerry added.

Link agreed. "But I think the colony would benefit more if we left him with Junior and the shuttles. Another candidate would be our combat medic, Mike Bennet. But," he held up a hand before the two doctors could self-combust, "I wouldn't even mention it knowing that when John and Nancy got through with me, I would need a medic myself. So, we will start our scout force with one two-man team"

"And," Alex asked, "I presume you have a mission in mind for our scouts?"

"I do. I propose that we send them after the Wedgies."

That brought a growl of approval from both inside and outside of the council chamber.

The next morning a huge crowd gathered in front of the Starduster Cavern to see the colony's first scout expedition on its way. Davy Crocket might have just walked off into the wilderness with his trusty rifle and what he could carry but the colony was determined that its scouts were going to have the advantage of every scrap of modern technology that was available. A full support team was on hand. The scouts would cover the first fifty miles in Dusty 1 with Junior tucked up in the cargo bay and a wildly excited Geek Squad and their drones on board.

Mike Bennet was also on board with a full medical kit. Audrey McPherson wasn't happy about her husband going off into the wilderness for who knew how long and had briefly considered joining the expedition in the medical role but with two young children and her duties in the clinic common sense prevailed.

Common sense was nowhere to be seen in her young son Peter. He begged, pleaded to come along, even tried to sneak aboard Dusty. His parents and Jerry Smith were convinced that if the expedition had left on foot young Peter would have followed. He had done it before.

Andy and Jerry didn't say much about all the fuss being made over this first scouting mission; they had been patrolling around Cliffside for months. They just said their goodbyes and got aboard the shuttle.

Ben Riley flew the shuttle fifty-seven miles south west of Cliffside to the clearing that they had selected as the place to start the scout. In a well-rehearsed drill practiced many times on Sanctuary Riley landed and, after waiting a few minutes to see if anything was going to attack, Linda Murphy and three deputies deployed around the shuttle while everyone waited again. When nothing big, mean and nasty or even little, mean and nasty charged out of the woods Marshal climbed up Dusty's side and lifted off in Junior. This time he was followed up the side of the shuttle by the Geek Squad Olga, Kevin and Bobby with their drones.

The Geeks may have been excited about being part of

the expedition and being so far from Cliffside for the first time but that didn't dampen their professionalism. They quickly and efficiently set up their control station on top of Dusty and the three drones spread out over the trees with Marshal and Junior following along behind.

Without any fanfare McPherson and Smith shouldered their packs and plunged into the forest. They hadn't said anything about all this support back at Cliffside but they had their doubts about how much use it would actually be. In their opinion, shuttles moving in and out in their immediate vicinity and drones and robots flying around overhead would only scare off the Wedgies they were trying to find. Marshal pretty much agreed with them and hung back with Junior.

McPherson and Smith took their time moving slowly through the fairly open undergrowth under the big trees, always keeping alert for any sign of Wedgies and any predators whose path they might cross. The scouts were in their element and the day passed quickly as they made their slow methodical way.

The same couldn't be said for the Geeks who were becoming increasingly frustrated at their inability to get down below the leafy canopy and the fact their sensors continued to register nothing. Marshal hung back with Junior and kept silent.

As dusk started to settle Marshal called the drones back to the clearing and everyone waited for McPherson and Smith to call in to be picked up for the night. Marshal smiled to himself 100% sure that wasn't going to happen. He put Junior away in the cargo bay, climbed down and slid into the copilot's seat and went to sleep.

The Geeks and some of the security team wanted to call the scouts but that was absolutely forbidden. The last thing the scouts needed was a Vid ringing when they were hiding from a predator.

It was full dark when Andy and Jerry finally called but instead of requesting a pick-up for the night, they said that they were comfortable in a tree and for everyone to go home and have a good night.

Riley lifted the shuttle and looked at Marshal. "You knew that didn't you. They don't want any help do they?"

"Nope." Marshal replied. "Well maybe a resupply every five or six days or so."

The crowd gathered around the Starduster Cavern was disappointed when the shuttle landed and the scouts weren't on board and Olga wasn't surprised when Marshal told her that the shuttle probably wouldn't be going out again tomorrow. The scouts were on their own. If they wanted help or additional support, they would ask for it.

That was the message that Alex passed to the staff the next morning. She knew that everyone was concerned and wanted to help but she reminded them that out there was the scouts world and it would probably be best to let them proceed at their own pace.

The staff accepted that and more or less the colony did also. Marshal smiled when he thought that most of the colony would probably be terrified at the thought of being on their own at night in the forest.

It was three weeks later on a Sunday afternoon when Andy and Jerry drifted into the Starduster Cavern. After Alex and the staff had been quietly summoned and before the news of their return became general knowledge, the scouts made their first report.

After leaving the shuttle in the clearing they proceeded toward the southwest. Progress was slow because they kept looking for the robot and the drones. They didn't think that either one would aid the mission but they were willing to give them a chance but the trees were so close together that neither platform was able to penetrate below the leafy canopy. In fact, they reported they only caught sight of the drones a couple of times and they never did see the robot.

That part of the forest consisted of mostly fir and pine with practically no underbrush. With so little vegetation available, game was sparse and there were few predators.

After six and a half days steadily moving to the south west they reached Big River, they figured about a hundred miles as the crow flies from Cliffside. In that time, they had seen no sign of the Wedgies. That was when they called in to Alex and it was decided that rather than keep on going upriver, they would turn east and follow the river downstream until they were opposite Cliffside then turn north.

Everyone including Marshal looked at Alex. That was the first time that anyone including Marshal had heard of that Vid conversation.

The scouts went on describing the terrain, vegetation and animals they encountered along the way. What they had seen was not remarkably different from what they normally encountered around Cliffside.

Andy and Jerry had reconnoitered a huge triangle a hundred miles on a side but the bottom line was that they hadn't encountered any Wedgies or any sign of them.

Gradually over the next days and weeks the colonists put the thought of Wedgies behind them and the life of the colony went on.

CHAPTER 18

Bob Sullivan stepped back and watched the tree fall onto the great pile of brush that they were calling the berm. It was just a ring of downed trees, brush and anything else that the colonists could lay their hands on to make a circle of brush around the fields where the crops were planted. A natural barrier to keep the larger grazing animals away from the crops and so far, it seemed to be working. Sullivan looked at the tree he had just felled, almost perfect he thought. There was a knack to cutting trees to make them fall exactly where you wanted them but he was learning. He looked down at his blistered hands. *Getting better,* he thought then he smiled to himself. *You're getting soft since your days on the ranch, Bob.*

Swinging an ax was a lot different from punching cattle but the leather gloves that Mr. Roberts had given him sure did help a lot. He smiled again. Uncle Henry would have liked Mr. Roberts.

He had no way of knowing but at that moment a couple of miles away, sitting in her office in the Great Cavern, Alexandria Cummings was thinking about young Bob Sullivan. She liked Sullivan. Once Jordan Roberts had decided to make gloves for the lumberjacks and farmers Sullivan worked overtime to help the Fosters get the tannery up and running and once it was, he picked up his ax and went back to cutting trees. Now,on her desk, hand written on a half sheet of paper, was a letter signed by Sullivan. A proposal that the colony send an expedition out onto the prairie to establish a ranch and capture horses. Alex smiled as she reread it. It wasn't even really a proposal; it was more like just a thought. The colony needs horses, the note said. Sullivan hadn't said why the colony needed horses or where these horses were or how a ranch could be established out on the prairie or how the horses were to be captured, trained or even transported. Just that the colony needed horses and presumably Bob Sullivan was just the man to get them.

But she wasn't necessarily against the idea and she knew a lot about Bob Sullivan. One day about a year before they left Earth Sullivan had turned up at the Project Voyager hangars asking for a job. His arrival wasn't completely unexpected. Sarah Williams had asked her mother Martha if she would ask Alex to give him a job. And how, her mother had asked, did Sarah know Bob Sullivan? So, Sarah had to explain that Sullivan worked at the stables where she kept her horse and that he knew all about horses and that he took special care of Rosebud and that they had gone riding a few times together and that she thought that he was just wonderful. Martha had gone out to the stables, met Sullivan and was suitably impressed.

It was hard not to like Bob Sullivan but Martha Williams wasn't about to let her only daughter be charmed by just anyone. So, she did a little quiet checking mostly by just listening while Sarah, Bob and their friends sat around the campfire at the stables and talked. Bob Sullivan had packed a lot of living into his twenty-four years and he wasn't at all shy about telling his life story.

He had been born on a ranch just east of Santa Fe, New Mexico the youngest of five children, all boys. The ranch was called the Flying S and had been in the family for almost two-hundred years and was run by his father and his two uncles. His mother died when he was only four and his dad never remarried. His two uncles were both bachelors so Sullivan chuckled, it was just us guys. He said that he rode his horse to school every day and by the time he was in his teens he was training horses to the saddle in the family corral.

He admitted that he was restless on the ranch and soon after graduating from high school he hit the rodeo circuit riding bucking broncos at county fairs all over the southwest.

Someone asked him why he quit and he admitted that at a county fair in Abilene he had gotten too cocky and had been thrown and stomped and broke his leg. He went back to the family ranch to heal and that's when he went to work for Uncle Henry in the saddle shop. But when he was healed, he went back on the circuit but this time it was different. The bunch of cowboys he fell in with were older, rougher, drank a lot and after he got accidently involved in a brawl with a bunch of oil riggers just outside Odessa, Texas he gave up the circuit.

He still wasn't ready to go home so he just kept drifting west from ranch to ranch, stable to stable until he ended up at Sand Flea. "And," as he finished his story he took Sarah's hand, "here's where I met Sarah."

That drew good natured "Oohs" and "Uggs" from their friends but Martha Williams gave a contented smile. Bob

Sullivan might not be the smartest most handsome man you could hope to find but he seemed like a decent man and looking at his background he could have turned out so different and he was obviously in love with Sarah.

Of course, Martha had passed all that along to Alex.

When Sullivan finally turned up Alex had played it straight and asked him what his qualifications were. She even kept a straight face when he said that he was a rancher, that he knew cattle and horses and he was a pretty fair hand at saddle making. But he was honest enough to admit that those skills weren't much in demand when building a spaceship and that he really wanted a job to be near Sarah. Alex liked him right away and even without Sarah's anxious looks from the kitchen she probably would have hired him anyway. She sent him over to the motor pool for Pedro's approval and the rest, as they say, was history.

Alex tucked the note into her pocket when she went to meet her husband for dinner and afterwards showed it to Marshal and Link.

"Not a bad idea." Marshal said. Then he held the sheet of paper up by the corner between a thumb and forefinger. "A little light on specifics maybe but not a bad idea."

Alex and Lincoln laughed and Link said, "I agree. Not a bad idea at all. Might let off a little steam. Some of our younger members are getting a little restless."

"Do you think it could be done?" Alex asked.

Link and Marshal looked at each other. Link said, "I don't know. Never thought about it. Why don't we drift over to the McPhersons table and run it by them? Get some different thoughts."

The happy hard working McPherson clan were involved in just about every aspect of the colony and by any measurement major contributors to the success of the colony.

When Alex, John and Link walked up to the table they were warmly greeted and when they were seated the Colonel asked what was on their mind. Alex laughed and said that the Colonel knew her all too well and passed him the paper.

"I got this from Bob Sullivan. Do you know him?"

The Colonel shook his head as he held the paper so his wife could read it and then passed it across the table to Andy and Audrey. While they read Andy said, "I know him. He's one of our security augmentees. Seems like a good kid."

Link added, "One of our better ones. Always on time. Takes good care of his weapon."

Audrey snapped her fingers. "I remember him. The last time Mike and I had our little mobile clinic down at the farm he came in to have his hands treated. I remember because his hands were in terrible shape. Horribly blistered. I don't know how he could keep working but he never flinched when Mike worked on him. When we were finished, he thanked us very much, accepted a pair of leather gloves from Jordan, picked up his ax and headed back towards the berm."

Billy and Erin were looking at the paper. "Tough kid," Billy commented.

"Twenty-four." Alex said. "Been around a little, used to ride the rodeo circuit. You know him, Erin, Sarah's partner."

"Oh! That Bob. Sorry, I didn't make the connection. Yes, great guy."

Alex smiled. "Okay now that we've all agreed that Bob Sullivan is a fine young man, what do you think of his idea?"

"Well," Andy said, "he's not going to live out on the prairie. If the big cats or the wolves or who knows whatever other predator didn't eat him the herds would surely run over him. And if he did manage to catch his horses, how is he going to keep them?"

Audrey said, "What about medical? Ranching isn't the

tamest of occupations and these horses he proposes catching are big, wild and because we are on Sanctuary probable mean. Aggression is an animal trait here. People are going to get hurt."

Link, Marshal and Wright nodded in emphatic agreement.

Erin added, "Alex, if we did establish a ranch out on the prairie, we would have to support it. There's plenty of meat out there but humans can't live on meat alone."

Alex had been listening. She looked across the table to the colonel. "Any thoughts, Alex?" she asked.

McPherson smiled back. "You know, Alex, I served in the Air Force and the Space Force for almost thirty years and I can't begin to count the times when some young lieutenant came to me with an idea on how things could be improved, changed, done differently, done better and I learned over the years that rather than just squash the notion it was better to let them develop the thought. Many times, maybe most times, when I made them dig into the nuts and bolts of their proposal, they realized on their own that the idea was impractical or unfeasible. But not always. Sometimes solid developmental or operational changes resulted.

"Listening to the difficulties that were raised around the table I don't know if the notion of a horse ranch is feasible or not but my advice would be to let him run with it. Develop a plan. Encourage him to talk to the staff. Experts in all the disciplines that are going to impact his project. Personally, despite all the difficulties, I think it's a good idea and I can think of at least one possible positive side effect that it might have."

Alex raised an eyebrow.

He pointed over his shoulder with his thumb. "The Carson's.

Alex and everyone else at the table looked at each other confused by the seeming non-sequitur.

McPherson smiled. "Okay," he said, "your first lesson in Pentagon Infighting 101, divide and conquer. The Carson's, Floyd and Faith and Charlie and Faye came to Voyager as Visions Unlimited nominees and as such everyone has assumed that they are in Lasseter's orbit. Even Lasseter. Right?"

There were nods around the table.

The colonel went on. "I don't think that that's necessarily true. I think that their ties to the VU crowd are loose and that they kind of hang out with Lasseter's bunch because they don't have anywhere else to go. I think they're good people. Rich people who grew up with a silver spoon in their mouths, sure, but deep down they are good people. Did you know that Floyd and Charlie are cousins?"

That brought a murmur around the table. Apparently, Alex was the only one who knew that.

"And," the colonel went on. "did you know that Faith and Faye are sisters?"

No one knew that, not even Alex. "But," Billy asked, "what's all that got to do with Sullivan's ranch?"

"Because," the colonel said, "they are all horse nuts."

"How could you know that?" his wife asked.

"Floyd told me. He was working down in the wood shop a couple of weeks ago and he told me that all four of them had grown up with their own saddle ponies and before Earth went to hell in addition to their regular jobs, they ran a stable. I'll have a word with Floyd. So, Alex, my advice would be to call Sullivan in for a little one on one and point out to him that his proposal needs a little fleshing out."

The next morning a very somber Bob Sullivan walked out of Alex's office and crossed the cavern to the table where a very anxious Sarah Williams was waiting. Sarah looked up at his sober look and asked, "She said no?"

Sullivan gave a rueful smile. "No. No, she didn't say no but she didn't say yes either."

"Well, what then?"

Bob gave himself a shake. "What the Director told me, sweetheart, in the politest of terms mind you, was that I'm a jackass. That if I wanted to build a ranch and go catch horses or anything else, I needed more than a proposal on a half sheet of paper. If I wanted her support, the colony's support, I needed a well-thought-out plan and when I developed the plan, she would be willing to put it before the staff for consideration. It was embarrassing."

Sarah leaned across the table and gave him a hug. "Cheer up, honey," she said. "She didn't say no. So, we'll make a plan."

"Make a plan." Bob repeated. "I don't know how to make a plan. Do you?"

"No. So we ask people. Get help, advice. I don't think Ms. Cummings expected us to do this all on our own anyway."

A slightly more cheerful Bob Sullivan hugged her back. "Okay," he said. "You're right as always. Where do we start?"

Sarah thought for a moment and said, "Let's go talk to Mr. Marshal. He's been around. He's been all over this planet so maybe he can point us in the right direction."

When Bob and Sarah walked into the Starduster Cavern Marshal nudged Billy Wright. "Right on schedule," he said with a smile.

Two hours later Sullivan's head was spinning. After talking to Marshal and several other people who had stopped by to listen, ask questions, and offer advice, he felt even more like a jackass than he had before when he realized that he hadn't really thought about the practical problems of his proposal. Someone asked where the horses were and like a fool, he had replied that they were out on the prairie. When the laughter died down Wright pointed out the prairie was a mighty big place, thousands and thousands of square miles and he had to admit that he had no idea exactly where the horses were.

When Marshal asked him how he was going to round the horses up seeing as they didn't have any horses of their own to drive them and they surely couldn't do it on foot. He had to admit that he hadn't thought about that either but cheered up a bit when Marshal waved his hand around the cavern and told him that other drivers might be available, things like Stardusters, robots, even drones.

Jerry Smith and Andy McPherson joined the conversation and Smith had asked where he was going to hold the horses once they were captured. And many more questions like how were the ranchers going to survive out on the prairie? Where were they going to live? What were they going to eat?

As the conversation went on, Sullivan and even Sarah were getting more and more discouraged when Marshal said "Don't be so down hearted, kids. These are questions that need to be answered. Problems that need to be solved. Not necessarily game stoppers. That's what your plan is all about. Objectives. Problems. Solutions. And if I may put forward a suggestion, the first thing you need is intelligence of exactly what you are facing. Suppose we take a reconnaissance flight out on the prairie tomorrow and you can see for yourself what you're up against. Bring all the people who are interested in the project. Pack us a lunch, Sarah, and we'll make a day of it."

Sullivan's mind was spinning when he left the Starduster Cavern to alert the other members of what he thought of as the horse group, or the ranchers, for their morning flight.

That evening Alex held a mini staff meeting at the McPhersons table. Alex was determined to provide all the support that was possible for the ranch project but at the same time she wanted the ranchers to identify problems and solve them on their own. For the morning flight they decided on just one Starduster, Dusty 1, with Junior in the cargo bay. Riley would fly with Marshal in the copilot's seat. They discovered that two of the proposed ranchers were security personnel so McPherson and Smith would go along to round out the security team "and to provide a little adult supervision," Jerry said. Mike Bennet would provide medical support and Ellen Nolan who was a member of the Geek Squad as well as being a potential rancher would provide drone support. Alex also decided to include the Fosters for whatever insight they might provide.

Alex shook her head. With twenty people the shuttle would be crowded but she didn't think that anyone would mind.

It was a half excited, half apprehensive group of ranchers that gathered around the shuttle the next morning. As Alex had predicted the shuttle was crowded but the old hands were happy to occupy the cockpit and sit on the floor in the entryway and let the ranchers, thirteen of them, sort themselves out in the ten plush passenger seats. Marshal looked back and smiled. Alex and Alex would be happy to know that the Carson's were fitting in nicely.

Sarah William's lunch, which seemed to Marshal to be more than enough to feed a battalion, was stowed in the cargo bay.

Riley took Dusty down Little River and followed the river out across the prairie all the way to the Big Lake diverting to the right or left whenever he spotted a large herd of grazers or a pack of predators. The ranchers' excited chatter gradually diminished as the enormity of the grasslands, the size of the herds and the number and variety of predators became a reality to them.

Around noon Riley set the shuttle down on a small hill not far from where they had their encounter with the Terror Bird and to impress the need for security and constant vigilance, he waited for a full five minutes to see if anything was going to attack before he opened the passenger hatch and the four security personnel deployed. When they determined that all was clear Sarah laid out the lunch and standing in that sea of grass Marshal had to admit that the prairie at this time of year was a beautiful sight. The grass was waist high and in the gentle southerly breeze rippled like the waves of the ocean. Not a constant, consistent wave but a hundred separate eddies of changing colors running away from the viewer and always in the background there was a low whisper as the wind brushed the top of each stalk

It was a partly cloudy day with great billowy white clouds pasted against a cobalt blue sky. Just beautiful. And somewhere off in the far distance the waving green merged with the blue and white.

Bob Sullivan stood on the edge of the lunch circle gazing out on the sight. Marshal walked up next to him, put an arm around his shoulder and said, "It is beautiful, Bob, but you know you can't live out here."

"I know." He sighed. "I guess building a ranch and living out here was just a dream."

"Don't give up," Marshal answered. "Grant has an idea."

"What?"

"You'll see."

Sullivan wondered what Marshal meant. He didn't

need any more evidence that the prairie was a dangerous place. While the ranchers sat in the waist high waving grass having their lunch four were constantly on sentry duty while Junior or the drone or both of them kept watch overhead.

And Marshal made sure that Grant Foster told the story of the Terror Bird attack and the stampeding bison. For years back on Earth Grant Foster had his own Vid series and told his and Maryanne's adventure stories to millions of avid listeners and he told them very well. When he was finished the ranchers looked at big Andy McPherson and tried to picture him hanging on the end of the ladder while the bison thundered by underneath.

They lingered over lunch for over an hour seemingly reluctant to admit that their dream of a ranch on the prairie was just not practical. Their spirits were considerably lifted however when Grant suggested an alternative. Instead of living out on the prairie he told them what about setting up their ranch on the western edge of the grasslands up against the foothills and using the many box canyons that cut into the hills for corrals.

Why not? And their enthusiasm rebounded immediately.

After a little discussion Riley flew the shuttle back to the edge of the prairie and starting at Little River flew for almost two hundred miles north along the base of the foothills landing whenever the ranchers requested to explore a particularly promising canyon. And at every stop Ellen Nolan flew her drone gathering sensor recordings.

They kept at it until it was too dark to see and reluctantly turned west back toward Cliffside.

For the next week or so the notion of a ranch on the prairie kind of faded into the colony's background. The ranchers all went back to their regular jobs but Bjorn let the ranchers set up their computers in a corner of the cook house and every minute of their free time was spent either with their noses buried in the computers or talking to various staff members, taking notes, making lists.

Ten days after the reconnaissance flight Sullivan requested a meeting with Alex and she tried hard to be the stern leader and not to show her pleasure when four very nervous, anxious young people turned up in her office. This time instead of a half page proposal the ranchers had a twelve-page plan that they insisted was only a draft, complete with computer graphics, that covered every aspect of the proposed ranch. But, Sullivan insisted, it was only a draft. There were still some problem areas and to answer their remaining questions they would like to make another shuttle reconnaissance flight.

Alex readily agreed and the next morning Dusty 1 with Junior on board in the cargo bay along with, of course, Sarah's very generous lunch, was waiting in front of the Starduster Cavern. The same twenty people who had made the first flight, with the exception of McPherson and Smith who were out on a scout and were replaced with Kurt Jaeger and Linda Murphy, milled around anxious to be off.

Sullivan sat in the metal seat right behind Riley and Marshal. No sightseeing this time. The ranchers had identified three sites that they wanted to check out and Sullivan knew right where they were.

Riley flew down Little River and turned north at the base of the foothills.

"Not far," Sullivan said, "only about twenty-five miles." He paused and pointed. "There, that canyon that looks like it has a double opening. An opening inside the opening."

Riley and Marshal were a little puzzled at that description but as soon as they turned toward the canyon, they saw what he meant.

"Oh, that looks perfect, Bob," Marshal said.

The entrance to the canyon was a twenty-five or thirty yard opening in the line of hills. Beyond the entrance to the canyon a grassy meadow stretched for a quarter of a mile before the canyon walls closed in to create a second opening of no more than twenty-five or thirty yards. And beyond that opening the canyon spread out again to perhaps a half mile or more and ran back into the hills for another five. The canyon floor was covered in lush grass and the canyon walls were steep, maybe a hundred feet high and rocky.

"Where would you like to set down?" Riley asked.

Sullivan thought for a moment and answered. "I think back to the first entrance, please." And as Riley turned the shuttle, he slid out of the jump seat and went back to the rest of the ranchers.

Linda Murphy took his place and looked at the canyon and the prairie beyond. "Cougar country," she said.

"What?" Riley and Marshal said in unison.

"This looks like good country for cougars. They live up in the rocks but hunt out on the prairie. Just like my uncle's place in Montana."

Riley turned the shuttle back toward the canyon and prepared to land in the opening but before he could tell the eager ranchers to sit back down and wait a few Murph pointed forward and said, "See? What did I tell you!"

Riley and Marshal looked where she was pointing and saw a very large tawny colored cat bounding down the hillside and it looked like it was coming right for them.

"Well, damn!" Riley said. "That stupid animal is going to attack us." He lifted Dusty just as the big cat launched itself twelve feet into the air. It even made a swipe at the shuttle as it passed by underneath.

Riley held the shuttle a hundred feet or so but the big cat showed no sign of leaving so he turned east and flew out over the prairie before ascending to a thousand feet and returning to the canyon entrance. The cat was still there. "Geeze!" Riley exclaimed. "If we want to land, that critter has got to go."

"I agree," Murph said, "but I'd rather not land while it's still here. Probably charge right through the door before I could get a shot off."

They all nodded and Grant said, "Why don't we go checkout the other two sites. We can come back here later. Maybe the nasty kitty will have found something else to do by then."

Foster's prediction turned out to be accurate. Four hours later after checking out both canyons and having lunch Dusty 1 again hovered over the canyon's entrance with no sign of the big cat.

"What I like about this canyon," Sullivan said, "is the double opening, like an hourglass. I figure that we can run the horses all the way to the back of the second opening and we can set up our tents and maybe later build a ranch house here in the first opening. We'll be off the prairie and I think if we build up against the north wall, we'll be out of most of the weather too."

They spent the rest of the day exploring the canyon and the surrounding area and it was a happy group of ranchers that piled back into the shuttle for the return trip.

The site was perfect.

This was going to work.

Less than a week later a much more confident Bob Sullivan stood in the Conference Cavern and made his pitch for colony support for a ranch. His detailed briefing was a long way from the handwritten half page that he had first given

Alex. When he was finished, the council was all for it and with only one modification, a rather large modification, approved the plan. The modification came from Alex who wasn't going to leave her young ranchers living on the edge of the prairie in tents through the winter so as soon as possible the ranch house would be built.

The ranch became the colony's thing and everything seemed to happen at once. Under Grant and Maryanne's direction the ranchers went through the supply cave and selected tents, sleeping bags and everything else that they might need for an extended camping trip and moved out to their canyon. As soon as they were settled a request for some help in building the barriers to close off the canyon openings was approved and half of Whit Latham's lumber pile was loaded into the cargo bays of all four Stardusters and forty lumberjacks and carpenters filled the passenger compartments. It took less than a day to finish both barriers complete with swing gates. Once the barriers were finished Sullivan asked that one shuttle be left behind for reconnaissance. The ranchers needed to find a herd.

From the air, finding horses proved to be surprisingly easy. Riley lifted off from the ranch with Marshal in the copilot's seat and all thirteen ranchers chattering excitedly in the back. Almost immediately They spotted a big herd of horses—which was immediately rejected.

"Too big," said Sullivan from the jump seat. "A herd that size would be too much for us to handle." They flew on discovering two more herds but both were also rejected for being too big. They were now over a hundred miles from the ranch and Sullivan said that they had better turn back. The farther away from the canyon the harder it would be to drive the horses.

They were almost back to the ranch when they saw

the small horse herd moving along the edge of the prairie. A single stallion, eight mares, and what looked to be four foals and four yearlings. After a frantic series of com calls a plan was thrown together for a horse hunt the next day.

What followed was a kind of semi-organized chaos. Riley landed at the ranch and unloaded Dusty including Junior then he flew to Cliffside and loaded Paul Mahoney and his robot, the Geek Squad and three drones and a full security team headed up by Link Lincoln himself. They offloaded at the ranch and Riley went back to Cliffside to get Tony Simmons and his robot. To their surprise Alex had sent ten farmers and lumberjacks to help with the gates or whatever else might be necessary.

The next morning the first horse herding crew in Sanctuary's history set forth to capture some horses. A unique herding team to say the least. One Starduster planet-to-orbit tourist vehicle, three construction robots and four drones. The Geeks took their command station up to the top of the canyon wall and would control the drones from there. Riley, with Sullivan in the copilot's seat, flew north along the foot of the hills with the three robots and four drones in company.

The small herd was just about where Sullivan had predicted it to be grazing along the edge of the prairie. The hopeful herders went out over the grassland and circled north to approach the horses from that direction. The first thing Sullivan had said was to see how the horses reacted to the various drovers. He sent the drones first and the four drones fanned out behind the horses and disappointingly to the humans they were pretty much ignored. Sullivan said later that the horses probably thought that they were some strange kind of bird.

Marshal and Junior were next. Marshal held Junior about fifty feet above the ground and came slowly up behind the horses. That got a reaction. The horses definitely did not like Junior and moved away from the robot to the south and when the herd started to drift out to the east over the prairie Sullivan had Riley fly parallel to them. The big black stallion did not like Dusty either and moved back toward the hills.

"Good. Good," Sullivan said, "not too close. Just keep them going another five miles or so then we'll pick up the pace."

Marshal smiled to himself. Sullivan was working this all out in his head as they went along and doing a heck of a job. Just then Sullivan said, "Okay, we're getting close. Robots, start crowding them a bit. Get them running." That was easily done and Sullivan turned to Riley and said, "Mr. Riley, you have the really hard and tricky part. I would like you to set the shuttle down just past the gate so the horses have to turn into the canyon but we don't want them to break out to the east into the open prairie. Can you do that?"

Ben Riley was having the time of his life. "You just watch me!" he shouted. No one could handle a shuttle like Ben Riley. The robots had the horse herd in a full gallop now and Riley kept the shuttle just abreast of the big stallion crowding him a little toward the hills. The canyon was coming up fast and Riley timed it perfectly. The shuttle shot forward just ahead of the horse herd, slewed around to the right and thumped down just past the gate.

The stallion practically fell all over himself to keep from crashing into Dusty. He frantically looked around but there were robots behind and to the left of him now and he had nowhere to go but to the right into the canyon. He thundered through the first gate with his small herd right behind. The ranchers and the muscle from Cliffside immediately closed the gate behind them. The robots popped over the barrier and chased the horses through the second opening and the gate closed behind them. The herd was trapped.

But Bob Sullivan had one more trick up his sleeve. He'd worked it out beforehand with the ranchers, Marshal and the robots and it worked. The big stallion charged across the upper canyon until he came to the end. Confused, he must have suddenly realized that he was trapped in a box canyon. He looked back toward the opening and saw that there were no robots. He charged back toward the opening, the gate opened and he raced through it. Before his mares could follow the gate slammed shut again but the stallion was helpless because there were those flying things behind him.

The robots chased him through the outer gate and for an hour out onto the prairie. Poor guy, Marshal thought. Talk about having a bad day. But a bad day for some could be a good day for others. The ranch had been a community effort and a real moral boost for the colony. The ranchers had their ranch and now they had some horses. Big, aggressive horses. Marshal wondered what was going to happen now.

CHAPTER 19

Dawn was just breaking as Alex sat with her husband in the cafeteria nursing her second cup of coffee while watching the sun rise bright and clear through the non-polluted air of Sanctuary and then slowly climb over the forest to the east to reveal the cleared farmland between the forest and Cliffside. She missed having her second cup at her desk but the building of the wall to seal the Great Cavern had started in the northern corner where her office was located so if she wanted a view she had to move over to the cafeteria.

Reading her mind John said, "Enjoy it while you can, Luv. Pretty soon we'll have to go outside for a view. Look on the bright side, though. Olga's going to set up a camera so you can still enjoy the view on a Vid screen at your desk and when winter comes, we'll be snug, warm and dry in here, out of the weather."

Alex sighed again. "I know, and of course I wouldn't have it any other way but I will miss watching the view live you might say."

"Yeah, me too. Hey, who's that?" he asked, watching a woman walking off toward the farm. Since the farmers had settled a mile or so to the east and started building their own houses, not many of them stayed overnight in the caves—especially with Roberta stuffing them down in the cookhouse—it was kind of unusual to someone going in that direction so early in the morning.

"Laura Chaucer," Alex answered. "Her sister is sick so she's been spending a few days up here, helping out and taking care of the kids..." Her voice trailed off and turned into a gasp as Laura screamed, threw up her hands and collapsed to the ground.

"What the —?" Marshal exclaimed as he surged to his feet.

Before he could move toward the cavern opening another woman was running toward Laura.

She never made it.

With a brief shriek she pitched forward with a spear in her back. At the same time Marshal heard the warning bell. Two clanks and then it was silent.

"Shit!" he muttered.

With the sound of the cow bell the whole cavern was stirring. Link came running up with Andy McPherson and Jerry Smith right on his heels. As he asked "What's happening?" and started to go outside. Marshal grabbed him by the arm. "Wait, Link! Better not go out there." And he pointed to the bodies of the two women. "Those two were hit by spears. I think from above."

McPherson cautiously stuck his head out and tried to look up. "You think that it's Wedgies?"

"I don't know what else it could be," Marshal answered.

Smith said, "If it is Wedgies and they're up on top of

the cliff they have us in a bad way. If we try to get out to do anything they'll nail us for sure."

"Too right." McPherson agreed.

Alex looked at Lincoln. "I think that the first thing we need to do is to spread the word for everyone to stay inside and away from the cave openings while we try to figure out what to do."

"Right, boss," Link said. "Should have thought about that myself." Several of the deputies were now gathered around and he ordered, "You heard the lady! Spread out along the opening and don't let anyone outside."

"And," Alex added as she headed across the cavern toward her desk, "don't try to be heroes. Keep your heads inside. Chief, I'll contact the other caves and the farm while you and Andy and the rest figure out what we're going to do about this. I want recommendations. What about your deputies manning the guard post on the top of the cliff and our lookout who rang the bell?"

"Damn," said Lincoln. "I should have thought of that too." He tried to contact his three deputies who were manning the guard post at the top of the cliff and received no response. Link sighed to himself when he got no response from the lookout post, either.

Smith chuckled. "That's why she's the boss Chief. So what are we going to do?"

Link looked around at his senior deputies. "Damnifiknow. If anyone has any brilliant suggestions, now's the time to hear them."

Everyone looked at each other—nothing, then Marshal snapped his fingers. "Junior!" he exclaimed. "Remember the last time we met the Wedgies, they really reacted to Junior. If I can get down to the Starduster cavern, maybe I can do something."

Link asked, "Junior's in the Starduster cavern?"

"Right."

Andy said, "That's the better part of a hundred- and fifty-yards John, right down the cliff face. You'd never make it."

"Well, I might have a chance if you create a diversion."

Jerry snorted. "The only diversion I can think of is for one of us to go outside. Ah! I see your devious little plan; we get pointy things stuck into us here so you don't get pointy things stuck into you down there."

Marshal laughed. "Not quite what I had in mind, old buddy. Let me see if Brian's in the shop."

"How is that going to help? Ander's blacksmith shop is in the northernmost cavern right next to the river. It's about as far away from the Starduster cavern as you can get."

Ignoring him, Marshal thumbed his com. "Brian, you there? Oh, hi, Helen. What? You got the word and you're all safe inside. Good. Drag Brian away from his hammer, would you? I need to talk to him."

A few seconds later Anders said, "Yup." Brian Anders was a man of few, a very few, words.

"You know the situation?"

"Yup."

"I'm in the Great Cavern and I need to get down to the Starduster cave without getting stuck full of javelins. Do you think that you could create some kind of distraction that would draw the Wedgies attention—without getting yourself stuck full of spears, of course?"

Anders was silent for a few moments then he said, "Yup!" and hung up.

Link asked, "What did he say?"

"He said 'Yup'."

"What?" Before he could say more, he was

interrupted by a very loud clanging and crashing from the vicinity of the blacksmith cave.

"Damn!" exclaimed Smith. "He must be throwing every piece of junk he's got out onto the rocks."

"Smart," said McPherson. Then he turned toward Marshal but Marshal was already gone.

After a couple of minutes, the clattering noise stopped and Anders came up on the com. "Okay?" he asked.

Link answered, "Great idea, Brian. Hang on a minute. John, are you okay?"

"Yeah fine, no spears came my way. I don't think they even saw me."

"Good. Where are you? Did you make it to Junior?"

"No, I'm about halfway. I ducked into the Conference Cave, that one's still open. Tell Brian to do it again and I'll go the rest of the way."

"Did you get that Brian?" Lincoln asked.

"Can't," Anders answered. "Every piece of junk that was loose in the shop is lying out there on the rocks. Got a couple of useless apprentices here though that I can throw out if they'll do."

Everyone smiled knowing that Brian Anders loved his apprentices and would fight dire wolves naked to protect them.

Link answered, "No better not do that. I don't think Alex would like that too much."

"What wouldn't Alex not like?" she asked as she walked up to the group.

Someone said, "If the blacksmith threw his apprentices out of the cave."

"What? Why would he do that?"

Someone else said, "To create a diversion."

"A diversion for what?" she scowled. "Chief, do mind

telling me just what is going on?" It didn't take a rocket scientist to see that she was just a little pissed.

Link hesitated. "Well, Alex, it's like this... John thought—"

At that, Alex looked around and not seeing her husband she glared at Link and demanded, "Where is he?"

Big old Bart Lincoln was like a little kid with his hand caught in the cookie jar. "Well Alex, John thought that if he could get down to the Starduster cavern and Junior—"

"He's out there? You let him go out there?" Before he could answer she was on her com. "John, where are you?"

An infuriatingly calm voice answered her. "Oh! Hi Luv. It's working. I'm at the Conference Cave. Give me another diversion."

An exasperated Alex exclaimed, "You big oaf! If you get yourself stuck full of spears, I'll never speak to you again."

Despite the seriousness of the situation the ridiculousness of that statement brought a laugh from everyone within ear shot including her. She shook herself and said, "Please be careful, my sweet."

"Me? I'm always careful, Luv, you know that."

Before she could answer, Jerry Smith came running up holding two bed rolls. He flipped one to a puzzled Andy McPherson and said, "Come on!" Moving to the cavern opening he added, "Ready, John?"

"Ready."

"Go!" and he waved the bedroll out of the cavern opening like a big towel. It was immediately pierced by a spear. McPherson got the idea and sent his bedroll out. As he jerked it back in another spear rattled off the rocks.

A jubilant shout came over the com. "Made it!"

Marshal raced into the cavern and up to his robot. "Okay, Junior," he said as he crawled inside, "time to get your scary face on."

A moment later an Earth made twenty-first century construction robot swept up the cliff face and confronted two very startled who-knows-what-century Wedgies. The pair of them stumbled backwards so fast that one of them actually fell over backwards. Marshal ignored them as he turned Junior to the north and raced along the edge of the cliff scattering Wedgies while whooping and shouting like a madman.

Down in the cavern Alex turned toward Link. "What's my goofy husband going to do? Junior doesn't have any weapons."

Before Link could answer the air was split by a clicking, whistling scream and a Wedgie crashed onto the rock shelf in front of them.

McPherson exclaimed, "How did you do that? Did you scare him so bad he jumped?"

"Nah! Remember that old movie they made back around the turn of the century about the magic ring and all. Those flying dragons that picked up the good guys defending the castle and dropped them. Well, that's what I tried to do with Junior except that Junior wasn't strong enough to pick him up so we kind of pulled him over the edge and dropped him."

"Seems to have worked. Are you going to send down any more?"

"Nah! I don't think so. They're all running for the trees. Ah, Chief, it looks like the three deputies that were on watch are all down."

Lincoln sighed and said, "Yeah, I expected that." He paused for a moment. "You said that the Wedgies were running for the trees? Good! That's good, John." McPherson held up his hand. "Yeah, Andy?"

"Alex, you said that you wanted recommendations? Let me put John on hold for a minute and I'll tell you what I have in mind." Alex nodded and Andy asked, "Did you get that, John?"

"Got it. What do you want us to do? The boys are with me now—five robots."

McPherson answered, "Good, John. For the moment don't chase them. Just keep them away from the cliff edge while we come up with a plan. Okay?"

"Gotcha!"

Andy looked at Alex and Link. "I don't think that we should just chase them away. I may be wrong but by the way they reacted to John and Junior I'm willing to bet that these are the same bunch of Wedgies that we chased off before and, in my opinion, if we let them go now, they'll be back."

You could tell that neither Alex or Link liked where McPherson was going but for the safety of the colony, they could see the wisdom in his suggestion. Alex sighed and Link shrugged.

"Andy, what do you propose?" Alex asked.

"Hammer and anvil. Jerry and I will take—um—ten deputies up the river past that small burn area—you know the one, Chief, that's about half a mile upstream? We'll set up a blocking position. Chief, you get all the deputies you can lay your hands on and deploy them along the cliff top and drive the Wedgies towards us. John, you and the rest of the jockeys keep the Wedgies in play but away from the cliff top and the river while we get into position."

No one answered for a minute while they processed McPherson's proposal. After a few minutes everyone slowly nodded.

Marshal said, "Got it, Andy." Then added, "Paul you're closest to the river. Keep them from looking over the edge while Andy's bunch comes up."

"Right!" Mahoney replied. "Coast is clear. Anytime, Andy."

McPherson just grunted. He and Jerry were already on the move with ten deputies and they wasted no time reaching the rocky river bank and starting upstream. The gorge that Little River had carved through the rocks made them invisible to anyone, or anything, above that wasn't looking directly over the edge. A few minutes later what McPherson was calling the anvil team was climbing the rocks that led up the river. "Still good, Paul?" he asked.

"Still good. The Wedgies are all in the edge of the trees looking at the robots. As far as I can see there aren't any near the river but I can't see very far upstream so be careful."

McPherson replied, "Roger. John, just keep them interested for another ten or fifteen minutes until we get into position."

Marshal answered, "Right! Link and his bunch are just coming up the rocks now."

Lincoln came up on the com. "Andy, John, we're going to spread out along the cliff top. Andy, let me know when you're in position and, John, I'm depending on you and your robots to keep us from getting stuck full of javelins."

While the two groups of deputies moved into position and the robots darted and retreated toward the Wedgies, Olga Sorenson came up on the com. "Mr. Marshal, we're here with all six drones. What do you want us to do?"

"Good girl!" Marshal answered and thought for a moment. "Send two up the river bank to screen Andy and spread out the rest between the robots and the trees but don't get too close—those spears will bounce off a robot but they would probably be deadly for a drone."

"No problem," Olga laughed and two drones sped up

the river past Mahoney and the other four proceeded to completely ignore Marshal's advice as they darted forward and backward at the Wedgies.

"Geeze, Olga!" Marshal exclaimed but all he heard was laughter from the drone operators.

McPherson passed the burn area, brought his blocking team up out of the river bed and started moving south along edge of the burn. He was pleased that there was plenty of cover as he positioned his anvil team into three groups along the western edge of the burn. Knowing he could depend on Jerry to not let any Wedgies get around him, he sent him and three deputies to the southern end of the cleared area.

He was just as concerned about the river bed but he smiled as he told Linda Murphy what he wanted. Murph had been one of Lincoln's deputies for years even before she joined Project Voyager. When she smiled and said that no Wedgies were going to use the river to get around her, he knew that he could depend on it.

McPherson deployed his deputies in the center, the main blocking position and told Link he was in position.

"Okay," Lincoln said. "Andy, get your people burrowed down deep. There's going to be a lot of bullets coming your way. I don't think the Wedgies will get through the trees as far as you but I don't want any friendly fire accidents. John, Olga, up and out of the way."

The blocking team hugged the ground while five construction robots and six drones swept up into the air as three dozen twenty-first century automatic weapons sent a deadly hail of destruction into the tree line.

"They're running, Chief!" Marshal exclaimed. "Those that are left anyway."

"Right!" Lincoln answered. "My people, stay put and stay down. You ready, Andy? They're coming your way."

The Wedgies burst through the trees into the burn area.

"Wait for it," McPherson said. "Let them all get clear." When the lead Wedgies were halfway across the burn McPherson yelled, "Fire!"

The three strong points opened up with a dozen automatic weapons and the Wedgies went down like mown wheat. But not all of them. You had to hit a Wedgie in the head to take him out for good. "Damn!" McPherson said. "Link, about six or seven made it back into the woods."

"Not good. What do you suggest?"

"We're going to have to flush them out. Either I move toward you or you come to me."

Lincoln thought for a moment and said, "You hold your blocking position. I have more people so we'll move toward you. Okay people, did you all get that. We are going to move in a line through the trees and try to drive the Wedgies toward McPherson. Keep the line straight, keep contact with the people on your right and left and watch where you're shooting."

McPherson said, "A suggestion Chief, before you get going why not give them another burst. Maybe get them moving."

"Good idea. Everyone got that?" He waited a few moments. "Heads down, Andy, and... fire!"

A second hail of bullets swept through the trees. All was quiet for a minute then Link heard rifle fire from ahead to the right and also to the left. McPherson came up on the com. "Are you all right, Murph?"

"Yeah, we're fine. Two tried to break down to the river. Didn't make it."

McPherson chuckled. "Right, Murph. What about you Jerry?"

"Same here. Two tried to head south, we got 'em."

"Blocking team stay in position. We're clear, Chief."

Link asked, "Andy, how many do you think are left?"

"Not sure. Not many, I think six or seven got back into the woods after the first skirmish and we just got four. But I can't be sure. Some of the ones that went down might just have holes in the bark"

Link said, "Right. Keep your heads down." Then he looked up and down his line of very nervous colonists. "All right, people, try to keep the line straight, maintain contact with those on your right and left and let's move out slow and easy."

With the robots and drones floating over the trees the line of colonists slowly moved into the forest. The good news was that due to the thick foliage overhead the ground was fairly clear consisting of mostly knee-high ferns of some kind that thrived on the steady drip of water from the canopy a hundred feet or more above. The bad news was that the thick cover blotted out most of the light and the trees grew so close together that they could only see ten or twelve feet in any direction. Most of Link's inexperienced deputies quickly lost contact with each other.

Grimly determined, the Voyagers moved deeper into the woods. All were startled by a burst of gunfire from the right side of the line toward the river. A long silence followed and just as Link was going to demand a report a sheepish voice said, "Ah sorry, Chief. I thought I saw something."

"Who's 'I' and where are you?" Link demanded

"Ah, Sam Teutopolis, Chief. Sorry. And I'm on the bank above the river."

Lincoln tried to remember who Sam was and realized he was one of the miners. "That's okay, Sam," he answered. "Better to shoot a tree than to miss seeing a Wedgie."

There was another burst of fire from ahead and a female voice said, "Ha! Sneaky bastard."

McPherson asked, "Murph? Are you okay?"

"Oh yeah, Andy. Fine."

"What happened?"

Murphy answered with a chuckle, "Sneaky Wedgie got down into the river. Might have gotten away with it too except that most logs don't float upstream."

McPherson shook his head; Linda Murphy was something else. "Stay sharp, people. There's still more of them out there. I can feel it."

He had no sooner uttered those words when there was a scream and the rattle of gunfire in the woods. In the quiet that followed everyone seemed to be holding their breath waiting. Just before Lincoln was going to demand a report a hesitant voice said, "Ah, Chief."

"Who's that?" Link demanded. "Who's talking?"

"Charlie Briggs, sir," a choked-up voice answered.

Right. Young kid, Starduster mechanic apprentice Link mentally cataloged. "Kurt, are you close?"

"Almost there, Chief."

"Are you alright Charlie?"

Briggs blubbered, "Ah, yes sir, but Mark... Mark sir, he's dead."

Mark Roberts, another young Starduster apprentice. Made sense, they would have been together. Softly Lincoln asked, "What happened, Charlie?"

Even over the com Link could tell that Briggs was trying hard to hold back the tears. "We were moving along with everyone else and a tree stabbed Mark. Only it wasn't a tree, it was a Wedgie. We walked right past it." He snuffed a bit. "I shot it, sir."

"Head shot?"

"Yes, sir."

"Good, that's good Charlie. You there Kurt?"

"Yeah. The kid's gone, Chief."

"Damn! Take care of young Briggs, will you?"

"Right, Chief."

Lincoln said, "Okay, people, let's get going."

The ragged line of colonists moved forward again. When they were almost to the burn area McPherson yelled, "Chief, get your people down! There's three of them coming out of the trees."

"Everyone down!" Link ordered as Jerry Smith's southernmost team opened fire. A brief rattle of automatic weapons was followed by silence then Smith said, "Clear, Andy, Chief. They're down."

McPherson said, "Good, Jerry. I suggest you hold your position, Chief, and we'll come to you."

"Right. You heard the man, people. Hold your fire."

The anvil team came out from behind the logs and stumps that had provided them shelter and moved across the burn carefully checking every wedgie they passed to ensure that they were really down. After they joined up with the main body the reinforced line walked back toward the cliff top.

Thirty-four Wedgie bodies were counted during this final sweep. As far as the Voyagers could determine none had escaped.

"Good work, people," Link said. "Now comes the unpleasant task of cleaning up." He thought for a minute. "Okay. Everyone, we're going to walk back to the burn picking up every Wedgie along the way and drag them out into the open area. Jerry, Murph, can you get the ones who tried to break around you?"

"Can do."

"Check."

As Lincoln had said it was an unpleasant task but in the end all the Wedgie bodies were recovered, stripped, piled into a heap and burned. The artifacts were collected and turned over to the scientists for study and the last sad chore was to collect their human dead.

So far, Lincoln thought, the colony had been extremely fortunate. There were only four markers in the little cemetery by the river but after today there would be seven more.

CHAPTER 20

Marshal racked up the coffee cups and started walking with Alex toward the entrance to the Great Cavern. This, he thought, was going to be an interesting morning. After yesterday's attack on the colony Alex had called a staff meeting for 0800 this morning to decide the way forward. That was smart, Marshal thought, seeing as right after the attack half the colony wanted to charge off into the woods going who knew where after who knew what and it took all of Alex's and Chief Lincoln's persuasive abilities to prevent them from doing just that.

Waiting overnight gave everyone a chance to think about what had happened and what action if any the colony should take. Smart. But Alex was smart. Visions Unlimited hadn't picked her to be the director for Project Voyager at random and the Voyagers hadn't kept insisting that she was their leader because she was incompetent. But whatever plan she had in mind she was keeping to herself. That was fine with

Marshal. She brains—me brawn. That arrangement had worked out fine so far.

After the Wedgie attack and skirmish Alex had quietly circulated around all yesterday afternoon and long into the evening talking to as many people as she could and calming people down. But at the same time, she listened to their opinions, feelings. And those opinions and feelings ranged from "let's arm everyone and go wipe the Wedgies out" to "let's get on Voyager and go back to Earth".

Marshal was sure that the proper course of action was somewhere in between those extremes but how Alex was going to get several hundred angry, scared or vengeful humans to embrace a unified response was a mystery Marshal was glad he didn't have to solve.

He had had his own conversations with people whose opinion he valued; both Andy and his dad Colonel Alex McPherson, Link Lincoln, Jerry Smith, Ben Riley and the robot jockeys, Al Wilson and the boffins up in Wisdom. They hadn't all agreed on a way forward but for several reasons they were all pretty much in agreement on what had happened.

By the way the Wedgies reacted to the colony and especially the robots, the consensus was that the attack had been made by the same Wedgies that had attacked the colonists two months earlier. These Wedgies were probably joined by all the able-bodied males in their clan or village or whatever. It had been two months since the first encounter so the scientists and the scouts estimated that this village was anywhere from two to three hundred miles away. Depending on the terrain and how fast the Wedgies walked or ran to get home and how long they talked about their encounter and what to do about the creatures they had encountered before they headed back. Based on their previous scouts, Smith and McPherson were convinced that the Wedgies' village or whatever, was up in the mountains to the west. Finally, everyone Marshal had talked to seemed to be in agreement that the humans had killed every Wedgie that had attacked the colony—no survivors—so the colony wasn't in any immediate danger.

But it was obvious that not everyone saw it that way. Yup! It was going to be an interesting meeting.

Alex and Marshal walked up to the rather large group that was gathered in front of the Great Cavern and after greetings were exchanged everyone started drifting toward the Conference Cave. Early on Alex had wanted a larger setting for staff meetings other than her office so she just picked another cave and called it a conference room. Colonel McPherson and the wood workers had knocked together a table and some chairs and the Conference Cave was where staff meetings and any other meeting had been held since the colony's earliest days.

As they approached the cave Alex's senses began to tingle. Something was going on. She glanced at her husband—he had that look. The crowd hadn't dispersed, they were buzzing, anticipating something and she could sense that it wasn't the results of the Wedgie attack and the upcoming meeting. No, something was going on. Something was afoot as Sherlock would say and everyone was in on it except her but before she could say anything the crowd in front of the cave parted and she was staring open mouthed at a new vastly upgraded conference room or conference cave. It was the equal of any corporate conference room that she had ever seen on Earth and it was dominated by a magnificent forty-foot-long solid oak table with more than a dozen matching chairs. Beautiful.

Her surprise obvious, Alex just stood there speechless and the crowd broke out into laughter and cheers. She looked at the Colonel. "How did you—when did you——?"

"Well," McPherson answered, "it wasn't easy. We did want to surprise you but we couldn't find a time to do it with you around all over the place all the time. So, we decided to do it in the middle of the night and then the Wedgies attacked and you were up half the night talking to everyone. But we couldn't keep it under wraps any longer so after everyone settled down last night we went ahead."

"Yeah," added Marshal, "by the time you got to sleep and I could slip away they already had it down here on anti-grav and were putting the final touches on."

McPherson went on. "The table is a solid piece of wood that came from a single tree and we didn't even have to cut it down. It blew down in that big wind storm we had a couple of months ago. The chairs, all of them, are from the same tree."

Alex ran a hand over one of the chairs. "They are just beautiful and they match perfectly."

"You can thank Ryan for that." McPherson said. "And all done by hand and eye too, no jigs, computers or lasers. Each piece turned individually on a power lathe by hand. Beautiful work."

Alex shook her head. Ryan Lasseter was a very complicated man and she had never been able to like him and she was sure that the feeling was mutual. They were on the most formal of terms. It was Ms. Cummings and Mr. Lasseter whenever they interacted. But despite the fact that his was the constant voice for abandoning the colony he was a gifted wood carver who did his share and more to improve living conditions for the colonists. He and Alex McPherson got along just fine. Very complicated.

"Well, ladies and gentlemen," she said, "if you wanted to surprise me you certainly succeeded. Now if the staff would join me let's put this magnificent piece of carpentry to work."

The staff trooped in and settled gingerly into the new chairs but the crowd outside didn't disperse. There must have been fifty or so colonists gathered around the still open entrance to the conference cave and Alex knew that there were three or four hundred more looking at the Vid screens in the Great Cavern and down at the farm. Yes, she thought, they are still scared, apprehensive—no reason they shouldn't be. We have to proceed slowly.

She planned to open the meeting by thoroughly reviewing yesterday's attack but before she could call on Link for a report on the actual attack itself Lasseter jumped in with his standard pitch to abandon the colony.

Alex noted that the usual groans that followed his complaints were muted today. The colony was scared. Seven humans were gone, including fourteen-year-old Jimmy Paterson who had died at his post ringing the bell to warn the colony. Dozens of rumors were circulating as to what was lurking out there in the deep woods. Well, she thought, tell it like it is and she motioned for Lincoln to go ahead.

Link reviewed the fight with the Wedgies emphasizing that as far as they could be certain no Wedgies had escaped. Marshal and the RJs and Olga and the Geek Squad agreed.

Ty West reported for the scientists and the medical department and stated that from their study of the artifacts and the bodies they were pretty certain that these Wedgies were the same group, probably augmented by every able-bodied male in the clan or whatever, that they had encountered earlier and agreed that every Wedgie that had attacked Cliffside lay dead in the pyre above the cliff.

Andy McPherson spoke for the scouts, reassuring the listeners that over the past few months they had thoroughly scouted the area within a hundred miles in every direction and there were no Wedgie habitations within that area so it was their opinion that the group that attacked the colony had to come from farther away most likely from the west.

At a nod from Alex, he went ahead and proposed that he and Jerry Smith undertake a scout up into the mountains far to the west to see if they could find the village or any sign of Wedgie habitation.

Surprisingly that suggestion didn't encounter as much resistance as one would have expected from the group rage of yesterday. There were still a few hot bloods in the colony who wanted to mount a punitive expedition. But not many and none on the staff and after a little discussion a fully supported scout was agreed to.

The next morning things were quiet around the McPherson breakfast table. The entire McPherson clan was in the habit of sharing breakfast before they scattered for the day and seeing as they were involved in every aspect of colony life, they probably wouldn't see each other until dinner and maybe not even then. They were usually a laughing boisterous group but today was different. This morning they were quieter. Today Andy McPherson was going off to see what lay in the mountains and great forests far to the west and of course they were concerned about his safety. But they were cheered by the fact that he wouldn't be going off into the unknown for weeks or months. No, with twenty-first century support he would never be out of touch or contact. For this scout Alex had pulled out all the stops and assigned a full support team.

The only non-McPherson that joined the family most mornings was Jerry Smith. Jerry was pretty much a loner happiest when he was out in the forest exploring the wonders of Sanctuary with Andy. The female McPhersons—Joan, Erin and Audrey—kept trying to match him up with someone and for a while he seemed to have his eye on the school teacher Mary Henderson but when it became pretty obvious that Dave Allen (even though so far Allen was too shy to do anything about it) had the inside tract there the McPhersons kind of gave up on his love life and just adopted him into the clan. Of course, he was probably already in anyway. After many scouts together he and big Andy had become more like brothers and Andy's son Peter shadowed "Uncle Jerry" every minute that he wasn't in school. Even sometimes when he was supposed to be in school. Twice Smith had caught young Peter following them when they started out on a scout and he was pretty sure that a couple of times he hadn't caught him.

Despite the clan's fond feeling for him, Jerry had drawn frowns from Peter's mother and grandmother when he told them that Peter was a born scout who was wasting his time in school.

Smith and all the McPhersons had to smile at Peter's antics this morning as wild with excitement he begged to be included on the scout. After a firm no from not only his mother and father, his grandparents and even his hero Uncle Jerry, Peter disappeared. No one thought about him until they were walking out of the Great Cavern and Audrey asked where her son was.

While everyone looked around Smith laughed. "Audrey, if I know your son, he's hiding somewhere up the trail waiting to follow us."

Audrey McPherson looked at her husband and asked, "Is that true, Andy?"

"Probably, honey, and it wouldn't be the first time either." He sighed. "Outside of tying him up I can't think of any way of keeping him out of the forest. That boy is a born woodsman."

Before Audrey could protest, Smith said, "Don't

worry, Audrey he'll be back soon." Then he chuckled. "I don't think Peter realizes that the first hundred miles of this scout are going to be by air."

That made them all smile and Audrey relaxed a little.

Linda Murphy said, "Audrey, if you like I'll go fetch him."

Audrey McPherson smiled her thanks as Jerry said, "Good luck, Murph. Better go quiet. If that boy doesn't want to be found you'll have a hell of a job finding him."

"Nah! Piece of cake. I'll just stand in the middle of the trail and yell that the scout has gone—by shuttle."

After quick final hugs Dusty 1 lifted off with Ben Riley at the controls and John Marshal sitting in the copilots' seat with Junior tucked away in the cargo bay. Dave Allen sat in the jump seat behind them with a full sensor suite at his fingertips and Olga Sorenson with a couple of drones and Kurt Jaeger and two deputies sat in the back. Ann Turner and Ty West had opted to monitor the scout from Wisdom.

Might as well send the first team Alex had said when they were planning the mission. Jerry and Andy had initially objected to all the backup on the grounds and that the sight of a Starduster might freeze the Wedgies into immobility which is probably why no Wedgies had ever been spotted from the air. The scouts had the same basic objection to Junior and the drones but they had worked it out. Once the scouts were dropped off about a hundred miles west of Cliffside the scouts were on their own and the support was on call. "Hell," Jerry said. "We might want to go home for a shave and shower every once in a while."

Riley flew Dusty over the seemingly endless forest looking for a place to set down when Marshal asked, "Ben, what about that burned off area up ahead?"

"Might work. Dave, get Andy up here."

McPherson came forward and the four men survived the burn area and the forest beyond. Riley asked. "What do you think, Andy?"

"Fine with me. Can you set down? Looks pretty rough."

"Yeah. I think so. What do you see, John?"

"Clear area up ahead—off to the right. Pretty close to the trees though."

"Yeah. Well, here goes. Tell everyone back there to keep a close eye on the tree line."

Riley gently settled the Starduster toward the ground but just as he was about to touchdown there was a frantic chorus from the passenger section of "Up! Up! Take it up!"

After nine months of flying near or around Sanctuary Riley didn't ask any dumb questions, he just lifted Dusty straight up as fast as he could.

Marshal looked back to the cabin. "What was it?"

Jaeger answered, "Bear. Big one too. Just came charging out of the woods."

Riley said, "Yeah. Typical." He looked at McPherson. "Where to?"

McPherson shrugged. "Doesn't matter. North or south. Just get us about a mile away."

Riley looked at the seemingly endless forest and asked, "Andy, how in the hell are you going to find Wedgies in all that? It's like looking for a needle in a haystack."

McPherson smiled. "A needle in a haystack? Ben, we're looking for creatures that look like trees in a forest. We're looking for a needle in a needle stack."

"You're looking for a tree in a forest," Marshal muttered.

"So how are you going to find them?" Riley asked.

"Probably won't, not unless we get damn lucky."

They flew north for a couple of minutes and set down without incident. As McPherson and Smith went down the ladder Andy turned and said, "Remember, don't call us, we'll call you. That's all we need is to have our Vids chirp when we're trying to avoid a pack of dire wolves." Everyone chuckled as the shuttle lifted and the two men walked to the forest and disappeared.

Smith and McPherson walked for a few minutes then stopped and just looked around, looking, listening, smelling, as Jerry Smith always put it "becoming one with your surroundings". They didn't say anything but they were both extremely happy to be finally out on their own. Of course, they knew that everyone at Cliffside from Alex Cummings on down were only trying to help with all their offers of support but they didn't understand the forest and the creatures of the forest. Neither did Smith and McPherson really and they knew it but they did learn more and more each day with each scout and this scout far into the western mountains was one that they had wanted to take for months.

The scouts soon settled into a routine. The two men would travel westward during daylight then find a substantial tree where they could spend the night high off the ground and hopefully out of the reach of anything big, nasty and unfriendly. They would contact Dusty a couple of times a day to report progress or lack of progress and almost always whoever they were talking to would urge them to come aboard Dusty for the night or even go back to Cliffside and pick up the scout in the morning. Of course, they always declined. The people who wanted the scouts to come in just didn't understand. They noted that one man aboard the Starduster, John Marshal, never mentioned not spending the nights in the forest. Himself an ex-Army scout, he understood.

That determination to remain in contact with their

surroundings paid off in an extraordinary stroke of luck on their twenty-first day of the trek. Smith and McPherson had spent the night in a mighty oak nestled in the crook of a branch that was large enough that they could both stretch out. As dawn broke and they prepared to descend to resume their search, Jerry reached out, touched Andy's boot, put a finger to his lips and pointed down.

McPherson looked down through the branches. He wasn't sure what he was looking for when he sucked in a breath. Part of the forest was moving fifty feet below him. What looked like the tops of trees were moving. He could only catch glimpses through the foliage but he was sure that they were Wedgies. He was also sure that what he was seeing was only a small group, maybe ten or twelve individuals evenly divided between large and small, adults and young.

After a careful check of their surroundings and the wind direction they climbed down and began to follow them. As far as they could tell the adult Wedgies were all female and they were obviously foraging, gathering nuts and berries and placing them into shoulder bags that each of the adults and a couple of the larger young carried. As they moved slowly through the woods they chattered, the humans assumed it was chattering, back and forth in their click-whistle language.

Jerry pointed to the ground and to the bushes that the Wedgies had just passed through. Andy nodded. Even though the Wedgies had made no effort to conceal their trail, except for the bare berry bushes they had left behind there was no more sign of their passing than a leaf on the wind.

McPherson signaled a halt and when he figured the Wedgies were far enough ahead, he said, "What do you think, Jerry? It's early so they probably just started out so the village or whatever they call home is probably back there somewhere." Then he pointed toward the foragers and asked,

"Should we trail that group or backtrack?"

Smith looked right and left and said, "We've never been able to spot a village. Let's see if we can find out where this bunch came from."

"Right."

The two men moved back along the Wedgies trail guided only by the partly bare nut and berry bushes the foraging group had picked over and just over a half hour later they practically stumbled into the Wedgie "village." It wasn't really a village or even an encampment. It was nothing, just a partially open part of the forest where a bunch of Wedgies were. No huts, lodges, teepees or shelters of any kind. There were no fire pits or obvious gathering places. Just tree-like creatures standing among other widely scattered trees. McPherson shook his head and thought, *no wonder we never saw the Wedgies from the air. Even now that we know where to look and what to look for, the Wedgies are hard to see.*

Jerry pointed to a large tree just back from the semi clearing. Andy nodded and they were soon in a perfectly concealed observation post forty feet above the ground. Jerry used the binoculars and Andy punched in notes on his pad. "Well," McPherson said, "I guess we'd better report in."

Marshal had to laugh out loud when Andy McPherson's cryptic text of *Contact. Details to follow.* reached Dusty 1 and was relayed to Cliffside and Wisdom. People went nuts in both locations. Marshal laughed again when the scientists and the staff realized that they had a million questions and couldn't ask them. It even got funnier, in Marshal's opinion, when the scouts made them wait all night and all the next day before texting, *Request pick-up* and giving coordinates that were nowhere near where everyone thought they were.

"Jokers," Marshal laughed. "Probably Jerry's doing."

It was full dark when Riley set the Starduster down at the designated location and Kurt and the deputies fanned out around the boarding ladder and waited for the scouts to come in. They adjusted their night vision goggles but all they could see were the trees around the clearing and all they could hear were night sounds of the forest. They waited. Where were the scouts?

Kurt Jaeger almost jumped out of his skin when a voice in his ear said, "Took you long enough to get here."

Jaeger spun around to see a grinning Jerry Smith standing right next to him. "Geeze, Jerry, don't do that."

Smith laughed and said, "Don't complain. It could have been him."

Jaeger spun the other way and almost bumped into big Andy McPherson. "Geeze!" he said again.

Marshal was sitting forty feet up on the edge of the shuttle's open cargo hold. He didn't think there would be any call for Junior's services in the pitch blackness but it was a nice place to sit. He chuckled. Smith had pulled the same stunt on him when they were on a scout back on Earth.

One thing you couldn't keep in the colony was a secret and the news of the scout's discovery spread like wildfire. By the time the shuttle returned to Cliffside a couple hundred colonists were milling around on the stone apron. It took a little pushing and shoving to clear a space big enough for Dusty to land and not being able to see anything directly beneath him Riley was holding his breath as the laughing colonists waved him down.

Even before the boarding stairs touched the ground hundreds of questions were shouted at everyone on board. McPherson and Smith hadn't said much on the return flight so the crew was as much in ignorance as anyone else but that didn't save them from the questioning crowd.

Alex started to tell everyone to go to the Conference Cave but looking at the shouting crowd she changed her mind and pointed at the Great Cavern. Two or three hundred colonists managed to squeeze through the four doors that pierced the wall that now closed the entrance to the cavern. Alex made her way to the rock with the scouts in tow.

She climbed up on the rock and said, "You all know why we are here so without any more words let's hear the report from our scouts."

A hush of anticipation spread through the Great Cavern

McPherson stepped up onto the rock—other people might climb up but McPherson stepped up—and began to briefly describe their scout and how they had stumbled across the Wedgies. The colonists were hanging on his every word and kept pressing him for more details. They were fascinated by the fact that the Wedgies had no shelters. They just lived in the open and while they knew about fire, except for rudimentary cooking, they didn't seem to use it.

But the fact that seemed to intrigue the colonists most was the fact that the Wedgies didn't lie down to sleep but just kind of dug their feet into the ground, spread their arms out and stopped moving.

When he was finally able to finish, he reiterated his and Smith's opinion that due to an unimaginable stroke of luck the group of Wedgies that they had found were associated with the ones who had attacked Cliffside.

Just as Alex was about to open the floor for discussion on what to do next there was a commotion outside the cavern as a shuttle landed and Ann Turner and Ty West made their way to the rock. Alex welcomed them and asked if they had anything to contribute. When they didn't, Alex continued asking the colonists what they thought should be done, if anything, about the Wedgies. The discussion ranged from sending the Chief and his deputies in and wiping them out to move them or just leave them alone.

When it was obvious to one and all that Link and his deputies weren't about to go in and massacre females and young, less drastic measures were considered and after more than an hour of suggestions, counter suggestions and some outright nutty ideas the bottom line seemed to be that even though the Wedgies were the better part of four hundred miles away in the mountains to the west the colonists were uncomfortable with leaving them where they were and wanted them moved. Exactly where they didn't know.

Marshal scratched his head, that didn't seem to make sense. This group of Wedgies was already four hundred miles away. How far was far enough? And, no matter where this group of Wedgies went, they would still know about the humans and Cliffside. He shrugged and asked, "We have no communication with the Wedgies except throwing spears and shooting back. How would you get them to move peacefully?"

While most of the colonists pondered that in silence Ann Turner turned to Alex and said, "Actually, Ms. Cummings, Ty and I have some thoughts on that."

A puzzled Alex answered, "Well then why don't you come up here and tell us about them."

Turner did and the colonists loved it and two days later all the pieces were in place.

As dawn broke over the Wedgie group or gathering, or whatever you wanted to call the non-village in the thin forest, the Voyagers were in position. As the Wedgies started to wake up—or whatever tree-like creatures do—and move around, they suddenly noticed something on a tree stump at the northern edge of their meadow. A great clicking and whistling broke out with much twig-like finger pointing. What was it? It was kind of like one of their own. It had a head, a body, arms and legs but it was obviously not one of them.

What they were seeing was big Andy McPherson wearing fur boots and leggings, a fur hat and wrapped in a great bear skin robe.

The aberration on the stump slowly raised its right arm and pointed toward the south.

The movement caused a stir among the Wedgies and one of the apparently older males reached for his throwing stick and a javelin. There was a loud noise as Jerry Smith in concealment in the bushes at McPherson's feet took aim and fired. There was a bang and the throwing stick shattered. The oldster jumped away from his broken throwing stick as if it was a poison snake.

The Wedgies click-whistle increased in volume while they pointed at the stick, at the sky and at McPherson.

At ten thousand feet and a few miles away Alex, Turner, and West watched. All of today's actions were predicated on the assumption that this group was associated with the group of Wedgies that the colonists had first encountered and that the stories that the Wedgies from the first encounter with the humans told them would match today's events.

In the stories would have been the fact when the first noise was heard a Wedgie died. Today when the noise was heard just a throwing stick was shattered.

The Wedgies chattered and as they moved forward toward McPherson again there was another noise as Jerry fired a round over their heads. The Wedgies stopped chattering and pointing. At the second noise nothing happened. Hopefully just like the stories they had heard. But the Wedgies hesitated, seeming reluctant to take the next step. According to the stories when the Wedgies moved forward again something dreadful happened, one of their members had been killed. But nothing dreadful happened. They milled around.

McPherson stood on his stump and raised his hand again pointing south.

Reluctantly as if compelled to do so the Wedgies slowly moved forward and true to the stories of the first encounter a monster appeared. That's when Marshal in Junior rose up from the bushes behind McPherson and hovered over his head.

That was the last straw for the Wedgies. They turned as one and fled and in an instant the semi clearing was empty. Alex turned to Olga who was working a joystick and monitoring a Vid screen "Can you track them?" she asked.

Olga had one drone moving parallel to the Wedgies line of flight. "Yes, Ma'am, as long as they're moving. It's when they stop that they're hard to find."

West frowned. "Olga, what direction are they headed?"

"South. Ummm, more southeast."

"That's what I thought."

"Yes," Alex said. "Can't have that. Ben, call everyone in and we'll jump around in front of them."

Apparently over their initial fright the Wedgies were still moving but slowly to the south east when they came to a clearing and saw that the thing was now standing in front of them again. Standing on a rock at the far end of the clearing and right in their way. The group stopped so quickly that they fell all over themselves.

Andy lifted his arm and pointed toward the southwest.

The Wedgies hesitated for a few minutes then slowly turned and moved off in that direction.

The humans herded the Wedgies to the south for two weeks and almost a hundred miles to an area of small streams and rivers. As the days had gone on Alex and the scientists had agreed that this area, a collection of small streams that Al Wilson insisted were the headwaters of Big River, would be the boundary line. The Earthmen would drive the Wedgies to the south of the headwaters of Big River. As long as the Wedgies stayed south of this network of rivers the humans figured that was far enough.

The Wedgies crossed the last stream and the next morning when they stirred to life and looked north there was no fur clad monster pointing them onward and a few days later when a small group attempted to cross back over the southernmost tributary, they found the fur clad thing waiting for them.

This time they got the message.

CHAPTER 21

Much to his wife's increasing annoyance Marshal kept twisting in his chair and staring across the cafeteria. "John!" Alex finally exclaimed. "What is the matter with you? You haven't been listening to a word that I've said. What are you looking for?"

"They're up to something," Marshal muttered. "I can feel it."

"What are you talking about? Who's up to what?"

Marshal pointed across the cafeteria. "Those two."

Alex tried to pick out who her husband was referring to across the crowded tables. "Who?" she asked again.

"Those two," Marshal said as though the two he was referring to should be obvious to anyone. "Simmons and Mahoney."

"Tony and Paul?" she asked. "What have they done?"

"I don't know. But they're up to something. Probably something to do with the festival."

"My sweet, everybody in the colony is involved with something for the festival."

Marshal muttered something under his breath.

Alex shook her head. She really didn't know what her sometimes exasperating, sometimes goofy, but always lovable husband was on about. As far as Simmons and Mahoney went, in her opinion, in the seven months that the colony had been in operation Tony and Paul had become two of its more valued members. In fact, Cathy Jackson and Erin McPherson couldn't say enough good things about them. It seems that they had attached themselves to the food service section and whenever they weren't engaged in official colony work and were on their own time, they were more than willing to take their robots and as many of the Bug Brigade as they could fit inside the spheres, off into the wilds to find or fetch whatever spice or edible the kitchen staff desired. Bjorn and the farmers loved them too because whenever the two RJs and the kids went off on these expeditions, and had the time, they would plant the seeds or starter shoots the farmers gave them starting little plantations all around the colony. The Johnny Appleseed's of Sanctuary Mahoney called them. Also, whenever they went on these foraging expeditions their robots always carried an empty storage bin which always came back full of whatever fruits, berries or nuts were in the area.

Alex looked at her husband. "My sweet, Tony and Paul have been among the hardest working members of the community. If we had knights here Cathy and Erin would be proposing them for knighthood. And, look at the kids. Tony and Paul have given them jobs, something meaningful and useful to do. The kids love them. The parents love them."

Marshal nodded to his wife as if she had just proved his suspicions. "See! Exactly! It's unnatural! Back on Earth they never did anything for Voyager when they were on the ground. To Simmons and Mahoney, Sand Flea was just a way station between working in orbit on the spaceship and Las Vegas."

"Well," Alex said. "It's a new life. A new planet. The boys have found a new direction."

But Marshal wasn't buying it. "I don't believe it, Luv. They're up to something."

Her exclamation of "John!" was only met with more muttering.

Alex thought the boys probably were just thinking about the festival; after all, everyone else was. She tried to remember how the idea of an official holiday, a fall festival, came about. She thought that it originated with the kids in school asking the teachers if there was going to be a Halloween here on Sanctuary and there was no doubt in any adult's mind that the kids wanted Halloween. They probably didn't care what it was called as long as they could dress up and go trick-or-treating. So, the parents got together with the school teachers, Evie Porter and Mary Henderson, and decided on a costume party at school with suitable treats of course. But then as word of the kid's costume party spread through the colony many adults, just being larger versions of kids at heart, wanted a chance to dress up and party too.

Early on the colonists had decided that along with the Earth calendar Earth holidays did not apply on Sanctuary. They would have their own holidays. Holidays that had meaning here on this planet. The winter holidays of Earth passed while almost everyone was still in orbit in cryogenic hibernation but since the colony had been active Memorial Day, July 4th and Labor Day had passed without acknowledgement. Everyone seemed to agree that that was good, the only problem was that so far, the colony only had one, count them, *one* holiday and that was New Year's Day way back in Month One. It was now Month Seven (Alex thought that if the colony continued its unimaginative way of naming things the months would be One thru Twelve forever).

So, the idea grew from a costume party for the kids to a costume party for everyone. From there it went to celebrating the harvest. Great! And with singing and dancing too. Even greater! The artisans thought that the Harvest Festival would be a superb showcase for arts and crafts. Excellent idea and that was included. What about competitions? The lumberjacks were right there. With only three modern, solar powered chain saws available the woodsmen were relearning the old skills of the woodsman's trade and were anxious to show them off. Excellent. And races for kids too.

There were many who felt left out when competitions were discussed. They were the ones that had skills that they were proud of but skills that didn't lend themselves to competition. No problem. We'll have demonstrations mixed in with the competitions.

There were so many talented individuals, Alex couldn't believe where all the musical instruments came from, bands were formed—at least four who were going to perform for the evenings dancing—that a talent show was included and after much discussion the only judge would be the audience itself.

And food. Lots of food. This led to more potential competitions.

Alex shook her head again. She was now the unofficial, but very official when it came to allocating resources, CEO of this run-away freight train called the Harvest Festival. One thing that you could say for the colonists on Sanctuary was they weren't ones to let the grass grow under their feet. Once it was decided that there would be a festival, events progressed with alarming speed. The dates—because it grew into a two-day affair—were quickly settled. After considering the phases of the moon, made more difficult here on Sanctuary with two moons, they rejected lunar involvement. The Harvest moon, the first full moon after the autumnal equinox, might come too soon before the harvest was actually in and the Hunters Moon, the second full moon after the equinox, might come too late. No, a date on the calendar would be better and the third weekend of the seventh month, what would be October back on Earth, was chosen.

Next was the venue. There were really only three choices: the stone shelf in front of the caves, the ranch or the farm. The farm was the unanimous choice and with less than a week to go the carpenters were putting the finishing touches on a horseshoe shaped amphitheater with a wooden stage in the open area and bleacher seating for six hundred people. A vast open area stretched off to the west toward the caves for the competitions and demonstrations. Everyone in the stands would have an excellent view of what was going on.

On either side of the amphitheater from the river road north of the farm to the pig pens at the farms southern edge were four more wooden platforms for dancing and on the southern end of the amphitheater, away from river road, the farmers had emptied one of the canvas green houses and set up tables for the artisans. Further on were two long trestle tables. Alex knew that there was no way six hundred people were going to sit there to eat and the tables would probably be used for displaying the wares from the two cooking competitions—which quickly became three when the BBQ competition split into two events thanks to the never-ending war brought forward from Earth to Sanctuary between the pork people from the Carolinas and the east coast and the beef people of Texas and the great plains. Alex smiled, to her it didn't matter, it was all good. The other culinary completion was going to be pies. André was selected to judge the BBQ. Link Lincoln was also selected to be a judge but he begged off because, no mean hand around a grill himself, he planned to be a contestant. That left André as the only judge much to the consternation of the contestants who sniffed, asking, "What does a Frenchman know about BBQ?"

The judges for the pie baking contest were, of course, Cathy and Erin. Some of the ladies blanched a little at that. They would be tough judges and no one was going to win it due to a popularity contest.

Many of the colonists wanted Alex to be the judge of everything but she managed to avoid everything except the costumes. Even then she only agreed if the panel was expanded to include a couple of people who really knew something about design and fashion, so Joan McPherson and much to his surprise Jordan Roberts joined Alex as judges. After much discussion the costume judging was broken down into just two categories: kids twelve and under and the rest with special prizes given for humor, originality, or whatever other category the judges thought up. Joan and Jordan agreed with her that there would be lots of those.

The morning of the first annual Sanctuary Harvest Festival dawned with a thick layer of cloud covering the land and an anxious Project Director checking with Al Wilson... again.

"No, Alex, I don't think it will rain," Al reassured her. "It's going to be cloudy but cheer up. It might even break up a little this afternoon."

Slightly reassured Alex smiled when her husband said, "Don't worry about it, Luv. Sure, it would be better dry but this crowd is going to party today no matter what." And with that he was off.

Marshal went and cranked up Junior. He really didn't have anything to do today so he along with everyone else were helping where they could.

A couple of hours later Alex left her desk and started down the river road towards the farm. There were soon a dozen or so people waking with her laughing, talking, greeting each other. This, she thought, is the way it's supposed to be. A beautiful, uncrowded, unpolluted world where humans could just enjoy nature's bounty. The crowd grew as they approached the amphitheater and then magically dispersed as each colonist found a seat and at exactly noon Alexandria Cummings stood on the wooden platform and smiled up at six hundred cheering colonists.

"Good afternoon and welcome to the first annual Sanctuary Harvest Festival."

That brought loud cheers and greetings back at her.

"This weekend we are putting work aside and we are going to have a party and my heartfelt thanks to you all— you've earned a party!"

The roar of approval that greeted her startled a flock of birds on the far side of the farm into flight. Alex went on.

"It's been a hard seven months. We've had our successes, our failures and our losses but we are still here becoming more settled and stronger every day and making Sanctuary our own. Yes?"

Another roar.

"The harvest is in and even with just the experimental plots our farmers have raised enough food to feed the whole colony for a year."

Cheers.

"But enough of that, you all know your

accomplishments and take pride in them as you should. I'll now turn you over to your Master of Ceremonies, Colonel Alexander McPherson."

A roar of approval greeted that and only intensified with laughter when McPherson said in a ringmaster's voice,

"Ladies and Gentlemen and children of all ages, welcome to the Harvest Festival. You all know the agenda; this afternoon will be competitions and demonstrations of all kinds followed by the BBQ judging and dinner. Then the pie judging and dessert."

The crowd roared their approval.

McPherson continued. "Then we will take a break until 1900 to give everyone time to get into their costumes then we'll have the costume judging right here followed by music and dancing until you drop."

The happy noise from the stands made it clear that the colonists heartily approved.

"All right," McPherson said, "first up in today's competitions will be our younger Sanctuarians. Will all those fourteen and under who wish to compete please step forward to the cleared area beyond the stage."

About thirty kids jumped out of the stands and ran across the stage. While the crowd cheered, they were painfully aware of how few children there really were. True, many women were pregnant and the docs were expecting a baby boom in a couple of months but in the future, there was going to be a tremendous generation gap.

The children were quickly organized by age and to the cheers of six hundred roaring adults the running, jumping and throwing began. Boys against boys. Girls against girls, and boys against girls with loud roars of approval when the girls more than held their own. The next to last competition was javelin throwing using a modified version of the Wedgies throwing sticks. There were *Ooohs* and *Ahaas* when a husky fourteen-year-old named Bill Thomas hurled a javelin almost two hundred yards.

There were some looks of concern, too. If one of their youngsters could do that, how far could a full-grown Wedgie throw one?

The last event for the youngsters was a cross-country foot race—up the river road to the caves, cross in front of the caves and then return on the south side of the cleared fields. About two and a half miles altogether. All the kids ranging in age from sixteen to six took off in a single body with the cheers of the adults ringing in their ears. Of course, the older, bigger kids broke out in front and as they went up the road and soon they were strung out by size with little Sally McPherson, age six, bringing up the rear. Some of the parents began to grumble that it wasn't fair to the little ones but the Colonel reassured them that all that was taken into consideration and prizes would be awarded by age. In fact, the judges had planned that for every youngster that finished there would be a prize.

The crowd began to buzz when they realized that the bigger, older kids weren't having it all their own way

There were a couple of smaller figures mixed in with the larger ones.

They began to cheer when it became clear that one of the younger members was pulling away from the rest. No not so much pulling away as the rest were falling back. The small figure didn't speed up or slow down; he just kept the steady pace that he maintained throughout.

Young Peter McPherson crossed the finish line a good ten yards ahead of his nearest competitor to the obvious pleasure of his father and Jerry Smith. Jerry had coached the boy how to pace himself and was pleased with how well Peter had listened.

While the youngsters had been racing the final touches were put on the venue for the lumberjack competitions. Most of the colonists had never seen woodsmen at work and were amazed as their skills were displayed and their cheers and enthusiasm drove the lumberjacks on.

They cut logs manually with an ax and saw almost as fast as they went through them with a chainsaw. But the hit of the day was the pole climb. Up a forty-foot pole, ring a bell and back on the ground in less than a minute. The colonists loved it.

The BBQ was a great success. First place in the pork category had been won by the saw-mill operator Whit Latham and the beef prize went to Hank Ferguson the supply chief—and as much as André tried to get their sauce recipes from them, they weren't talking. The BBQ and everything else that had been prepared during the afternoon's festivities quickly disappeared.

Dessert had to wait. There were over fifty pies in the pie competition and Jackson and McPherson were not going to be rushed in their decision. When they finally declared Helen Nordstrom the winner and opened up the table the pies disappeared in a heartbeat.

The colonists also disappeared as everyone went to get into their costumes for the evening activities.

At 1900 sharp the colonel stepped to the center of the stage and invited all the children to join him. Then the adults.

It was a madhouse. Most of the colonists had gone to great lengths in their costume design and execution and all wanted to be in the competition. Alex, Joan and Jordan had tried to establish categories such as funniest, scariest and best design, but the categories spilled over into each other. In the end, it was hundreds of contestants parading across the stage with the judges selecting the ones that caught their eye and figuring out a category for it later. Over fifty prizes were awarded and everyone seemed happy.

Then, still in costume, the colonists and the musicians moved to the dance platforms and the party began. Old fashioned square dancing on the large platform, Texas line dancing on another, ballroom dancing on yet another. There was something for everyone and it seemed that most of the colonists moved from venue to venue.

Alex and John walked from stage to stage greeting everyone and as they progressed toward the trestle tables, they heard singing. Loud singing. Most of the young men and many young women were there and were having a great time. Before Alex or Marshal could comment Tony Simmons hailed them and thrust a mug in their hands. "Have a sip!"

Expecting some of the fruit juice that had been prepared they both took a deep swallow and immediately dissolved into sputtering and coughing much to the delight of all the youngsters present.

"Tony," Alex gasped, "what is this?"

"Just a little apple juice."

Marshal said, "Apple juice my foot—that's applejack! That's what you two have been up to these past couple of months. I knew it! All that goodie, goodie stuff was just a cover so you could collect apples."

"Who? Us?" Tony and Paul said innocently.

The applejack was a great success and the party went on far into the night.

As Alex and John walked toward the next dance platform they were met by Evie Porter. She jabbed her finger into Marshal's chest. "Where," she demanded, "is Dave Allen?"

A bemused Marshal said, "Dave? I have no idea."

"Well," Evie said, "you go find him and bring him—" she pointed to the tables by the dance platform, "—over there." And she turned and walked away.

"What," exclaimed Alex, "was that all about?!"

Marshal shook his head. "I don't know but I guess I better try to find Dave."

Alex laughed. "Well that shouldn't be hard. Look."

Marshal looked back toward the amphitheater and saw Allen and several others walking toward him. He took Allen by the arm and started steering him toward Evie Porter. "You, my friend, have been summoned," he said.

"What?" Allen got out.

Marshal didn't answer. He and Allen walked up to Evie and with a curt nod of her head said, "Good!" and turned to reveal a brightly blushing Mary Henderson sitting on the bench behind her. Porter took Mary's hand, pulled her up off the bench, put her hand into Allen's and, pointing toward the dance platform, ordered, "Dance."

Alex laughed. Before Allen and Henderson knew what hit them, they were dancing. Alex gave Evie a hug. "Well done, Evie."

A slightly confused Marshal asked, "What just happened?"

Evie Porter snorted. "Those two young idiots are in love but both of them are too shy to do anything about it."

"Oh!"

The dance ended but Dave and Mary didn't return to the table. In fact, a hugely smiling Dave and an absolutely glowing Mary didn't return until the band took a break.

The next day everyone was back in their seats at noon. Colonel McPherson stepped to center stage but before he said a word Ben Riley in Dusty 1 opened the show by sneaking up on the crowd from behind and roaring over the horseshoe shaped stands at well over the speed of sound creating a thunderous sonic boom. The momentary gasp was followed by cheers and laughter. Many of the colonists, especially the farmers and lumbermen were not familiar with the capabilities of the Stardusters and were amazed as Riley put the shuttle through its paces. Riley always complained that the Stardusters were flying bricks and that people shouldn't expect him to fly them like a helicopter but he made his own arguments mute as he touched down vertically as light as a feather, held the shuttle a few feet off the ground and turned in a full circle. Then he lifted straight up until he was out of sight and an instant later returned with another sonic boom.

The colonists ate it up.

Many more demonstrations of artistry and skill followed and the colonists loved them all.

Next up were the farmers who after showing off the capabilities of all the attachments that came with the two "Little Giant" tractors wowed the crowd with the sheer size of the fruits and vegetables that they were growing on Sanctuary. Tomatoes the size of cantaloupes. Three-foot ears of corn. Cabbages with the head the size of a pumpkin and leaves that extended five feet all around.

The ranchers even made a presentation. They hadn't progressed far enough to have horses to ride but Ellen had made a Vid that showed the ranch, the first round-up, efforts in separating and taming the animals. The gasps and cheers really came at the shots of the ranchers standing right up next to the horses and especially of Faye Carson, all five foot two of her, with her hand on the bridle of a mare that stood a full eighteen hands tall.

The colonel stood in the center of the stage. "And now, ladies and gentlemen, a demonstration from our

Scouts." Oh yeah, the crowd loved the scouts especially after the word spread (both factual and embellished) of what they had done to the Wedgies.

When McPherson waved his hand toward the back of the stage and the fields beyond, the colonists looked and saw nothing, just the fields and brush extending all the way back to the cliff. After a few minutes began to mumble.

"It's not a trick," McPherson said. "I assure you our scouts are out there and will join me here on the stage shortly."

Six hundred pairs of eyes redoubled their scrutiny of every tree, bush and blade of grass. Someone exclaimed, "There over by the road I saw something move." Everyone including the colonel turned to look. Nothing, and after a few minutes they turned their attention back to McPherson and gasped for standing next to Colonel McPherson on an otherwise empty wooden platform was Jerry Smith.

The *Ooohs* and *Ahaas* got louder as they began to ask the where's and how's which were then followed by thunderous cheers. But McPherson raised his hands and said, "Jerry here says that you just weren't paying attention but you have another chance; in fact, you have two chances. Andy is still out there somewhere and the scouts have taken on Andy's son Peter, the young lad that won the footrace, as an apprentice. Peter is still out there also."

The six hundred pairs of eyes were straining in their sockets trying to look everywhere at once when a sighting was again reported by the river road. Everyone looked. Again, there was nothing until they looked back to the stage and were astounded to see Andy McPherson standing next to the colonel and Smith.

They laughed and cheered and said to themselves, "Okay, surely, we can find the kid!" and then broke into laughter and applause when young Peter stepped out from behind his dad.

The last demonstration of the day was the RJs and their robots. They didn't need any introduction. They were everyone's favorite. Even though there were only five of them it seemed that they were everywhere contributing to every project in the colony. Colonel McPherson pointed toward the cliffs. The robots flew down from the cliffs in formation, five abreast, and hovered over the stage. Then they demonstrated the dexterity of the mechanical arms by picking individual grapes from a bunch and peeling an orange. They concluded by demonstrating maneuverability by doing a robot dance— kind of an improvised Virginia Reel with only five dancers.

The colonists loved it all and it was a laughing happy crowd that dispersed down to the food service area. No BBQ tonight. Cathy Jackson and Erin McPherson were in charge of tonight's menu. The entire meal was food from the farm... and it was delicious.

The talent show lasted into the wee hours of the morning. Everyone who wanted to perform was given a chance. Musicians, singers, dancers, even a couple of magicians. The crowd loved every act, even the ones that weren't very good. Many were excellent and the crowd demanded encores.

The morning sun was just cresting the horizon to the east when a happy, contented Alexandria Cummings walked with her husband back toward the cliffs. The second official holiday on Sanctuary, the Autumn Harvest Festival, had been a rousing success.

CHAPTER 22

The morning after produced a few sore heads from Tony and Paul's applejack but by any measure the Harvest Festival was a great success. A spirit of togetherness spread through the colony and the Voyagers were anxious to complete the last major project of the season. Before Al Wilson's projected wind and rain hit Cliffside and the winter storms swept down over the prairie, they had to finish the ranchers' ranch house. Alex smiled as she watched the colonists mill around the four Stardusters. Although the colony had carpenters, cabinet makers, engineers, masons and many other disciplines they didn't have any home builders and before they built the cook house down at the farm no one had actually built a house before. But they learned and now the entire community was going to throw itself into building a ranch house out on the edge of the prairie. And they were going to complete it from start to finish in only two days.

And about time too Alex thought. Getting the ranch

house built had to be the most frustrating project the colony had undertaken. One delay after another.

First it was the local predators around the rancher's canyon. The big cat that they had encountered on their initial exploration of the canyon hadn't gone away and Alex had been forced to augment the ranchers with a half dozen deputies so a twenty-four-hour watch over their hard-won horses could be maintained.

That solution was unsatisfactory. It was like the ranch was under siege.

Finally, Linda Murphy, who had spent her summers "chasing mountain lions" on her uncle's ranch in Montana, made a presentation to the staff and convinced them that as long as the horses were there the predators would be also. She also said that the only cure was to hunt the varmints out and that she was just the girl to do it.

Her presentation went over so well that the staff was insistent that the colony's entire resources be put at her disposal. Poor Linda almost had a heart attack at the thought of dozens of farmers and lumberjacks, with guns blazing, blundering around the foothills and finally convinced the staff that a small team would be better—preferably just her. Thinking back on it, Alex had to laugh. Murph had done such a good job of convincing the staff that the critters had to go that now the staff was determined to support her with everything the colony had whether she wanted it or not. It was like the colony wanting to support the scouts. It was hard to convince them that less was better.

They finally decided that there would be five hunters; Murph who would be the team chief, Grant and Maryanne Foster and the two deputies, Byron Atwood and Sid Jenkins, who lived out at the ranch. The hunt would be supported by one shuttle, one robot and Ellen Nolan and the drones already at the ranch.

Despite all efforts to keep the mission low key a large crowd had gathered to see Dusty 1 lift off with Junior tucked away in the cargo bay and Murph and the two Fosters the only occupants in the luxurious passenger section.

Two weeks later the team was back at Cliffside.

Alex never asked for or received an official report of the hunt but from what her husband told her it was a pretty hairy adventure.

Without wasting any time as soon as the shuttle arrived at the ranch, Murph established a command post in one of the rancher's tents and laid out her plan for the hunt. Ellen Nolan would remain at the ranch and act as coordinator between the various elements of the hunt. The hunting party would be on foot with Nolan keeping her drone over them. Marshal and Junior would search a mile or so farther out and Riley would take whatever ranchers could be spared and search still farther out. They would spend their nights at the ranch.

Two hours after landing they lifted off toward the first search area that Murph had identified a rocky outcrop about five miles up in the rugged foothills west of the ranch.

Alex remembered how her husband had shaken his head as he told her that following Murph's directions he had circled the hunting party and taken Junior low and slow over the jagged hills. Rough country. Forest along the many creeks and small rivers and on the sides and tops of the hills and bare rocks down below in the hollows and gullies. He thought a big cat or a bear or just about anything could be right below him and it would probably blend in so completely with its surroundings that he would never see it.

The rest of the story she had pieced together from talking to the surviving members of the hunt.

An hour or so after Riley dropped them off the ground party was approaching a rocky hill side that Linda thought might be good cat country when Ellen broke in on the com. "Murph, the horse herd in the big canyon has just been attacked by a large cat. Floyd thinks that it's Big Kitty."

"Well damn," Murphy said. "Here we are out looking for it and it attacks us. What happened?"

"Not exactly sure. From what I'm hearing it snuck down the canyon wall, attacked the mares and when the guys shot at it, it went back up the wall."

"Do you know if they hit it?" Murphy asked. "And do you know which way it went after it got to the top of the wall?"

"Hang on," she said. A couple of minutes later she answered, "They're pretty sure they hit it at least a couple of times and they think it went west."

"Okay, Ellen, thanks. Ben, John, did you get that?"

"Got it," Riley answered. "What's the plan?"

"I'm going to hunker down here. You and John scout the country between me and the ranch. It looks like the big kitty could be running right towards us."

Murphy checked the wind. It was blowing from the east which was good, she thought. With any kind of luck, the cat wouldn't have any idea that they were there. She spread her small force out along the rocky hillside and waited.

Fifteen minutes passed. Twenty, with no sighting and with nothing but negative reports from Marshal and Riley. Murphy began to get nervous. She looked over to her right to Maryanne Foster. Maryanne shrugged and then screamed, "Down, Linda! Get down!"

Murphy dropped as Maryanne brought her elephant gun up and fired across Murphy's position. The blast took the big cat full in the chest killing it instantly, but not before it had savaged the deputy to Murphy's left. Young Byron Atwood was dead before they could get to him.

Alex sighed. Atwood was a good kid. He had graduated high school when they were at Sand Flea and joined Chet Barton's Project Voyager security force and when the Barton's decided to remain on Earth, he joined Link's force to go to Sanctuary. Tragic. One more marker in the little cemetery.

After a day to pull themselves together at the ranch Linda took her team and went back out on the hunt again. Although they had killed Big Kitty on the first day Murphy kept them at it for another ten days and during that time they bagged two more cats, a bear and decimated a pack of wolves.

Murph said that she was pretty sure that the ranchers wouldn't be troubled by predators for the near future but Alex shook her head again—Murph was probably right but the cost was high.

Once the cat problem had been tackled, there was a problem with the lumber needed to build the ranch house. Timber was abundant around Cliffside but scarce on the edge of the prairie and the one grove of pine that was discovered not too far from the rancher's canyon had been wiped out by a wildfire. So, after an extensive search around the rancher's canyon came up empty, they decided that all the timber for building the ranch house would have to be cut in the vicinity of Cliffside, finished in Latham's saw mill and then ferried out to the ranch in the Stardusters cargo bays.

It was during this time that the building materials were being assembled that the Wedgies attacked and then there was the Harvest Festival.

But all that was behind them. The building materials had all been assembled. In fact, the entire ranch house had been built in Whit Latham's lumber yard, all the pieces had been carefully marked and labeled and the ranch house disassembled. Now two thirds of it were neatly laid out ready for shipment while the other third was tucked away in the Stardusters' four cargo bays.

At Alex's signal forty laughing chattering colonists piled into the shuttles. There would be two more shuttle trips after this one before everything needed was in place at the ranch. Alex took the jump seat behind Ben Riley and her husband, gave Marshal a kiss on the cheek and they were off.

The shuttle pilots didn't spare the horses and all four Stardusters were on the ground and being unloaded in less than an hour and the colonists went to work. For everything that had gone wrong up to now the actual building of the ranch went off like clockwork. The shuttles were unloaded in record time and lifted off for the second load and less than five hours later they were back with full cargo bays, one more robot and forty more Voyagers.

When the last load arrived just before sundown the foundation and outer framing was complete. Bonfires appeared all over the canyon floor and a spirited drawing was held to see who would get to spend the night stretched out in the Starduster's luxurious seats. The losers laughed and soon a hundred Voyagers were asleep on the ground by a couple dozen campfires clustered around the four shuttles and the ranch.

Alex and John sat high off the ground on the edge of Dusty 1's cargo bay as the happy noises slowly faded away. Marshal waved his hand out over the canyon. "Quite a difference from a few months ago, Luv," he said. "Back then they were uncertain, unsure. Now look at them! Ready to tackle dire wolves barehanded."

Alex laughed. "Well maybe not that confident, my

sweet, but, yes, I know what you mean. Isn't it wonderful?"

The next day the ranch house was completed right down to the last bed in each of the twelve bedrooms that were built off of the long hall that ran west along the canyon wall from the cook house and the last set of tables and chairs in the common room. With the job completed the colonists were anxious to be off. Not willing to wait for the shuttles to make three round trips, thirty colonists piled into each of the four Starddusters and made it back to Cliffside in one trip.

As it turned out they had completed the ranch just in time. As Al Wilson had predicted the windy, rainy winter settled in around them and outside activities slowed down to a crawl.

Alex sat at her desk with her fingers steepled under her chin in her typical thinking position when she looked up at a soft knock on her office door frame (the door was never closed) to see Colonel Alex McPherson and Sam Teutopolis standing in the doorway.

A bit surprised she recovered and said, "Gentlemen, come in. Have a seat." Indicating the chairs in front of her desk. "To what do I owe the honor of this visit?"

McPherson smiled. "Just wondering if you had a minute?"

Alex's senses were at full twitch. These guys were up to something. "Sure. Shoot."

"Ah," McPherson said. "It's more like something we would like to show you."

Now thoroughly intrigued, she asked, "Do I need my coat?"

The men nodded and they went out. The wind was picking up, Alex noticed and she said, "Al says wind and rain for tomorrow."

McPherson laughed. "Wind and rain for the next six

months probably."

Teutopolis snapped his fingers and said, "We care not for wind and rain."

McPherson gave him a look and he said no more.

Alex wondered what that was all about as the trio turned into the machine shop cave. McPherson said, "What we want to show you is in the wood shop."

Before a confused Alex Cummings could point out that the wood shop was the next cave over, they were walking toward the back of the machine shop and Alex was being greeted on all sides by "Hi, Alex," "Hey, Boss," and a formal but polite "Ms. Cummings," by smiling people who, she could tell, were in on a secret that she wasn't privy to. Like her office desk and the conference table and chairs she thought, but before she could comment on it, she was standing at the back of the machine shop's cave and looking at a tunnel that hadn't been there before.

"After you, Madam Director," McPherson said.

Alex walked through the short tunnel into the wood shop. The surprise on her face must have been evident because all the carpenters and machinists crowded around laughing and talking delighted that their surprise had worked.

"What? When?" she sputtered.

"Been working on it for weeks." McPherson said. He put an arm around Teutopolis's shoulders. "Sam here is the brains behind it."

"Aw," he said blushing. "I just got tired of walking out in the rain."

Alex smiled. "Well I'm tired of walking in the rain too." She thought for a moment and asked, "Do you think you could cut tunnels between the other caves? Maybe create a corridor that runs the whole length of Cliffside?"

McPherson hesitated. "Well I don't know. None of us

are geologists. We wouldn't want to go digging around and bring the whole mountain down on top of us. The idea for this tunnel came from Sam here. He did some mining back in Colorado."

Alex turned to Teutopolis. "Well, Sam?"

A clearly flustered Sam Teutopolis said, "I don't know, Ma'am. This was pretty straight forward. A short distance through hard rock." He waved his hand. "About the rest of the mountain—I don't know."

Alex patted him on the shoulder. "Thank you, Sam. You're an honest man." And she was on her com. "Ann, where are you?"

Ann Turner answered, "I'm up at Wisdom. What's up?"

"I'm just wondering if any of you bright scientists know anything about geology."

"Geology!" Turner exclaimed. "I don't know. Not me, that's for sure. I took an undergraduate course once but all I remember is that diamonds are good. Why?"

Alex laughed and said, "The Colonel and his merry men and women have just cut a connecting tunnel between the machine shop and the wood shop and I'm wondering if it would be possible to connect all the caves."

"Hey, that's cool. Stay out of the rain."

Alex said, "How about asking around and bringing anyone with any knowledge of geology or mining to the staff meeting tomorrow."

"Okay!" came the enthusiastic answer.

The next morning, she and Marshal walked along the cliff face with Wilson's promised wind and rain pushing them along. "It would be nice to show up at a staff meeting not looking like a drowned rat," she grumbled.

"Isn't that what this meeting's about?" Marshal laughed as they hung their ponchos on the drip rack and took their seats.

Alex looked around the table and said, "Before we tackle any new business, especially the topic that everyone is buzzing about, I would like to make sure that we are all in agreement on next month's mid-winter festival."

The mid-winter festival had been under discussion for weeks but had kind of gotten pushed aside by other events. Everyone had pretty much agreed that a mid-winter solstice festival would be the third official holiday on the Sanctuary calendar.

Since the beginning the colony was determined that Earth holidays didn't apply to Sanctuary. That decision was fine for the adults but there were thirty kids who had insisted on celebrating Halloween, which had become the Harvest Festival. Now these same kids were making it crystal clear that they wanted Christmas. At least they wanted a Christmas Tree and presents. So, in their practical way the Voyagers had compromised. They would have a Winter Festival celebrating the mid-winter solstice but with elements of a traditional Earth Christmas thrown in. There would be decorations, Christmas Trees, presents, and a community sing along. Even Santa was going to make an appearance and let the smallest kids wonder how his reindeer flew to Sanctuary.

There were nods around the table. Most of the adults were also looking forward to Christmas. "Then I would like to get on with two new items."

The staff kind of looked at each other. They knew they were there to talk about the tunnels. They wondered what the second was.

Alex went on. "The first item is, of course, the possibility of opening up tunnels to connect the caves. As I'm sure you all know by now, Sam Teutopolis here has drilled a tunnel between the machine shop and the wood shop. The question is, can we open up connecting tunnels between the other caves, maybe even creating a corridor that would run the length of Cliffside from the Blacksmith shop to the Starduster Cavern? So, any thoughts?"

"Well for openers," Colonel McPherson said, "I can tell you that a tunnel from the wood shop to the Blacksmith shop won't be necessary. Brian's not interested."

"Why?" Doc Nancy asked.

"I guess he just feels that it's not necessary. You know that he and Helen and the apprentices live in the shop and hardly ever come out. They don't even come up here for meals." He nodded to Cathy. "Cathy and Erin give Helen the supplies and she feeds them down there. Brian says that they never worry about the wind and rain. Heck, they never even closed off the entrance to the cave."

There was a general chuckle around the table and Marshal added, "You know it's a long way and there's nothing between here and the Starduster Cavern. It might not be practical to bore a tunnel between those two and Evie told me that she didn't want people traipsing around in the back of her classroom."

Another chuckle and Cathy Jackson said, "Alex, after you mentioned the possibility of connecting the caves, we took a quick look at our food service facilities and at first glance we didn't see where we could cut a tunnel. We've used the entire south wall of the Great Cavern for the kitchen, the serving lines, food storage and freezers."

Nancy Watson sniffed. "Ignore these nay-sayers, Alex. John and I think that it's a wonderful idea. Maybe cut down on the number of colds that we've been seeing. And we would love to see a connecting tunnel between the dispensary and the Great Cavern and the dispensary and the medical college."

Alex nodded and looked around the table. "Any other comments?"

Hank Ferguson said, "A tunnel between the Great Cavern and supply wouldn't be a bad idea. Keep stuff out of the rain."

Alex looked toward the scientists and Ty West shrugged. "I don't know how much help we can be, Alex. Neither one of us are geologists and you just sprang this on us yesterday but we'll be happy to give it a look and maybe we can contribute something."

Alex had been sitting quietly absorbing the comments and she smiled and said, "Thank you all for your comments and I think they have at least given us a direction to proceed." She looked at the staff. "Before our next meeting I would like you to survey your work areas and determine if a connecting tunnel is practical or even desirable. Ty and Ann, I would like you to get with Sam and do the same thing. Everyone, take your time and we'll revisit the subject next week."

After the nods and murmurs of agreement rolled around the table she went on. "Now for the next item. I would like to see us explore the southern half of this continent."

That got everyone's attention and in the general discussion that followed Alex and the scientists pointed out that with Wisdom as their only satellite in permanent orbit over the middle of the northern hemisphere, any definitive coverage of the southern hemisphere was impossible from space.

Wisdom was in communication range and Wilson and the scientists shared with the staff what they knew about the southern hemisphere of Middle Finger which wasn't much. "A thousand miles or so south of the equatorial green belt the eastern edge of landmass takes an abrupt turn to the west and keeps narrowing all the way down to the southern tip of the continent. There is a high mountain range on the west coast with its western slopes almost constantly covered in clouds. Under the clouds is probably a coast line that is all cliffs and rainforest. Desert to the east and rolling tree covered hills on the southern edge of the green belt. And that's about all we can see from here."

They kicked ideas around the table for a while but it was obvious that if they wanted to learn more about what lay to the south of the tropical green belt the way forward was to do a series of fly-bys to map the entire southern half of the continent followed by actual landings in selected locations.

Once decided on a course of action the colony moved with its usual speed and a week later Riley and Marshal with Dave Allen in the jump seat monitoring the sensors were again on a fly-by approaching the west coast of Middle Finger only this time it was the southern coast of the continent. And just as they had remembered from the flights of almost a year ago, they were in the middle of a violent storm, wind and rain lashing the shuttle.

"A bit of Déjà vu all over again," Dave laughed.

Initially the flight from the ocean did seem to be a repeat of their flights over the northern half of the continent. The coast consisted of the same two-hundred-foot cliff and behind it a rainforest but here in the southern hemisphere the mountains were higher. Not as high as the massive range they had encountered on Index but at least a couple of thousand feet higher than the mountains to the north.

Dusty 1 swept up the west slope of the tree covered mountains, crested the snow-covered peaks and looked ahead at hundreds of miles of rolling tree covered hills. "That looks like the jungles of South America." Allen said. "Like Peru or Colombia."

"Yeah! It does kind of," Riley said. "I wonder if there's coffee down there."

"That will sure make Alex happy if there is," Marshal said. "We've just about used up everything we brought from Earth and my lady does love her morning cup of coffee."

The first leg of today's flight was planned to skirt the southern edge of the tropical jungle with the return east to west flight path five hundred miles to the south and it was immediately obvious that as Al Wilson had said the southern half of Middle finger was very different from the north. Once they crossed the mountains onto the lower foothills the terrain never did flatten out into a prairie or plateau but continued on as rolling tree covered hills as far as they could see. In the northern hemisphere there was a fairly distinct break between the prairie to the north and jungles of the south. Prairie, a narrow belt of savannah then the tropical jungle. But here?

"Where's the edge of the green belt?" Riley jokingly asked.

The only answer he got was a chuckle from Marshal and Allen.

"What kind of trees are those?" Riley asked.

"Don't know," Marshal answered and Allen just shook his head.

The shuttle crew had no way of knowing what kind of animals might be living below that dense green canopy but there were birds. Millions of colorful birds.

After three hours they came to a huge river, maybe ten miles wide at this point, that flowed out of the jungle to the north and off toward the southeast and after crossing the river the green hills picked up again and continued on until they rolled up into the mountain range that bordered the east coast of the continent.

Riley took the shuttle out over the ever-churning ocean, turned south, gave the controls to Marshal and said, "Well, I certainly didn't expect that."

"No," Allen answered. "It's like the Great Smoky Mountains from coast to coast. Or from mountain range to mountain range, only with a jungle flavor."

"Yeah," Marshal agreed. "The only break in all that green was that big river. Hey! Do you think that it could be Big River?"

"Geeze, John," Riley said. "We must be four thousand miles from Cliffside. That would be one hell of a long river."

The three men thought about that as Marshal took over the controls and turned to the west five hundred miles south of their first pass.

Coming in from the ocean the east coast was a repeat of the west—a wave pounded cliff marked the coast, then a rain drenched forest and the mountain range. Not a very high range, only four or five thousand feet max followed by the rolling green hills. The trees were still unfamiliar but they seemed different from the ones that they had seen just five hundred miles to the north.

After just a few hundred miles they came to the big river only now it was twice as wide, twenty to twenty-five miles at least. The tree covered hills continued on the west side of the river all the way to the western mountains. The crew shook their heads. Anything could be down there but all they could see were trees and birds. Birds and trees.

As day was ending Marshal brought the Starduster over the western mountains and into the seemingly never-ending wind and rain that lashed the west coast.

The next day everyone on the space station had their nose buried in a computer. Of course, the main item of interest was the river. It was massive.

Al Wilson shook his head. "We'll know more when we get coverage further to the south," he said, "but right now it looks like that river is going to cut across the entire continent from northwest to southeast."

A week later after a day's delay when a huge storm swept across the southern end of the continent and two more days of back-and-forth fly-bys, Al was proved to be entirely correct. Even more than he anticipated. A little more than a thousand miles south from the path of the shuttle's first east to west pass the east coast curved sharply to the west and the Big River quickly ended as it flowed into this indentation of the ocean. As the sensor coverage of the continent continued further south the Voyagers could see that the continent continued to narrow and was only a couple of hundreds of miles wide when it finally ended as a string of rocky outcrops extending out into the Great Southern Ocean.

Alex flew up to Wisdom the next day and between her, Wilson and the scientists they determined a course of action to try to digest this mound of data. Surprisingly due to its curve to the west the landmass of the southern hemisphere was less than half the size of the northern half of the continent but even at that it was a huge area and with so many diverse and distinct environments it was going to take weeks—maybe months—to determine sites suitable for future exploration.

The scientists loved it and wasted no time diving into the project.

CHAPTER 23

Alex couldn't believe that the mid-winter solstice festival had already come and gone. In the weeks before the staff had been flooded with suggestions for everything from the venue to what events would be included. In the end it was decided that due to the weather the festival would be held in the Great Cavern and to accommodate everyone the carpenters would replicate the viewing stand that they had built for the Harvest Festival inside the Great Cavern itself. To save as much space as possible they built it right up against the outer wall. That had blocked two of the four doors and disrupted food service but no one, except Lasseter, of course, seemed to mind.

A stage was constructed inside the open area of the viewing stand and a twenty-five-foot-high fir tree was set up behind the stage. Then the magic started happening. Without any direction or coordination decorations appeared both on the tree and throughout the Great Cavern. Some were quite sophisticated like the glass ornaments that were made from the three-D printers in the machine shop or the beautifully painted porcelain figures created by the potters but most of the decorations were just small labors of love from individual colonists. Everything from decorated pine cones to intricately woven garlands.

The festivities kicked off at noon on the twenty-first day of the ninth month on what would have been December back on Earth with performances by anyone who wanted to show their skills and talents. Lots of singing with audience precipitation but there was also a magician and a juggler. Like the Harvest Festival every act, even the ones that weren't very good was greeted with thunderous applause. Of course, there was music and dancing later in the evening on the stage and anywhere else the dancers could find an open space on the stone floor of the Great Cavern. The kitchen staff outdid themselves with traditional delicacies from many cultures. Alex chuckled to herself, if that seemed contradictory to the notion of not carrying over Earth traditions the Voyagers were not going to deprive themselves of a good treat.

Even Santa made an appearance in the form of André the French chef. If anyone thought it odd that Santa was French the children didn't mind and roly-poly André was the only colonist that had the right physical appearance and was dressed in a magnificent Santa suit that Jordan Roberts had made. But all apprehensions aside, André pulled it off perfectly and explained to the kids that not even another planet could stop him and his reindeer from making his annual delivery.

But that was all a couple of weeks ago. Now Alex sat at her desk thinking about what was next for the colony. It was now month ten and what would have been called January back on Earth. No matter what they called the month, it was still the middle of winter and as Al Wilson had promised the weather, so far at least, hadn't been severe. No blizzards or deep freezes but even so it was pretty nasty. Cold but not freezing, but very wet and windy and a dark gray sky overhead through which the sun never shined. But that was outside. Inside the caves and caverns, the farm's cook house and the colonists' individual houses and even inside the ranch every colonist was snug, dry and warm. And that Alex thought to herself was no small accomplishment.

The problem wasn't their physical comfort but mental. Now that the festival was over and no one could go exploring, people were getting bored.

Alex was realizing that the most unfortunate aspect of both the exploration of the southern part of the continent and the possible tunneling operations was that they involved so few people. A half dozen maybe a dozen would be working on tunnels and the mapping and possible selection of sites for exploration would be done by the scientists up in Wisdom. The Mid-Winter Festival had been a great diversion, but it was going to be a long winter and they needed to focus on something else. The one thing Alex could say for her Voyagers—when they got steam up for a project there was no stopping them. And that thought made Alex smile.

Her thoughts were interrupted by a commotion out in the Great Cavern. She walked to her office door and saw everyone either moving toward or pointing at the southwest corner of the cavern. Damn! That's where they were digging the tunnel to connect the Great Cavern to the dispensary.

Alex moved with the crowd but everyone seemed to give way before her and she was soon standing at the tunnel entrance. Chief Lincoln came up beside her. "What happened?" he asked. "A cave in?"

"I don't know, Chief. I just arrived myself,"

Alex answered.

Link looked around and saw some of his deputies in the crowd. "Well, Alex, give me a minute and we'll get a little order here. Gail, Linda, Kurt, see if you can't get everyone back a bit. Clear the end of the tunnel."

"Right, Chief," the three responded.

Link went to the mouth of the tunnel and said, "Please, would everyone who's not a miner exit the tunnel?" And in just a moment the tunnel was clear and Lincoln beckoned to Alex. Mike Bennet, slightly damp from his run from the dispensary, joined them as they walked the few yards into the tunnel.

"What happened?" Bennet asked. "I was over in the dispensary and I got a com call to get over here."

"I don't know, Mike," Alex answered.

The three of them walked the few yards toward where the miners had been working.

"Geeze!" exclaimed Bennet.

"Yeah!" echoed Lincoln.

Alex didn't say anything but stood in open mouthed wonder at the sight before them. The miners had been tunneling south to connect the Great Cavern with the hospital but it looked as though a huge section of the west side of the tunnel had collapsed revealing what appeared to be another cave that stretched away into darkness. Sam Teutopolis sat on the mound of rubble with his head in his hands sobbing over and over, "George! George!

Bennet went down on his knees beside him and said, "Easy, Sam, easy. Are you hurt?"

Teutopolis couldn't stop shaking. In a strangled sob all he could manage was, "George! George!"

Bennet looked up at Alex. "He doesn't seem to be injured but he's definitely in shock."

Alex knelt down on the other side of Teutopolis, took his hand and said, "Sam, it's me, Alex."

Teutopolis looked at her with vacant eyes.

"Sam, you were digging with George Reynolds?"

A nod while Alex, Mike and Link looked around. There was no sign of Reynolds.

Bennet quietly asked, "Sam, where's George?"

Teutopolis jerked upright, grabbed Bennet's shoulders and screamed, "It took him! It took him!"

"Easy Sam, easy. What took him?"

A distraught Sam Teutopolis was babbling, "It came out of the dark, grabbed him and... just took him."

Link was immediately on his com and a few moments later, Smith and McPherson appeared with their rifles. Link of course already had his as he motioned with it for Alex and Bennet to move Teutopolis away from the opening. The three deputies took up positions at the gaping black mouth and trained their flashlights into the darkness. The best technology of twenty-first century illumination was quickly swallowed by the vast inky blackness that loomed before them.

Alex and Bennet sat Teutopolis down on the far side of the tunnel and Alex asked, "Sam, can you tell us what grabbed George?"

Teutopolis looked at her and reason seemed to come back into his eyes. "Ms. Cummings, I don't know."

"Take your time Sam and just try to tell us what happened."

Bennet gave him a drink of water and Teutopolis seemed to come back to himself. Still shaking he tried to describe what had happened. "We were working side by side when the wall next to George just collapsed. George turned to look into the opening when this *thing* just shot out of the hole and grabbed him. It was so fast. It happened so fast…"

Alex squeezed his hand. "Sam, can you tell us what took George?"

"I don't know. I don't know. It was big, as big as George and… and red. But it was shapeless, just a blob. But fast, so fast! It hit George and then it and George were gone."

While Teutopolis was telling his story Link had been on his com and soon Murph and Jaeger appeared dressed in full field gear with similar items for McPherson and Smith.

Alex McPherson pushed his way through the crowd, assessed the situation and soon several engineers arrived and work lights were set up at the cave opening.

Link looked at Alex and then at the opening to the cave and at Alex's nod spoke to his four deputies. "Let's be clear. This is a quick in and out to look for Reynolds. We don't know what's out there so don't take any chances." He paused and thought for a moment. "One hour; half an hour in, half an hour back. Okay?"

His deputies grimly nodded as they entered the new cavern. Soon even the light from their flashlights was swallowed in the darkness.

An hour later they were back and could only just shake their heads when Alex asked about Reynolds. McPherson started to give Alex a report but she waved him off and said, "I think we should take this down to the Conference Cave and let the entire staff and the whole colony hear it."

In just a few minutes Andy McPherson was standing at the head of the conference table looking at a crowded room of very anxious faces. He had given many briefings in his military career but he couldn't remember any that had generated as much interest as this one. And he couldn't think of any briefing he had previously given where he had less to say. Every chair in the Conference Cave was occupied and there were a couple of people standing just inside the door. A few times in the past, especially before the cave was closed, several dozen colonists would be clustered outside but not today, not in this weather. Today a few hundred people were focused on the big Vid screen in the Great Cavern. And he was sure dozens more were focused on the screen down at the farm's cook house and probably the ranch too. Too bad that he didn't have much to tell them.

Alex called the meeting to order. "Just to be sure that everyone is in the picture, earlier today the miners tunneling from the Great Cavern to the hospital broke into what appears to be a huge cave and something attacked them. George Reynolds, we fear, was killed. Chief Lincoln immediately secured the cave entrance and sent a security team into the cave to attempt to recover Reynolds. Unfortunately, the attempt was unsuccessful. The main purpose of this meeting is to hear the deputies report on what they did discover. Andy."

"Ms. Cummings, ladies and gentlemen, on entering the cave we proceeded due west looking for any sign of Reynolds or whatever it was that took him. I'm Sorry to say we saw nothing. What we did find was a cave environment that is totally different from what we have here at Cliffside. Instead of the dry, relatively smooth caves that we have here, the cave on the other side of the wall is a vast cavern. If anyone has been to Carlsbad Cavern, you'll understand what this one resembles. Unlike our Great Cavern, this cavern is damp. Wet in some places, with water continually dripping from the cavern's roof. The floor is a jumble of rocks and other debris. I asked Doctor Turner about the dampness and the debris covered floor and she speculated that the floor may once have been smooth like the Great Cavern but sometime in the distant past the roof collapsed. If such a collapse occurred that could account for the debris and for the moisture.

"I was never a spelunker but this cave seems to me more like what we would expect a cave or cavern to be back on Earth. We couldn't move more than a few feet in any direction without having to climb over or detour around rocks of all sizes. There are stalactites and stalagmites, we even saw a few full columns."

Andy paused to collect his thoughts before continuing. "There is insect life of all kinds. We weren't equipped to collect samples but we saw a variety of crickets, roaches, worms and spiders. We saw two different species of lizards but what we didn't see was any animal big enough to attack a man.

"As to the size of the cave the total blackness seemed to soak up light like a sponge and our lights never penetrated to the sides of the cave or in some instances to the roof but we all had the impression that the cave or cavern whatever you want to call it was huge."

McPherson looked around the conference table. "I, we, will try to answer any questions you might have but quite honestly I think I just told you all we know."

"Thank you, Andy," Alex said. "So ladies and gentlemen, I guess the question is what do we do now? I, for one, am naturally curious about what this new cave system might have to offer but on the other hand there is something or possibly more than one something that is incredibly dangerous in there. The choices would seem to be: do we seal it up or explore it?"

Surprisingly it was Ryan Lasseter who spoke up first. "I insist that the entrance not be sealed until Brandon and I have a chance to evaluate the possibility of valuable minerals."

That rather strange pronouncement resulted in a slightly shocked and puzzled silence around the table. Finally, a thoroughly confused Hank Ferguson exclaimed, "What the hell are you talking about, Lasseter?"

"I'm talking about the possibility that the cave may contain precious metals, gold, silver, maybe even gems."

Of all the possibilities that the cave might have to offer the idea of gold was probably the furthest from everyone's mind and a wave of laughter swept around the conference table with several commenting that Lasseter was nuts.

"What do you want gold for?" Hank asked. "Are you going to buy something?"

A red-faced Lasseter jumped up and said, "You fools who are staying on this miserable backwater of a planet can laugh, but when I arrive back on Earth a sack full of gold will be very useful."

Alex asked, "Mr. Lasseter, what makes you think that there may be gold or other precious metals in the cave."

"Ever since you people," he waved his hand around the table and practically sneered the words, "started digging tunnels Brandon and I have been evaluating the rock structure and we think that there is a very real possibility that there may be gold or silver in these hills."

"By Brandon, I assume you mean Brandon Johnstone?"

Lasseter gave a jerky nod.

Alex went on. "And do you and Mr. Johnstone have any particular expertise in the field of gold exploration?"

This time Lasseter gave a sneering laugh. "Of course we do, Ms. Not-so-clever director. Brandon and I were partners in several mining operations in Alaska and the Yukon."

There was a shocked silence around the table and finally Alex quietly said, "If you and Johnstone have mining experience why didn't you share that experience with us when we were planning the tunnels?"

Lasseter snorted. "Why should we?"

There were angry mutters around the table and Lasseter realizing that he may have said too much headed for the door. "I'm going to explore that cave and don't you try to stop me."

"No one will try to stop you," Alex quietly said as Lasseter went through the door.

Link looked at Alex. "Shouldn't we stop him?" he asked.

Alex just shrugged. "On what grounds, Chief? This colony isn't a dictatorship. If Lasseter or anyone else wants to go into the cave, or into the woods or go swim in Big River with the giant croc-a-gators, who are we to stop them?"

Sitting against the wall Smith quietly said, "With any kind of luck the big red blob will get him."

"Now, now, Jerry," Alex smiled and went on. "Well ladies and gentlemen, shall we explore the cave? I must admit that I'm curious about what's in there."

And that settled that.

Two days later an exploratory team that looked for a while like it was going to contain half the colony because everyone was curious as to what lay back in those caves, gathered at the back of the Great Cavern. It seemed that despite the very real danger lurking in the darkness everyone wanted to go but common sense quickly dictated that only the scientists and the people needed to support them were really required. Link decided on a six-person security detail that included his top deputies McPherson, Smith, Murphy and Jaeger along with Leo Daniels and Julie Grayson.

Alex was determined to accompany the mission so that meant Marshal was going, too. His skills as shuttle or robot operator would be useless in the caves, but he was an auxiliary deputy assigned to protect Alex.

No one even asked if the Fosters were going. Of course, they were. Even though their particular skills probably wouldn't be required in a cave, the Fosters were the Fosters and always seemed to be handy in tense situations.

And without anyone specifically mentioning it, Mike Bennet showed up with his medical kit.

"Well, Chief," Alex said, "I guess we're as ready as we're going to get. Have you heard anything from Lasseter and his party?"

"Not a word. Gail here," and he nodded toward Gail Hendricks who was guarding the cave entrance. "Was on duty when they went into the cave two days ago."

Alex turned to Hendricks. "Don't know what I can tell you, Ma'am," Hendricks said. "There were six of them and they just kind of brushed past us as if they were daring us to stop them."

Alex and Link looked at each other and Link said, "Two days ago just after noon, Alex. Just a couple of hours after the staff meeting. Lasseter must have left the meeting, grabbed his people and gone into the cave."

"Yes, I know." Alex was quiet for a moment and then asked, "Gail, how were they equipped?"

Hendricks thought for a moment and said, "Well they each had a rifle and a backpack but they didn't have any way near the gear that you have." And she waved at the completely outfitted team with its two grav sleds piled high with supplies that were waiting to enter the cave.

Alex sighed and said, "Yes. Well, I hope they're all right. One last question, Gail. Which way did they go?"

"Off that way," she pointed. "To the left."

"Thank you, Gail." And then almost to herself, she

added, "Two days and no contact." And she sighed again.

Link said, "Try not to worry about them, Alex. There's not really anything you or any of us can do and like you said, we couldn't have stopped them. I'll keep trying to contact them and if they do need any help, we'll do the best we can."

"Thanks, Chief," she said. "They may not be our favorite people but they're still our people." She stepped up to the waiting team. "Well, Andy, what's our marching order?"

"I assume you and the rest of these eggheads," he smiled as they all shook their fingers at him, "will be collecting specimens along the way so we'll space you out, each with a deputy." He looked at his security team. "Jerry, up ahead to scout. Kurt, watch the back door. Alex and John might as well stay up front with me and you other three," he pointed to the three remaining deputies, "pick an egghead."

Everyone chuckled and McPherson went on. "Let's not wander too far off the line of march and let's try not to get too strung out. Mike, you can throw your stuff on one of the sleds and, Fosters, do your thing."

And with that they plunged into the unknown cave complex.

After an hour of climbing over rocks, Alex realized that sitting behind a desk hadn't been the best training for scrambling around in a cave. She followed McPherson as best as she could but no two steps were flat and obstacles that the big man in front of her more or less just stepped over or around, she had to scramble over. But they were in no hurry and Marshal was right behind her to lend a helping hand and to contribute a willing pair of legs to fetch a new specimen jar.

The cave was just as McPherson had described, a very damp jumble of rocks and rubble with walls and roof out of sight or touch. As Andy had said it was kind of like Carlsbad

Cavern. There were stalagmites and stalactites but not as many as she might have expected.

A type of lichen covered practically all surfaces with a multitude of crickets, roaches and beetles feeding on it. They in turn, were food for larger predators like spiders and centipedes and on up the food chain were pale lizards—some up to two feet in length.

"The lizards have been here a while, but not as long as the centipedes," Maryanne commented.

"How do you mean?" Marshal asked.

"They've lost their pigmentation, but not their eyes," she answered.

"Oh," Marshal answered and didn't know what to say beyond that.

Progress was slow as the scientists filled their specimen jars like kids on a candy hunt not knowing which one to pick first. They stopped for lunch in a relatively clear area where their lights could pick out a few stalactites giving them a rough estimate of the height of the roof. At least fifty feet was the consensus and one place being as good as another they spent an hour searching around for specimens. Just as McPherson was getting ready to resume the march Fisher said, "Everyone stop. Check yourselves and those around you. Make sure you don't have any of these crawling on you."

What "these" looked like was a brown and black centipede about eight inches long.

Fisher continued. "Poison, I'm sure of it. I caught it crawling up my pant leg and I think that those little white spiders we caught a while back, the ones about the size of your thumbnail, might be poison too."

Alex and Marshal looked at each other. Neither one of them were fond of bugs especially after their time at Sand

Flea. Alex mumbled, "Bugs, and now poison bugs."

Marshal said, "Well, onward, Luv." And they resumed the march deeper into the cavern.

Day and night were meaningless in the blackness of the cavern but McPherson called a halt at what would have been early evening and they made camp for the night. There was enough wood around to make a campfire and Marshal asked where the wood came from but no one could give him a satisfactory answer. On the plus side Leo Daniels turned out to be an accomplished camp cook. He gathered everyone's rations and turned them into quite an acceptable meal.

But despite that and everyone's attempts to remain upbeat and positive it was a restless uncomfortable night for all. They couldn't see anything, couldn't hear anything, but there was something out there. Something monstrous. They knew it. They could feel it.

CHAPTER 24

Even a rainy winter dawn would have been a welcome sight but it would never come in the blackness of the cavern. The scientists had entered the cavern on a wave of excitement for new discoveries and now they went forward with more dogged determination than enthusiasm. Even the excitement of finding new specimens was wearing thin. And it wasn't just the fear of unknown dangerous animals that haunted them. It was the oppressive darkness that enveloped them.

Andy McPherson admitted later that he didn't know what made him look up at that precise moment to see a worm-like shape looming over Jerry Smith. "Down, Jerry!" he shouted and his rifle was instantly in his hands firing at the indistinct shape.

Smith and McPherson had been a scout team for almost a year and Jerry dropped instantly at Andy's command. Before he hit the ground, his own rifle was in his hands and he was firing up at, as he said later, a huge circular mouth that was ringed with hundreds of needle-like teeth.

It had been a few years since Marshal had been in the military but the scout-sniper instincts were still there. "Down, Luv!" he shouted to Alex and an instant later he too was firing at the creature whatever it was.

The three automatic weapons literally cut the worm-like creature in half and it collapsed on the rocks next to Smith.

McPherson reached down and helped Smith to his feet. "You okay, Jerry?"

"Yeah. Scared the hell out of me though."

The rest of the humans gathered around the remains. It was obvious that it was a worm of some kind but this worm was about eighteen feet long, at least that was how much of it was out of its hole, and four or five feet across. Like any worm it didn't appear to have any features except the mouth at the front. A great circular opening that as Jerry had noted was completely ringed with thin, six inch long, needle-like teeth. Julie Grayson spoke for everyone when she asked, "What the hell is that thing? Is that what killed George?"

The scientists were quiet for a moment and finally West said, "Julie, I'm not sure what it is. What I am sure of is that there's nothing like it living on Earth or as far as I know in Earth's fossil record. What it is, I think, is some kind of a tube worm but of a monstrous size and looking at those teeth, a carnivore. And to answer your second question, no, from the description that Teutopolis gave a creature like this isn't what took Reynolds."

"Great!" Grayson muttered, "now we have two potential man eaters to worry about."

After the scientists had satisfied themselves with samples and photographs, the team started forward again but they hadn't gone more than a hundred yards when they encountered another of the worm-like creatures.

A shout and a burst of rifle fire from up ahead and Jerry Smith's triumphant "Ha!" told the rest of the team that he had taken care of the problem himself. When the team came up, they found Smith standing next to the remains of another of the worms.

What was left of this one had crashed down on the rocks and lay half across the partially open area they were following. They humans stepped gingerly around it as they made their way forward.

Once past the worms McPherson halted the team and told everyone to take an early lunch while they assessed their situation. While the team nervously nibbled on their rations McPherson reviewed their options.

By his best estimation, he said, they had come a little more than two miles into the cave and outside of the worms no new creatures had been encountered since the initial discoveries when they first entered the cavern and they had not found Reynolds or whatever it was that had taken him.

"So," McPherson said, "I guess the question I have is do you want to continue on or head on back? It's up to you, of course, but I feel that I'm responsible for your safety and I don't know how many of those worm critters or who knows what else is out there."

Alex smiled. "Our call, eh, Andy? Fair enough." And she and the three scientists gathered for a quick meeting. When they were finished Alex spoke for the group. "We appreciate your concern, Andy. We really do. But we are scientists and we learn things by going forward, sometimes into dangerous situations. And we do realize that it's not just us," and she waved her hand at the rest of the team. "What we suggest is that we go on for the rest of the day or whatever you figure day is down here, camp for the night and start back tomorrow. Is that acceptable to everyone?"

There were nods all around even from Marshal who wanted to get his wife out of this pitch-black hole ASAP.

A few hours later, what they estimated was probably midafternoon up where there was sunlight, they halted when Jerry Smith came back from his point position and rejoined the group. "There's open water up ahead," he announced. "I didn't have enough light to tell if it's just a small pond or a lake but I think it's big. I only had this one flashlight but the water stretched from side to side and out ahead as far as I could see."

"How far ahead is the lake?" McPherson asked'

"Not far." And he shined his flashlight forward. "Just beyond that jumble of rocks there's a clear area, almost like a beach, and then the water."

The team moved cautiously forward but at McPherson's urging they settled themselves among Smith's jumble of rocks where they could see the "beach". Shining their lights forward they could see a black body of water stretching out before them.

"Let's spread the lights out," Fisher suggested. "Maybe we can get an idea of the size of this thing."

The team separated as best as they could among the rocks and aimed their flashlights toward the water. The dozen lights that were spread out along the shoreline produced mixed results. They seemed feeble against the blackness that surrounded them but even with that small bit of light it was clear that this was no small pond but a lake in the middle of the huge cavern. Just how big they couldn't tell. There was nothing but inky black water to be seen to the right and left and as far forward as the light would penetrate. McPherson called his deputies over to assess the situation but before they could gather the three scientists, they, with Alex and the two grav sleds were already out on the open beach area spreading out and happily collecting samples.

McPherson looked at his deputies, Marshal and the Fosters and shrugged. "Well let's spread out behind them and give them as much cover as we can. And don't forget to keep checking the rocks behind us."

The guardians, the deputies, Marshal and the Fosters, positioned themselves as best as they could between the scientists and the rocks trying to keep their lights on the eggheads, the water and the rocks all at the same time. When their lights were spread out like that each individual beam seemed puny, feeble against the all-enveloping darkness.

For the guardians it was a very nervous two hours before the scientists were satisfied and packed away their sample jars. A suggestion by the scientists to camp on the beach was quickly vetoed by McPherson and the group moved back into the rocks for the night. After a hasty meal the team settled down to get what sleep they could before they started the trek back to Cliffside.

A couple of hours later Marshal woke from a fitful sleep. He wasn't sure what had awakened him but he felt that something was wrong. He quickly glanced over at Alex to reassure himself that she was okay then he looked around the campsite. Everything seemed alright there too. The fire had burned down to embers so the only light were the thin beams from the guards' flashlights. But everything appeared as normal as was possible in a deep dark cave. Then he noticed the glow of another light toward the lake. Marshal went toward the light and found Jerry Smith crouched behind a boulder looking out into the darkness over the lake.

"Jerry."

"John."

"See anything?" Marshal asked.

"Nothing. But there's something out there, John, I can feel it."

Marshal crouched down beside him and added the beam of his flashlight to Smith's to try to penetrate the darkness. Marshal was about to say that he couldn't see anything when Ty West joined them. Marshal laughed. "I guess no one can sleep."

West said, "Well not me anyway. What's up?"

"Jerry thinks that there's something out there in the water."

West added his light and a moment later pointed directly out in front of them and whispered, "Yes."

Marshal saw it too. Just beyond the edge of light he thought he could see a huge black shape moving in the dark. As the shape moved toward the beach, he was sure that it was an animal of some kind. Some grossly misshapen animal.

"It's a frog!" Jerry exclaimed.

The moment Marshal thought that it couldn't be a frog as it was nearly fifty feet long, the creature advanced toward the beach. Frog! It was enormous and seemed to be all head and the head seemed to be all mouth. A gaping, dripping gash sliced the creature's head from side to side.

The three men stared in shocked silence as the frog thing flowed silently forward, stopped at the edge of the water thirty feet away and seemed to look directly at them. But the creature couldn't be looking at them Marshal thought, as far as he could see the thing had no eyes. Then something that looked like a tongue started pushing its way out of that huge mouth.

"Down!" yelled West and the three men dropped behind the boulder as a huge red blob shot over their heads and smacked into the rocks behind them.

Jerry came up shooting and he was soon joined by the others. They poured round after round into the huge creature but the bullets seemed to have no effect. Of course, the noise of the rifle fire woke the camp and soon a dozen rifles were blazing away at the massive blob.

West was shouting, "Keep down! Keep down. Get behind a rock. Stay out of its line of sight. I'm certain it can see us."

Alex calmly asked, "Ty, what are we dealing with here?"

West answered. "Infa-red. I think it sees in infa-red and that tongue shoots out the same as some species of iguana that we have back on Earth."

"Right," McPherson said. "Everybody got that?"

There were murmurs of "aye" and "check" and everyone kept firing but with no apparent effect. A waste of ammunition McPherson thought but what else could they do. It wasn't until Maryanne hit it in the area of that darting tongue with a round from her hand cannon that the creature took notice and slowly backed into the lake and disappeared out of the range of their lights.

As the creature disappeared into the darkness the team hesitated and, seemingly drawn by some unknown force, everyone slowly moved out of the rocks towards the lake as a babble of voices demanded to know what it was that they had just seen.

"Quiet please, everyone," McPherson said. "I know we all have a million questions but that thing, whatever it is, is still out there and maybe has relatives. And I wouldn't be surprised if that's not the thing that got Reynolds. So, everyone off this beach and back to the campsite and pack up. I want to be on the move back toward Cliffside in ten minutes. We can ask questions while we're walking."

When everyone stopped to think for a moment McPherson was absolutely right, they really didn't want to be standing out in the open looking for something with a tongue that could swallow a man whole.

They packed up and were on the march toward the safety of Cliffside in five minutes.

Marshal felt the trip back was like walking in a nightmare. The kind where you try to move fast but find your feet are stuck to the ground or you are waist high in water. No matter what he did he couldn't seem to make any speed. The path ahead was just one rock after another and his imagination took over as the darkness seemed to close in around them. Behind them was a huge toad-like monster that, if McPherson was right, had traveled all the way to the cave entrance to take Remolds.

Was it stalking them? How fast could it move?

Ahead of them were the carnivorous worms, poisonous insects and who knew what else. With the demons of the known and unknown prodding them they naturally wanted to move fast. A couple of them mentioned abandoning the sleds but that suggestion was violently vetoed by the scientists. Without those specimens the entire trip would have been for nothing. McPherson agreed, pointing out that it wasn't the grav sleds that were slowing them down as much as the terrain itself. They were literally climbing over a rock pile. It wasn't as noticeable during the outbound journey because they were moving at a leisurely pace stopping to collect samples as they went. Now that they were trying to make speed every stone, every boulder, every jog through a rock pile became an obstacle.

Marshal nodded. Andy was right. Going into the cavern he had kept his rifle in his hands with the flashlight clipped to it. Now as they were trying to make their egress with speed, he needed both hands to scramble over the rocks. Everyone had their flashlight in one hand and their rifles slung across their backs in order to keep their remaining hand free for climbing. Not a very good position to be in if something large and unfriendly attacked them. Also, he wanted to keep a light on the next rock that he was going to touch to avoid any nasty or possibly poisonous insect.

And to make this nightmare even more fun they had neglected to include gloves on the equipment list. Soon everyone's hands were scraped and bleeding.

Marshal and Alex rounded a boulder to find McPherson and Smith waiting for them. At Alex's questioning glance Andy said, "We're coming up to the place where Jerry killed the second worm. Alex, why don't you go back with the group and please send up the Fosters. John, you stay up here with me and Jerry."

The Fosters joined them a few minutes later and the five of them began a cautious advance toward the worm's rock pile. Jerry played his light on the rocks ahead. "Look Andy. The carcass is gone. That big worm I killed yesterday is gone."

"Geeze!" exclaimed Grant. "That worm must have weighed a couple of tons. That's some scavenging in twenty-four hours."

"Maybe his worm buddies ate him," Marshal said.

Maryanne looked around and said, "Or maybe the big toad got him." As she spoke, she kept scanning around the top of the rocks ahead of them. "Look!" she exclaimed.

All five lights concentrated on the spot she indicated and revealed a worm slowly rising out of its hole but before it could attack them, even before the humans could get their guns up to fire, a red blob shot out of the darkness fastened onto the worm and jerked it up out of its hole. Then the blob and worm disappeared back into the inky black.

They stood in shocked silence for only a moment before McPherson shouted, "Okay, team, show's over! Let's go!" And the humans needed no more urging than that. Driven on by what they had just seen and their own inner terrors all caution was thrown to the winds and they charged forward with reckless abandon.

Vorarephobia. Marshal was shocked that a word he'd probably only heard once in his life popped into his head so clearly, but he knew its meaning: the fear of being eaten alive.

Five hours later they were in sight of the lights at the caves opening. Running as best as they could, certain the frog thing right behind them, they bolted towards the exit.

Link saw them coming, heard McPherson's frantic calls on the com and cleared the entrance. One thing Link had done in their absence was to close the entrance down to just the size of a doorway. One by one the team members tumbled through the gap into the tunnel shouting to everyone to get back away from the tunnel and into the Great Cavern. The colonists might not have known exactly what was happening but they didn't dawdle and as the team members came through the opening there was plenty of space for everyone to clear the tunnel.

Andy McPherson was the last one through and some instinct made him dive. He hit the ground rolling toward the Great Cavern just as a red blob shot through the opening over him, smacked against the tunnel wall and withdrew.

Link was on his knee next to McPherson. "Close, Andy. Too close."

"I agree, Chief. If you want my recommendation, close that opening off. Preferably with about ten tons of solid concrete and forget that there was ever a cave back there."

Everyone within hearing range chuckled and Lincoln

said, "I couldn't agree more, Andy."

But not everyone agreed.

An exhausted Ty West struggled up off the floor and said, "You can't close the opening—the grav sleds are still out there."

"What?" a thoroughly confused Link asked.

"The grav sleds with all our specimens are still in the cave. They wouldn't fit through the opening."

Before the Chief could give his rather pungent opinion as to what he thought about that an exhausted Alex Cummings said, "Chief, you can put whatever guards on the door as you deem necessary but the door remains open until we recover those sleds and until we determine the fate of Lasseter and his party."

Link was also about to reply what he thought about that when McPherson said, "She's got a point, Chief. Two points in fact. We didn't drag that stuff all the way back from black lake just to give them away to some big frog and as much as we may not like Lasseter, he is one of our people. We can't seal him in that cavern if he's still alive."

Lincoln let out a breath and said, "You're right of course, Andy, Alex. Sorry. I guess I was just so happy to get all you clowns back in one piece that all I could think of not putting you in danger there again."

"See?" Julie said as she nudged Leo. "I told you that he loved us."

That brought a laugh from everyone and a wag of the finger from Link which brought another laugh.

McPherson was still lying on the floor of the cave. "I need a nurse." And his wife Audrey said, "It's about time, now shut up and let me get to work on you." And she leaned in to give her husband a big kiss.

The next day Marshal pushed his wife across the Great

Cavern in her office chair. West, Turner and Fisher were willing to take their chances going out into the cave to unload the sleds but Alex wouldn't hear of it. No, her solution was to enlarge the door to accommodate the sleds, throw out grapples to snag them and just pull them in. It worked like a charm.

Now there was only Lasseter and his party. Lasseter had gone into the cave two days before Alex's team so they had now been gone for six days and despite continued efforts to communicate with him and his team there had been no answer.

Alex smiled at just what wonderful people the Voyagers were. Once they realized that she was going to sit there by the tunnel entrance until she determined the fate of the Lasseter party the wood carvers brought her a table to work on and Olga showed up with her personal computer and a vid screen. In no time she had a mini office on the far side of the cavern.

One thing Alex did do was that as soon as the sleds were recovered, she immediately ordered the entrance closed back up to door size and now they waited. The question was, how long was it reasonable to wait? Half the colony wanted to wall the entrance up right now and to hell with Lasseter. But there were five people out there with him and all six of them had wives, people who cared about them. Earlier this morning two of the wives had come by to talk to her and she had assured them that as long as there was hope the entrance would remain open. Alex had asked if they had been in contact but they said no. They're com calls weren't answered.

She held out for two more days until finally Chief Lincoln convinced her she was putting the colony in danger by not sealing up the cave. Alex understood. She sympathized. But she had to make the call and Marshal knew that if she sealed it up and left someone alive there, she would never forgive herself.

Calling a staff meeting Alex laid it all on the line. The fact was that six of their number had gone into the cave eight days ago and had not been heard from since. She didn't minimize the dangers lurking in the cave or the danger that she was putting the deputies, including her husband, in guarding the entrance.

She tried to answer their questions. Had the toad thing come back to the entrance since she had made her escape?

Yes. Twice that they were sure of and maybe more that they couldn't confirm.

Was it the toad thing that had taken Reynolds?

Not 100% sure but yes pretty sure.

And the million-dollar question, was Lasseter and his party still alive?

That was the question and Alex admitted that she didn't know. But when further pressed had to also admit that no one had heard from anyone in the party since they entered the cave eight days ago.

The vote, not counting Alex who abstained, was unanimous, even Marshal who knew more than anyone what she was going through, voted to seal up the cave.

Alex sighed and said, "Okay, I hear you. Tomorrow at noon we seal it up."

That statement caused a ripple around the table. Why wait? Do it now.

"Please," Alex said. "Indulge me one more time. Noon tomorrow and please anyone who can try to contact the party and warn them of the deadline. Please give them one more chance to get out of there."

The staff grumbled. Probably most of the colony

grumbled but they went along.

Nothing happened during the night and the next morning a couple of hundred colonists found a reason to be in or around the Great Cavern. Would the Lasseter party make it out before the cave was sealed forever? Were they even alive? Pretty morbid but it was rumored that bets were even made.

Alex sat at her little desk where she could see the tunnel entrance and the opening into the cave. Leo Daniels and Julie Grayson were on duty. That team was shaping up nicely, Alex thought.

Leo suddenly shouted, "Down, Julie! Stay back! There's something out there."

Just as he said it a big red blob came through the opening and quickly withdrew.

Julie looked across the opening at Leo. "Thanks, sweetie. I owe you one big time." She gave Leo a playful smirk. "Payment will be later."

Alex was on her com. "Lasseter, if you're out there do not approach the cave entrance. One of those toad things is just outside."

There was no answer but Alex kept trying.

From her position lying and looking toward the left side of the entrance Julie said, "There's something moving out there. Out on the fringe of the light."

"A toad?" Leo asked.

"No smaller. It's people! Lasseter and his group; they're running toward us. No! The toad got one of them. The rest are still coming."

Chief Lincoln was standing by the tunnel entrance and shouted, "Everyone back! Out of the way. Leo, get over on this side and be ready to pull them out of the way when they come through. Julie, you too."

The first man through the entrance was Ryan

Lasseter. He hesitated a little at the entrance but Daniels quickly grabbed him and shoved him into the Great Cavern. He let out an indignant yell as he sprawled at the foot of Alex's desk.

Julie had the second man and he was quickly out of the way. The third man got the idea on his own and dived toward the tunnel entrance. As the last man came through fifty voices were hollering "Down!" He might have just stumbled but he did fall toward the Great Cavern just as the toad's tongue passed over him.

Alex looked down at Lasseter who was struggling to get up and finding it hard with the obviously heavy pack on his back. Alex asked, "Mr. Lasseter, there are only four of you, where are the other two?"

"That thing out there grabbed Henry and you people just stood here and did nothing."

Before anyone else could answer or maybe just quietly tear Lasseter apart Alex asked, "Johnstone. I don't see Mr. Johnstone."

"He died," Lasseter replied.

Mike Bennet who had been quietly checking men asked, "Died? What from, Mr. Lasseter?"

"How the hell do I know? I'm no doctor."

Bennet persisted, "How did he die, Lasseter?"

It was clear that Lasseter just wanted to get away. His three companions had already left but he was hemmed in by the colonists. "I don't know. He just died. We were walking and he said he thought something bit him, then he said he didn't feel good then he sat down and died. Now get out of my way!" And he pushed his way through the crowd.

The crowd muttered about going out of their way to save a bum like Lasseter but Alex was happy with the result. Lasseter was a bum, or more specifically a certain part of a bum, and probably his friends, too but Alexandria Cummings would sleep well knowing that she hadn't left four men to die in the darkness.

CHAPTER 25

The two Starbusters circled the clearing like a couple of buzzards around a road kill with every eye in both shuttles scanning every tree and the tree line surrounding the simi open area that they had selected for a landing. You couldn't really call it a clearing, there were too many trees and bushes for that. As far as they could determine from the sensor data obtained in the fly-bys it seemed as if there were no clearings here in the eastern foothills of the great range of mountains that dominated the west coast of the southern hemisphere. Here more than two thousand miles south of the equator the land was a continuous carpet of green, rolling, semi-tropical jungle so this partially open space was going to have to do.

Back and forth, they went over the open area, trying to make sure that each one of those trees was just a tree and not a Wedgie. Of course, they couldn't eliminate all the risk. The Wedgies could be out of sight in the fringe of the forest just waiting to unleash their deadly javelins.

If there were Wedgies or more unfriendly animals than they could handle the Stardusters would probably just move on. The humans figured that it really didn't make much difference where they landed. This wasn't a combat mission. The main purpose of today's mission was to begin to catalog the flora, and fauna too if they encountered any, of this part of the continent so within a few hundred miles one place was as good as another.

To cover as much ground as possible all the biologists were present and divided into three teams. Well, four if you counted Julius Rosen. The professor might be a brilliant biologist but as absent minded and as easily distracted as he was, roaming around a planet like Sanctuary he was a danger to himself and anyone around him. He had insisted on joining the expedition and in all fairness, they couldn't deny him that so they created a team that consisted of just the professor and Kurt Jaeger to hopefully keep him out of trouble.

The other three teams had four members each and were headed up by the three remaining biologists, Ann Turner, Ty West and Glenn Fisher. Also present in the two shuttles was Mike Bennet for medical support should any be needed, Olga Sorenson with a couple of drones to add to Marshal and Junior's overhead surveillance, the Fosters Grant and Maryanne, and two scouts, Andy McPherson and Jerry Smith, who planned to do a little exploring of their own.

The remaining seats were occupied by additional deputies with the exception of the jump seat directly behind Riley and Marshal in Dusty 1. That seat was occupied by Alexandria Cummings. Alex chuckled to herself. When she had announced that she was going to accompany the mission it seemed that the entire staff had thrown up their hands in alarm declaring it was too dangerous, the colony couldn't afford to lose her, blah, blah. But Alex wouldn't be moved. She had stayed up in Wisdom during the initial landings. No more. She told them she had gone into the cave and she was going to join this exploratory mission and that was that.

The two shuttles finally settled in the middle of the open area and patiently went through their landing routine. Wait five minutes to see if anything big and nasty, or on Sanctuary little and nastier, decided to attack them. If nothing happened then deploy the security force around the Stardusters and get Marshal and Junior, and in this case Olga's drone also, airborne. Only when they determined that the local area was clear of everything except birds and bugs did the rest of the Voyagers disembark.

As soon as all the Voyagers gathered, they split up into their pre assigned teams.

Ann Turner's team was the same as it had been on previous landings, her and Maryanne with Chief Lincoln and Linda Murphy for security. The rest of the Voyagers had taken to calling them "Link and his girls", but no one was going to argue that it wasn't a tough, competent team. After all, they were the ones who took down Big Daddy.

Grant Foster teamed up as usual with West but, with Kurt baby-sitting the professor, Leo Daniels and Julie Grayson joined them.

The last team built around Glenn Fisher had three deputies but one of them, Charlie Edwards, had been in his sophomore year at Cal Poly when the country collapsed and he ended up at Project Voyager with his parents so he had been recruited to double as an assistant to Fisher.

Alex hesitated uncertain about which team to join. It was clear that the colonists didn't want her to join any team but to stay at the shuttles. Alex, determined to be part of this expedition, was starting to dig her heels and even get a little angry when Marshal landed Junior got out and whispered in her ear, "Why not ride with me, Luv? The view's better and I guarantee it's less buggy."

Alex smiled, thanked everyone for their concern and climbed into Junior. Her husband was right: the view was much better from a couple hundred feet in the air. They looked down as the four teams started off in the four cardinal directions. McPherson and Smith had disappeared into the forest as soon as they had landed. All four teams stopped at the forest's edge and started collecting samples and then one by one disappeared from Alex and Marshal's view into the semi-tropical forest.

"I can't see them," Alex commented.

"Me neither," her husband answered. "Canopy's too thick. What about you Olga? Anything?"

"Nothing on visual, Mr. Marshal. The canopy's too dense but the infa-red is going crazy. There must be a million animals down there large and small. I can just barely separate the humans from the background."

"Do the best you can, Olga, and if you can give the teams a heads up if you see anything large around them."

"Yes, sir." She hesitated a minute and said, "There is a large heat source just to the north of Dr. West's group."

"You got that, Ty?" Marshal asked.

"Yeah, but I don't see anything."

Grant moved up next to him. "Anything?" West asked.

"Nothing," Foster answered. "Can't see more than fifteen, twenty feet in this jungle."

Daniels and Grayson had moved in behind them and Julie pointed. "That tree with mottled bark, about twenty feet up, that big branch on the left. I think there's something there."

The three men stared at where Julie was pointing and

then Julie's *something* moved. Apparently aware that it had been seen, a big jaguar-like cat launched itself at the four humans. Three rifles rose as one and fired and at least a dozen bullets must have hit it in midair. A wide-eyed Ty West still had his rifle over his shoulder when the cat crashed to the ground at his feet.

Link was immediately on the com. "Everyone off the net," he ordered. "Which team fired?"

Seeing as West was still standing open mouthed gasping for air like a beached cod Foster answered, "It was us, Chief, West's team. We were attacked by a fair-sized cat. Kind of looks like a jaguar. No injuries here and thanks for the heads up, Olga."

Marshal could picture Olga Sorenson sitting cross-legged with her drone control station on top of Dusty 1. Yeah, she was loving this. He smiled at Alex as he added his congratulations. "Good work, Olga, keep it up. The infra-red is the only eye that we have in this jungle. If you can keep the drone moving from team to team."

Before Olga could answer Alex pointed and exclaimed, "What's that, John? It looks like an eagle or a hawk and it's diving on the drone."

Olga heard Alex's warning at the same time but it was too late for her to react. The eagle hit the drone sinking its talons into the soft plastic. As soon as the bird realized that what it had caught wasn't something it wanted it tried to let it go but it couldn't free its talon. The eagle could have probably just flown away with the drone but apparently being free of it was more important. The bird fluttered over the tree line landing in the open area near the shuttles while it battered the drone with beak and wings trying to free itself.

Olga was off the top of the shuttle in a shot running to save her drone oblivious of the shouts to not get too close to what was obviously a very dangerous bird. But it didn't matter. Before Olga could reach the drone, the eagle had managed to disengage its foot and was flying away over the forest.

With a frown Olga picked up the remains of her drone just as Junior arrived.

Alex asked, "What's the verdict Olga? Is it repairable?"

"Not a chance, Ms. Cummings. The drone is torn to pieces and it looks like the sensors are damaged too. Sorry."

"Not your fault." Alex said. "Do you have another?"

"Yes, ma'am, but it's visual only. In fact, this was the only IR sensor we had left."

Well, that's a bummer, Alex thought but she said, "Well nothing we can do about that. How about getting the other drone up and we'll do the best we can?"

"Yes, ma'am."

Alex went on. "Okay. Did everyone get that? As far as aerial surveillance goes all we have is visual and we can only see glimpses of the ground so be careful."

If that announcement bothered the teams, they didn't show it as a chorus of "right" and "no problem" greeted her.

"Good crew," her husband said.

Alex sighed. "Yes, but I hope they don't get too over confident." She sighed again. "Anyway, my sweet, if we can't help them how about checking something out for me?"

"Sure. What?"

"You see that big tree? The one sticking way up above the rest. Now back on Earth that would probably be a fig. Let's check it out."

Andy McPherson came up on the com. "Please everyone stop wherever you are and check your surroundings. If you see a large tree that looks like it's wrapped in vines and has a partially cleared area around it, stay away from it. The vines are part of the tree and we have watched the one we are looking at reach out and grab a lizard. We think the tree is carnivorous."

Fisher immediately answered. "Yes, there's one right in front of us. We were just going to check it out. Carnivorous you say?"

Smith said, "Yeah, Glenn. Look around and see if you can snag a lizard or something and toss it in close. And be careful we don't know how far those vines can reach."

"Okay. Hang on."

In just a minute Edwards had a two-foot-long iguana and at Fisher's nod threw it towards the tree. It hit the ground but before it could move a vine whipped out, encircled it, then vine and iguana disappeared up into the tree's leafy branches.

Fisher had filmed the entire event so everyone saw what had happened. The net was silent. Finally, Marshal said, "Well, damn! Venus Fly Trap on steroids."

That didn't even raise a snicker and Alex said, "I think that's enough excitement for one morning. Let's work our way back to the shuttles and we'll think about lunch."

"But first, my sweet," she said, "I want a fig."

"Your wish is my command, Luv." And Junior delicately snipped off a branch that was heavy with whatever fruit the tree produced.

They returned to the clearing and waited while the scientists sorted out their discoveries, packed them away and waited while Marshal, with Alex's laughing assistance, and Junior lifted them and stowed them away in the shuttle's cargo bays. Any thoughts of having lunch in the vicinity of the steaming buggy jungle were quickly put aside and a couple of hours later the exploratory team was contently sitting on a large rock outcrop high up in the western mountains a thousand miles southwest of their original landing site enjoying the remnants of a very leisurely lunch.

Sentries were posted and the robot and the drones had made their customary sweep around the area. Now only the drone was up keeping watch. Junior was parked behind a small stone as Marshal and Alex sat on the other side looking out to the east over the barren desert terrain of the southern half of the continent.

"Pretty in its way," Marshal said as he continued to gaze out at the brown and tan vista that stretched down and away from him. Out in the distance the hills gave way to a narrow prairie. The continent was only about twelve hundred miles wide this far south of the equator as the east coast kept bending to the west until it ended in a chain of rocks that extended and disappeared into the great Southern Ocean.

If he wanted to, he could turn on his vid and see what the drone saw but the drone was patrolling close in and the view out to the east was much more interesting. Marshal thought of Olga Sorenson behind him sitting cross-legged on the top of Dusty 1 with her little control panel happily flying the drone. He didn't have to look to know that there would be one or two or more of the expedition's young bachelors up there with her trying to chat her up. Marshal chuckled to himself as far as he could see they were wasting their time. To Marshal's knowledge Olga showed no interest at all in any of the young men of the colony. Their interest was understandable. Olga Sorenson was the classic Nordic blond. Tall, blue eyes, nice figure. But Olga was a Geek. A Geek's Geek. If any of these ardent suitors didn't look like, smell like or act like a computer—forget it.

He returned his attention to the view as Alex nestled into his shoulder and murmured, "Yes, my sweet, very pretty." But her thoughts wandered in other directions. Yes, there were several areas of the southern half of the continent that were very attractive for a possible settlement but that probably wasn't going to happen, at least not in her lifetime. There was really no need for it. True they had found useful items, citrus and figs, cocoa and coffee, but nothing that modern science, biology and genetics couldn't replicate back at Cliffside and the farm.

No, she thought, except for the occasional foraging or scientific expedition the southern hemisphere of Middle Finger could wait. What was more important right now was the coming of the new year and the knowledge that she was going to lose Voyager. Of course, ever since she made her promise that after a year anyone who wanted to could return to Earth and Ryan Lasseter had opened his mouth, she knew that she was going to lose their ship. The question was how much of it? Some of the colonists were determined to return to Earth and that question hung over her like a dark cloud: how many?

She didn't understand Lasseter. No, that wasn't right. She did understand people like him—arrogant, self-centered individuals who were absolutely convinced that they were always right. What she didn't understand were the people who listened to him, followed him, believed him.

Over the last year Lasseter had kept up a steady drum beat of half-truths and outright lies aimed at undermining the Voyager's faith in the colony and in themselves and promoting a return to Earth. An Earth, he said, that was still green and lovely with a fully functioning advanced civilization. Everyone knew that that wasn't true, that's why they were here, but that inconvenient truth never slowed down the rhetoric.

His most persistent theme was that the colony was living in primitive conditions in caves. That of course was partly true. About two-thirds of the colony were still living in caves but you could hardly call the living conditions primitive.

The caves were completely sealed from the elements and were heated and air conditioned with indoor plumbing. And the walls of four of the caves, the conference cave, the dispensary, the medical college and the school house had been covered with beautiful wood paneling.

Lasseter would go on his vid show (and here Alex sighed to herself. When they, Olga mostly, had set up their one Vid channel to carry the staff meetings and Al Wilson's weather reports, it had quickly expanded to evening movies and documentaries, educational demonstrations of all kinds, cooking, weaving, tailoring, and when Lasseter had demanded equal time, the staff had reluctantly granted it) and say that the colony was going to starve. That there wasn't enough food to last the winter. A claim easily disproved by just enjoying three hearty meals a day or looking into Cathy and Erin's well stocked pantry. Some people still believed it.

As her husband told her when she mentioned it, "Think of it as a religion or a cult, Luv. People who believe in the leader, the god or gods, the guru, whatever, believe. And no amount of facts or evidence is going to shake that belief. Sure, it sounds nutty to the rest of us but committing suicide to join a spaceship following a comet or going to another country to feed your children poisoned Kool Aid makes perfect sense to them. Lasseter has his followers. Why I don't know but when our year is up, they are going to demand to return to Earth."

Alex sighed again as she looked out over the beautiful landscape of Sanctuary and thought to herself, *Let's hope we can keep the loss down to just Voyager and not lose either of the cryogenic cylinders and R3.*

CHAPTER 26

Alex stood on what was, since the beginning of the colony in Cliffside, called Speakers Rock. It was just a finger of stone that jutted out from the side of the Great Cavern near the northeast corner where Alex had her office. There wasn't really anything special about it; it was just a rock. The masons could have ground it away without a trace in half an afternoon. But the rock had historical and sentimental value to the colonists. Alex had stood on this stone the very first time that she had addressed all the colonists a little over a year ago and despite the occasional call to replace it with a proper speaker's platform it seemed assured that Speakers Rock was here to stay. The only concession that had been made was to let the masons smooth and polish it and cut a couple of steps in the side so the speakers didn't have to actually climb up onto the rock.

Alex looked out over the crowd, if you could call it a crowd. There were only about thirty or forty colonists gathered to wish the Voyagers well on their return journey to Earth and they were mostly all friends of the two robot jockeys, André and the Geek Squad. As far as Alex could tell

Lasseter and his thirty followers had no friends. In fact, if truth be told, the vast majority of the colonists were glad to be rid of them.

What a difference a year can make, Alex thought. What a difference even a couple of months can make. The first time she had stepped on Speaker's Rock the colonists had just woken up from their twenty-year sleep and twenty light year journey through space. The Earthlings that had crowded in the Great Cavern that day had been a tentative and fearful group contemplating getting started on their new planet.

The last time Alex had been on Speaker's Rock was to address a loud, happy and boisterous gathering just two months ago to celebrate their New Year. That had been the first of April by Earth reckoning, but on Sanctuary it had been Day 1 of Year 2.

Alex smiled as she remembered every bit of that day. "Good morning!" she had called out to the crowded cavern.

"Good morning, Alex!" they had roared back. Somehow six hundred people had managed to stuff themselves into the Great Cavern and the sound of their greeting reverberated around the cave.

Alex had continued. "Or should I say 'Happy New Year!'"

Joyous echoes wishing Alex and everyone else a Happy New Year sounded for several minutes.

When the crowd had quieted Alex went on. "One year ago we stood here confused, uncertain, apprehensive of what the future might hold and we faced a decision. We were adrift on an alien, primitive, unfriendly planet facing a future that fueled by our fears held terrors on which we could only speculate. But despite voices that spoke for caution and an immediate return to Earth we decided—you decided—to give Sanctuary a year. One year to determine if we could not only survive on this planet but to see if we could thrive. So, our year has passed. A hard year with our successes and sadly our losses but the question remains the same—do we stay or do we go?"

The roar from six hundred voices was deafening. "WE STAY!"

Before a suddenly teary-eyed Alexandria Cummings could answer, Ryan Lasseter had bounded up the steps onto the Speaker's Rock and was shouting at the colonists, "What's the matter with you? There's no future here on Sanctuary, can't you see that? Look at you. You're living in caves, in log houses. You're struggling just to stay alive. We need to return to Earth, back to civilization. A year ago, the Director said that those of us who wanted to return to Earth could do so," and he pointed at Alex. "Where is that promise now?"

Before a furious Alex could answer the crowd was shouting Lasseter down.

"Shut up, Lasseter."

"You don't know what you're talking about."

"Get off the rock."

But Ryan Lasseter was in full rant and kept demanding Voyager be returned to Earth. When the crowd was finally able to shut him up Alex stepped forward again.

"As usual, Mr. Lasseter has only a slight acquaintance with the truth. A year ago, I promised that anyone who so desired could return to Earth. The truth is that I have kept my promise. At this moment Voyager sits in space three-hundred miles above us, fully functional and ready to take everyone who wants to go back to Earth. A year ago, we agreed to give Sanctuary a year and at the end of that year we, all of us, would decide individually whether to make Sanctuary our home or return to Earth. You just told me in no uncertain terms how most of you feel."

The colonists vehemently agreed with her.

"Thank you," Alex said. "I feel the same way but," and she looked at Lasseter, "not all of us do. There are those of us who do wish to return to Earth."

Before Alex could continue another growl rose up from the colonists. In the din she caught "Tough!" "Let 'em stay!" and "We don't owe them anything!"

Alex held up her hands again. "Please! Let's be fair and reasonable here. We do owe them—I owe them. A year ago, I made a promise—a promise to you all that at the end of our trial year anyone—*everyone*—who wanted to return to Earth could." Alex gave Lasseter a hard stare. "And despite what Mr. Lasseter says I have kept that promise. Voyager still orbits above us, intact and capable of transporting anyone who wants to return back to Earth."

Lasseter jumped up again and spat, "That's a lie! Voyager is not intact. The supply cylinder has been dismantled and the robot maintenance facility has been taken apart."

From the crowd at the foot of Speaker's Rock John Marshal couldn't contain himself any longer. "Lasseter, you are a complete idiot! The supply cylinder has nothing to do with Voyager being able to return to Earth. That section carried supplies for us here on Sanctuary and was emptied out months ago. What was dismantled and brought down here was an empty shell. As for R3, there are three sections. We took one section apart to use down here on the planet. The other two sections are still attached to Voyager."

Admitting that there was such a thing as inconvenient facts to contradict his view of the world was never in Ryan Lasseter's DNA. He continued to insist that Alex had lied and that Voyager was incomplete. Then he seized on the fact that five robots had been converted to planetary use was more evidence that the Director never intended to send anyone back to Earth.

Before Alex or Marshal could respond to that nonsense the crowd shouted him down again.

Shaking her head Alex said, "Ladies and gentlemen, Mr. Lasseter is wrong. As I said before Voyager is intact and as much as I would have liked to recycle the cryogenic pods and cylinders for use here on Sanctuary I haven't done so. So, enough talk. Voyager *is* ready to return to Earth and each and every one of us has had a year to reach a decision. Stay or go?"

Again, the roar. "*Stay!*"

Alex smiled. "It would appear that the majority vote to stay. However, we are not unanimous and despite what Mr. Lasseter said I will keep my promise. Voyager will return to Earth with those who wish to return. I imagine most of you have already made up your minds but to properly configure Voyager for the return trip I will need to know the exact number of returnees. So would those who wish to go step over here with Mr. Lasseter."

There was hardly a ripple in the crowd. Lasseter's followers had already been clustered around him. Alex leaned down to her husband, pointed to Lasseter's group and asked, "Can you get a count, my sweet?"

A few moments later Marshal answered, "Thirty. Thirty-one counting Lasseter."

"Thank you, my sweet." A chuckle went through the crowd both for the pet name that Alex used for her husband and for the relatively low number of colonists that had chosen to return to Earth.

Alex turned to address the crowd again but before she could speak a disturbance in the audience distracted her. Two people were having what apparently started as a private disagreement but was now escalating into a very public shouting match with embarrassed spectators edging away from the arguing couple and creating a small circle around them. What made everyone hold their breath was that the combatants were Dave Allen and Mary Henderson. Dave and Mary had been everyone's favorite love match for months. They had even built a cabin together down the river road and to see them engaged in a public fight was an embarrassment to all.

Finally, Allen shouted, "Fine, stay in this backwater if you want! I'm going back to Earth." And he turned and made his way stone faced through the crowd toward a smirking Ryan Lasseter while a sobbing Mary Henderson wailed, "The children. I can't leave the children."

Allen walked up to Lasseter and said, "I don't like you, Lasseter, but I'm going back to Earth so, if you're in charge, I'll accept that."

Lasseter just smiled and a shocked silence rippled through the crowd as the word was passed.

Clearly momentarily at a loss for words Alex cleared her throat and said, "Well, that alters things a little. The reason that I wanted a head count of returnees was that there are forty-six cryogenic pods in the spaceship Voyager itself. If there are forty-six or less returnees the strap-on cryogenic cylinders won't be required. But," and she looked at Allen, "it would appear that not everyone has made up their minds." She paused for a moment to make a quick decision. "We will extend the deadline for commitment to Voyager for two weeks."

The crowd just shrugged at that. It seemed clear that they had made up their minds.

Alex continued, "But it does seem clear that both of the cryogenic cylinders won't be needed so I want to make a proposal." She looked out over the crowd. "Is the staff present?" That brought a laugh from the crowd as the various staff members scattered throughout the Great Cavern acknowledged their presence. The Colonel, Whit Latham, the Chief, Cathy Jackson, the Fosters, the Docs, Marshal, Bjorn, Hank Ferguson... and Lasseter.

"I think we have a quorum so I'm calling an impromptu staff meeting. I propose that we authorize Fred and the robot jockeys to start dismantling the cryogenic cylinder that the RJs call the Italian Job in order to recycle the material down here to the colony. Any discussion?"

Lasseter shouted, "You can't do that! That cylinder might be needed for the return to Earth."

A clearly exasperated Alex Cummings said. "Mr. Lasseter, Voyager will still have the other cryogenic cylinder, the San Diego Job. That's two-hundred and seventy-three cryogenic pods in addition to the ones in Voyager. Look around, do you really think that there will be more than three-hundred of us who want to return to Earth?"

But Lasseter kept on arguing and complaining despite the hoots and shouts of laughter from the colonists. When he finally shut-up enough for Alex to get a word in she said, "Are there any other comments that staff members care to make?"

Colonel McPherson answered from the crowd. "No, Alex. We're good. In fact, I make a motion that we vote on it right now."

That brought a chorus of seconds from the rest of the council. All except Lasseter, of course, who kept sputtering, "No! You can't do that. This is improper." Then, more and even louder shouts came from the crowd for Lasseter to shut up.

Alex paid no attention to him and said, "A motion has been made and seconded that we dismantle the cryogenic cylinder called the Italian Job. All in favor of immediately starting to dismantle the Italian Job signify by saying aye."

Probably all the council members except Lasseter said aye but who could tell with six- hundred or more voices roaring aye. The colonists were loving this.

"Nays?" Alex asked.

Lasseter said, "Nay." And maybe one or two of his minions squeaked out a nay but they couldn't be heard over the laughter that rolled through the Great Cavern.

Alex again looked out over the crowd, and with a smile said, "I think the ayes have it." The colonist's laughter echoed through the cave again and over the din a voice was heard saying, "Now that's my kind of a staff meeting."

Alex scanned the crowd and asked, "Fred! Are you here?"

Fred Thompson answered, "Right here, Alex."

"You heard the people, Fred. How long do you think it will take to detach the cylinder?"

"Ah! Piece of cake. Two weeks, a month at the outside."

"Thank you, Fred. Please get started as soon as you can." Then Alex went on addressing the crowd. "That moves our departure date by a month and gives everyone an opportunity to re-think their decision. I'll give you two weeks. If anyone wants to change their mind and return to Earth, you have two weeks to think about it. If you do want to return you have to tell me by then. If at that time there are still less than forty-six returnees, I am going to propose to the staff that we dismantle the San Diego Job and the rest of R3."

Lasseter went ballistic. Ranting and screaming about stranding the humans on Sanctuary, dictatorial tactics and anything else he could think of.

The crowd either laughed or ignored him.

Colonel McPherson spoke up from the middle of the

crowd. "Madam Director, I don't think that we have to wait for two weeks to vote on that proposal—we can do it now."

The colonists roared their approval so McPherson went on. "We have a quorum of the staff here. I make a motion that if after the next two weeks no more than forty-six colonists have opted to return to Earth the Director has the authority to strip Voyager down to its original atmospheric configuration for its return to Earth."

There was a chorus of seconds.

Alex asked, "All in favor?"

"Aye!"

The two weeks following the New Year's gathering had been ones of growing apprehension for her. Would anyone else follow Dave Allen?

As it turned out six of the originals from Sand Flea did—and Alex had been surprised at each one.

The first was just two days after the gathering. Alex looked up from her desk to see Tony Simmons and Paul Mahoney standing in her doorway.

"Come in, boys." Alex smiled. "What can I do for you?"

"Uh, Alex... Ms. Cummings," Tony stuttered. Staring at his shuffling feet he couldn't look Alex in the eye. "We, myself and Paul, we want to go back to Earth in Voyager."

Alex was so startled she blustered, "What? Why?" Then she silently kicked herself. She had promised herself that she wouldn't question anyone's decision or try to talk them out of whatever they decided, but this coming from Tony and Paul was a shock. Why would they want to leave? They were the youngest of the robot jockeys. The good time boys. Everyone loved them. Back on Earth they had spent every minute of their down time, and every penny of their generous paychecks, up in Las Vegas. And, their partying ways hadn't diminished here on Sanctuary. Tony and Paul had been the culprits who provided the applejack for the ruckus Harvest Festival party last year.

She shook her head again and quietly asked, "Why, boys?"

They seemed embarrassed and finally Paul said, "There's no action here."

A puzzled Alex asked, "No action?"

Tony added, "Alex, we miss the bright lights, the glitter, the gambling, the women."

Alex said, "There are nice girls here."

That statement reduced Tony and Paul incoherent fumbling and mumbling and Alex finally got it.

"Oh! I understand. But you realize that when you return to Earth forty years—forty-one years will have passed? There might not be a Las Vegas anymore."

The boys just smiled and Paul said with a wisdom far beyond his years, "Alex, as long as there are human beings breathing on Earth there will be a Las Vegas."

The next day Alex was surprised again when she looked up to see Tony and Paul again in her doorway but this time with André in their wake.

She said, "Don't tell me. André, why?"

There was no embarrassment in the French chef's reply. "Ah, Madam Director, what can I say? I am a creature of the night, yes? And the ladies have been too long without André."

Alex smothered a laugh and didn't bother to say that there were ladies here on Sanctuary also. She thought there are ladies and then there are ladies. Instead, she said, "And didn't consorting with the wrong lady almost get you killed?"

André shrugged. "A mere trifle, Madam Director. Besides, all those ladies will be gone and there will be new ladies."

"Yes," Alex replied. "Ladies who weren't even born when you left Earth."

"Oui! Yes! As always, Ms. Cummings, you understand completely. They need André."

There was no pricking André's bubble and Alex just smiled. "Well, all I can do is wish you good luck and I hope you're not disappointed."

The final three were probably the greatest shock of all and one that could seriously affect operations on Sanctuary. Nothing could have surprised Alex more than to see Olga and the boys, Kevin Young and Bobby Burk—the Geek Squad— standing in the doorway to her office with Olga's brother Bjorn standing behind them.

Oh no! she thought, but she smiled and said, "Come in, come in. Grab a chair. What can I do for you?"

Before anyone else could speak Bjorn Sorenson said, "Ms. Cummings, I've tried talking some sense into my sister here but she seems determined on returning to Earth. Maybe you will have better luck."

Alex replied, "Sorry, Bjorn. I promised myself that it wasn't my place to try to talk anyone into going or staying. Those are individual decisions, although in this case Olga you and the boys have been valuable members of the community. I will miss the drones and your expertise in keeping our computers running."

Olga smiled. "Ms. Cummings, you know more about computers than we ever will and you will still have the drones. In fact, we haven't been operating them for weeks. It's all been Marty and Ellen and the other people that we have been training."

Alex smiled back. "Been thinking about this for a while, have you?"

Olga nodded.

"May I ask why?"

"It's the computers, Ms. Cummings, and the games. We're Geeks. We live on that stuff. We know every computer on Sanctuary by heart. No challenge. And we haven't seen a new game in over a year."

Alex sighed. "I understand, Olga." And she smiled at Kevin and Bobby. "I just hope that you're not disappointed when you return to Earth."

In the following two months the robot jockeys worked like demons to strip Voyager down. There were only six robots still configured for work in space and the robot jockeys did need to sleep sometime but to keep the work going the ground the jockeys moved up to orbit so they could work around the clock to get the job done. The two cryogenic cylinders and R3 now floated in space next to Voyager and Wisdom.

While the work in space was going on Alex, and it seemed that at one time or another everyone else, had to deal with Lasseter and the very real and imagined problems that he and reality posed for getting the returnees and Voyager ready to return to Earth.

First and foremost was the fact that while Alex could program Voyager to travel twenty light years through space and obtain orbit around Earth, she couldn't land it. If they wanted the spaceship to actually land on good old Terra Ferma, someone had to physically fly it down through Earth's atmosphere and land it. Voyager needed a pilot. And as the fates would have it of all the returnees Ryan Lasseter was the only qualified pilot. Of course, he had never flown anything the size of Voyager but he did have extensive experience flying his own executive jet aircraft back on Earth. To get Voyager safely back on Earth someone was going to have to give Ryan Lasseter a crash—to use a bad word—course. And the only person with the experience to do that was Colonel Alexander McPherson.

If McPherson was returning to Earth, he could fly Voyager, but the Colonel made it very clear he wasn't going anywhere. So, he agreed to teach Lasseter all he could about flying something the size of an overgrown 747 and landing it in one piece.

As friendly as the Colonel and Lasseter had been in their cabinet making collaborations, working on something outside of the wood shop was something else. The experience of trying to teach Lasseter how to fly Voyager almost drove Alexander McPherson mad.

Every time McPherson tried to tell or show him something Lasseter said that he already knew that or that he knew a better way to do it. It was only after McPherson set up a jury-rigged simulator and Lasseter crashed a few times that he began to listen.

Next was supplies. It seemed that Lasseter wanted about half of everything that the colonists had—food, clothing, weapons, ammunition, equipment... everything. And each and every item had to be negotiated separately. Alex was willing to be reasonable and ensure that the humans returned to Earth as self-reliant as possible but she wasn't going to deprive the colony of anything needed on Sanctuary for something that Lasseter thought that he *might* need on Earth.

But Lasseter was Lasseter. He knew what he knew and he wanted what he wanted and he brought every request up in the staff meetings. Sometimes over and over again.

First was clothing. Lasseter had never liked the one-piece flight suits that had been issued initially to all the colonists and didn't want to return to Earth looking like, as he said, a mechanic. Well to be fair a lot of colonists felt that way and over the past year shirts and pants, halters and shorts had begun to appear. Anyone could have them. All they had to do was find the material and then convince someone with tailoring skills to make it.

And as a gifted tailor, Lasseter's former valet, Jordan Roberts, was in high demand. Alex was convinced that if Sanctuary ever went to a market economy Jordan Roberts would be a millionaire. While the returnees were looking around for Earth-like clothing the colony took great delight in the story (probably highly embellished) that circulated that when Lasseter went to his former valet and ordered him to make clothes for him and his wife Jordan told him to get lost.

Probably the biggest fight was over weapons. Lasseter, of course, wanted guns for everyone with thousands of rounds of ammunition. Given the state of Earth when Voyager left twenty-one years ago and speculating on what it might be like twenty more years in the future about half the staff agreed with him.

The other half which consisted of Chief Lincoln and all the ex-military members, such as the Colonel, Marshal and Hank Ferguson, were unmoved by any thoughts and speculation about what the conditions on Earth might or might not be. Link made it clear that his responsibility was the security of the colony here on Sanctuary and he needed every rifle and especially every round of irreplaceable ammunition.

Alex later reflected, that it was a strange discussion, more like bartering in a mid-eastern bazaar

Lasseter: "I want thirty-eight rifles one for each of the returnees with a thousand rounds of ammunition each."

Lincoln: "Out of the question. That would be thirty-eight thousand rounds of ammunition. Can't spare it. I'll give you two rifles with a full magazine in each one."

Lasseter was furious. "That's only forty rounds!

Unacceptable." And they went on from there.

Lasseter: "Thirty rifles with five-hundred rounds each".

Lincoln: "Two rifles with two magazines, forty rounds, each."

Lasseter: "Two dozen rifles with five magazines each."

Lincoln: "Six and two."

They finally settled on a dozen rifles with two magazines each. Link didn't like it and Lasseter was furious so all in all Alex figured that it was a pretty good compromise.

Then there was the problem of food. Lasseter wanted thousands of rations to sustain the returnees who would be awake for a year at a time on the return journey. When Alex explained to him that they had learned on the trip to Sanctuary that keeping a duty crew awake wasn't necessary and that everyone could be in cryogenic hibernation for the return journey, Lasseter wasn't buying it.

It took a trip up to Wisdom and Voyager with Alex and Dave Allen sitting down with Lasseter in the cockpit and explaining how the return flight program worked for him to accept that it wouldn't be necessary for anyone to remain awake. Alex was sure that if it was just her trying to convince him as paranoid as he was, he wouldn't have accepted it. It was only Allen's presence that swayed him and even at that he said that he was going to remain awake when Voyager left for Earth and he still wanted rations. Rations for the trip and rations for the first year on Earth.

That brought a howl of derision from the rest of the staff. All except Cathy Jackson who said, "Fine, Ryan. Just let me know what you need and I will see that it gets aboard Voyager."

In the shocked silence that followed Lasseter said,

"See? We can all be reasonable."

"Don't worry," Cathy grinned after Lasseter turned on his heel and left. "I'm going to generously provide him with the leftover MREs. You know, those military rations that everyone hated on their journey to Sanctuary."

"Cathy, you little devil!" Marshal grinned at her.

Finally, it was here. The day of departure arrived. Alex shook off her thoughts and again looked at the sparse crowd and the returnees, Lasseter, Allen, André, Tony, Paul, the Geek Squad and the other thirty returnees with a heavy heart. Most of them wouldn't be missed but some---.

"Well, ladies and gentlemen, are you ready?" she asked. "If so, we can board the shuttles. It will be a little crowded but we have all four Stardusters working today and it's a short flight."

It was almost eerie. There were thirty-eight humans embarking on a journey of twenty light years back to Earth and no one said a word.

Alex took her seat in the cockpit of Dusty 1 next to her husband. When the tell-tales indicated that the steps were up and secured Marshal looked over and asked, "Ready, Luv?"

Alex gave herself a little shake and smiled. "Yes, my sweet. Ready."

It was a quiet flight up to Wisdom. The Stardusters docked one at a time and the returnees were escorted through the space station, the tube connecting Wisdom to Voyager and into the cryogenic section.

Both Doctor Watsons were present and after a quick check the returnees striped and went into their individual tubes. On Lasseter's instance a slightly embarrassed Dave Allen personally checked each pod setting. All were on call. They would not come out of hibernation until someone manually recalled them. Only Allen and Lasseter's pods were set to automatically open when Voyager achieved orbit around the planet Earth.

When all thirty-six were in hibernation Dave Allen went into his pod leaving only Ryan Lasseter awake.

The doctors and the rest of the colonists went down the connecting tube to Wisdom and Alex and Lasseter were left alone.

Alex asked politely, "Well, Mr. Lasseter, I think that's everything. Is there anything else you require?"

"No. No. I know all this stuff. I could have built spaceships, you know."

Alex just gave a little shrug. She was used to Lasseter's I-know-more-than-everyone-else nonsense, so she just said, "Then I'll be saying goodbye, Mr. Lasseter. Goodbye and bon voyage."

Lasseter just grunted something in reply.

Alex slipped into the access tube and waited a moment until she heard the hatch being secured from the inside then she floated the rest of the way into Wisdom. She heard someone secure the hatch behind her and said, "Okay, Fred, you can uncouple us now."

Lasseter must have been watching the monitors closely. As soon as Thompson had the tube detached from Voyager the spaceship began to move away.

The humans in Wisdom looked at each other. It was done. The way it had happened was a bittersweet departure with someone like Ryan Lasseter at the controls. But it was done and now for good or ill Voyager, their last possible link with planet Earth, had departed and the future was in their hands here on a planet called Sanctuary.

EPILOGUE

In the two months since Voyager departed for its long journey back to Earth, life went on in the colony. People went to work; a couple babies were born and occasionally someone would comment on the fate of the returnees. Of course, unless they collided with a rock or were boarded by space vampires, that fate was in limbo for the next twenty years. Still, the colonists couldn't help but wonder what their life would be like once they arrived back on Earth, especially with someone like Ryan Lasseter deciding who to contact and where Voyager would ultimately land.

Alex woke up and stretched like a lazy cat in a sunbeam and turned toward her husband. "I need you this morning, my sweet."

"Well yeah, sure." Marshal replied as he moved closer.

"Not that, you big oaf!" She laughed as she punched him lightly in the shoulder. "Although it would be nice. No, we have to get up. Things to do today. I need you to fly me up to Wisdom."

"Up to Wisdom? Oh yeah! Sure. Why?"

"Ummm... Later, my sweet."

After they showered and dressed, the two moved into the cafeteria for breakfast. Marshal could see that his wife was more than a little distracted. It was like she was going over a checklist in her head.

"Now let's see," she mumbled. "I need one of the docs. Ah! There's Nancy." She waved and Nancy Watson walked over.

"Morning, Alex, John." Doc Nancy said and looked a question at Alex.

"Nancy, I need either you or John this morning. There'll be a Starduster out in front of the Great Cavern in about an hour and a half," and Marshal nodded that he'd be ready. "Would one of you be there please?"

"Sure," Nancy replied. "What's up?"

But Alex was already walking away. Nancy now looked a question at Marshal who could only shrug.

"Don't ask me. I don't know any more than you do. She told me to have a Starduster ready to fly up to Wisdom and that's all I know." Then Marshal hurried off to catch up with his wife who was now standing at the edge of the cafeteria seating area scanning the noisy and bustling breakfast crowd.

"Are you looking for someone, Luv?" Marshal asked.

"Yes, Mary Henderson," she answered. "Do you see her?"

"Nope," he said, glancing around. "Don't see her. Probably already over at the school."

Alex pulled out her Vid and was punching a combination and Al Wilson appeared on the screen. "Well, good morning, Madam Director. To what do I owe the pleasure of your smiling face on this fine day?"

Alex laughed. "Ah, Al, you old smoothie! I'm planning on coming up to Wisdom this morning. Just giving you a heads up to be expecting company"

"Great. Always glad to squire the director around. What's up?"

"I'll tell you later, Al. I'll be up in a few hours."

Wilson laughed. "Alex, what's up? What's going on?" But Alex had already punched off and was scanning the cafeteria again. "John, my sweet, do you see the Chief?"

Marshal shrugged again. "Nope! I don't see him, either."

Alex then began walking away towards the McPhersons' table. Whenever possible the closely knit McPherson clan gathered for breakfast before the day's activities separated them. There was hardly an endeavor that the colony engaged in that there wasn't a McPherson helping it along or in some cases guiding it along. A chorus of "Heys" and "Good mornings" rang out as Alex and Marshal walked up to the table. Alex smiled and looked at the patriarch of the clan.

"Alex, I need you this morning."

"Sure," the colonel said. "What's up?"

Not answering directly, she said, "There will be a Starduster out front in about an hour. Please be ready to take a little trip." Before the Colonel could get another question in, Alex was turning toward Andy McPherson. "Andy, I don't see the Chief."

Andy answered, "No. He went down to the farm earlier to check out their new training arrangements. Is there anything I can do?"

"As a matter of fact, yes. I need..." and she *ummmed* for a moment, "...three armed deputies to be on that shuttle.

Can do?"

A clearly confused Andy McPherson said, "Sure!" And before he could ask any of the many questions boiling up in his mind Alex was already walking away toward the food service line leaving a bewildered Marshal facing the stares of an equally bewildered McPherson clan.

"Don't ask me," Marshal shrugged again. "Me just pilot. I don't know any more about what's percolating in that brain of hers than you do. The one thing I do know is that she's got Doc Nancy lined up, she's looking for Mary Henderson and I am going to have a Starduster sitting outside as soon as I have breakfast. See ya!"

A couple of people had heard Alex's exchange with Doc Nancy and several more colonists overheard the conversation at the McPherson table so by the time Alex and Marshal sat down with their breakfast trays the cafeteria was buzzing like a disturbed hive of bees. But whatever was going on, Alex wasn't talking. After only one cup of coffee Marshal headed toward the Starduster/robot cave to pick up the shuttle.

Just as Marshal was walking away Mary Henderson came up to the table. "Were you looking for me, Alex?"

"Yes indeed," Alex answered. "There will be a shuttle out front in a few minutes and I would like you to be on it."

"Me? Alright."

The colonists that heard that exchange were even more puzzled than before and the buzz intensified.

Alex walked out of the Great Cavern just as Marshal was setting Dusty 1 down. Some of the people that Alex had designated were waiting along with a large crowd of the just plain curious. Doc Nancy and the colonel were already there and Andy McPherson walked up with Jerry and Murph.

Alex said, "It seems that you brought the first team,

Andy. Good. But if all goes as planned, we won't need you."

A clearly befuddled Andy McPherson smiled back. "Well, I brought half of the first team anyway. Kurt is with the Chief down at the farm."

Alex just smiled. "We are all here so let's get on board."

And without another word she went up the ladder, turned left into the cockpit and slid into the co-pilot's chair next to her husband leaving a group of mostly pretty bewildered people following in her wake.

Marshal saw the tell-tale light go out that said that the stairs were up. He lifted Dusty up and set a course for Wisdom. It was a quiet flight. Alex wasn't talking and although everyone else was bursting with curiosity, no one was asking.

After docking with Wisdom, they floated into the meteorological section where after hasty greetings Alex was bombarded with questions not just from her passengers but from everyone who had been up in Wisdom.

Finally, Alex said, "Please, just be patient. All your questions should be answered in about…" and she looked at her Vid, "…seven minutes."

That answer was just as confusing as no answer and while they were digesting that bit of non-information Ann Turner exclaimed, "Al, look at the screen. What's that?"

Wilson replied, "What's what?"

"That blip. It looks like there's something in orbit with us."

That pronouncement had everyone looking at computer screens or out the windows and talking at once.

"What is it?"

"It's catching up."

"It looks like a space station."

"No, it's a spaceship."

Al Wilson turned from his monitor and looked at Alex. "It's Voyager!" he exclaimed. And a dozen humans watched in shocked silence as Voyager slowly closed in on Wisdom, matched velocities and came to rest next to the space station.

Before the storm of questions could begin Alex said, "Well, you didn't really think that I was going to leave Voyager in the hands of someone like Ryan Lasseter, did you?"

The babble of voices trying to answer that rhetorical question became silent when Alex continued. "No. Voyager's return was planned from the moment it was obvious that Lasseter would be more or less in charge of the ship. But let's give credit where credit is due. I never could have pulled this off without the help and personal sacrifice of Mary and Dave."

All eyes turned toward a blushing Mary Henderson. "Well," she said, "I didn't really do anything except have a very lonely four months. It was all Dave."

The colonists were all trying to talk at once.

"What?"

"What do you mean a lonely four months?"

"What did Dave do?"

Finally, Ann Turner pointed an accusing finger at Mary and blustered, "That big bust up with Dave—it was all a fake!"

Alex said, "Yes, it was. And it was pulled off by two of the best actors that ever walked on any stage."

"So instead of programming Voyager to return to Earth you programmed it to come back here," Marshal commented.

"Well, yes and no, my sweet. Yes, I wrote the program to bring Voyager back here but with someone as paranoid as Lasseter watching me like a hawk, I couldn't have installed it. Lasseter is no dummy and he knows enough about programming to know that the program I wrote and presumably installed would take Voyager to Earth and he certainly wasn't going to let me tamper with that. No, the real program, the one to bring Voyager right back here in two months couldn't be installed by me. For that we needed a mole, someone on the inside and Dave Allen volunteered."

Turner looked at Alex and said, "So the big bust up was your idea?" and she looked at Mary. "And you went along with it?"

Before a blushing Mary could answer Alex said, "No, actually the big bust up was Mary's idea. She thought it would give Dave more credibility with the ignorant, arrogant, male domineering, sexist bunch that were returning to Earth. And she was right, too. Dave was accepted into Lasseter's inner circle and in effect became his right-hand man. Dave was the one who programmed all the cryogenic pods so that he and Lasseter would wake up first when Voyager was in Earth's orbit. In fact, no one else would come out of cryo until they were called."

Marshal just shook his head. "Brilliant, Luv, and my hats off to you Mary... and Dave, of course. But why wait so long to bring Voyager back?"

Alex grinned. "Well, maybe I was being a little overly cautious there. I wanted to be sure that Lasseter and all his minions were in cryogenic hibernation when Voyager returned. Not everyone was when Voyager left. Lasseter was awake. While there wasn't anything he could do to prevent Voyager returning back to Sanctuary even if he had realized that it was happening, an angry Lasseter is a dangerous one. Remember, all the visible Gutman Drive controls on the flight crew's council don't really do anything. We installed those when we were worried that Vice President Collins and his goons might take us over. But I didn't want to risk having Lasseter do something really stupid and possibly damage Voyager's operating systems."

She turned to a wide-eyed and thoroughly stunned Andy McPherson. "And that is why you, Linda and Jerry are here. Just in case some of those nut cases are still awake and possibly hostile. Once you have ensured that the coast is clear Nancy and I will go on board and wake up Dave. Then we'll do a little checking, reprogramming and recalibrating of the cryogenic pods and set Voyager on its proper course to Earth."

"So, my sweet," Alex said to Marshal, "I think that the first move is up to you, and Sam, of course. Do you think you could get the access tube from Wisdom attached to Voyager?"

Marshal laughed. "Sure and that will be the first time this morning that I knew what I was doing."

Everyone laughed and soon the clear sphere of the construction robot floated into view as Marshal detached the personnel tube and stretched it out toward Voyager.

But Alex wasn't finished. "Colonel, once we are on board, I would like you to check the atmospheric flight controls just to be sure that no one has done anything really stupid that would prevent Voyager from flying down to Earth. I can't really imagine that that would happen but please check just to be sure."

The Colonel smiled. "I wondered why I was included on this trip. I'll check, of course, but I don't really expect to find any problems. Lasseter is too good a pilot for that plus the fact that he wouldn't do anything that would risk his precious butt."

Alex laughed along with everyone else and added, "Oh, Colonel, please use the right seat. I'll need the left."

Marshal's face appeared on the Vid. "All set, Luv."

"Thank you, my sweet. You might as well wait out there. We shouldn't be too long. I guess it's up to you now,

Andy. Please be careful."

McPherson said, "No problem, boss. I'll just go up there and knock on the door."

Linda Murphy snorted. "Not you, you big lug! You'd plug up the whole tube. This is a job for me or Jerry. Probably me."

But while she was talking Jerry Smith had already floated up the tube to Voyager and was undogging the hatch.

"Watch it!" exclaimed McPherson. "There might be someone unfriendly awake in there."

Smith snorted. "Nah! Not a chance. If Lasseter was awake that arrogant, self-loving a-hole couldn't have kept his mouth shut this long."

Smith was right. He floated into a silent Voyager with Murph and Andy right behind him. Nothing stirred. Thirty-eight humans blissfully slept in cryogenic hibernation. Colonel McPherson headed for the cockpit; the security team floated in the command section while everyone else headed for the cryogenic pod occupied by Dave Allen.

Doc Nancy said, "Ah, Alex, I usually do this with a cryogenic specialist."

Alex said, "Go ahead, Nancy. I'll monitor the gauges."

In a moment the yellow mists cleared and Dave blinked his eyes as Mary wrapped him in a bear hug and a long kiss. "Well," he croaked a minute later, "I guess it worked."

"Like a charm," Alex grinned. "And now if you and Nancy would check all the other pods to ensure that they are all stable. Oh! And please wake up Tony and Paul."

Marshal blustered over the comm, "Simmons and Mahoney? What do they know about all this? Were they in on the plot, too?"

"Sadly, no," Alex answered. "They really are going back, but instead of Lasseter, those two are going to be the ones who automatically come out of hibernation when Voyager reaches orbit around Earth."

Marshal asked, "Why didn't you tell them?"

"Are you kidding? Those two happy-go-lucky play boys? No. I was afraid that they would accidently spill the beans."

Everyone laughed.

"Great," Marshal said. "They really hated it when they found out that Lasseter was going to be awake when they were still in hibernation."

Everyone went about the missions that Alex had tasked. She personally briefed the robot jocks, Mahoney and Simmons, on what she expected them to find when they reached Earth. She even had the RJs and the security team search Voyager to make sure that Lasseter and his minions hadn't hidden any weapons away anywhere. Then she slid into the pilot's chair, called up the hidden computers and re-activated Voyagers to return to Earth.

Less than an hour later it was all accomplished. Voyager would automatically return to orbit around the Earth with thirty-eight humans in cryogenic hibernation. Once orbit was successfully achieved Simmons and Mahoney would be awakened. Where Voyager went from there was up to them. Armed with meticulous checklists that Doc Nancy and Allen had hastily prepared, who came out of hibernation next and in what order was also up to them. Of course, once they decided where Voyager was going to land, they would have to wake Lasseter seeing as he was the only pilot. Alex was sure that Tony and Paul could handle Lasseter and if they needed backup, there was always the Geek Squad.

After triple checking the programming, pod settings, flight controls, weapons and anything else they could think of, the colonists floated back down into Wisdom and Marshal uncoupled and stowed the access tube. Alex waited until he floated into the met cylinder then she looked around at everyone. With a sigh, Alex punched a code into her Vid. Nothing happened for a few moments then Voyager slowly moved away from the space station on her twenty-year journey to rendezvous with Earth.

Everyone was quiet. No one said anything but everyone thought it. The same thought that they had had two months ago: Their last tie with Earth had been severed and the colony was truly on its own.

"Look!" Turner suddenly exclaimed. "A meteor is heading towards Sanctuary.

Voyager was momentarily forgotten as everyone stared at the line of fire slashing down toward the planet.

Al Wilson suddenly looked up from his instruments, his eyes wide. "It's not a meteor. It's a spaceship. And it's going to land on the southern edge of the greenbelt about forty-five hundred miles southeast of Cliffside. Alex, we've got company."

Made in the USA
Columbia, SC
03 June 2024

36166494R00251